THE
BATHWATER
BRIGADE

JEFFERSON J. SHUPE

ISBN 978-1-7360121-0-9

ACKNOWLEDGMENTS

Thank you to my editor, Josie Hulme. I needed that teaspoon of encouragement for every cup of (very constructive) criticism. Thanks, Caleb Nelson, for the insights on the first draft, and for being the chief proofreader on the final.

I send my thanks to the slew of beta readers, and my sympathy to the earlier ones. Your suggestions have been invaluable. I have started this project multiple times over the years, and many of you have been my sounding board since the beginning, helping me finally land on the format that felt right.

My siblings have been overwhelmingly supportive, with some of them offering to review and give input on each draft along the way.

I have to mention my father, Jon, for modeling the genuine respect and understanding for everyone that I've tried to portray in this book. And my mother, Loretta, for inspiring me to dream.

Thanks to my kids for bringing their homework to the attic office, keeping me company while I type. Especially to my daughter Aly for her perspective and advice, and our long chats about the very topics in this book.

And a special thanks to my wife Stacie, for your belief in good ideas, skepticism of my bad ones, and picking up more slack than usual. I'm finally going to clean the garage now, I promise.

For Aly.

(Quite literally.)

THE
BATHWATER
BRIGADE

JEFFERSON J. SHUPE

PROLOGUE

"SUSPECT RUNNING WESTBOUND ON GRANT," Officer Lambson said steadily into her car radio, but her heart pounded. Blue and red flashes reflected off the windows of white painted houses as her black F-150 roared through the deserted residential street. Strands of blond hair had worked their way out of her tight bun over the course of her shift and swept her cheek.

Her eyes darted from the suspect to the road ahead and back again. He had abandoned his green flannel shirt on the broken sidewalk a few blocks ago. His dark skin and clothes now made him almost invisible in the moonless night. Her vehicle overtook him, and the rear profile of the sprinter quickly became a side one. He raced the truck with his hands open. For an instant, he was illuminated as he dashed under a street-light. Her glance caught his desperate grimace, and the bulging veins on his head and neck. He had the height of a man, but not the build. Late teens, she guessed. Another kid who will visit a jail cell before a college dorm. Groaning, she clutched the gear selector and prepared to hit the brake.

But before she could make her move, he made his. Grasping a fence post, he launched to the right and disappeared down an unlit alley too narrow for the truck to follow. It sliced between backyards of the tiny, run-down homes of New Brig's industrial district.

"Now northbound toward the Belmont factory," she radioed. "Cutting him off on the other side. Block the alley entrance near Empire."

A string of events during the chase had separated her from her junior partner. She was seasoned and fearless, but there are several reasons why you don't want to confront a dangerous suspect alone. "You'd better hurry," she muttered.

At the end of the street, she ignored the stop sign, slowed just enough to keep her four tires on the road, and skidded around the turn toward the giant metal landmark.

She peered between the homes on her right as she drove by. Nothing. She sped to the looming factory. The truck's headlights glinted off corrugated metal sheds as she closed in.

The dilapidated parking lot was empty except for a dumpster and a rusty Ford Bronco. Opposite her was a chain-link fence topped with strands of barbed wire, which connected the back of the factory on her left to the alley on her right.

"I'm at the factory," she radioed.

She braked hard, her truck sliding on pebbles of pavement. She slammed the transmission into park and opened the door. Large fans whirred at the top of the building and made an aggravating metallic squeak. A sticky note fluttered on her dashboard, a child's drawing—the outline of a police badge with a smiley face inside. She stepped from the truck and instinctively pulled out her Glock 22.

Over ten years a cop, and she had only pulled that trigger in training exercises. Would this be the day? She blinked, swallowed hard, and allowed her training to force those thoughts from her mind as she fixed her eyes on the alley.

The suspect burst into the open space and turned.

No way out.

He faced her, his back to the fence and his chest heaving. His hands trembled.

She was motionless except for her wide eyes darting between his hands and his gaze. His right hand was empty. The other, she wasn't sure.

Two beams of light bounced wildly on the factory building. Flashlights from the alleyway. This would be a textbook takedown: suspect sees no hope of escape and surrenders.

"Get down!" She pitched her voice to overpower the clamor of the factory fans. "Hands up!" She stepped toward him, keeping her defensive stance and her weapon drawn.

He looked through the fence behind him, and then back at her.

"Get down! Now!" Another step forward. Then she begged quietly, "Please, just do it. Stay alive."

The bouncing lights on the factory wall became smaller and brighter. Help was nearly there.

He jerked to look behind the fence once more, and then burst ahead, sprinting toward her and the truck. A glint of light reflected from something dark in his left hand.

"Stop!"

As if the factory fans had heard her command, they suddenly halted. At least, she no longer heard them. Her grip tightened, pushing the Glock forward with her left hand, and pulling it toward her with her right. Four times she felt it kick back in her hands. She heard the clink of the brass against the side of the truck and the tiny reset click of the trigger.

He crumpled to the ground, face down, palms up and empty, arms at his side.

The fans faded in again. The officers arrived from the alleyway. They had weapons drawn and shouted commands of their own. He hadn't moved since the gunshots. And neither had she.

One of the officers grimly walked up to her. "Lambson. You all right?"

She nodded.

He put a hand on her shoulder. "You can holster. We've got this."

She put her weapon away, moved near her truck, and waited for other support vehicles to arrive.

More flashing lights, red and blue. A dog barked.

She couldn't think.

She sank to the ground with her back to a tire, rested her elbows on her knees, and buried her head in her hands.

And for the first time in her fourteen years with the force, she sobbed.

CHAPTER ONE

SWEAT DRIPPED from Jace Kartchner's chin. He cursed the long sleeves of his black Fort Riley shirt. Heat radiated from the sidewalks, and it felt like he'd just walked into the bathroom after one of his brother's twenty-minute showers.

He put his phone back into his pocket once he could see the Union Building. A tan, clean-shaven guy leaned near the entrance, arms folded, one foot planted on the sidewalk and the other against the sandy red brick wall. He wore khaki shorts, sandals, and had brown hair to his shoulders.

Jace stopped and waved a hand in front of the guy's sunglasses. "You asleep?"

A slight smile appeared. "I should be."

Jace clasped right hands with Rob Thomas, his best friend since third grade. Rob slapped Jace on the back, and then wiped his hand on his shorts. "It's like you just climbed out of the pool," he grumbled. "Long sleeves in south Texas? Dark colors. Let me guess...long winter underwear?"

"Didn't think we'd be spending the day outside," said Jace. "So where are the others?"

Rob moved his sunglasses to the top of his head and checked his watch. "Give them a minute. It's early. Cale is technically in the Central Time Zone, but you could say we run on Pacific."

Jace had been awake for three hours already, though it had been well after midnight when he pulled his green sedan into the parking lot at Stoddard Hall, an old dormitory where half of the rooms were vacant. He'd hauled his clothes, trombone case, and blue hardtail mountain bike up two flights of stairs to his tiny new home.

Rob grimaced at Jace and held open the glass door. "We'd better wait inside. In those clothes out here, you've got about thirty minutes to live."

Their footsteps echoed in the tile hallway, which had a new smell to it, like fresh paint. The bowling alley, ice cream shop, and the old arcade were empty. Three guys stood at one of a dozen pool tables in a large carpeted area to the left. A security officer sat on a soft bench in the corner. He looked up from his phone and exchanged nods with Rob.

Jace couldn't help but smile. He'd looked forward to this for years. He was officially off to college with his best friend, a few states away from their home in Richard Springs, Kansas.

Although they were born only two years apart, Rob was a year ahead of Jace in school. At the closing bell of elementary school, they would dash to Rob's house, two white kids making marble runs in the sandpile. They used their wooden rulers to gauge the height of their bike tires from the pavement as they flew off speed bumps in the grocery store parking lot. One of them measured in inches, but jubilantly announced the number in feet as the other clanked to the ground and skidded to a stop. As teenagers, they watched *The Office* late into the night and jumped their family minivans off those same speed bumps.

"How's Jed doing?" asked Jace, referring to Rob's older brother. "He's a cop now, right?"

"Yup, in Oklahoma. Loves it. You hungry, man?"

"Sure," Jace said.

"I'm buying. Just this once."

Jace followed Rob to what was apparently the only food place on campus open at 10:30 in the morning. The sign read *Sweet Rolls...and a little bit more.* Jace ordered one with raisins and walnuts, and Rob got a plain one and a fried egg.

While they waited at the counter, Jace took a stack of napkins from Rob's outstretched hand and wiped the sweat from his face, neck, and arms. Despite having spent the summer hauling bales of hay, Jace wasn't quite as muscular as his friend. His straight, dark brown hair usually swept the tops of his hazel eyes, but now it was damp and matted, and he scraped it away from his forehead.

"How are the criminal justice courses coming?" Jace asked.

Rob raised an eyebrow. "Fine. You still doing computer science?"

"Yup."

Rob gave him a thumbs up. A worker handed them their food on flimsy paper plates, and they sat across from each other at a square table in the far corner. Rob put his fried egg on top of his sweet roll and cut into it, glancing outside the window while he ate.

"So, you want to tell me about the prank?"

Rob held up a finger. "These aren't pranks. They're operations."

Jace narrowed his eyes. His metal chair scraped loudly on the tile as he scooted closer to the table. "I watched that video you sent me. Of that anti-cop group. Zero...something?"

"Zero Supremacy. We call them Zeroes. Here, I've got a better one to show you. This was last week, right here in New Brig." Rob whipped the hair from his face, pulled up the video on his phone, and leaned forward.

"Hey Rob!" A smiling Polynesian student with black basketball shorts, a red T-shirt, and curly black hair walked to their table holding a plate with two sweet rolls. He was tall, and Jace guessed he was over 300 pounds. He had a deep, raspy voice. "So, this is Jace?"

"Hi, Eli. Yup, that's him," Rob sighed, with mock disappointment. Jace met Eli's outstretched arm in a fist bump. Eli sat next to Jace, smiling. He seemed to have a genuine face that told you precisely what he was feeling.

"Trombone, right?"

Jace nodded.

"Piccolo." Eli followed this with something that sounded almost rehearsed. "I know what you're thinking. A big guy like me should play the tuba or the bass drum. But how many band instruments can you fit in your pocket?"

According to Rob, everyone involved in the operation was also in the Cale University Concert Band. That's how they had met. Rob and Jace had been in band together since junior high school. Rob played percussion.

"We're watching the Kodiak video," Rob said.

"Good." Eli nodded, chewing his food.

Rob angled his phone toward Jace, who switched seats to watch. It showed a group of people about Jace's age standing close together. They were milling about, restless. There were at least sixty of them—maybe a hundred. Guys and girls, different races. Nearly all of them wore red shirts or hoodies and baseball caps low to their eyes.

It was night. They were talking with each other, but not loudly. There were occasional smiles and laughter, but you wouldn't call the group cheerful.

Other figures moved in the background. Bystanders, apparently. They were difficult to see, except when briefly illuminated by street-lamps as they walked. Some scurried away, but others stood to watch, their backs to the brick walls of the buildings.

Everyone was waiting for something.

Someone in the video had a bullhorn. "Let's go." The sudden piercing, tinny voice made the Zeroes flinch. The red sea began to move. Though they weren't in step with each other, it looked like a march. The camera moved with them. Some in the crowd held their phones high and slowly panned from front to back, as if they were part of some historic event.

The person taking the cell phone video moved to the front of the group, the picture bouncing as they ran. A young white woman with short, light blond hair and dark red lipstick turned, walking backwards. She screamed at the Zeroes behind her. "Drop racist cops! Drop racist cops!" By the third time, everyone had joined in.

Jace glanced up. Rob and Eli were watching him.

"Where are they going?" Jace asked.

"Just watch," said Rob.

Occasionally there was a sound of something being dropped or knocked over, or broken. A car alarm went off. Three young men yanked on the pole of a stop sign, pulling it down. An old woman yelled something at the crowd, and about ten of them stopped to confront her.

A new chant had begun. "Stephen Dies!" yelled the girl. They roared their response, "Gina Fries!" This was repeated for a minute or so.

The light had grown brighter and more consistent as they marched into a more prominent section of the city.

Two of them, their hoods shadowing their faces, hefted a metal garbage can from the sidewalk and threw it at a large glass window, which cracked as the can bounced off and hit the cement with the sound of a large church bell. After two more tries, they broke through. Sparkling glass crystals covered the ground like a diamond carpet. Their friends cheered, and they both crept through the jagged window frame. One of them hurled a metal stool at a counter, knocking over a computer monitor.

A police officer darted in and tackled the most violent one. The other Zero looked as if he wanted to dive onto the officer, but hesitated. Everyone was yelling. More Zeroes approached the window, but new police officers jumped to block them. A few policemen went inside to help the wrestling officer. By the end, four Zeroes were arrested, and one police officer had a bloody nose and cuts to his arm.

The video ended.

"That's what we're fighting," Rob said solemnly, his caramel hair draped over one eye and his jaw firmly set.

"It didn't even show everything," said Eli. "The Zeroes went all the way to the police station."

Jace raised his eyebrows and scratched his neck. "That's...interesting." He looked down at his half-eaten sweet roll and pushed his plate away.

Rob and Jace had a history of pulling pranks. After the new principal had disappointed Elliot High School with strict enforcement of new, unreasonable rules—including no hats—they had managed to disguise a sound system at the closing assembly, complete with two large subwoofers. To the delight of the students, Rob had started the *Jaws* theme from his phone each time the principal approached the microphone.

Until now, the worst they'd faced was suspension from school.

"All the yelling about Stephen and Gina," said Jace. "Is that Stephen Hobbs? The guy who got shot last year?"

Rob and Eli glanced at each other. Eli coughed.

"It was national news, Jace," said Rob. "Still is."

"I don't really pay attention..."

Rob squeezed his eyes shut for a moment, then leaned closer. "Okay. Stephen Hobbs was a kid running from the cops. He looked like he had a weapon and ran at one of them, and she shot him. Gina Lambson. Zero Supremacy went crazy. Riots, vandalism, arson..."

"The Zeroes think she only shot him because he was black," added Eli.

"Ah," said Jace, nodding. "Any evidence for that?"

"From what I can tell," said Rob, "she followed her training exactly."

"And this has been going on since last year?"

"It calmed down for a while, but Gina is finally on trial. So, they're getting worked up again."

"Are Zeroes normally this violent, then? I thought a few of them had gone rogue or something."

"Nah, they're all the same. Violence is their big thing."

Jace slouched and folded his arms. "So you think we can do a better job fighting Zeroes than armed police officers can?"

Eli laughed. "It's not hand-to-hand combat. We're smarter than that."

"In fact," said Rob, "You won't come within two hundred feet of a Zero. I promise."

Jace furrowed his brow and nodded. He gazed at the pool game down the hall before looking back at Rob and Eli. "So, what are we doing?"

Eli scooted his chair closer.

"Did you notice what business they broke into?" asked Rob.

"No."

"Kodiak Security Bank."

"A bank? I thought they'd have bars on the windows or something."

"They do now," said Eli.

"Guess what statement they gave to the press after this happened?" Rob said.

Jace shrugged. "We want all of them arrested?"

"No. Nothing."

Jace's eyes widened. "Really?"

"Not entirely true," said Eli. "They said they appreciate free speech expressions or something like that."

Jace laughed incredulously. "Wow."

"The businesses around here are ridiculous," said Rob. "They won't stand up for themselves. They're encouraging Zero Supremacy."

"Welcome to Operation Coward," said Eli proudly. Rob put a finger to his mouth. "Sorry," whispered Eli.

"The Zeroes are getting together a week from Wednesday," Rob said.

"How do you know?" said Jace.

"He's got connections," said Eli.

"They're coming to Victor Square, a different part of town," said Rob, "and they are going to be right next to another branch of the same bank."

"We don't think they're planning to smash it up," said Eli. "Probably coincidence."

"And I thought they could use a welcoming committee," said Rob.

Jace tapped his fingers on the wooden tabletop. "Does your brother know you're doing this?"

"Yeah. Jed's pumped. He hates Zeroes. He has to deal with them, too. They're making things a lot more dangerous for the police who are just trying to do their job."

"Do your parents know?"

Rob leaned back in his chair, put his hands behind his head, and smiled a little. "Sort of."

"Your mom came by on Sunday. She made me promise to keep you from doing something stupid."

"Well, you already failed. I bought you breakfast."

Eli chuckled as he wiped his face with a napkin.

"It's just us, then?" Jace sighed.

Rob checked his watch and glanced around. "We've got one more.

I'd rather have all of us here when we explain the plan, though. Can you stay after band rehearsal Monday?"

"Sure."

"Oh, and can you dress like you're in Texas? If one of my team won't stop sweating at the operation, Zeroes are going to get suspicious."

CHAPTER TWO

THE BAND ROOM had a black ceiling and high, brown carpeted walls to absorb the echo. A hundred black chairs stood in perfect semi-circles, four rows deep, like an army at attention. A carpeted podium in the center was their captain. At the back were marimbas, timpani, bass drums and a gong.

Jace felt at home. It even had that faint carpet smell, reminding Jace of when he'd collapse onto the living room floor after a long day of school. However, everything here was larger, more polished, and less dented than the band room back at Elliot High.

Jace was early. He sat at the back, hunched over, trombone case at his feet. He pulled a small metal object out of his pocket. It was twice as long as it was wide, about the dimensions of a car key fob. The corners and edges were rounded, and in the center on both sides was a tiny grid of holes for gripping. He leaned forward in his chair and studied it while turning it over.

"So," said Rob just behind Jace's ear, changing his voice to sound like Jace's mother. "How is your first day of school?"

Startled, Jace dropped the metal item, and quickly grabbed it off the carpet.

"What's that?" said Rob.

Jace handed it to him.

Rob smiled. "Another toy your dad made, huh? It's cool he does that. I have a few at home still." He turned it over, lightly squeezed it, and pulled at the edges. "This one's not much of a toy, though."

Jace chuckled. "We're all grown up. They're tokens now."

"Right." Rob shrugged, tossed it back to Jace, and worked on removing the black timpani covers.

The trickle of students had increased. A tall trombonist with a maroon button-up shirt and rough, curly blond hair introduced himself as Howard Foster and asked Jace to scoot down to his third-chair seat. Howard looked like he was in his thirties. "Trombones," he sighed. "The worst seats in band. We hear the percussion the loudest."

Rob winked at Jace as he flipped a drumstick and caught it.

"So how long have you played trombone?" asked Jace.

"Long enough."

Eli sat on the front row. He smiled and waved, and said something to Jace, which was totally inaudible for the noise of instruments playing random bits of music. Someone played nimble arpeggios on a marimba, and the trumpets were showing off.

Dr. Kline entered the room, a short and swift-moving figure carrying several large black binders under his arm. He had neatly combed brown hair, a trim and graying beard, and glasses that looked a little small for his face. Without talking to, or even looking at anyone else in the room, he strode directly to the director's platform as the volume dropped to zero.

"We'll begin with Tunbridge Fair."

Jace reached for his music folder and glanced up. Dr. Kline was ready to begin—and so was everyone else. How was Jace the only one not ready?

There was no movement at all, and barely any sound. Jace froze to fit in. He hoped that Dr. Kline would begin the song so he could finish preparing his music unnoticed. That always worked in high school.

"We're waiting," said Dr. Kline, looking at the wall behind them.

As quietly as possible, Jace retrieved the binder from his backpack. The only sound in the room was him turning the pages.

The band director took a deep breath and suddenly raised his arms.

He launched into the piece at a furious pace—twice as fast as Jace had practiced on his own. The band had completely shaken Jace loose by the tenth measure.

Though Jace had a few songs he could play well, which he used to his full advantage at his scholarship audition, he had never committed to being a great trombonist. He groaned inwardly at the work it would take to catch up to everyone else at the university level.

At the end of the piece, Howard leaned over and whispered, "I think the bigger question here is: how long have *you* been playing the trombone?"

After rehearsal, Rob directed Jace and Eli into a soundproof practice room with four chairs, a round table, and a large window. Jace leaned against the wall in the corner, his hands in his pockets. Rob and Eli sat in chairs, Eli resting an arm on the table, and Rob laughed hard with his chair tipped back against the wall.

"Jace, that was hilarious though. When Kline was ready to go on Tunbridge, and you just froze." He held his arms out in a random, motionless pose, with only his eyes moving about nervously. "It's like you were hiding from a T-Rex that can only see you if you're moving."

Eli laughed, too. He was nearly silent, head back and shaking.

"Yes, I need about ninety hours of practice before next rehearsal," Jace said, hanging his head. "I'd rather talk about the operation. What are we doing as the welcoming committee for the Zeroes?"

"We're making a sign," said Eli, a huge grin still on his face. "A big one."

"I hope you're an artist," said Jace. "Rob's stick figures are worse than his handwriting."

Rob nodded to someone outside the window. "We're getting some help on that, actually. From India."

"Outsourcing the artwork?" said Jace. "Smart."

Eli grinned.

A girl with jeans, a red tank top, and disapproving glasses stepped into the practice room and shut the door behind. Her wavy hair looked unnaturally dark against her pale skin. Something about the way she dressed made her seem ten years older.

She set her backpack, keys, and phone on the table. Then she took a deep breath and smiled. "Hi. I'm India. Clarinet. You must be Rob's friend."

"For now, yes."

"I hope you didn't feel too bad about being put on the spot today." India pulled a binder from her backpack. "Dr. Kline has a way of making awkward situations much worse. He's a brilliant director, though."

Having played trombone in junior high, Jace was no stranger to awkward situations. "Yeah. I met with him in the Spring for a scholarship audition."

"Did you get it?" asked Eli.

"Half tuition."

"Nice," Eli said, looking surprised.

India flopped into a chair and flipped through her binder. "Deepest apologies for not meeting you a few days ago." She glared at Rob. "Gives a girl fifteen minutes' notice on a Saturday morning."

Rob shrugged and tipped his chair firmly onto the floor. "Is it done?"

She held her notebook to him, still glaring.

Rob laughed out loud when he saw it. "That's perfect!" Eli and Jace looked over his shoulder and laughed, too. It was a sketch of a wide banner that read, *Kodiak Security Bank Proudly Welcomes Zero Supremacy.* The *Zero Supremacy* lettering was bright red. There was an illustration of a handshake below it. One cartoon arm wore a suit coat, while the other had a red sleeve. At the bottom was a simple line of smaller text: *Please don't hurt us!*

"So, what does Zero Supremacy even mean?" asked Jace.

Eli answered. "They think America is powered by white supremacy, wealth supremacy, male supremacy...that sort of thing. And, apparently, yelling and violence is supposed to change that."

India looked at Jace over her glasses. "Did they show you the video where a kid hit a policewoman in the face with a brick? Real gentlemen, those Zeroes."

"We have long rolls of heavy-duty paper," Rob said. "We're going to paint it Thursday night at my place."

"You're actually going to help paint this time?" asked India.

Rob smiled again. "Of course!"

"So," said Jace, "we hang this up the night before their big protest."

"No..." Rob said. "We're going for more attention than that. You're going to like it. And if I remember correctly, you're not afraid of heights...?"

"India is our getaway driver," said Eli.

"We need a getaway?" said Jace. "Like, an escape?" His mouth twisted.

Rob folded his hands behind his head after brushing his hair back. "I told these guys you'd help us. It looks like you're not sure." He and Eli watched Jace while India scrolled on her phone.

"Well...I'm *not* sure."

"About what exactly?"

"Mostly, if..." Jace squinted at the recessed light on the dark ceiling. "If she's innocent."

"Gina Lambson?"

"Yeah." Jace shrugged. "If what she did was justified."

Rob blinked.

"I mean, I understand why you're defending her. She's a cop. Practically your whole family are cops. But I guess I just want to see what the jury says before I take a side."

Rob leaned forward. "Ask me if I know."

"What?"

"If she's innocent. Ask me."

"Do you?"

"Nope." Rob sat up straight. "I mean, I've looked into it and I have some *very* strong suspicions. But I want justice done, same as you. If she's guilty, she's guilty."

Jace slowly nodded.

"Look. You saw the videos. And it's not just Zero Supremacy. All of New Brig is going crazy. Everyone is arguing and marching, and most of them are against her. Influencing public opinion. *They* are the ones taking a side without all the facts."

"Yeah."

"You don't sound convinced, Jace. What's up?"

Jace slumped into the chair next to him. "Remember Pauliston last year? Iowa."

"Sure. What does it have to do with this?"

"That cop literally beat that guy to death," Jace said. "On video. And it looks like the cop really *was* racist."

"I know. Homicide. The cop's in prison where he belongs." Rob slapped his hand on the table. "Jace, this was *not* Pauliston. Not even close."

India and Eli glanced at each other.

"I know it wasn't. But, if the people of New Brig have decided that they are seeing a pattern with white officers shooting black people..." Jace trailed off, struggling to find the right words.

"You mean there might be bigger societal issues to solve in America? Systemic problems? That kind of thing?"

"Sure."

Rob dropped his head and nodded. "All right. Let's say that America has these huge, embedded race issues that somehow cause police to be more likely to shoot a black person than a white one. Who are the Zeroes targeting right now?"

Jace paused. "Gina Lambson."

"Exactly. Our city asked her to put her life on the line to protect us. They trained her and handed her a gun and a disappointing paycheck. And from everything I've seen in this situation, she did *exactly* what her training required her to do. There might be someone to blame here, but it's not her."

India set her phone down and watched.

"The trial has to be just about what one officer did," Rob continued. "Not some big thing about justice for all cops and all black people, trying to balance the cosmic scales or something. How is she going to get a fair trial if people are obsessed with that instead of the facts...of...this...case?" Rob pounded his fist on the table at each of those last four words, as if frustration had been building for weeks.

"I'm with you," said Jace. "But do you think America shouldn't have that conversation, then, about whether there is some problem with the system?"

"Sure. Have whatever conversation you want. But not while you're pointing your finger at Gina in a courtroom. Those are separate things, man."

Jace exhaled deeply, and slowly nodded. "So, you're not out there saying Gina is innocent. You're just telling the Zeroes to shut up and to leave it to the justice system."

"Yes! Exactly. I'm not trying to get her *out* of the grasp of justice. I'm all for it. *Actual* justice. For Gina, the one on trial. And if we can quiet the Zeroes a little, maybe justice will have a shot."

Eli and India nodded, and looked at Jace.

"I've got your back either way," Rob said. "But we need to know. Are you in this or not?"

They watched him. India lifted an eyebrow.

Jace folded his arms and looked at the brown carpet. Then he smiled. "Only if I can help plan the next one."

CHAPTER THREE

THE NEXT MORNING, Jace sat in the center of his required botany class, his interest in plants hovering around zero. Every desk was taken. It was ten o'clock, but no professor. Students whispered and glanced around the dull room. The ceiling was alabaster, it smelled like books and paper, and the whiteboards provided no contrast to the sterile, glossy walls behind.

Jace slouched and spun a pen on his desk.

"Hey!" someone whispered. Jace felt a poke in his back. He turned to see a girl with long, straight brown hair and dark eyelashes over almond-shaped eyes. "I dropped my pencil," she said.

He found it underneath his desk, examined it, and then eyed her suspiciously. She wore a plain blue long-sleeve shirt and her sterling earrings and necklace with a silver moon contrasted with her olive skin. "How do I know this is yours?" he said.

"I dropped it. Just now." At his continued hesitation, she briefly leaned forward and whispered, "You can trust me."

He held the pencil out of her view. "There is a number on this pencil. Can you tell me what it is?"

"Um, is it the number two?"

Jace feigned disappointment and put the pencil on his desk.

"Great," she said. "So...you'll give it back?"

He narrowed his eyes, opened a notebook, and flipped to a clean sheet of paper. "I'd better get your name," he sighed, "just in case."

She raised an eyebrow and smiled. "Mari."

"M-A-R-R-I?"

"Just one R."

He wrote it down and glanced up. "Last name?"

"You know where you can find me." She leaned forward again and patted her desk. "You can include our class schedule in your police report."

He nodded and handed her the pencil. "I'll leave Social Security Number blank for now."

A thin student in a gray sweater, thick-rimmed glasses, and smooth hair combed to the side walked to the chalkboard. He had been sitting on a windowsill at the back of the room. "Welcome to Botany 1250, Plant Biology," he said. "I'm Professor Adelson."

He introduced the course and his expectations on assignments. "One last thing." He pulled a microscopic piece of lint from his sweater. "Here we will study not just the plants themselves, but their environments and the threats to their existence. Humans need plants. But paradoxically, we seem intent on destroying them.

"Next month, Germany will host the World Climate Summit where the United States will *hopefully* vote to pass the Planet Survival Accord. I'm sure most of you have heard, but the accord is an agreement for nations to cooperate and take much-needed action to save our environment. We'll discuss the accord next week in detail, and we'll also track the summit carefully in class.

"Now." He clasped his hands. "Each year I'm blessed with one freshman who knows more than all the climatologists and meteorologists in the world." There were a few chuckles around the room. "With all the material we need to cover, we won't have time to discuss the existence of climate change, or whether the Earth is round. That is, except for today."

Professor Adelson straightened. "Please raise your hand now if you are that prodigy climate change denier. We'll wait."

Quiet footsteps in the hallway echoed through the closed door.

"Anyone not convinced that the Earth has been warming up? Or that humans are causing it?" He leaned against his desk in the corner and folded his arms. "Don't worry, this won't hurt your grade. Free pass, today only."

Jace hoped a gladiator would rise. He'd enjoyed irritating his more annoying teachers in high school. In fact, the perfect storm had arisen three years earlier when he and Rob had an algebra class with a teacher who was especially condescending. They'd pulled pranks and squandered class time, arguing with her about the parts of story problems that had nothing at all to do with math.

Today, though, the gladiator certainly wouldn't be him—he had no points of disagreement. Oh, he'd seen climate change disputes before. Is a warmer world all that bad? And are humans really causing it? They were logical questions, some of them. But the thought of a college student defying thousands of scientists...

The young professor jerked his head, smirked, and looked directly at Jace. "Yes?"

Jace hadn't raised his hand, or even moved. He stared at Adelson as every student in his peripheral turned in unison.

He felt he had to say something. Maybe a joke. As he opened his mouth to suggest that Santa Claus could use a break on his heating bill, a girl's voice directly behind him brought a wave of relief.

"Yes, I have a question."

Students grinned and murmured.

"It's about that Planet Survival Accord."

Jace looked behind. Mari sat as tall as her short frame would allow, her hands calmly folded on the desk. She glanced at Jace and winked.

Adelson folded his arms, his smirk remaining. "Please."

"I've been thinking about it," she said, "and I just have one question: who should be in charge?"

He leaned forward. "In charge of...?"

"Deciding what we do about the climate. Of making it all happen."

The professor scratched the back of his head with a pained look on his face. Jace wasn't following, either.

"It's national governments, global committees..." Adelson shook his head. "I'm not sure what you're asking here. You'd like to be in charge *yourself*?"

The class laughed, including Mari. "No. I'm wondering whether governments will be best at solving this, or private industry."

Adelson tilted his head and raised a hand to his chin. "You think private industry can solve the climate crisis."

"Yes."

He looked amused. "Please explain."

"Well, inventors are great at solving problems, right? Large and small. They've been the Earth's best friend for centuries, helping us do more with less."

"Why can't we do both? Pass the Survival Accord to allow governments to do what they can, and see what your inventors do in the meantime. Team effort, you know? Fight for our planet with all we've got."

This seemed reasonable. Students nodded and began turning away from Mari. That wasn't as exciting as Jace had hoped.

She wasn't done, however.

"The way I see it, we *can't* do both," she said. "I've looked at the accord. It will bring new regulations and taxes and wealth transfer."

"A small price to pay for saving the Earth."

"Sure—if that's really the best way. But those things hurt businesses, entrepreneurs, and inventors—you know, private industry. So, what if it turns out that those guys are much better than global governments at reducing human harm to the planet?"

The class faced her again, with renewed interest.

Professor Adelson took a step toward her, holding up the syllabus. "This is a science class. Do you have a *science*-related question for us?"

"Oh, but it *is* science-related." She sat a little taller. "The accord's proposals go deep into political, economic, and social sciences. If we want to be successful, we have to consider those, too." She furrowed her brow. "Whether the climate is changing isn't the only question on the table. Even if we're all in lock step on the science and the causes and everything, we should still hash out the details of what we do and how."

She backed down a little. "But we can keep this just to earth science if you like." Jace could tell she was being genuine in her offer.

The professor put the marker to his chin and gazed at the desk in front of him, as if he were deciding whether to continue.

"So, we're just going to *invent* our way out of this?" He looked up. "Improving the efficiency of a refrigerator is a drop in the ocean. It will take a million inventions to turn the tide here."

She smiled. "Luckily, the earth has a million inventors."

Eyebrows raised and heads nodded.

"You'd like us to do *nothing* for the climate, then," Adelson challenged.

"I didn't say that. Again, it's a matter of who. And what." She shifted. "How did we get millions of people to stop chopping down trees to heat their homes? We didn't create a law for that. We didn't *have* to. And last semester I studied the horse crisis of the 1890's. Manure and even dead horses clogged the streets of the big cities. It was a serious health and environmental situation. Thankfully, they didn't pass a City Survival Accord that slowed—or stopped—the invention of the automobile. I really do think we'll invent our way out of this if we can keep from creating policies that will discourage it."

"On-line shopping made it so we don't have to drive as much," offered another student.

The professor frowned. "You think there is some revolutionary discovery just around the corner? Let's hear it."

"It could be perfecting solar technology," Mari said, "or quantum cell phones, or something else entirely that we've never considered. Maybe it will give us cleaner energy or make it so we don't have to use as much. It could be just a lot of smaller inventions that add up, you know? We have quite a track record of improving the climate with big new inventions and small improvements. When we analyze trends to predict the future, we should take that into account along with our climate models. Sometimes it feels like we assume that one hundred years into the future we'll have the same technology as today."

A student near the door raised her hand. "You said that we can't invent and tax at the same time," she asked Mari. "Why not?"

"Businesses and regular people have ideas all the time," Mari answered. "They save up money and spend late nights in the garage working on it. The more we tax them, the less freedom and resources and incentive they have to try. I believe there's a reason that far more inventions come out of America than from countries with heavier taxes."

The student nodded thoughtfully. The grins had long disappeared. This wasn't the smackdown of some anti-science home schooler. It was less fun, he supposed. But more intriguing.

The room was silent while Professor Adelson seemed to gather his thoughts. Mari waited patiently.

Adelson picked up his dry erase marker again and slowly paced at the front of the room.

"Private industry," he mused. "Capitalism."

He pointed the marker at Mari. "Capitalism is precisely what got us *into* this mess."

The class turned to Mari, who gave no response. She was shockingly calm, in fact.

Adelson continued. "Capitalism is responsible for the oil fields, where humans are drawing the very blood from the earth and shipping it across the oceans of the world in polluting tankers. It's responsible for every device that consumes fossil fuels."

Jace sensed that Mari had more to say, but chose not to.

Professor Adelson gained speed and volume as he walked. He went on about working conditions in the Philippines and a growing gap between rich and poor. He complained about flashy sales at used car lots, pointless vacations, and seas littered with plastic.

He stopped pacing and faced Mari. "You'd like to convince the world to fix the climate with *capitalism*? Be my guest."

He slapped the marker on his desk in a mic drop sort of way. While there was a scattered, brief applause, most of the students appeared to be contemplating.

"Thank you," Mari said, brightly. "I'll give it some more thought."

That was all.

The professor appeared almost angry at how Mari had brushed his monologue aside. From her response, you would have thought Professor Adelson had just given her advice on Chapstick flavors to try. No tears or asking forgiveness, no fighting back or admission that she had been wrong. The awaited Roman gladiator had turned out to be more of a Greek philosopher.

Adelson opened his mouth to speak, but then shut it again. Then in his quiet, polished tone, he reviewed the test schedule.

Something had happened between Mari and Professor Adelson, but Jace couldn't explain what it was.

Jace and Mari loaded their backpacks and left the classroom at the same time. Standing up, she was shorter than expected.

Mari, looking worried, motioned for Jace to come closer as they walked into the hallway. She pointed to a guy a few paces ahead of them. "I saw him using three separate pens during class. He couldn't possibly own all of them. You should check into it."

Jace coughed and stifled a smile. "Thanks for the tip, ma'am. You're a model citizen."

They followed the crowd toward the outer doors. Jace turned sideways to avoid someone. "So, why did you stop?"

"What do you mean?"

"When he piled onto capitalism like that. Seemed a bit harsh." He leaned down a little to hear her over the noise.

"Honestly, there was some truth to the things he said. And I think he was talking more about big-corporation crony capitalism than the simple free market, like I was. But I think he's forgetting that it wasn't Congress that created the solar panel."

"It seemed like there was more you could have said."

"Oh, right." She smiled. "Yes, we probably could have gone on forever. I didn't want to take up too much class time. Plus, did you really think a student could win an argument with a professor? You struck me as smarter than that, detective..." She trailed off, inviting a response.

"Jace."

"Right."

They squinted in the sunlight as they left the building and stopped a few paces from the door.

"I sort of wanted to hear what you would say next," Jace said.

"Really? What was interesting to you?"

"Well, the whole idea of a bunch of ordinary people solving big problems is cool. I hadn't thought of the climate being something that, you know, entrepreneurs could tackle."

She smiled. "Regular people have more power than they think."

"Adelson sure doesn't think so."

Mari laughed. "No, he doesn't! Not in that way, at least. We need to have a little faith and trust our entrepreneurs."

"Unless we regulate and tax them out of business with the Planet Survival Accord."

"Exactly! Some ideas that seem good can end up making things worse instead of better."

"And you think the accord will make things worse," Jace said.

"Probably."

She seemed so confident. And at the same time, humble.

Jace adjusted his backpack strap. "I still don't get why you cut it short in class."

"I told you. I wasn't going to win."

He laughed. "Then why did you start?"

"Mari!" A tall blond girl interrupted the discussion from the other side of the entrance.

Mari turned her head and waved. "Just a second!"

She looked at Jace for a moment, a smile creeping to her face.

"Want to know why I started that discussion?" She leaned up to him and lowered her voice. "I wasn't talking to the professor."

More confused than ever, he watched as she hurried to her friend, turning back to give him a wave. He smiled with one side of his mouth, as if even his face was unsure how to react.

That conversation needed a sequel.

CHAPTER FOUR

AFTER WEDNESDAY'S BAND REHEARSAL, Rob and Eli brought Jace to one of their favorite hangouts, Emmie's Place, just outside of campus. The enormous cafeteria-style restaurant served food on gray trays, smelled like cheese, and the kitchen was so noisy that Jace felt like he was right there with the cooks and the dishwashers.

Jace set his tray on the table, sporting an impressively large cheeseburger. He sat down and took a massive, satisfying bite.

Rob swallowed and gave Jace a thumbs up. "You were much improved at rehearsal."

"Still a long ways to go, though."

Eli choked on his drink and stared at Rob's plate. "What on earth is on your sandwich?"

"Sliced banana."

Jace grinned. "Don't tell me this is the first time you've seen him do this."

"No," said Eli. "Still freaks me out, though."

"He's always looking for the next big dish. The lazy way. Just mixes things you wouldn't think are good together and tries them out."

"Hey!" Rob said. "Lots of delicious things are discovered this way."

"I thought you learned your lesson with the sauerkraut and applesauce," said Eli.

Rob shrugged. "Why did that guy climb Mt. Everest?"

"I don't think you'll get the Presidential Medal of Freedom for discovering a way to turn lasagna into breakfast food. What are you going to do? Open your own weird restaurant?"

"Maybe," Rob swallowed. "Or a cookbook, TV show. I need to finish my menu first."

Eli shook his head. "So, how's the banana burger?"

Rob, chewing again, gave a thumbs down.

Just as Rob pulled out a checklist for Operation Coward, three girls appeared in the doorway, one of them with long hair, noticeably shorter than the other two.

Jace sat up straight. The girls walked to the back of the line. Jace stood and slowly pushed his tray to Eli. "I'll be back in a minute."

"Just because I'm big, doesn't mean I want to eat everybody's food," Eli called. "That's offensive." He grabbed two of Jace's fries.

Trying not to look like he was in a hurry, Jace sped to the end of the line before anyone else got in. The girls were talking and hadn't noticed him. He waited for a break in the conversation.

"Oh. Hi, Mari!" He hoped he appeared more natural than he felt.

She turned around, surprised. "You, again."

"Mari *is* your name, isn't it? It occurred to me that a pencil-stealer probably wouldn't use their real one."

She smiled. "Yes. It's Mariana, actually. And this is Amber and Holland. Guys, this is Jace. We have botany together."

He nodded to them. "I'm new here. So, what's good?"

"The French Dip!" Holland and Mari said it together and laughed.

Amber said, "I like their grilled chicken. You have to try it with onions, though."

He turned to Mari. "Hey, I have a question for you."

She switched places with Amber. "Just warning you, I haven't even looked at the homework."

Jace nodded and spoke a little quieter. "So earlier, you said you weren't talking to the professor. You may not recall, but I was there. You guys talked for like ten minutes, so..."

"Yeah, I might have been too cryptic," she chuckled.

"Who were you talking to, then?"

"Well, *you,* I guess. Like I said, we both know I could never win an argument with Adelson in front of the class. I brought up those ideas to help the other students think."

"Ah. To get us on your side, against the Planet Survival Accord."

She folded her arms. "No, not really. To be honest, I'm not entirely sure I'm *right.*"

Jace tilted his head. "You sure sounded confident in class today."

"I *am* confident that there are some important ideas left out of the conversation. That's the reason I brought it up. And if people don't have all the information, you can't blame them for making bad choices."

"Hm."

"I don't know for sure that there should be *no* global government action to help the planet. I'm obviously not the smartest person in the world—or even in the room. I just want to make sure other sides of the story get out there, too. I'm fine if the rest of the class supports the accord, as long as they understand those entrepreneur trade-offs."

"Very humble of you," said Jace sincerely. "I think it actually strengthens your argument, admitting that you don't have all the answers."

"Well, thank you!"

"So, do you do this a lot? Talk to the professor-but-really-the-students?"

"Once in a while. I've been learning how to do it right."

The line had moved enough to place them in front of the trays, and they each took one.

"You should have kept the argument going with Adelson," Jace said, smiling. "He was getting pretty annoyed."

"I've tried that before. I've learned that being too long-winded or confrontational doesn't help. The professor and I can each take a few pawns, just enough to let the class see that there is a board and a game where maybe they didn't know one existed before."

They stepped in front of the grill, greeted by the sound and smell of sizzling beef, and an old man who asked for their order. The girls selected their favorites. No longer hungry, Jace stroked his chin as he scanned the prices. He ordered another cheeseburger—no fries this time.

Jace leaned over, gripping the metal bars near his tray. "So, what are you? Conservative? Liberal?" He guessed conservative, but he wanted her to say it.

She cocked her head. "Let's find out. What does 'conservative' mean to you?"

"I don't know," he hedged. "Republican?"

"Conservative meaning people that love freedom and independence?"

"Sure."

"Or do you mean the kind that are closed-minded? Afraid of change? Or racist?"

"Woah, I don't know!" He wished she would talk quieter. The man had been holding the cheeseburger plate out to Jace. At the mention of "racist" he pulled back and eyed him with a frown. Then he slowly handed it over.

"I don't think conservatives are racist," Jace mumbled.

"I don't, either. But some people do. When you say conservative, liberal, progressive, right, left, or whatever else, there is a long list of traits in your head that you associate with it. When you say that word to someone else, they think of *their* list, which probably doesn't perfectly match yours. That's a problem.

"If you can't tell, I don't like labels. Could you perhaps allow a modern woman more than one word to describe her complex array of views and opinions?"

"Please." He bent forward in a mock bow, knocking his tray off and flipping it face-down onto his shoes. The tray landed with a clatter. Conversations stopped and heads turned. Rob stood and clapped from across the room. Jace closed his eyes and his cheeks flushed.

Mari's friends turned. "What happened?"

Jace cleared his throat and glanced at the burger. "Didn't meet my standards." Mari stifled a laugh.

The napkins were out of his reach, but Mari was already fetching some. All three girls busily helped him clean up the mess. He stood holding a tray with a pile of dirty napkins and cheeseburger parts scattered on the tray as if diners here were expected to assemble their own meal.

The man behind the counter looked at him in the same distrustful way as before. "Another cheeseburger?" Jace didn't even want *this* one. With the girls watching him expectantly, he sighed and nodded.

He turned to throw away the mess on his tray. The man called after him. "No, leave it there until you pay."

"Pay for both cheeseburgers?"

"Of course." The man had apparently prepared the second one during the cleanup and handed another plate to him right away. Jace set it on the tray next to the obliterated one.

Mari watched, amused. "Talk about this a different time?"

"Probably," Jace said. "One last thing, though."

"What?"

"You said that this is all something you learned. Where did you learn it?"

"You have a lot of questions, Jace. But then, you *are* a detective." She smiled and played with a lock of her hair for a moment. "I'm not sure you're ready for the answer." She stepped to the cash register.

Jace wasn't sure whether she had just flirted with him or brushed him off. He scratched his head and risked one more question. "I know where you sit in class. But in case I need help with homework, could I get your number?"

"Homework, huh?" Mari said with a wink. "All right." She had been so cryptic in their conversations that Jace wouldn't have been surprised if she'd responded with a calculus problem. She delighted him by giving exactly ten digits.

The girls waited while he paid for his second and third cheeseburgers, and the four of them carried their trays through the maze of tables, toward some empty ones at the back. Eli saw them coming and put one of his two trays of food on his lap.

"I'll...sit with my friends over here," Jace said awkwardly.

"Oh, cool," Mari said. "Hi, everyone."

"We're in band together," volunteered Eli.

Mari stopped while her friends found a table. "You're in a band? Which one?"

"Cale University Concert," Eli beamed.

Rob chimed in. "You know, trumpets and flutes and stuff."

Jace smiled tightly. He'd never experienced the upside of telling a girl he was in band. Once, he had even searched—unsuccessfully—for an oversized guitar case he could cram a trombone into.

"Oh. Well, enjoy your food!"

Eli put Jace's old tray back on the table. There were still a couple of fries left.

"A few more giant burgers," Rob mused. "Why not?"

"I've got another combo for you to try," Jace said. "I mixed a cheeseburger with a dirty floor."

Rob hesitated. Jace could only recall a few times Rob turned down a strange food combination offered to him.

"Not today."

That night, Jace was halfway through his calculus assignment when he reached for a snack. He frowned. Two granola bars instead of four.

Adam, his roommate, sat on the floor with his back to the bed, squinting at a tablet inches from his face. They had spoken little, and when they did, it was always Jace that began the conversation.

Jace sat back in his chair and unwrapped one of the bars. He noticed Adam's headphones were covering only one ear.

"Can I ask you something?"

"What."

"If you had up to five sentences to describe yourself politically, what—"

"Democrat," Adam interrupted, without looking up.

"Oh. Cool."

Jace pulled out headphones of his own and went back to work.

CHAPTER FIVE

JACE FLIPPED through the pages of his textbook, waiting for another session of botany to begin.

"Hey," Mari whispered behind him. "What band instrument do you play?"

He turned. He hadn't noticed her come in. "Oh, hi. Trombone."

"The big slidey thing, right?" She held her fists in front of her and moved one of them forward and back.

"Perfect. Looks like you play too."

"Ha. We guessed trumpet. We were close, right?"

"Definitely." He turned sideways in his desk. "Hey, question for you."

"Keep in mind that I have a weekly question limit, Jace," she said, "and you're getting close."

Mari looked into his eyes with her hands folded on her desk, the same way she did when addressing Professor Adelson two days ago. She wore that same necklace with the moon.

"As I recall," he said, "you were about to tell me where you learned to think and talk. You know, about what you said to Adelson last time."

"I'm pretty sure I said I was *not* going to tell you."

Jace held up his hands in a shrug. "I guess we remember things differently."

"Are you really interested, then?"

"Yeah."

She tapped her pencil to her cheek. "Okay. Now this will sound weird, but I have a test for you."

His expression dulled. "There's not like a book or a link you can give me?"

"There is. Sort of. But it's better if you experience it first, and I want to see if you've got what it takes."

Jace leaned his elbow on the edge of her desk, rested his chin on his hand, and muttered, "The more you talk, the more questions I have."

She opened her backpack. "Give me a minute."

Jace faced forward. A few minutes later, she set a ruled sheet of paper on his shoulder. He grabbed it. There were two columns drawn in pencil, labeled *Different* and *Similar*. At the top, the title read, *Rabbits and Horses*.

Jace turned it over. Nothing on the other side. Then he flipped it back to the front and studied it, hand to his chin.

"Well?" she said. "Self-explanatory?"

Adelson entered the room and began writing on the board.

"So," Jace slowly whispered, "you want me to list some similarities and differences between rabbits and horses."

"Very good! You *are* a detective. Yes, write everything you can think of."

"Why those animals specifically?"

"They're random. It's just so I can see how you think."

"Hmm." Jace raised his eyebrows and shrugged. "All right."

"Let's begin," Adelson announced. He started into a review of plant tissues that took the entire hour.

"This class wasn't nearly as exciting as the last one," Jace said to Mari as they stood from their desks. "I was kind of hoping you'd stand up and make the case that rainforests really aren't that cool."

"I think I'll let you take that one on."

He handed her the sheet of paper as she lifted her backpack to her shoulder.

"Oh. That was quick."

She read the list in its entirety. Under differences he listed size, tail, rideability, rabbits live in a cage, and, hoping for a laugh, horses are easier to hunt. His list of similarities was equally generic. He thought he had nailed it.

He wasn't expecting the genuine disappointment on her face.

"Did I pass?"

"No." She handed the paper back to him.

Jace frowned. "Did I write the wrong things?"

"You didn't write nearly enough. I said to write *everything* you can think of."

Frustrated, and a little embarrassed, Jace walked her into the hall.

"I suppose you can try again," Mari said. "If you want."

Jace shrugged.

They talked about their plans for the weekend, a stilted conversation about Jace's bike ride with Rob, and Mari's baking. He walked with her as far as the front doors of the library, even though his next class was in the opposite direction.

"Enjoy your studies." Jace scuffed the toe of his shoe against a cement step.

Mari looked as if she wanted to say something but changed her mind. She gave him a quick smile. "See ya."

Jace still held the test in his hand. As he reached the bottom of the steps, he dropped it in the trash.

CHAPTER SIX

"NICE WARM-UP," Jace panted. "But any time you want to start riding, let me know." The gears grated on his mountain bike, then clicked loudly into place as he tried to pass his friend.

Rob looked to the side, his long hair flying from underneath his helmet. "You're still here? I thought I'd lost you back at campus."

As they approached Oak Bend Park, Jace tipped his yellow polarized glasses down to behold the true colors of the forest. Nothing but fresh air, trees, and grasses, cut through by smooth dirt trails, some gullies, and a highway overpass in the distance. It was late on a cloudless morning and the sun, riding high in the sky, made the sweat pour down his face and back.

Rob took a sudden left onto a narrow single-track that Jace hadn't seen coming. Jace followed, his back tire fishtailing as he made the turn. The steep trail curved on banked corners and short, choppy hills put air under Jace's tires. Adrenaline rushed through him as he flew down the trail. At the bottom, Jace shifted gears again and allowed his muscles to recover for the inevitable climb. The single-track looped back up to the main pathway.

They rode to where the ground met a wall of the overpass—the highest point in the park. Here, Rob finally stopped and adjusted his fingerless gloves. The whir of the wind and Jace's squealing brakes had silenced, replaced by a chorus of chirping birds and the constant, low drone from the overpass.

They sat in the shade with their backs to the cool concrete and looked out into the trees. It felt like this was the very border between nature and civilization. They removed their helmets and Rob shook out his hair before tossing Jace a protein bar.

"Well, this is Oak Bend," said Rob. "Aren't you glad I told you to bring your bike to Cale?"

"Definitely. I just should have left the trombone behind."

Rob laughed. "I know, it's not high school anymore. But you've really been doing better."

"Howard's still way ahead of me."

"Well, he's probably been playing thirty years."

"Thirty years?"

"Nobody knows how old he really is." Rob sipped from his Camelback and looked out at the treetops in the distance. "So, tell me about her."

"Who?"

"That girl at Emmie's. Did you say her name is Mary?"

"Mah-ree." Jace split a long blade of grass down the middle. "I don't know, just a girl in my class."

"You don't buy eight burgers at once for just a girl in a class."

"True. Okay, she's fun. Interesting. She argued with our botany professor for ten minutes on the first day. He was totally confused."

At this, Rob raised his eyebrows. "We should take the girls to a movie or something."

"Woah!" Jace held up his hands. "It's not to that point yet. She might even have a boyfriend."

Rob nodded, amused. "Well, have fun getting all that figured out."

"So, what's the situation with you and India, precisely?"

"Yeah, we're together."

"Would she agree if I asked her?"

Rob shrugged. "It's casual. We don't sit around talking about relationships. At least, not while the Zeroes are still making trouble, screaming for blood. There's work to do."

Jace nodded and reached for another blade of grass. "So, how's she doing?" Jace asked. "The police officer, I mean. Gina Lambson."

Rob looked in the distance, twirled the hose of his Camelback, and sighed. "Not good. Jed knows one of the cops on her force and says she can't sleep more than two hours at a time. Even if she's cleared of everything, she doesn't even know where to start rebuilding her life."

"The trial starts in, what, four weeks?"

"Three."

"Man. I bet she just wants it to be done."

Rob nodded. "If we play our cards right, we can help give her story a happy ending. Well, as happy as it *can* be."

"Think we can make a difference?"

Rob shrugged. "Hope so. But it's not always about making a difference. Sometimes it's just knowing you took a stand."

The two friends weaved their way through the hodgepodge of old and new buildings on campus at the end of their ride. Jace looked forward to trading his hard seat for a cool shower. They rode down the main walkway, and Rob's bike squeaked to a stop.

"There's your girl."

Three students carried chairs and cardboard boxes to a white plastic folding table at the edge of the sidewalk, where Mari perfected the symmetry of a tablecloth.

Straddling his bike, Jace took a few steps forward. "Hi, Mari!"

She smiled. "Jace, how are you?" Rob winked at Jace as he drank from his Camelback.

"Remember Rob from Emmie's?" Rob moved up next to Jace.

"Oh, right," she said. "One of the band. Do you play trombone too?"

Rob violently sputtered and coughed. "Heavens, no."

"He can't play a real instrument," said Jace, "so they let him hit things in the back."

Mari grinned. "Percussion, I'm guessing."

A light breeze flipped over part of the tablecloth. Jace laid his bike on the grass and sprang to help.

"Thank you!"

"Perfect place for a group study?" Jace said, gesturing up at the sun. "Great idea."

Mari laughed. "Not exactly. Here." She handed them each a half-page flier from a box.

Jace read the title aloud. "America and Race—We've come a long way." Mari was always doing something unexpected. "A celebration of race relations?"

"Sure, why not?" said Amber, who had just arrived. She wore white pants and a blue top, and her short blond hair angled toward the table as she placed frosted red, white, and blue cupcakes in a grid. She was followed by two guys Jace had never seen before.

"So, you're saying everything is good now?" asked Jace.

Amber exchanged looks with one of the guys. "I told you they'd say that!"

A black student with jeans, a red polo, glasses, and an easy smile introduced himself as Kendric. The other said his name was Dylan. He was exceptionally thin, with angular facial features and perfect, dark hair. He wore basketball shorts and a T-shirt. His pale skin indicated he was not used to spending time in the sun, and the contrast was striking when he stood next to Kendric.

"No," Amber said, "we're not saying everything's just fine. And sometimes we take a step backward between the forward ones. But if you look at the big picture, we've made a *ton* of progress."

"Hmm..." said Jace, nodding. Rob gave no reaction. Kendric and Dylan crouched at the front of the table and taped a banner with the same title as the flier.

"It's healthy to recognize how far you've come," Kendric said, "even if you still have a way to go."

"Yeah, maybe," said Jace.

"Maybe?" Kendric stood. "If you have an F at school, your parents tell you to shape up, right? So, you work up to a B. Your parents still want you to get the A, but don't you think some positive feedback is helpful for the progress you *have* made?"

"Sure. Has it really gotten a lot better, though? With race in America, feels like we're maybe at a C minus."

"I think this kid has been watching too much TV." Kendric glanced at Dylan and smiled, then turned back to Jace. "Ever had a history class? Look at this timeline."

He pointed near the bottom of the flier which listed a series of events, starting with the beginning of North American slavery on the left. Moving along the timeline there were dates like the Emancipation Proclamation, the ending of segregation, and the Civil Rights Act. At the other end, the election of a black president. The arrow kept going, however, and above it read, *More progress to be made!*

"I'm black, obviously," Kendric said. "If you and I took a time machine back to this point, you and I probably couldn't be in the same school together. If we visited *this* time," pointing to another spot, "I might get beat up just for trying to vote. And if we went all the way back here? I just might have a chain around my ankle.

"Oh, we've still got issues." Kendric took a step back and held his arms out. "But look at me. Can you think of one thing I'm actually not legally allowed to do in America that you are? Because I can't. How is that not progress?"

"Excellent point," Jace said. He glanced at Rob. "This is about the Stephen Hobbs thing, isn't it? The black man shot by police."

"In a way," grunted Dylan as he struggled with a shade canopy. "A lot of students are attending anti-police protests. They say cops are looking for any excuse to shoot a black man. It makes the job of the police much harder when people think that. Trust goes out the window, the residents stop calling and talking to the police to solve crimes, and it's just more dangerous for everyone."

"Yes!" Rob said loudly and clapped as if he'd been waiting for someone to make this point for days. "Thank you."

"Do you think they shot him because he was black?" asked Jace.

Dylan shrugged. "Who knows for sure? They say she had a black boss once that fired her, she could have been prejudiced."

"Ridiculous," said Rob. "From what I can tell, she did what they train any cop to do."

Kendric nodded. "I've looked into it, too, and I think you're right."

"You're out here supporting the police, then," said Jace.

"No, we're not," said Amber, holding up a flier. "This is all we're saying."

Dylan, who had just finished with the canopy, walked over to Jace while fixing his hair. He motioned toward the others. "They get a little extreme sometimes in their neutrality. So, you into politics?"

"Sort of. My parents are."

"Liberal? Conservative?"

Jace paused. "Not much of a 'labels' guy."

Dylan grinned and briefly glanced at Mari, who was rearranging the cupcakes that Amber had already arranged. "I respect that. Following the Senate race at all?"

"Not really."

"You should look up Senator Weaver. If he doesn't get reelected..." Dylan shook his head.

Jace looked at Mari, who cheerfully handed a cupcake to someone walking by. "I'll check him out." But he'd already forgotten the senator's name.

The display was complete. Dylan took a picture. Mari offered Jace and Rob a cupcake.

"No thanks," said Rob.

Jace didn't really want to eat dessert right after his ride. However, it was probably Mari that baked it, and he wasn't going to turn that down. "Thanks!"

She walked back to the table and Jace looked back at the flier. "Hey. Why is the signing of the Constitution on your timeline of positive progress on race?"

"Sometimes we forget that slavery was here before our country was," said Kendric. "Ever heard of Frederick Douglass? Probably the most famous escaped slave ever. He didn't like the Constitution at all. But once he actually studied it, he called it a glorious liberty document."

"Doesn't it say that a black man is worth like half of a white man?"

"Race technically isn't mentioned in the Constitution at all. But for a non-free person, it was three fifths."

"Oh." Jace was confused. The black student he was talking to didn't have an issue with this?

Kendric smiled. "How I understand it, the South wanted to count slaves for representation. The North didn't want the South to have that much power because then slavery would stick around longer. So that was a compromise that they could get the South to agree to."

"You think it was a *good* thing to not count slaves the same as free people?"

"For their particular situation, I think so." Kendric nodded. "There was another compromise, too. The Constitution promised that Congress wouldn't try to stop importing slaves for another twenty years, but left the door wide open after that."

"I wouldn't have compromised."

"I know what you mean. But no compromise, no country. They found they'd have to solve some of their problems later. If they stayed under King George, they *definitely* would have still had slavery. In fact, in an early version of the Declaration of Independence, one of the grievances that Thomas Jefferson listed was that the king was pushing it onto the colonies."

"Thomas Jefferson. The slave-owner."

Kendric laughed. "Yes, kind of a mind-bender isn't it? He inherited slaves and the state of Virginia wouldn't let him free them. He and George Washington both wrote against slavery, but they did own slaves. A paradox, I guess. If you look at the big picture, though, those two men advanced the cause of human freedom light years ahead, for all races."

Rob walked off the sidewalk to the shade of a large tree and sat on the grass. Curious, Jace stayed near the table and leaned against his bike. Students walked past. Some slowed to read the banner. A few took fliers.

A girl in a white T-shirt and large sunglasses looked up from the flier. "Where did you get these stats?" she demanded.

Dylan replied, "It says at the bottom. The Economic Policy Institute."

The institute had compared numbers between 2018 and fifty years previous, separating the numbers by 'black' and 'white'. Things like high school graduation, life expectancy, poverty rate, and household wealth. It showed that while white people still had better numbers on average, black people had significantly narrowed the gap.

"Obviously not where we want to be yet," said Dylan. "But moving in the right direction, wouldn't you say?"

Dylan then pointed out a small chart from the Migration Policy

Institute showing that the United States had by far the most international migrants in the world. "If American life for immigrants of color is as bad as some people say, would we have so many coming here?"

She ignored his points. "Why are you only saying good things about race in America?"

Dylan stood from his chair and ran his hand back through his dark hair. "There is definitely good and bad. We think both stories should be told. The bad is already being covered pretty well here on campus, so we're sharing the other side today. I'm Dylan, by the way."

"You're doing a lot of damage, you know, to the progress that a lot of us are trying to accomplish."

"In what ways?"

"White people will stop caring about their privilege and all of that. There's a whole layer of oppression in society that we don't even see."

Dylan pointed toward the Union Center. "Do you see that display case? There is an announcement about a seminar on microaggressions, one on cultural appropriation, and a symposium that has something to do with race and power. Believe me, nobody at Cale has forgotten about the things that we still need to work on." He gestured toward the table. "We're four students at one table on one afternoon just here to remind people that we've made a lot of progress, too."

"Are you going to be attending those seminars?" she challenged.

"Yes. At least one of them. We should go together."

At that, she walked away.

Kendric laughed. "What was that, Dylan? Stop trying to get a date. People are leaving our table."

"I meant that we would *all* go together." He winked at Amber. "Don't worry, babe."

"At least offer them a cupcake next time!" said Amber.

More students walked by the table. A Hispanic guy looked over the flier and gave Amber a high five before taking a cupcake. A group of Caucasian girls talked with Mari.

There seemed to be a three-way split among support, disagreement, and confusion regarding the message. Jace wished they would all come talk for a while, to understand where Mari and her friends were coming from.

Shouted insults had peppered their conversations with other students. Mari and her friends were called white supremacists (mostly by white people) and bathwater scum. A girl yelled that whites would be the minority in American in thirty years, and they just shrugged. Another screamed "Drop racist cops!" They never yelled back, and mostly smiled in response.

A tall, thin woman with glasses and blond highlights slowed to a stop. She was easily over sixty and wore high heels and a red dress. She looked at the display, then at Mari and her friends.

Amber stood from her chair. "Mrs. Thompson."

The woman snatched a flier and scowled at it. "This had all better be accurate."

"It is, ma'am," Kendric said.

The woman paused as if she wanted to say something more, then crumpled the flier in her fist and walked away about as quickly as Jace thought possible in high heels. Amber shook her head and gave a knowing look to Dylan.

A hefty black student drew Jace's attention back to the table. He wore a large blue backpack and an orange striped shirt. Two others were with him, one white and one black.

"We've come a long way?" he said. "Tell that to Stephen Hobbs."

Rob stood from his spot on the grass, coolly walked over, and folded his arms. "Think he would disagree?"

CHAPTER SEVEN

"THE TAXPAYER-FUNDED murder of an unarmed black man?" said the student. "Yup, we've reached race nirvana. Time to celebrate."

"He wouldn't listen to the police officer," Rob said. "He was charging at her with something in his hand."

"A cell phone."

"She didn't know that." Then he spoke firmly and slowly. "She had to shoot."

Jace saw an intensity in Rob that he normally only saw in the drum line. Amber watched with her hands awkwardly at her side.

The student matched Rob's belligerent stance. "So there isn't another way that the police can interact with a black man? Just shoot him. Got it."

"Would have been the same if he were a white guy," Rob replied.

The student doubled over and laughed. Then he held out his hand to Rob. "Look around you, man! Watch the news. This ain't happening to whites."

Most of the passing students stopped to watch.

"That's not the point of the flier," said Amber. "I think you both have some—"

But Rob interrupted, ignoring her. "This year in Texas, more whites have been shot and killed by police than blacks."

"Well, that would make sense, wouldn't it? There are a whole lot more of you whites here than there are of us. How about you adjust those numbers proportionally? We are a much bigger target of police. Look at the prisons."

"Fine, let's talk statistics," said Rob. "Let's look at which race commits more crime."

The gathering crowd loudly said, "Oh…"

Dylan stepped between them and gestured toward the grass. "We'd rather not discuss this here. Gentlemen?" They ignored him, too.

"Why would I trust police statistics?"

"Cops aren't racist killers," Rob insisted.

"I can't believe you, man! You remember Pauliston, right?"

"There are bad people in every part of society," Rob said. "And we deal with them. You're acting like that officer escaped justice or something."

"My grandparents remember actual lynchings."

"They lynched whites too. Especially whites who fought against slavery and for civil rights."

"Next you're going to tell me that whites were slaves."

"Actually, they were, in other parts of the world." Rob unfolded his arms and put them to his side. "And the first slave owner in America was a black man. Most of us whites don't have any slave holders in our history. Actually, lots of our ancestors died fighting slavery in the Civil War."

"You're missing the point," the student said, gesturing to his head. "Think, man! You don't seriously mean to tell me that blacks have it as good as white people, right?"

A few began filming with their phones. Some cheered when Rob spoke, but more cheered for the other guy. Mari looked at Jace and motioned with her eyes toward the argument. He shrugged at her. She nodded. So, he chimed in from the sidelines.

"Right," Jace said. "There are black TV channels, but can you imagine if we had ones just for white people?"

The student laughed again. "What do you mean? *Every* other TV channel is for white people!"

Rob said, "There are certain words that you and I could say, right here today. They would kick me out of school immediately, but not you. I'm not seeing the bias against black people here."

Jace nodded. "Affirmative Action doesn't help me very much. Even if you and I are just as wealthy, you get a boost, and I don't."

The student threw his hands in the air. "Well, excuse me for accepting a tiny offering to help balance things a little."

"I get it..." began Rob.

"*How* can you possibly get it?" Rob's opponent clenched his fists. "You'll never have any idea what it's like to be us."

"I didn't say I know what it's like to be you," Rob replied. "I mean that I understand the intellectual point that you're making."

One of the student's friends pulled at his elbow.

"I hope I don't see your cop friends," the black student said.

Rob answered calmly. "Follow the law, do what the cop says, and you'll be fine. Just like everybody else."

"I'm not joking."

"Neither am I."

The crowd began to disperse and the tension was dissipating. However, one of the angry student's friends dashed to the table and swiped a third of Mari's cupcakes to the ground. A few steps too late, Jace rushed to stop him. His shoe caught the leg of the canopy, and he fell onto the table. It tipped over. He landed on his back, legs in the air.

They laughed, and Jace closed his eyes for a moment while he fumed. He rolled over and stood, facing away from everyone. He wasn't hurt, but he almost wished he was.

"Good thing those cupcakes cushioned your fall," said Dylan. Jace looked behind him and saw white and blue frosting smeared on his back and down his left arm. He took off his bike helmet.

"Are you all right?" said Mari.

Jace nodded, still facing away from them.

"Okay," said Kendric. He sounded tired. "Let's pack this up."

. . .

48

Mari and her friends salvaged the fliers that were still pristine, and gingerly picked up the large chunks of chocolate cupcake from the sidewalk. Rob and Jace carried the frosting-smeared table off the sidewalk and dragged it upside down on the grass.

"That was an impressive dive," Rob said. "That guy learned his lesson: never come between Jace Kartchner and a treat."

"Shut up."

"You're protective of Mari."

Jace rolled his eyes and shook his head.

"You know I'm right," Rob added with a grin. "One of them is a Zero, by the way."

Jace frowned and pointed. "One of Mari's friends?"

"No! One of the guys we were arguing with. I've seen him on their videos."

"Really." Jace's smile spread across his face in slow motion. "Nice to know we'll be continuing the conversation in a few days."

"Amen to that."

Rob and Jace helped load the table into the car.

"Sorry about all this," Jace said.

Mari glanced at him. His efforts to clean up resulted in grass clippings stuck to his bike jersey. "That's all right. I wasn't planning on all of them getting eaten anyway." She suddenly looked exhausted.

"Does he always do this?" Amber asked Rob. "Every time I've seen Jace with food, he has gotten it all over himself."

"He likes to make sure it *feels* right before he eats it." Rob was the only one who laughed. With a short wave, he pedaled south.

Jace apologized once more before Mari's friends piled into the car. Mari waved them away, insisting she'd rather walk. Jace fetched his bike and caught up with Mari. She gazed just ahead of her feet. He rode slowly next to her, occasionally jerking the handlebars to stay upright.

"Seriously, I feel terrible."

"I told you, don't worry about it."

"Rob sure got into it at the end. Kind of like you with Professor Adelson."

"Hm. I prefer a little less confrontation, though."

Jace nodded. "Definitely. They were complete jerks."

"I didn't mean just them."

Jace frowned. "You got some very different reactions today." He laughed. "'Bathwater scum' was my favorite. Is that something they say in Texas?"

She kept walking.

"Mari?"

"He was right."

"Okay, I think you're being too down on yourself."

She gave a feeble smile, and hesitated. "Do you have one of those fliers still?"

"Yeah." He stopped his bike and pulled a folded one from his pocket.

"What do you see in the bottom corner?"

It was a simple outline of a toy.

"A rubber duck."

"Ever heard of the Bathwater Brigade?"

"No," he said slowly.

"It's a club on campus we're a part of. Me, Amber, Kendric, and Dylan."

"Oh. That makes sense. I was wondering why four friends just decided to set up a table like that." He looked at Mari. "So, is this that same club where you learned how to talk to professors and stuff?"

She chuckled. "Yeah, this is it."

"Weird name."

"I know. After Kendric joined, he added a 'Bathwater party' event to his calendar. His parents called him the next day, all concerned. The event popped up on the shared calendar, and they wanted to know what kind of crazy stuff he was getting involved in at college!" She laughed, then she studied Jace. "You've heard of the saying, 'Don't throw the baby out with the bathwater,' right? It's when you do something that seems good but has a tragic consequence."

Jace pondered for a moment. "So, where's the water, what's the baby, and who's throwing it out?"

"Society is moving," she said. "Our values and traditions are shifting. A lot of it is great. But when we're in a hurry to make big changes, we can easily lose some important things along the way—and regret it later.

We might not realize there's a baby in that tub of dirty water, or maybe we just haven't thought of a better way to go about it."

"So, you're basically searching for babies in the societal bathwater before it gets tossed out."

She smiled. "It's not a glamorous job. But it's an important one that nobody else seems to be doing. It's our mission to find ways to make the progress we're going for, and keep the baby, too.

"Amber likes to say we're smart shoppers, metaphorically speaking. We check the price tag on social transformations, making sure we have the best option before we run the credit card."

Jace leaned an arm on his handlebars and pointed at Mari. "When you asked Professor Adelson who would be in charge of fixing the climate, you were trying to make sure we didn't ruin entrepreneurship. The free market. That was the baby."

"Exactly. I want us to be aware of some side effects of huge government programs and taxes. We really don't have any idea how important entrepreneurs are to our lives. If we tie their hands by restricting the free market, it would affect us a lot more than we realize.

"But, maybe we'd decide it's worth the trade-off, and deliberately throw the baby out, too. I just want everyone to know it's there. I want America to see our situation clearly for what it is before we make these huge, far-reaching decisions."

Jace raised an eyebrow. "Throwing the baby out on purpose? That's a little dark."

"Okay, if it were an actual baby, of course we'd save it at all costs. But here it just means something that's valuable. Is this making sense?"

"I think so."

"Take the race fliers. Of course it's good to push for a more equal and welcoming society for all races, but there are ways we can try to go about it that make things worse. For instance, broadly characterizing police as racist. With that approach, trust between the police and the community is the baby that's getting tossed out in our efforts to achieve those other good things. That lost trust and hesitancy on the part of the cops can have deadly consequences."

Jace politely smiled at a jogger who went around them on the grass. "So why didn't you tell me about it earlier? Why is it a big secret?"

"Well, technically, the club is on the Cale website listed with all the others. But earlier this year we had to go underground. You know, meet in secret. Some people don't like what we have to say and what we're trying to do. You saw a few of them today."

Jace nodded emphatically.

"They started coming to our club meetings in the spring for some reason. And, you know, we love talking to *everyone*. We try to get as many perspectives as possible, so at first, we were like, great! But they started disrupting things. You know, yelling, pulling fire alarms, all that stuff. We couldn't even hold our meetings. It's a group called Zero Supremacy."

Jace tilted his head and raised his eyebrows.

"Looks like you've heard of them," Mari said.

"Yes. Though hopefully I'll never be within two hundred feet of one."

She gave him a strange look, and they started moving again.

"Why do people have to be like that?" said Jace. "Why are they afraid of talking about ideas with you, especially when they are welcome to come and say what they think?"

"I really don't know. I think they're convinced that things are so bad right now, and their ideas are so important, that they're feeling desperate."

"That's a very kind way to put it." Jace scanned his front tire for thorns as it rotated. "So that's why you had me do that rabbits and horses test thing. To see if I was serious enough to learn more about the club?"

"Yes. I liked how you're full of questions and slow to judge. I wanted to see how interested you were in the club, and if I could trust you. Once in a while, we let in someone new."

They were now next to Stoddard Hall.

"Hey. Sorry again about the table. Probably looks like I hopped on my bike and tried to summit a wedding cake."

Mari smiled weakly. "Well, see you around." She turned and walked away.

"Don't worry," Jace said quietly. "We'll pay them back."

CHAPTER EIGHT

ELI CLOSED the hatch of Rob's blue SUV and nodded at India. The three boys, wearing baseball caps and old clothes to look like maintenance workers, had just finished hauling the long cardboard tubes and duffel bags inside the back doors of the office building. It was early afternoon.

India leaned out of the open window on the driver's side, wearing bright red lipstick and large, dark sunglasses. "I'll be back as soon as I get the video," she said over the noise of the engine, the blasting air conditioner, and Led Zeppelin's *Ramble On*.

"Hey! Rob." She motioned for him to come.

He glanced at Jace and Eli with an embarrassed grin. He walked over and gave her a quick kiss. Then the three of them went inside as India drove away.

"It's great she's helping us," Jace said.

Eli nodded. "Has she told you that Florence Hughes is her grandma?"

"Florence Hughes?"

"It's the name in big letters on the Fine Arts Building where the band meets!"

"Oh. Never noticed."

"She's super rich. Every year, India gets to bring some of us to a dinner party at her beach house."

Jace nodded while peering down the hall out the glass front doors.

Rob looked at the pile on the entryway floor and lightly kicked a black plastic case. "Jace? Why do I see a trombone here?"

Jace grinned. "You'll like it. I had to add my own touch."

"You always do," Rob sighed.

Eli checked his watch, though he had done so thirty seconds before. "Fifty minutes."

"We'd better get up there," said Rob. "Follow me."

Rob and Eli grabbed the three long cardboard tubes and started down the hall. Jace picked up the heavy duffel bag and trombone and followed. The brown tiled hallway floor met full-length glass office walls on either side. Behind the glass, office workers glanced up at them from their computers.

"Don't you think we should take the stairs?" Jace whispered loudly.

"Don't whisper," said Rob aloud and without turning. "And no, we don't take the stairs. All your ideas will attract attention. Just act like you belong here and nobody will ask questions."

While waiting for the elevator, they smiled and nodded as two women walked by in business suits. They stepped off at the third floor, which was quiet and smelled of dust. Translucent sheets of plastic hung from the ceiling at the end of the hallway, indicating that a paint or construction project was underway. Rob retrieved a tall ladder from an unlocked closet and stood it up at an opening in the ceiling.

"Seems too easy," Jace said.

"It will get harder in a minute," Rob grunted from the top of the ladder.

A few feet above the ceiling, Rob opened the roof access hatch. Sunlight and the sound of distant traffic entered the office hallway. Jace climbed halfway up. Piece by piece, Eli handed the equipment to Jace, who pushed it up to Rob.

"Thirty-five minutes," Eli announced.

Rob draped a small blanket over the hot metal railing at the roof opening. Jace climbed out and looked around.

Multi-story office and government buildings bracketed the one they stood on and faced them from across the street. They were a few blocks north of the city center. They heard car and truck engines rev and idle, and brakes squeak at the stop lights. Normal, peaceful city sounds in the afternoon sun.

Eli trembled slightly as he lifted his sizeable frame onto the flat roof. He panted. "My triceps are going to kill me tomorrow." He oriented himself and pointed to the front of the building. "Lincoln is over there?" He picked up a long roll of paper and started walking. Jace followed.

"Guys," said Rob. "We're setting up over *there*." He pointed to the next building over.

Jace looked at his watch. "Really? You got the wrong building?"

"Did that look like a bank to you on the bottom floor?" Rob half smiled. "It's some software company."

Eli dropped the tubes onto the roof. "Does it matter which building we're on?"

Rob walked over to them. "Think about it. Once the Zeroes see the banner, they'll probably come up to the building we're on and either wait for us to come out or come inside looking for us."

Eli raised his eyebrows. "But they won't think to come to the next building over."

"Right. Come here."

"Why didn't you tell us earlier?" asked Jace.

"Because of this."

As they approached the side of the building, they saw a six-foot gap. Jace peered over. The pavement looked very far away.

Eli said, "I'm not going to try to jump that, Rob."

"Come on." Rob led them to the back of the building and up to three old wooden doors lying flat. Jace helped Rob make a bridge out of them by laying two doors side by side across the gap and placing the third door in the middle.

"See? Just walk across." Rob picked up two sections of the sign and walked to the other side.

Eli's mouth dropped open. "Rob? You know how much I weigh, right?"

"Sure. You said three hundred?"

Eli swallowed. "Actually, three fifty."

"Perfect," Rob said. "This bridge has been rated to three fifty-five." Rob rolled his eyes, stepped on the doors above the chasm and jumped straight up three times. Each time the doors bounced, they shifted slightly. Jace's heart lurched. Only six inches of the door was touching the roof on each end. "Super solid," Rob said.

"Let's just cross," said Jace. "Eli, don't stop to jump in the middle and you'll be fine." He carried the rest of the equipment himself so that Eli would only have his own weight to worry about.

Eli paused between steps and held his hands out like he was on a tightrope.

"You got it, man," said Rob. He took Eli's hand on his last step and patted him on the back.

Crouching near the four-foot parapet at the front of the building, they rolled out the three parts of the sign on the roof. It was identical to the drawing shown to Jace in the band room last week with the hand-shake between the banker and the Zero, except that Rob had added brass knuckles on the Zero's hand.

They used their large roll of duct tape to hold the sections together and fasten the top of the sign to the back of the short wall. They fixed wooden dowels to the bottom of the sign to keep it from flapping in the breeze. Then they rolled it all up and waited on blankets. The tiny black gravel that covered the roof still held the midday heat, and Jace felt like a sausage on a Texas-sized griddle.

"Is this going to hold together?" Jace asked.

"Definitely." Rob tugged at the stiff paper. "And it can handle a little wind. We tested it."

"Ten minutes," Eli said.

Rob sat with his back to the wall while the other two knelt and peered over.

Jace studied the reflection from the glass office building across the street. "Yup, we're definitely on top of Kodiak Security." He scanned Victor Square below. "Look. They're setting something up."

All three watched as two fold-up tables were set up at the back of the square. A young woman was setting large pictures on them. Portraits. A man tied about thirty green helium balloons to a nearby railing.

"Interesting," said Eli. "I thought the Zeroes were just going to come and chant some stuff and then leave."

"Me too," said Rob.

Jace said, "If this is about Stephen Hobbs, what are all those pictures?"

Rob studied the scene. "Interesting. Notice any patterns?"

On one table, the five faces were black. Eli nodded. "I think the one in the middle is Stephen Hobbs."

On the other table, the faces were white, some of them in uniform. Jace recognized one photo from the news coverage. Gina Lambson.

"All police shootings, do you think?" Jace asked.

"Yeah." Rob clenched his jaw. "They're making this into something much bigger than Gina Lambson and Stephen Hobbs. It's like they think she's part of a big conspiracy to kill black people. It's so sad. I'm telling you, what happened that night was about a police officer trying to follow her training. Not racism."

Jace said, "It would be nice if they were accurate and include some pictures of black officers, and white civilians who have been shot by police. It's not like the only police shootings are white-on-black."

"Exactly." Rob sat down again.

Below, the crowd grew larger, gathering in quiet circles. "Maybe these Zeroes aren't the violent ones," Jace said.

"They're *all* violent. And how much red do you see? The Zeroes aren't here yet."

"I wonder who these other people are," said Eli.

A black man paced near the tables with a megaphone at his side, stopping now and then to talk with someone in the gathering crowd.

Jace slumped down to join Rob. "So, do you guys *know* any Zeroes? Personally?" They spoke softly, even though there was no danger of being heard from the busy street.

Rob shook his head.

"No," said Eli. "I mean, some of them are Cale students. I have a few in my English class. They're always talking about this stuff at the back."

Jace nodded.

"Five minutes," said Eli, keeping watch on the south end of Lincoln Boulevard. "They should be coming from that direction, Jace.

They usually meet at the same place in town and then march from there."

"See anything yet?" said Rob.

"Now *there's* some red."

Jace peeked over the wall. "Five of them. One guy has a baseball bat." He frowned, knowing that within minutes he would become the enemy of the guy holding it.

Eli quietly began to laugh. "Rob. Rob! They're checking the bushes."

Rob grinned and turned to look. Then he laughed, too. "They really are!"

Two guys wearing red shirts and black pants were walking up and down the street, looking in and under the trimmed bushes that lined the sides. The one with the bat used it to move the branches.

"Why are they doing that?" asked Jace.

Rob gave Eli a knowing smile. "Tell him."

"It was from the operation two weeks ago, before you got here. We planted some remote-activated devices in the bushes on either side of the street during a protest where we knew they would be. And then we watched from a second-story window."

"Fireworks?"

"Even better. Bubble machines and speakers. We had a play list of eighties soft rock. You know, to calm the crowd."

Jace snorted, then laughed aloud. "I bet you didn't get your stuff back."

"Nope," Rob said. "They destroyed the bubble machines in about twenty seconds. But we almost got through the whole playlist before they figured out how to stop the speakers."

"How'd you manage that?"

"Each one was in a padded metal box with holes for the sound, padlocked shut and chained to a lamp post. They couldn't get rid of them or smother the sound. Eventually they dumped water into the holes. If we do it again, we'll find a waterproof speaker."

More red shirts and hoodies appeared down the street and made their way toward them.

"When do we do it?" asked Jace.

"Just before they start."

Jace assembled his trombone.

"I think we need a name to call ourselves," Eli said. "The Three...something."

Rob rolled his eyes.

Jace thought of Mari's display that the Zeroes ruined. "How about the Bathwater Band," he murmured as he attached the mouthpiece.

A few minutes later, there were about forty zeroes on the sidewalks. They were like a growing army of red ants, milling about, blissfully ignorant that their nest was about to be disturbed. Jace's heart beat rapidly.

Staying low, Rob crept to one end of the sign and motioned for Eli to get the other end. Jace took his place in the middle.

Rob pulled down on his baseball cap and counted to three. They flipped the sign over the ledge, and the heavy paper unrolled, bounced, and fluttered against the building. Jace kept his head just high enough to look at their reflection in the building across the street to make sure they hadn't hung it upside down. All good.

He didn't dare peek over at the Zeroes, but he silently laughed as he wondered what they must be thinking as they saw the giant banner. *Kodiak Security Bank Proudly Welcomes Zero Supremacy. Please don't hurt us!*

Rob and Eli each grabbed a smaller cardboard tube from inside the duffel bag. They aimed the tubes over the ledge on either side of the sign and gave them a twist, launching confetti with a loud pop. They heard a few cheers and brief, confused applause below as the confetti floated down.

Jace then performed his best and loudest 'sad trombone', the three descending notes you might hear on an old game show when the contestant loses. *BWAH, BWAH, BWAAAAAAAAAH.*

Rob grinned at Jace. "Nice touch!"

Then there were shouts.

"Now what?" asked Jace.

Rob whipped around, a smile creeping to his face.

"Now we run."

CHAPTER NINE

DOUBLED OVER, Jace carried the trombone and Rob took the duffel bag. They left everything else. They ran to the edge of the rooftop, the fine black gravel crunching beneath their feet.

Rob ran lightly across his worrisome bridge. Jace held his breath and slowed to a walk as he crossed. But Eli just stared three stories down.

"Eli," whispered Jace. "Hurry! They'll see us."

He didn't move.

"He's freezing up!" said Rob.

Eli appeared to be trying to say something.

"He's like the freaking tin man," groaned Jace.

"Eli!" commanded Rob. "Look at me. Get down and crawl. It's okay."

Eli sank to all fours but made no move to cross. They heard running below. "They're going to see us," Rob murmured in a singsong voice.

Jace set the duffel bag, now mostly empty, on the bridge. "Here. Hold on to this." Eli gripped it with one hand and inched across as Jace gently pulled. Rob and Jace glanced at each other. As soon as Eli cleared the gap, they helped him to his feet, and he plodded toward the opening in the roof. Rob quietly removed the doors from the gap.

Jace went down the ladder first. Rob dropped the trombone through the opening and it crashed to the floor.

"Rob! I wasn't ready!"

Eli trembled as he climbed down.

"You okay there?" asked Jace.

"Yeah. Sorry."

"The hard part is over now. You made it."

Jace caught the duffel bag. Rob closed the roof access door, climbed down the ladder, and calmly walked the ladder and the duffel bag to the closet. "They might hear you below, so don't run," he said. "Running equals suspicious."

They crept down the hall and into the elevator. Rob playfully pushed Eli and Jace off balance, both of whom were still too focused to smile.

Back on the ground floor, they crowded into the entrance at the rear of the building. There was no India and no SUV. Rob pulled his cap low and angled himself to get a view of the parking lot near the Kodiak building next door. "Yup, we've got Zeroes over there. They're going inside."

A man in a red hoodie ran past the software building entrance, startling Rob.

"You said I wouldn't be within two hundred feet of a Zero," Jace said. "That was about ten."

Rob pulled out his phone. "Where is she?" He put it on speaker and turned the volume low. "India," he said urgently. "Please tell me you're almost here."

"I'm across the street!"

"In my car?"

"Yes. I'm looking for another way. They've blocked things off."

Rob put a hand to his forehead. "You didn't see that coming? Why did you drive across the street?"

"You told me to take the video! I *had* to be across the street."

"I didn't tell you to *drive* there." Rob groaned. "You could have parked on this side."

"Will you stop complaining? I'll be there in a minute." Rob put his phone down. He'd lost his confident swagger. They backed away from the glass doors as more Zeroes ran past. Jace looked for a way to lock the doors while Eli stared wide-eyed at the sea of red outside.

They heard a growing chant. "Drop racist cops! Drop racist cops!"

India called Rob. He paced the hall as they argued.

"Maybe we should go back upstairs," said Eli.

Rob put his phone away and picked up the duffel bag. "She'll pick us up across the street. There are too many Zeroes over here."

Eli's mouth fell open. "There are a lot of Zeroes by the street, too!"

"We'll be fine," said Rob. "Just walk straight ahead and nobody will stop you. I doubt anyone got a good look at us on the roof, so it's not like they're going to recognize us."

They moved to the front of the building. Rob glanced at his phone. "She's not quite into position."

They heard a muffled megaphone through the closed glass doors. "Stephen Hobbs," a man said. "Look at this picture. He could have been your brother."

"My brother wouldn't give police a reason to chase him," Rob said under his breath. He tapped his foot rapidly, his gaze focused on the other side of the street.

The man with the megaphone continued. "If you're black, you know what it's like to be stalked by the badge. The police lured him into that alleyway. Was there any way they were going to let him out alive?"

"No!" the crowd shouted.

"They brought their dogs. They brought their trucks. And their guns. Like they were fighting some war. This was business as usual in America." He raised his voice. "It was there, at the alleyway, that they murdered Stephen Hobbs! Intentionally, and in cold blood!"

The crowd roared.

"They said they thought he had a weapon," the man said. "But what were all those deadly weapons that Stephen had on him? A wallet and a phone!"

"Come on, India," said Eli.

"But let me tell you," the man continued. "Those *are* deadly weapons to the police. A phone can record their corruption, and they need our wallets to fund it!"

"There she is," said Rob. "Let's go five seconds apart." He picked up the bag and strode calmly into the street.

Jace counted to five and followed. He ignored the Zeroes to his right as he crossed. India was parallel parked on a small street between two buildings, engine running. Rob put the bag in the back and got into the driver's seat.

As Jace stepped onto the curb, someone yelled, "That's the trombone guy!"

Jace's grip tightened on his instrument case and his body tensed. He jogged, then ran to the SUV without looking to see whether he was being chased.

"Get in!" said India from the front passenger seat. "We'll get Eli later." Jace tossed the trombone into the back. He looked behind and saw Eli running. Jace groaned.

"Don't run, you idiot!" Rob said under his breath.

Three Zeroes caught up to Eli and blocked his path. He looked around, panicked. More Zeroes arrived.

Jace hesitated.

Eli called out. "Rob! Jace!"

"Go!" Jace said to Rob and India. Then he shut the car door and ran toward his friend.

Eli towered over most of the Zeroes that surrounded him. His hat had fallen off and his curly black hair bounced as he tried to push his way to the car. They pushed back.

And then, he disappeared.

Jace dashed around behind, where fewer Zeroes stood, and shoved one of them out of the way. The Zero, a young man with a black bandana and red pants that matched his shirt, fell to the ground.

Eli was on his back, with blood on his face and on one hand. They were shouting at him.

The Zero with the bandana jumped back up and went for Jace. However, he stopped when a muscular security guard with a crew cut and a form-fitting black shirt stepped between them.

Eli sat on the ground. "Can you walk?" Jace asked, out of breath.

"Yeah. I'm okay."

Rob appeared. "No, you're not." He helped Eli to his feet.

Another security guard arrived and pointed at Eli and his friends. "Let's go." Then he pointed at one of the Zeroes—a short, skinny white kid with round glasses, black stud earrings, and a Zero Supremacy hoodie several sizes too large—and motioned for the first guard to deal with him. Jace exchanged glares with the Zeroes while he, Rob, and Eli followed the officer a short distance away.

Someone yelled, "White supremacists!" Eli briefly turned, walking backwards while he held up his arms at the crowd in an exaggerated shrug. "Don't you have to be white to be a white supremacist?" he yelled back.

The officer gave Eli a stern look and handed him a cloth. "I need y'all to wait here. Someone's bringing first aid. Unless you want an ambulance?" Eli shook his head.

The three of them sat, expressionless, on the edge of a large cement planter box. Bushes scratched the back of Jace's head. They watched as a dozen Zeroes screamed slurs at the security officer detaining their friend and began closing in on him.

Jace tightened his grip on the edge of the planter box. "Should we go help the officer?"

"No," said Rob reluctantly, nodding to his left. "They've got this."

A handful of police jogged up, shouldered their way through the crowd, and pushed them back. After an unsuccessful attempt to lead their members in another 'drop racist cops' chant, most of the Zeroes lost interest and rejoined the rally, though not before sending a few snide remarks toward Jace and his friends.

Drying blood caked Eli's black hair. He held the cloth to his face.

"Sorry about this," Jace said. "I probably should have gone last."

"Or left your trombone on the roof," said Rob.

The security guard repeatedly glanced at the boys while talking into his radio from twenty feet away.

"I'm okay, really." Eli jerked away each time Rob touched the cloth while inspecting his head wound. "They were kind of shoving me around and I fell on my face. Just scraped up, I think."

"You shouldn't have run, man," Rob said to Eli. "That's how they knew you were a part of it. You could have strolled around here all day, and nobody would have bothered you. We could have picked you up down the street sometime."

Eli smiled sheepishly. "Didn't think of that. I'll do that next time."

"Next time?" said Jace.

"Sure! Operation Coward was a success." Eli lifted his arm for a fist bump. Jace and Rob looked at the blood smearing his fingers, and he put it back down.

Cheers erupted from the crowd. Jace looked over to see what was happening. A few Zeroes had climbed to the roof and were tearing down the banner. It tumbled to the sidewalk in slow motion.

"Stephen's parents are here with us," yelled the man with the megaphone, "and they have something to say. Mrs. Hobbs?"

A woman accepted the megaphone. She spoke slowly with a strong southern accent. She was a little heavyset and wore a yellow dress. She looked tired, like a schoolteacher in May.

"Thank y'all for coming today. And it looks like your welcoming committee has been busy, too." She looked over at the banner on the ground, and the crowd laughed. She paused, and the smiles faded.

"My son wanted what was best for everyone, not just for him," she said. "And we're going to honor him by making things better. We're going to bring change."

The crowd applauded.

"My son was not perfect," she said. "But he was good. I wish I was there that night. I'd tell the police that he was kind. I'd tell them, 'Don't hurt him. Don't hurt him.'"

"I didn't know his mom was going to be here," said Jace.

Rob shook his head. "Same here."

Jace put his hands in his pockets, took a deep breath, and stared at the ground. The atmosphere of the event was completely different now, and though he would do it all again, part of him almost felt a little ashamed.

CHAPTER TEN

THEY DROPPED Eli off at his house. His scraped-up face was really starting to hurt. Then Jace, Rob, and India stopped at Emmie's.

"For future reference," said Rob, "it looks like Eli up high isn't a good thing."

Jace swallowed a bite of his swiss mushroom burger and glanced at Rob with tired eyes. "At least, when crossing rooftops on your home-made bridges."

"I know. I got nervous when the doors started cracking."

India, who had been resting her head on her hand, whipped upright. "They cracked?"

"I'm kidding! We can stay on the ground next time."

She folded her arms. "Ground or not, you'll have to arrange other transportation."

Rob frowned and shook his head at Jace as if to say, "Don't worry. She'll do it."

Jace slouched in his chair. "I sort of wish I stayed to watch more of what the Zeroes did—and said. You know, just to see."

"They don't have much to say." Rob set his corndog down and licked some ketchup off his thumb. "Nothing of value, at least."

"They do have catchy slogans, though. Drop racist cops again."

Rob rolled his eyes. "They're weird about it. They get in your face and demand you say it."

Jace shrugged. "We don't want racist cops, though, right? Seems like that's something we can agree on."

"If they stopped there, then yeah. But they aren't just going after the racist ones. If you spend a little time listening to them, it's pretty clear they hate *all* police. And go to the *Drop Racist Cops* website. It's not just about getting better police departments and fighting racism. They think cops shouldn't have any weapons at all. Crazy. And they have these demands about how they want American history taught in schools."

India tapped her thumbs on her phone, and then brushed her hands together. "There. My part in this is done. Just sent you guys the pictures and video." She sighed. "Eli's face will look pretty bad for a few weeks."

"It's a shame he'll heal by Halloween," said Rob. "He could have worked that into a great costume."

"That's not funny!"

Jace said, "Eli can still press charges if he decides to, right?"

Rob shrugged. "He knew what he was in for. And it feels sort of weird to go file a complaint when you're doing undercover operations. So far, we haven't gotten into trouble for going on the roof, and I want to keep it that way. Luckily the security officer didn't seem to know we were up there."

"Well, I didn't like it," said India. "Even if you *are* right." She rested her chin on her hand and pointed at a bowl on Rob's tray. "What's that?"

"I'm calling it Death by Peanuts. Peanut butter ice cream, with peanuts and Thai peanut sauce on top."

"Not funny," Jace said. "My sister's allergic. She would die if she ate it."

"Don't worry, I won't serve it to her. Actually, I won't get this again for me, either."

"Wasn't good?" said India. "Big surprise."

Rob watched his phone. "Got it!" He opened the attachment and Jace leaned over to watch the video. India had made a shortened clip that briefly showed Victor Square, then panned up to the top of the building. The banner had unfurled perfectly, and the confetti made them laugh out loud. Jace's hat and trombone slide could be seen as he played the short, comical tune.

"I'm sending it to my brother," Rob said.

Jace pulled out his phone as well, and swiped to a picture of him posing in front of the building. He texted that and the video to Mari.

We've been avenged!

A few minutes later, Mari texted back.

What did you DO?

He responded with a smiley wearing sunglasses. She replied immediately.

Call me.

Jace grinned. He excused himself, dumped his tray, and went outside with his phone to his ear.

"Hello?" she said.

"Hey, Mari!"

"What did you do?" she repeated.

She didn't sound happy. His face fell.

"Please tell me this wasn't about the stupid cupcakes."

"Well, yeah. Of course not," Jace fumbled, sounding far less reassuring than he wanted. "Like you said, Zeroes are making the community more dangerous. They're lying about the police."

There was a pause on the other end. "So, what was your goal?"

"I guess we were just calling them out on their crap."

"Making them look dumb? Making fun of them?"

Jace's confidence faltered. "Well, yeah. I mean, you said it yourself. We have to acknowledge the truth. Zeroes aren't doing that. So...we helped them."

More silence.

He added, "You know these are the same Zeroes that are ruining your meetings, right?"

She sighed. "I know. But Jace, how many people did you get to *think* today? Did you help any of them reconsider their position? Convince them that the police might not be as bad as they think?"

Jace chuckled. "Probably not."

"You and I might think they are misguided and that they aren't looking at all the facts. But what are they standing up for? In their own minds?"

"I don't know. Hating cops."

"Jace."

"Fine. They think they're standing up for justice."

"That's right. Are *you* for justice, Jace?"

"Well, not the kind they're talking about. Remember? The officer had no choice but to shoot. They're ruining her life."

"Maybe that should have been your message, then. I guarantee you, what they remember is that you declared yourself their enemy."

"I...guess?" Jace furrowed his brow and strolled along the sidewalk surrounding Emmie's.

"Listen. They probably see you as a person that supports racist police brutality and that mocks people just for trying to fix something they see as broken. Jace, they don't think you care about justice. Your absolute lack of nuance didn't give them a reason to think otherwise."

Jace tapped a railing with his palm as the silence built.

"I don't think you get it," she said. "Do you even know why we packed up the table the other day and left?"

"Sure. Those guys came and ruined it. They got confrontational, like you said."

"No," she said. "*You* ruined it. You and your friend."

Jace cleared his throat. "What?"

"*Yes*, Jace! We left because of you guys. Not because the table tipped over. You two were just as confrontational as they were. I would have liked to have had a very different conversation with them, but I never got the chance."

"We didn't start the argument," said Jace. "And how can you reason with someone that keeps on lying?"

"Jace." He heard the patience she was trying to hold on to. "They were all worked up. Sometimes when we're fuming like that, we say things we don't truly believe. But even if they do believe all of it, people usually aren't nearly as nuts as they seem at first. Once you get to know them, you'll see that they've had experiences and a thought process that makes their conclusions seem a lot more reasonable than they did at first, even if you still don't agree with them."

"Get to know them?" Jace laughed. "Well, *that's* not going to happen. Besides, you all were arguing too."

"Arguing?"

"Sure. You had disagreements with people. Isn't that arguing?"

"I'd say we were *reasoning* with them."

"Sure...whatever. Did Rob or I say anything that wasn't true?"

"You were technically right on most of what you were saying, but you weren't getting anyone to change their minds. Actually, you did the opposite. Those guys you spoke with are even more set against you now. The people at that protest, too. Don't you get it? You're making things worse."

"Then why did you give me that look at your table when Rob was talking? You know, to join in?"

"*Really*, Jace? I was trying to get you to *stop* him!"

"Oh." This revelation halted his momentum, but his last bit of pride wouldn't allow him to quit trying to defend himself. "But again, these are the same kinds of people that were ruining your club meetings. I met them today. You can't talk to them. They just yell at you and tell you that if you don't get it—if you're not on exactly the same page that they are on, right now—then you're not even worth having a discussion with. They say you're part of the problem and need to be shut down. They call you a racist."

"I highly doubt they're *all* like that," she said.

Jace briefly turned, talking quieter as an older couple passed him on the sidewalk. "Are you saying that I could actually bring them to my side? Did you *listen* to them?"

"You're sounding like Professor Adelson."

"Ouch."

"*Yes*, we can come together! That's what the Bathwater Brigade is trying to do. And you're doing the opposite."

Another brief silence.

"Look," said Mari. "Yes, there were some people that yelled at us that day. But did you see the girl in the green skirt?"

"Don't remember."

"She looked at our flier for a long time. She asked me and Kendric a lot of questions. I really believe we got her thinking. There were others like her, too. There could have been more."

"News flash," Jace said. "You weren't going to reach that guy that Rob and I were talking to."

"Maybe not. But you didn't give us a chance to try. You changed the whole tone of our table. Others walking by couldn't read and discuss with an open mind with your arguing going on. You made them pick sides. You were too busy building the walls that my club is trying to break down."

Jace frowned and squeezed the railing. "Wow. So, *I'm* your enemy now. Not the guys yelling lies at you."

"Don't be too quick to call them lies. Listen to their story and know where they're coming from to understand why they believe it." Then she added softly, "At least they believe in something."

"You're taking *their* side, then."

"You didn't see me in the crowd, did you? I'm not a Zero. But I try not to think in terms of sides, Jace. Life isn't that simple. When we assume it is, we do dumb things. Remember when we were walking back to our dorms and you said that Rob was talking to that guy the same way I was talking with Adelson? That was the moment that I knew you didn't get it."

Jace stopped walking, confused, with his mouth open.

"Look," she said. "Sorry to come across like this. You're not my enemy. You're a wonderful person. But I was hoping you were different. You can do what you want—act like one of them, get your friends to yell at and make fun of people who think differently. But don't expect me to be impressed."

"Okay," said Jace, not sure what else to say.

"And in the future? Don't come help at one of our tables."

CHAPTER ELEVEN

AS HE FLEW past the Union Center later that evening, Jace realized he had forgotten his bike helmet. He didn't care.

He had done what he thought was the right thing. Didn't good intentions count for something?

The sun was low as he entered Oak Bend Park, and Jace barely noticed that the clouds were breaking up. Panting, he traced the same route that he and Rob had taken the previous Friday, nearly flying off one of the banked curves. Sweat ran behind his yellow glasses and stung his eyes.

Gina Lambson *had* to shoot. Operation Coward defended her. Defended *all* good police officers, actually. Like Rob's dad and brother. How was that not the right thing to do?

Jace reached the wall of the overpass and let his bike fall to the ground. Sitting with his back to the wall, he ran his fingers through his hair as his chest heaved. His breathing gradually slowed. Birds chirped and unseen cars and semis quietly whooshed high above him.

He pulled out his phone. A missed text from his mom.

Hey honey, how is your week going?

He smiled at her timing.

You don't want to know. Ask me next week.

He put his phone back in his pocket. Moments later, the phone buzzed. He should have known his text would invite a phone call.

"Hey, mom."

"Hi Jace. So, what's going on?"

He sighed. "There are some people here that I strongly disagree with." He spun the back tire of his bike. "Well, let me put it this way: they're dead wrong. I'm just trying to find the best way to handle it."

"Do you *need* to handle it?" she said. "Can you just let them be wrong?"

"Maybe. It's kind of important though. A friend is telling me I should try to find middle ground, you know? But it's not going to happen. If you met them, you'd understand."

"A little vague on details," she said, laughing again. "That's okay, honey. But I have a question for you. Is it more important for you to win? Or to win them over?"

"I don't know, mom."

"Do you want to enjoy being right and pointing out how wrong they are? Or do you want them to understand your side, change their mind and join you? If you could have your wish, what do you want to happen?"

Jace knew the right answer but was stubbornly silent.

"If it's important, I think it's worth trying to win them over, even if right now it doesn't look realistic."

He stopped the spin of the wheel and ran his fingers along the tread of his tire.

"Jace," she said, "do you remember the year I taught second grade?"

"Yup, I was in kindergarten."

"I don't know if I ever told you kids about the teaching program that year. You probably remember I only taught half the days. Mrs. Froher taught the others. Well, let's just say that Susan and I disagreed on teaching styles—in a big way—and she was being very difficult to work with. But we had to be in sync so the class wouldn't get confused."

73

"What did you do?" Jace asked.

"I went to the principal. I had seniority. I wanted to have him tell her that we were going to do things my way."

"Cool. Did he solve the problem?"

"Not the way I wanted him to. He said that first he wanted to try to get both of us on board, willingly. He coached me on ways to work with Susan and made me promise to start by hearing her out completely. I wasn't excited about that, but I took her out to lunch and asked to know more about not just her plan, but her whole philosophy. She was thrilled. Want to know what happened?"

"Nope."

"Jace!"

"Kidding. Let me guess. You both compromised?"

"In a way."

"So you didn't get what you wanted," said Jace.

"Actually, it worked out even better. Once I really understood what she wanted and why, I changed *my* mind on a few things. We both did. I ended up getting most of what I wanted. And the weird thing is that she got most of what *she* wanted, too. And the teaching method that we landed on was better than the one I wanted at first."

"That's pretty cool." Jace smiled at the thought of inviting a Zero to discuss police training over lunch.

"It was. And having Susan on board with the plan made life so much easier than if the principal had made her do things my way. We were really successful with it. In fact, word got to the superintendent about our approach, and members of the state board even visited our classroom."

"I remember that picture." Jace watched as a white-tailed deer cautiously crossed the path in the distance. "I'm glad that worked out. But I really don't see any way that this other group and I are going to agree on anything."

"You might be right," she said. "But I would have said the same thing about Susan, too. It wasn't until I was pushed to work with her that it all sort of came together."

"Thanks."

"Just don't give up too quickly, Jace. What would Dad say?"

Jace rolled his eyes and then recited, "If it is to be, it is up to me." He grinned and knew his mom was smiling, too. "By the way, how's he doing?"

"He's fine. Doing more bids this week. Work is a little slow."

"Tell him 'hi' for me."

"I will. Love you, Jace."

"Love you too, Mom."

He rested his elbows on his knees and watched the auburn sky. Bright orange rays of sun shone through the rich textures of the clouds. It would be dark soon.

His ride home was calmer and more thoughtful.

Jace usually got a good night's sleep after a ride, but here he was, staring at the ceiling, wide awake. He checked his phone. 1:30 A.M. He sighed, willing his brain to shut up.

Would I rather win? Or win them over?

He blinked at the ceiling a few more times. Then, abandoning his pursuit of rest, he crept down from the top bunk and quietly found the switch for his desk lamp. Adam rolled over but didn't wake. Jace pulled out a blank sheet of paper and began to write.

Professor Adelson was already writing on the whiteboard when Jace rushed in. Jace's usual seat was taken so he stood next to Mari and waited for her to look up from her book.

"Oh, hey Jace," she said quietly. "Look, I'm sorry about yesterday."

"You don't have to apologize."

"Let's begin," announced Adelson.

Jace set a flimsy plastic yellow folder on her desk. On the cover was written, *Too little, too late.*

"What's this?" she whispered.

But Jace was already on his way to an available desk in the back corner. He set his backpack by his feet and glanced at Mari as he slowly pulled out his botany book, notebook, and pen.

She opened the cover, where he knew she would find a handwritten ruled sheet of paper. Two columns. Over one was written *Different*, and *Similar* was above the other. At the very top, the title was familiar. *Rabbits and Horses*. Jace had filled both columns to the bottom of the page. She clapped her hand to her mouth and turned what sounded like a laugh into a cough. She had to have just read the first difference listed: that horses were probably easier to hunt. That one was crossed out. Jace had listed many other obvious differences, such as lifespan, size, and type of feet.

Still examining the paper, she nodded. Jace had listed many similarities, too. Both were animals of prey, slept many times per day, and unless trained, they both jumped about the same height. She flipped to the next page. The list of differences stopped in the middle, but the similarities filled the column from top to bottom, mentioning things like habitat and food.

The similarities continued for two more pages. He had written that both had a hind gut where they digested food, followed by 'no idea what a hind gut is'. Both had teeth that never stop growing. Both lived in herds and could be territorial.

At the bottom of the fourth page, there was a note.

Sorry I didn't keep going on the differences. The similarities turned out to be more interesting.

Mari looked around and found Jace. She wasn't smiling, but her look of disappointment had vanished.

Jace loaded his backpack after class. Mari approached, holding the yellow folder. "You must have dropped your zoology homework."

"Are you kidding? I can only handle one life sciences class at a time."

"Looks like you've been busy. You did all this last night, then?"

"This morning, technically."

She sat backwards at the now empty desk in front of him.

"You want to come to one of our meetings, don't you?"

"You made it clear I have a lot to learn." He cleared his throat. "And I want to."

She closed her eyes and rubbed her forehead. "I'm not sure that's a good idea."

"So, you're ready to talk to a Zero, but not to me?"

"It's not the same thing, Jace."

"I've already blown it, then? There's nothing I can do?"

She let her backpack drop to the floor and groaned. "No, I'm not saying that."

"I gave it a lot of thought."

"Over the past, what, twelve hours?"

Jace smiled. "Well, yeah. Some of what you said yesterday makes perfect sense, and if I'm being honest, some of it doesn't. I'm not saying that I get it. At least not yet."

She blinked slowly.

"The thing is, I want to learn. Well, I don't really *want* to, but I think I should. You know?"

She gave no reaction.

He plowed on. "What I'm saying is, I need a bath."

A student two rows up turned her head to the side.

Jace smiled nervously. "I mean, I want to see the bathwater."

Mari put her finger to her mouth. She leaned in, her hair brushing his desk and eyes piercing him with a quiet, calm intensity. "Why?"

"Because I'm more interested in improving the world than my ego."

"You're serious about this?" She leaned back a little.

"Yeah," he said.

"You'll learn how to shut up?"

"I won't even talk unless I get permission."

She looked at the ceiling for a moment and then back at Jace.

"All right. What are you doing tonight?"

CHAPTER TWELVE

THAT EVENING, Jace used his phone to locate the greenhouse. It was in the far corner of the university's property. A good place for a secret meeting.

He mentally practiced band songs as he walked, miming the trombone slide movements when it appeared nobody was looking. Dr. Kline finally had that talk with him. The 'I expected more from you' talk. While Jace wasn't in immediate danger of being kicked out of the band, his recent performances didn't seem like material for Cale University. Or any university. Jace had promised to do better. He couldn't lose the scholarship.

The greenhouse was an enormous half cylinder laid cut-side down on the ground. It was made up of a hundred sections of clear glass. He tried the main doors. Locked. No one was around, and no lights were on inside. He put his face close to the glass and cupped his hands to block out the glare of the setting sun. The inside was one enormous room with rows of tables, each containing flowers and plants of all colors and sizes. He watched and listened, but all he could hear were the chirping birds outside.

"You are *really* into botany, aren't you?"

Jace spun around, his heart in his throat. Mari smirked at him from a few feet away.

"Only as much as you're into sneaking up on people."

"Nice comeback," she said dryly. "It's on the other side." They walked together toward the back of the building. Mari smiled up at him. Jace smiled back.

"So, there's something you should probably know," she said. "The others will be surprised that you're here. See, we all vote now when one of us wants to bring someone new to our meetings."

"Ah. You haven't voted on me, yet."

"Actually, after we talked at Emmie's last week, I thought it would be great to have you come to one of our meetings. I told the group about you, that you were open to other points of view, and that you ask interesting questions. And they gave you a thumbs up."

"Okay..."

"But that was before you and Rob showed up at our sidewalk display."

She trailed off, but Jace didn't need any further information. "It's going to get all quiet when I walk in, isn't it? The music will stop and everything."

She laughed. "Don't worry. We'll give you a chance."

He tucked his thumbs under his backpack straps and nodded. "I'm ready to learn something new."

The back door of the greenhouse was unlocked. Earthy smells greeted them, and mists from an automatic watering system rose above a long table of purple flowers. They went through another door immediately on their right. A long flight of cement stairs dove into the earth. The dim light of three sconces pushed feebly against the dark.

"When you said that the club went underground, you were serious." His voice echoed through the cement corridor.

"Just for now."

"I didn't know greenhouses had basements."

"This one does. I think it used to be a bomb shelter, actually. A guy named Wayne Berry arranged for us to use it. He lives around here and helps us out sometimes. He used to belong to the Brigade when he went to Cale years ago."

"Oh. Nice."

"He owns an Italian restaurant, too. He lets us hang out there once in a while, when we get bored with this place."

At the bottom of the staircase was a metal door with a keyed deadbolt above a silver knob. A little yellow rubber duck sat at the base of the door frame. Whether it had been placed there or accidentally dropped, Jace couldn't tell.

Mari entered first. Bright lights, the smell of cement, and conversation greeted them. Jace stepped into the back of a classroom-sized box. It looked like a classroom, too—from the waist up. Florescent bar lights hung on a white tiled foam ceiling, and bluish-white walls stopped about three feet above the cement floor. From the horizontal, dark stripes low on the concrete walls, Jace guessed there was occasional flooding.

About twenty metal folding chairs sat in a semicircle. Three more chairs faced them at the front, along with an empty easel. A jumble of equipment had taken over the front left corner. At the back was a metal filing cabinet and a tall glass-doored soda fridge, stocked with a variety of aluminum cans.

Mari approached six people at the front while Jace inspected the photos and artwork which hung around the back half of the room. He looked at a photo of about fifty students—wearing the denim and the big hair of the eighties—posing together outside. Some sat or crouched to make three rows. A label at the bottom stated, 'Bathwater Brigade—1987'. Above it hung a large, curious cartoon drawing of a man punching another smiling man, the first man's fist going through the smiling man's face, as if he were punching a ghost. Jace raised his eyebrows at the strange image.

He took a large step to his left and found a similar group photo, this one from 1985. Above that was another cartoon, this one showing two people at the base of Mount Rushmore, viewing it through those telescopes you put a quarter in to operate. One of them was looking through the telescope backwards, his face pressed up to the large end.

He made his way to the far back corner of the room, taking in the photos and artwork. 1989. 2003. 2015. A painting of a guy walking off a football field, removing his jersey while the other players stared. A large sketch of what looked like an old Medieval illustration showing someone in the process of emptying a large bucket filled with water—and a baby. The meaning of *this* one was obvious.

"Help yourself to the drinks."

A tall, smiling, bearded guy stood next to him and put his hand out to shake. Tattoos covered his muscular arms. His blond hair was almost shaved on the sides and his icy blue eyes smiled at Jace. "I'm T.J. Campfield."

Jace shook his hand, impressed by the strength of his grip. "Jace Kartchner."

"Awesome. Mari told us a little about you." T.J. slapped a hand on Jace's back. "Glad to have you here. I'm into architecture. You?"

"I'm majoring in computer science. Probably."

T.J. raised his eyebrows. "Great. We have a website that needs some work. Maybe you can give us a hand sometime."

"Sure," Jace said. "I'll need to take some classes first, though." He looked back at the wall. "So how old is the Bathwater Brigade, anyway?"

"It got started in 1976 by a Cale student named Clarissa Donnelson." T.J. pointed to a photo near the front of the room. "I don't know how much Mari told you about her." When Jace shook his head, T.J. went on. "There was a big push for socialism back then by a lot of the students here."

"So, she made this club to stop them?"

"Actually, no. Clarissa thought the socialists had some honorable goals—peace and equality and stuff like that. But when it came to how they wanted to accomplish those goals, she thought there were some societal costs that they didn't seem to be taking into account."

T.J. smiled like a proud parent. "Most students here at Cale were either one hundred percent against socialism, or a hundred and fifty percent *for* it. All they did was argue and yell at each other. Clarissa gathered a few students on each side of the issue, and they decided to explore together. They wanted to see if they could find a solution that would include a lot of what the socialists were looking for without tossing out what the other side thought were good, important things. So, they formed the Bathwater Brigade."

"The Brigade itself wasn't anti-socialist, then."

"Nope. Not pro-socialist either."

Mari was still at the front talking to Amber and a few others. Amber glanced at Jace now and then, her eyes narrowed. She didn't look happy.

"Did they have any luck?"

T.J. leaned against the wall, arms folded. "I guess it depends on what you mean." He shrugged. "No, they never solved the socialism thing. But they came up with a lot of creative ideas, new friendships, and it sparked something. A movement here at Cale University. They had built an environment for just about anybody to come share their ideas and break out of the team mindset. And they had developed a method to teach it."

Jace nodded slowly.

T.J. slapped Jace's back once more. "Stick with us for a few weeks and you'll see how it works."

"Cool," Jace said, gesturing to the nearest group photo. "Looks like it affected a lot of people."

T.J. grinned and his blue eyes flashed. "Oh, those are just the hard-core members. We had hundreds of students coming out to meetings, a printed newsletter...but that was before the trouble began. Anyway..." T.J. straightened. "We'll start in just a minute."

Jace grabbed an orange soda from the fridge and followed T.J. to the front of the room where there were still about five empty chairs. He sat on the end, next to Mari.

Amber sat alone on the other end, almost directly across from them. She crossed her long legs and set her phone on her lap. Her blond hair was in a wavy curl. Jace tried to catch her eyes so he could give her a friendly nod. It never happened.

Mari's whisper distracted Jace from his one-sided staring contest. "T.J.'s great, isn't he?"

"Yeah."

"Did he tell you he's the president?"

Jace chuckled. "No. I would have guessed, though."

"He's also Amber's brother."

"Interesting." He could see the family resemblance now that it was pointed out. But, by his interactions with them, they seemed to be opposites—one warm, and the other quite cold.

Dylan and Kendric walked in. They seemed surprised to see Jace but greeted him the same way T.J. had.

While Mari spoke with the girl next to her, Dylan crouched next to Jace holding a can of Coke, his bony arms resting on his jeans. He glanced at the ceiling and walls. "Welcome to Bathwater Castle." He popped open his soda and slurped the bubbles from the top. "Well, just the dungeon, I guess. Did Mari tell you why we're meeting down here?"

"She said that protesters were yelling and stuff."

Dylan nodded. "It was getting dangerous spring semester. We have just the core members—the leadership, basically—and a few others at the meetings for now. The rest of our members don't even know where we meet. It was this or shut down altogether."

"So, this is just temporary."

"Absolutely. We're not sure what our next move is. The momentum isn't going our way, and Cale administration hasn't been helpful."

"Dang. Any ideas on how to turn it around?"

Dylan smiled and looked at the floor. "They've had a few. Nothing that will do any good, if you ask me." His smile faded and he lightly tapped his soda can. "There *is* one path that could get us back in the open. But I don't think these guys would want to take it unless...well, things would have to get a lot worse for us before they'd consider it."

"Consider what?" said Mari.

Dylan blinked, then grinned. "Jace said he'd do my homework for twenty bucks per assignment. I'm politely trying to turn him down."

Jace smirked.

"You weirdo," laughed Mari. "Go sit by Amber. She looks lonely."

T.J. went to the front and gave Dylan a friendly slap on the back as he walked past. Then he looked at everyone and smiled.

"Let's begin."

CHAPTER THIRTEEN

T.J. WELCOMED Jace and a petite girl named Danica as newcomers—
or 'bathwater babies', as they called them. She had a shy smile and long
black braids that moved against her white T-shirt and smooth, ebony
skin.

Danica introduced herself as a freshman majoring in nutrition. "I've
wanted to come to Cale ever since I was a little girl. My mom was a
Bathwater member in the nineties."

Then everyone turned to Jace, who was trying to think of something interesting to say about himself. The only things that came to
mind were being known for living in the last house before you reached
the county landfill, and the kid who could hold a handstand the longest. And he didn't exactly want to tell them where he was from. He
knew from experience that at least one person in the group would
make that old, tired joke, telling Jace that he was not in Kansas
anymore.

"I heard about your club a few days ago." He shrugged.

After a pause, Mari said, "He's in the Cale Concert Band."

Amber explained that while they met underground, each new visitor
needed a sponsor—a longtime member to vouch for them. She was spon-
soring Danica, and of course Mari had sponsored Jace. The others

grinned at Danica and Jace, making Jace even more curious for whatever was coming next.

"I don't mean to imply that you're lucky to be in our presence," said T.J., "but we don't invite very many newcomers nowadays. Amber and Mari said you're cool."

"Cool?" said Dylan. "Mari, you just said he's in band."

They laughed at Jace's expense, but Jace just gave Dylan a sleepy smile.

The others introduced themselves. Amber was a gymnast—she could only come to Bathwater meetings in the off-season—but she was majoring in business. Mari's parents immigrated from Guatemala before she was born, and she was going for a degree in education with a minor in philosophy. Kendric wanted to be a civil engineer, and Dylan was on his way to becoming a dentist. There were a few others, but Jace quickly forgot all the new names.

"Let's get going," said T.J. "Today's topic is Sophia's Catering. We've all heard of the occasional baker or florist who has turned down weddings for gay couples. Well, for those of you fresh to New Brig, we've had our own cake incident. Kendric, you ready?"

Kendric removed the cover from a projector and on the wall behind T.J. appeared the words: *Gay Couple Sues Caterer*.

Mari whispered to Jace. "Kendric records the meeting and posts the transcripts on the website."

"Holland?" T.J. said. A frail-looking girl with long red hair took her place in one of the seats at the front of the semicircle.

T.J. set a worn poster board entitled *Rules* on the easel. There were four.

1. No Boxes
2. No Parties
3. No Egos
4. No Negativity

That last rule had a smiley face next to it, as if the poster board itself acknowledged that everything on it was, in fact, negativity.

Jace leaned over to Mari. "No parties? I'm not agreeing to that."

She patted his knee. "We'll explain later."

"All right, Holland and Kendric," T.J. said. "Let's set this up. What would you say is positive about this caterer being sued? Or put another way, what is the bathwater that society is trying to dispose of by allowing this to happen?"

Holland spoke up. "We're standing up against bigotry. We need to get with the times."

Kendric nodded.

"Great," T.J. said. "And when they take her to court for not making the cake for them, what is a baby that is being thrown out with it?"

"Freedom to be ourselves," Kendric said. Holland shrugged. Kendric moved into one of the seats at the front and faced the group. Dylan took over Kendric's spot in front of the laptop, adding two lines to the screen.

Bathwater: Bigotry
Baby: Freedom

"Outstanding!" The muscles in T.J.'s forearms flexed as he rubbed his hands together. "Go." He sat between Kendric and Holland, hands in his pockets with his head down.

Holland began. "Kendric, you're worried about the caterer, Sophia, being free to be herself. But what about gay people being free to be themselves?"

"I'm all for that," Kendric said. "As long as you're not hurting someone else, you should be free to do and believe whatever you like."

"But if you're a gay person and can't find anyone who will serve you, then are you really free to be you?" A few in the audience nodded.

"Let's be clear on this, though," Kendric said, adjusting his glasses. "Sophia didn't say she wouldn't sell them food. They were long-time customers of hers. She said she'd even make a generic cake and let them do the decorating themselves."

"Maybe she said that just because she got caught denying service to gay people," Holland replied.

"You think she hates gay people?"

She shrugged. "Probably."

T.J. raised a hand. "Straw man alert," he said without making eye contact. "Can't attribute other motives. You've got to take people at their word."

Holland nodded.

"It *is* possible," said Kendric, "to disagree with someone—even on their lifestyle—and still love them for who they are."

While both seemed passionate about the topic, they were surprisingly calm and respectful. Same with the audience—no one cheered or clapped. Jace ran his gaze around the semicircle. Did they have any opinions on this at all? He couldn't tell. They looked very interested, though, and would nod from time to time.

"Sophia is a business owner performing a public service, and can't discriminate," Holland said, holding her hands out to her sides.

"I agree," said Kendric. "Kind of." He tapped a finger on his chin. "Let's look at what 'public service' means. If you're running a government agency, then yes, you should have very strict rules to ensure that whatever you are offering is equally available to all citizens. However, Sophia's Catering is clearly a *private* business. You know, privately owned. And she should be free to decide what kinds of things she does with her company and her time."

Holland folded her arms. "Really. And she just gets away with it."

"Gets away with what? She never agreed to do it and didn't take their money. She might even lose other business because of it. Due to boycotts and stuff like that."

"So, you're saying that a private business owner should be able to hang a sign that says, *No Gays Here*?"

"She serves gay people all the time. But a custom wedding cake for a gay wedding is apparently not a product she offers."

"Well, that's a convenient distinction," Holland replied.

There was a pause, and T.J. held up a hand. "Should we swap some variables?"

Mari leaned over to Jace and whispered, "This is when it gets *really* interesting."

"Okay," said Holland, "let's flip this around. Kendric, I'm interested in your opinion as an African American. Since you're from the South, I'm guessing your grandparents remember *No Colored People Allowed* signs."

Kendric glanced at Danica, the other black person in the room, and sighed. "I've thought of that too. I mean, it's not the same situation exactly, but I can see how you could view it that way."

Kendric looked at the floor and pursed his lips, and Holland gave him a moment to process. "Hold on to that for a minute," he said. "Let's flip the variable of what's being asked for. Let's say Sophia is a member of Greenpeace. Involved in environmental causes."

"Okay..."

"A large oil company asks her to cater their corporate summer picnic."

"I'd think she should sell food to anyone, no matter who they are," said Holland.

"If it were a grocery store, I'm with you. But it's a little more than that. It's catering an event, and in a way, she'd be a part of it. Can she say no?"

Holland shrugged.

"Maybe I can give you a better example." Kendric sat forward in his seat. "I have a friend who is an atheist, and he thinks religion is bad for society. I'm a Christian, and if we get talking, it goes for hours. Anyway, let's say he starts a small print shop. Does graphic design and stuff."

"Got it."

"Suppose he has a neighbor who happens to be a pastor. They get along great, and my atheist friend makes copies for him all the time. One day the pastor comes into the print shop and asks him to design a better missionary pamphlet—you know, what they use to convince people to join their religion. But my friend feels that putting in his creative effort to design a document for something he feels strongly opposed to goes against the core of who he is on principle. And he'd just prefer not to do it."

Kendric sat back in his chair with his hands behind his head. "Is he allowed to politely refer the pastor to other graphic designers in the area? Or do we just haul him to court?"

"Ooh, never thought of it quite that way before." Holland folded her arms and looked at the ceiling. "But still, he'd be dumb to turn down the business."

"Maybe. Business is turned down all the time, though, for all kinds of reasons. I'm guessing there are hypothetical gigs that each one of us would turn down. For example, I'm good with a camera, but I've made it known that I refuse to take pictures for T.J.'s bodybuilding contest submission."

T.J. threw his head back and laughed. "Don't worry, I've reconsidered. Being crowned Mr. Cale would just make me sound like some wacky character that tries to get kids to eat healthy."

Kendric grinned. "Glad that's off the table! The point is, we all draw lines in the sand that we'd prefer not to cross. Can we be tolerant of someone else's lines that are different than ours?"

More thoughtful nods from the audience.

This went on for another ten minutes.

Checking his watch, T.J. stood and thanked Holland and Kendric. He turned to the audience and said, "Okay, what did they miss?"

A male student said, "The question of whether Sophia can be sued? It's simple. She broke the city ordinance that says she can't turn them down because of their sexual orientation."

"True," T.J. said. "But I'd say the question isn't whether she broke a law, but whether we should have that law in the first place."

Amber chimed in. "Because of my personal beliefs, I'd be uncomfortable making the cake, too. I'm honestly not sure what I would do. But is our goal for the gay couple to have the cake? Or for Sophia to *want* to make it for them?"

"Not sure I follow you," Holland said.

"When my parents would force me to apologize to that bonehead over there," said Amber, pointing at T.J., "it didn't change my heart. It made me resent him *more*, actually. Seems like society is already moving in a more inclusive direction anyway. And sometimes by trying to force it, we actually slow it down."

"Can you imagine how the couple feels, though?" someone said. "It's America, and somebody won't serve them because of who they are. Are we really okay with that?"

Dylan looked thoughtfully at the cement floor and pulled the tip of his hair in front of his eyes. "You know, who is persecuted more here? It's definitely a frustrating and probably humiliating experience for the gay couple. But they can get a cake somewhere else and have a great wedding and a great life. But Sophia might have to shut down her catering business because of all this."

He looked up at T.J. "Sophia's not trying to stop the couple from being who they are. You know, she's not telling other shops not to make that cake for them. But it seems like the couple or the city or whoever is trying to stop Sophia from being who *she* is."

Mari and Amber nodded.

"All right," said T.J. "Time to wrap it up. Dylan?"

The screen changed, and he created two sections. The first he gave the title *Common Ground*. Underneath he quickly typed *mutual respect*, *tolerance*, and *personal freedom*. The other title was *Solutions*. He enumerated, *make her do it*, *let her do what she wants*, and then asked, "what else?"

Jace had been quiet until now. He raised his hand. "How about she *chooses* to do it?"

Kendric smiled. "While that is definitely an option for Sophia, we're listing the options of how society and others could react to the situation."

"Someone else could bake them a cake?" said Danica.

"Actually," said Holland, "another bakery made them one for free."

"I like it," said T.J. He checked his watch. "Okay, we'll get the meeting notes on the website. Remember to leave a comment if you think of anything to add. Thanks everybody." The audience briefly applauded. Soon the chatter of conversation filled the room.

Jace and Mari both stood, and he leaned back in a stretch. "Hard chairs."

"Well, what do you think?"

"So, when do we vote on the solution?"

"We don't. Do you have the perfect answer worked out or something?"

He chuckled. "I'm not even close."

"Great! Mission accomplished."

He smiled flatly.

"You're more informed, right?" she said. "Better prepared to discuss this topic, and to start thinking about what kinds of policies or solutions you think are smart?"

"Definitely."

"*That's* the goal."

"But...we're not even going to declare a winner between Kendric and Holland?"

Mari laughed. "No. They were helping us look at all sides possible, not trying to win a debate."

Jace blinked. "That's cool and everything, but..." He held out his hands and dropped them back to his side. "That's it?"

She folded her arms. "Jace, do you complain to your calculus professor because you don't get to build an actual suspension bridge as part of class?"

"No."

"Don't worry, we'll see plenty of ways to apply this as we go through life. Have you heard of the Produce Production?"

"I think so. Is it the people who tell you how to run your farm?"

"Well, no, they don't *tell* you to do anything. They study and experiment on how to grow the best and healthiest food possible, even on the worst land. They share their findings with everyone, especially third-world countries, and they travel around to help. They've done *so* much good."

"Oh, nice. I know my parents are fans."

"The founder, Blaine Masters, was a Bathwater member twenty years ago. He gave a presentation here two years back and showed how he had to get support from farmers, unions, and a few key Republicans and Democrats so that he could get the access he needed and some roadblocks cleared. He said if it weren't for what he learned here, how to look at an issue from multiple angles, it never would have happened."

"Wow." He nodded, then looked at her. "So how about you? Personally. Any opinion on the whole catering thing?"

"Of course."

T.J. walked toward them.

"Let's talk after," she said.

T.J. put a firm hand on Jace's shoulder. "Danica wants to stay for the Bathwater Dojo. Did anyone tell you about that?"

Jace frowned. "The what?" Bathwater Dojo was one of the strangest terms he had ever heard.

T.J. laughed. "No problem. It's lessons on how to engage with people in conversation, and how to think. What we did just now puts into practice some of what we learn from the dojo."

This sounded like more of what Jace had come for. He glanced at Mari.

She grinned. "Don't look at me, goof. Do you want to do it or not?"

"Yeah, sure," Jace said.

"Great!" T.J. announced to everyone that they'd be starting the dojo in just a minute for the bathwater babies and whoever else wanted to stay. A few people left, putting away their chairs on the way out.

"Hey," Jace said. "What's the deal with Amber?"

"You noticed, huh?" Mari shrugged. "Yeah, she's not sure you're a good fit."

Jace frowned.

"Really, she'll be fine. Out in the real world, sometimes we'll be where others don't think we belong, and we need to learn how to handle that. It's good practice."

"Okay, everyone," T.J. called. "Dojo starts now."

CHAPTER FOURTEEN

T.J. PULLED a yellow strip of cloth from his pocket and tied it around his head. His gaze alternated between Jace and Danica. "To achieve the goals of the Bathwater Brigade, we *have* to know how to talk to each other about issues and principles. Especially to people with whom you seem to disagree. This is what the dojo is all about."

He held up a red book with gold designs and embossed lettering. "Lesson one. Sun Tzu authored *The Art of War*. He wrote that surprise leads to victory." He paced slowly in front of the chairs.

"He likes this part," Mari whispered with a smile. "So dramatic."

"Jace," T.J. said. "How are you with a Samurai sword?"

"Never held one."

"Great. Come on up." T.J. fetched a long canvas bag from the corner of the room.

Jace carefully set his open orange soda on the cement floor and stood. Thankfully, the weapons T.J. pulled from the bag were made of foam.

"Dylan, want to help us out?"

T.J. tossed one sword to Dylan and one to Jace. Dylan held his sword directly in front of him. Jace looked like he was ready to swing a baseball bat. They stood about ten feet from each other.

"Okay," T.J. said. "Jace, now don't swing too hard. These things break. But when I say 'go', show me how you might surprise your opponent. Ready?"

"Hang on." Jace thought a moment. "Okay."

"Go!"

Dylan held his sword steady and shifted his feet. Jace spun around and came at Dylan as if he were going to swing for his head. Then he quickly brought the sword around to the other side to hit Dylan's leg. Dylan easily blocked him.

"Great moves," T.J. said dryly. Jace laughed, along with the others.

"Okay, Dylan's turn. See if you can surprise Jace."

Dylan put his sword in the same position as before and nodded.

"Uh oh," Jace said, grinning.

"Go!"

Instinctively, Jace winced and brought his sword in close. But Dylan tossed his sword over the heads of the Brigade sitting in the chairs, then stood with his arms at his side and bowed.

"Okay, that *was* surprising," Jace said.

"Thanks, guys," T.J. said. Jace and Dylan took their seats. "Danica? Mari? Come on up."

T.J. went back to the canvas bag and returned with two sets of boxing gloves, handing a set to each. "Stand on opposite sides of the room and face away from each other. When you're ready, let me know and I'll tell you what to do. These can take a minute to take on and off. If you need help, let us know."

"I think I've got it," Danica said.

"Me too," said Mari.

They struggled for a full minute while their backs were turned, then announced that they were ready.

"When I say 'go', turn and come to the center. Ready? Go!"

Mari and Danica spun around and walked toward T.J. He handed them each a piece of paper and a pencil. "Here is a simple algebra problem that you need to solve. You can use these chairs to write. Show your work."

They immediately dropped their gloves, grabbed the paper and pencil, and went to work. It was obvious that neither of them had put the gloves on all the way.

"Smart girls!" said T.J. "You learn quickly, Danica. Usually one of us looks silly up here, trying to hold a pencil with boxing gloves."

Each handed their paper back to T.J. who crumpled them up without looking at them and tossed them toward a wastebasket near the bags. "Have a seat," he said.

When Mari sat back down, Jace whispered, "So we surprise them by not fighting?"

"Pretty much."

"Your opponent knows you," said T.J. "At least, they think they do. Society has trained your opponent on how to engage with those who challenge them—to come with their mind made up and ready for a fight. The thing is, though, you aren't playing that game. You play by different rules. In fact, they're not even your opponent at all."

Jace raised his hand. "I think I'm getting it. But can you give some real-life examples?"

"Sure," said T.J. "Let's say you want to talk to someone who seems to disagree with you about, oh, abortion. Doesn't matter which side of the issue. They're holding up their sword, ready for battle. They've identified you as the enemy and they're ready to cut down whatever you say, maybe even without thinking about it. They are going to try to convince you that they are right, or at least make you look foolish. Have you had these kinds of conversations with people? Even with friends or family members?"

"Definitely," Danica said.

Mari glanced at Jace, and he returned a sheepish look, reminded of him and Rob going to battle at her cupcake table.

"They've been trained in what they think are the rules of the game. Some of their arguments might not even make sense, but they play anyway. They throw what they can at you and won't give you any credit when you have a good point. Sound familiar?"

They nodded again.

"I used to be this way," T.J. said. "I knew what was true and what was right, and I'd blindly fight for it. At least, until I found the Bathwater Brigade."

Jace raised his hand once more. "So how do you surprise them exactly?"

T.J. gestured toward the audience. "Anyone?"

"Challenge stereotypes," Amber said. "Ignore the boxes and the lanes." She shifted and held up her hands. "So, with the abortion example, someone might tell me they are Republican or Democrat or something. Then I'll ask them more detailed questions about what they think about it. And often they'll act like, 'I just told you. I'm a Republican.' If you show them you're interested to hear what *they* believe, and not what their *group* believes, then it surprises them. Shocks them into thinking a little differently."

"Good one," T.J. said. "And you can start by showing them how it's done. Mention something on 'your side' that you may not agree with. It helps get them thinking outside the political box."

Holland raised her hand.

"Yes?"

"I don't know." Everyone laughed. "No, really," she said, smiling. "Saying 'I don't know' is unheard of when you talk about political things. Everyone acts like they have all the answers. If you say it first, then you take them off guard, and it gets them to think that maybe it's okay to admit when *they're* not sure about something."

"One more," T.J. said. "Jace, does it feel a little scary to toss your sword down when the other guy is still holding one?"

"Yeah, kind of," he said. "Because, what if they don't put theirs down too?"

"Here's a secret," T.J. said, holding up one of the swords. "Most of the swings don't hit you. They might bring up problems with a political leader that they think you idolize, or make assumptions about what they think you believe. But don't let that stuff bother you. Keep the conversation to the core ideas you're talking about and don't play that game. Don't get upset or do the same back to them."

T.J. stood in front of Jace and asked him to stand.

"Jace, what if you were to try to hit me right now? With your fists, or a sword, it doesn't matter. But it turns out you're not much of a fighter and you miss me completely."

"Are you asking me to try it?" asked Jace.

"Actually hitting T.J.?" Kendric chuckled. "Your funeral."

"No, I want you to think it through," said T.J. "When your fist unexpectedly goes through the air instead of hitting me, what happens to you?"

"I...fall over?"

"Right. Or at least you start to. You have to step and adjust your footing to keep your balance. That's what happens after their first few swings don't land. They move and adjust their footing just like we want them to. They prepare for a different kind of engagement than the fight they were expecting. And eventually, they put down their sword."

"Usually," added Mari.

"While I'm waiting for them to get the hint and lay down the weapon," Jace said, "what do I do about their swings that *don't* miss?"

T.J. smiled. "Ah, the final secret. That's for next time. But the thing is, those don't result in injuries. They're opportunities."

"That sounds so corny," Jace whispered as T.J. went to put the swords away.

"I know," Mari said. "But it's true."

CHAPTER FIFTEEN

IT WAS dark when Jace walked with Mari toward her dorm, and they went out of their way to follow the streetlamps.

"Thoughts?" she said.

"Interesting."

"Well, that was generic! Really, what do you think about the whole thing?"

Jace looked down and frowned. "It feels like you guys have some useful skills. I'd like to come back and learn more. It's a little weird for me, though, because when T.J. is going on about talking to your friends who just don't get it, it feels like he's referring to *me*."

Mari laughed and shook her head. "Don't worry about where you are right now, Jace. Every person in that room tonight has been there, too." She looked up at him. "I really think it's cool that you came tonight."

His chest swelled at the admiration in her eyes.

"What else?" she asked.

"That was an interesting chat about the wedding cake. I'm curious about your opinion."

The night was silent except for the sound of their footsteps and the distant rumble of a motorcycle.

"Have you ever been to the ocean?" she finally asked.

"Sure. Hasn't everybody?"

"Just checking. You grew up in the literal center of the United States."

"So why are we talking about the ocean now? Is this another analogy? You guys can't say anything without making an analogy about it."

Mari laughed. "So true! Sometimes we keep track just for fun. I think the record for original, relevant analogies made by one person was eight. It's a great way to learn and teach, though, even if we overdo it sometimes."

Jace grinned. "Okay, so we're at the ocean."

"Right. When you go on a pleasant day, it's calm high on the beach, and out in the ocean it's nice, too. But right where the beach meets the water, it's rough. If you're sitting down, the waves can knock you over, even on a calm summer day."

"Yup."

"We're all different. In America, we are pretty good about getting along. But once in a while you come across that line where cultures clash a little. Lifestyles, religions, heritage, values, that sort of thing. Someone gets offended or doesn't understand the other person. You know? It's inevitable."

Jace nodded. The sidewalk skirted a parking lot and the streetlamps reflected off the cars like twinkling stars.

"I think that's part of nature just as much as the waves hitting the beach. Sometimes we do things that others don't personally like. But unless we're actually harming each other, I think we are pretty good about figuring this stuff out ourselves."

"True. Aren't laws usually about stopping us from hurting other people, and not about making us do things *for* each other? Seems like forcing Sophia to design that cake goes against her rights. Still, I feel bad for a couple that gets turned away. That can't feel good."

"I know," she said. "Sometimes there's not a perfect answer that keeps people happy, but also respects everyone's rights, and you end up having to decide which is more important." She looked at Jace. "Why are you smiling?"

Jace shook his head. "I was just thinking about the last time I saw a wedding cake up close. Rob's aunt was getting married. Rob gave his five-year-old brother a plate and a fork and convinced him to walk right up to the table just as they were doing the ceremonial cutting of the cake."

Mari grinned. "What did they do?"

"They gave him the first slice, what else? Rob's aunt just glared at Rob. She knew he had to be involved. It was hilarious."

"You two are always causing trouble. It's never *you* stirring things up, though, right?"

"Usually not. I guess I did a little. That same aunt had a sign made for her office that said 'Interior Designer' under her name. I made a very tiny correction with a marker and changed the 't' to an 'f'. It took her an entire month to notice it."

Mari chuckled.

"He might not always do things the right way," said Jace, "but Rob is a good guy."

She smiled. "I know."

They walked in silence until Jace said, "I know you said you're keeping things small for now. But still, I was expecting more people."

Mari slowly nodded. Then a smile spread over her face and she pointed down a path between buildings. "Go left here. I want to show you something."

"What's this about?"

"Just hang on for a minute."

They approached the Physical Sciences Building with its massive observatory at the top. She steered him away from the entrance to the dark bushes on the side.

"Pull out your phone," she said. "Shine the flashlight over here. Raise it higher." On her tiptoes, she peered over the tops of the bushes. "There it is. Come on."

Mari pushed through a gap in the bushes. Jace followed. She stood beside a large gray square among the red and orange bricks and pulled back her hair, now sporting bits of leaves and twigs. Her adventurous eyes reflected the glint of his flashlight. She said nothing but looked expectantly at Jace and back at the cornerstone.

Jace read the inscription. Five important-sounding names that he didn't recognize, with 1987 centered below.

"Here. Let me help." Mari took his phone and moved it in a circle around the cornerstone. The shadows revealed a slight impression of a rubber duck below the year. "It's easier to see from a distance."

Jace chuckled. "Really? Nice. Who did that?"

"The architect." She pointed at the top name. "Louis Melick. He designed some of the newer buildings here and put a duck on each. I think there are six. If you ever walk through campus with T.J., he will point them out to you. Every time, in fact."

"Was Louis a brigade member, then?"

"No. But he likes to learn about the culture and purpose of the building and incorporate some of that into his design. When he learned about the Brigade, he was fascinated by it."

"The school was okay with him putting it on there?"

"Sure. Back then, the Bathwater Brigade had a bigger presence here. A lot of the students and even the faculty loved our free expression of ideas and our training on how to think and engage with others. Our club was never huge, but we were known and respected, even by those that never came to meetings."

"So cool."

They went back to the sidewalk, brushed themselves off, and headed back to the dorms. Mari stopped in front of a new three-story, red brick building with 'Miller Hall' in white lettering on the side.

Jace glanced around. "No duck on this one, I guess."

"Ha. You're always going to be looking now."

This wasn't exactly a date, but Jace wasn't sure how to end it. A wave? Handshake? A little-sister side hug? This seemed like a crucial moment with a girl that he wouldn't mind getting to know outside of class and the secret club.

"Next Monday, then?" Jace asked.

"We'd be glad to have you come again." She sounded sincere.

"Great."

Just as Jace started to lean in for a hug, Mari walked away. "See ya."

．　．　．

Back at his room, Jace was both exhausted and exhilarated, his mind racing with swords and wedding cakes.

As he set his backpack down at the base of his chair, he noticed an official-looking envelope in the center of his desk from the Office of Student Affairs.

"What's this?" Jace asked.

Adam was on his bed with his laptop open and headphones on. He didn't respond.

Jace opened the envelope and pulled out the letter inside. It was on Cale Administration letterhead. He noticed the words *Victor Square* and saw Dr. Janet Thompson's signature at the bottom with a large, swooping J.

His stomach sank as he read it through. When he was done, he set the letter on his lap and groaned. The university had found out about Operation Coward. He fisted his fingers in his hair. He had to complete campus service, whatever that meant. Probably doing chores, picking up trash, that kind of thing. Hopefully not in an orange jumpsuit.

"It had better not take more than a day."

"What'd you say, man?" Adam asked, pulling one earpiece away from his head.

"Nothing."

Jace scanned the notice once more. He was supposed to report to the administration office that coming Thursday to get the details.

He quietly folded the letter and placed it in his backpack.

CHAPTER SIXTEEN

ROOM 328 of the Administration Building looked more like a medical clinic waiting area—with its tall, leaning fronds, and the smell of magazines and apprehension—than a university office. It was empty other than a middle-aged receptionist who paused her cell phone conversation, took his name, and asked him to sit.

Though they had instructed him to wear work clothes, Jace felt out of place with his flannel shirt, pants with paint splotches, and a grungy Kansas City Chiefs fitted baseball hat. He reached into his pocket for his small metal token. Leaning forward, he surveyed its faces and corners and used the cuff of his shirt to polish away fingerprints.

Yesterday's band rehearsal had been the longest one yet. At least it felt like it. Kline had made Eli sit in his usual front-row seat, even though his scabs didn't allow for piccolo playing. For the full ninety minutes, Eli was forced to watch Dr. Kline glare at him and ferociously wave his arms a couple of feet from his face.

Jace had taken his friends aside and told them about his campus service letter. To their surprise, no one else had received one. In the fray, maybe it had appeared that Jace was fighting the Zeroes. Eli and India vowed to help. Of course, Jace declined. Rob, who never got in trouble for anything, didn't offer.

"Jace Kartchner?"

He hadn't noticed the woman enter the room. He stood, putting the token back into his pocket.

In high heels, she was a bit shorter than Jace. Still, she managed to look down at him through glasses perched at the end of her nose. The blond highlights of her soft, shoulder-length curls contrasted with her aging face. With a jolt of surprise, Jace recognized her as the irritated woman he had seen at Mari's cupcake table.

He cleared his throat. "Hi."

After a brief hesitation, she shook his extended hand.

"Come with me," she said. She marched through the hallway and into an office on the left. *Janet Thompson* was on the desk nameplate. Jace sat in a chair opposite her desk as she clicked her mouse, and then folded her hands in front of her. Her expression hadn't exactly been friendly before, but now it was downright grim. She spoke quickly, glancing at a sheet of paper in front of her.

"Mr. Kartchner, the New Brig Police Department has notified us that you were recently involved in an altercation in the city."

That was ironic. Didn't the police get that Jace had been defending them?

"You accosted a citizen there, unprovoked."

Jace's eyes flashed, and he gripped the armrests. "No. That's not how it happened. They were shoving my friend. He got hurt. I stepped in to protect him. I barely touched anyone."

"This is not a courtroom," Janet replied. "While it appears no formal charges are coming your way, I'm sure you can understand the relationship this university has with our host city. We must treat all incidents like this very seriously so as to discourage this sort of behavior in the future. To return to good standing with the university, you must complete forty hours of campus service."

"Forty?" Jace scowled. He didn't mind doing some time for the operation, but this was unfair.

She went on. "Unless you make special arrangements, you will work ten hours per week for the next four weeks. Five hours on Thursdays starting at 2 P.M., and another five on Saturdays at 10 A.M."

"What if I have class during that time?"

"You don't."

"All right." Jace slid down in his chair. "So, what am I going to be doing?"

"You'll meet with Mr. Oatley outside this building. He'll take it from here and track your time."

"Now?"

"Yes, he's there now," she said, turning back to her computer monitor.

Jace stood. Out of habit, he reached his hand out to shake, but he snatched it back and turned to the door.

"Jace," she said, still looking at her computer monitor. He turned in the doorway. "We have a high tolerance for personal views at Cale. But not *that* high."

He frowned. "You know we didn't start anything, right? It was them."

"Mr. Kartchner." She leaned forward and removed her glasses. "It's not just about you fighting someone. A group of people came together to honor a murdered, unarmed person of color. White students from Cale University mocked and disrupted it. How do you think this reflects on the university?"

Eli wasn't white. But he decided he'd let that slide. No sense in getting Eli in trouble, too.

"I don't think it was obvious that we were from Cale. For us, though, it wasn't about that guy that got shot. We were there because we're against Zero Supremacy. They tell lies about the police."

Her frown intensified.

"You think we're racist or something?" he continued. "I don't think you understand the situation."

"Why don't you examine your worldview puzzle?" she snapped.

Jace stared at her with his mouth open, having no idea what she was talking about.

She lowered her voice, and slowly said, "Starting right now, for every extra minute of my time you waste, I will add two hours to your service."

Jace considered keeping the conversation going for fifty-five more seconds, but he shook his head and left.

· · ·

In the building's north shade, Jace found a white vehicle that looked like a large golf cart with a yellow light on top. Reclining in the passenger seat was a weathered man in jeans, a gray long-sleeve button-up shirt, and a tan cowboy hat. He had boots resting on the dash, hands folded behind his head, and hat tipped forward mostly covering his eyes. Jace approached quietly.

"You Charles?" the old man asked, without moving. "Or Jace?" He had a thick southern drawl.

"Jace." After an awkward silence, he added, "So, what am I supposed to do?"

"Wash off your war paint, son. I ain't going to run through this twice. We'll wait till Charles gets here."

There was no one else around in work clothes. Jace sat against the brick building. He took off his hat and examined the jagged lines of the arrowhead logo.

A few minutes later, a skinny white kid came from the same direction that Jace had. He walked slowly, hands in his pockets, his body dipping a little with each step as if he were carrying something heavy or his stride was too long. He was unusually small. He had short hair, nearly shaved, round glasses, and black circular earrings.

Jace stiffened. He was ninety percent sure that it was the Zero Supremacy kid from the protest. One of the guys that roughed up Eli. Had the administration put him and Saint together on purpose?

"You Charles?" the old man asked him.

"I guess."

Mr. Oatley moved for the first time. He slowly put his feet down from the dashboard and exited the golf cart. He reset his hat and looked at the newcomer. Mr. Oatley wasn't much taller than him.

"You *guess*?" Mr. Oatley said, incredulous.

"I go by Saint."

The old man scratched his head under his hat. "You what, now?"

"Everyone calls me Saint."

"Ridiculous," Mr. Oatley exclaimed. "Did *you* choose that?"

"Yeah."

Mr. Oatley shook his head. Jace watched the conversation, still seated against the wall. Saint glanced at Jace and then looked away.

"All right," Mr. Oatley said. "They tell me we're going to do forty hours. They told y'all the times and everything?"

"Yeah," Jace and Saint both said together.

"Okay. Now you have a choice to make. We have two things that need to be done, and I don't care which one y'all want to do. We're either going to be fixing sprinklers or doors."

They said nothing.

"Well, which one?"

"I don't really know how to fix doors," Jace said, pulling his shirt down as he stood.

Mr. Oatley looked at Jace, dismayed. He leaned forward a little, scarred hands held up for emphasis, and yelled, "You don't *need* to know how to fix doors!" Jace recoiled slightly. "I've got all the tools. I'll show you. It ain't putting socks on a rooster."

Jace looked at Saint, who shrugged.

"Being indoors sounds better to me," Jace said.

"Well, I don't care which one you do. But y'all have about three seconds to make up your mind, or I'll just decide we're fixing toilets."

"Doors are fine," said Saint.

"That's more like it. Now hop in. We'll go pick up your tools and show you what to do."

Saint sat in front next to Mr. Oatley, and Jace took the back seat. Jace quickly discovered that to remain in the vehicle, he had to firmly hold on to the seat in front of him. Mr. Oatley walked slowly but drove the electric golf cart like a seventeen-year-old in a sports car.

Saint stared straight ahead, gripping a handle above his head as the cart jostled. Mr. Oatley shook his head as he drove. "Saint," he muttered to himself. "You used to just keep the name that's given to you."

Heads turned as they zipped and bounced through campus. Jace sat low in his seat and pulled down his cap. He studied the back of Saint's head. This would all go smoother if Saint didn't recognize him from the operation. Either way, it was going to be a long forty hours.

CHAPTER SEVENTEEN

MR. OATLEY PARKED at the Maintenance Building and led them to a room that was a mix between an office and a garage. One wall was lined with metal shelves containing heavy tools. One of the shelves had collapsed in a heavy gray heap, and it had been hastily barricaded with caution tape. All sorts of parts and hardware littered an enormous workbench, and the larger pieces leaned against the walls. The mugs and cups all contained nuts and bolts. Black smudges covered everything.

After some instruction, Mr. Oatley gave Jace and Saint each a tool belt with a hammer, flathead screwdriver, dry cloths, and various cans and tubes of lubrication. He also handed them a pack of green sticky notes to put on the locked doors so he could take care of them later.

"Can you two handle that?" he asked, doubtfully. His new workers nodded. "Start on lubricating the hinges and locks like I showed you. If you don't ruin everything you touch, then maybe another time y'all can help on the door closers."

"Door closers?" Saint asked.

Mr. Oatley rubbed his face in frustration. "It's that metal box up there on the back of the door that makes it shut by itself." He narrowed his eyes at the two of them. "Y'all know which part is the door handle, right?" When they nodded, he grunted. "Just checking."

He drove them a hundred yards to the Frank Moore Engineering Building where they were to spend the next four hours, starting on the ground floor. The three of them entered the lobby. Offices lined the hallway on the left side.

Mr. Oatley slowly walked toward the elevator with his much larger tool belt and a white plastic bucket. Halfway there, he turned. The boys hadn't moved.

"Well, aren't you two quick out of the chute." Then he yelled, "What are you waiting for?"

Jace walked to the first door and opened it.

"What in the..." Mr. Oatley began. He set his bucket down and threw his hands in the air. "Knock first!"

Jace had already seen that the room was empty, but he quickly closed the door and knocked anyway. Mr. Oatley picked up his bucket, turned, and shook his head as he trudged to the elevator.

Saint followed Jace into the small room, their belts clanking softly as they walked. It was bare except for some dry erase boards on the walls and a few chairs. Jace sighed and set his tool belt on the floor.

"You're supposed to leave it on, genius," Saint said. He paced to the window and back. "See? The tools follow me around. Amazing."

Jace rifled through the pockets on his belt without looking up. "Just making sure I know what everything is." He selected the can of WD-40 and the dingy white cloth and stood. "He said to leave the safety glasses on."

"Thanks, mom," Saint replied. "I can deal with Mr. Oatmeal or whatever his name is."

Jace shrugged and awkwardly applied the WD-40 to the top hinge. The liquid ran down the wooden door frame, and he did his best to wipe it up. "You going to help?"

"Well, I'd work on the lock and hardware, but you've got the door closed."

Jace opened the door a little and continued to the middle hinge. Saint still made no move to help.

"So, what are you here for?" Saint asked.

Jace had already planned what he'd say to this. "Disturbing the peace."

Saint finally applied some graphite powder to the lock and the hardware near the handle. Then they opened the door wide and closed it a few times. Silent and smooth. They wiped the hinges and hardware once more and left the room. Most of the offices were either locked or occupied, so they entered one of the empty classrooms in the center of the building and got to work.

"You're not going to ask what I'm here for?" said Saint.

"Oh, yeah. Why are you here, then?"

Saint gave Jace a penetrating stare. "For beating up your fat friend, Eli."

Jace turned his focus back to the hinges. "So, you recognized me."

"Of course I did, moron."

Jace finished the door. He had no idea how he was going to make it thirty-eight more hours with Saint—at least, without one of them heading to prison.

They finished five more classrooms, each having two doors to the hallway.

"I hope we're doing this right," Jace said. "Mr. Oatley will implode if we miss something."

"I was in the library this morning, actually. Saw a book that might help you."

"Yeah?"

"Yup. It's called *Door Maintenance for Nazis*."

"I avoid the Fascist aisle, so I've never seen it," Jace shot back. "But it's good to know where you browse." He shoved the tools back in his belt.

"Cute. Keeping a low profile, huh? You and your little Third Reich sleeper cell?"

"You have no idea what you're talking about."

"True, I guess I didn't ask. So, would you say you're more of an authoritarian, then? Or just a racist?"

"Are *you* more of a thug or a liar?" asked Jace. "'Saint' is a perfect name for someone who beats people up, by the way."

"Okay, look you idiot," Saint replied, deadly serious. "I didn't smash your stupid friend's face. Didn't get the chance, actually. We started pushing him around a bit, but he fell all on his own. And as for being a liar, I don't think lying to a racist counts. But I haven't even done that. Name one thing I've lied about."

Jace didn't hesitate. "That police are racist killers."

Saint folded his arms. "It sounds to me like you're willfully ignoring the evidence."

"And why would I do that?"

Saint gestured toward Jace. "No idea. As a white supremacist, Nazi, or whatever you are, you tell *me*."

The insults were getting increasingly annoying. "White people get killed by police, too," Jace said. "One black man being shot doesn't mean that all police everywhere are racist."

"Listen to me carefully," Saint said. He took a step forward. "Gina Lambson did *not* have to kill Stephen Hobbs."

Jace shifted his stance, squaring himself with Saint. "Yes. She did."

"Saint Charles," Oatley's crackling voice said from the other side of the classroom. "Didn't I tell you to wear the safety glasses the whole time? You don't want to get graphite powder in your eye. I don't need another injury on my watch."

Saint reached into his tool belt and put the glasses back on.

"If a duck had your brain, it would fly north for the winter!" Mr. Oatley walked up to them, his cowboy hat jerking slightly with each step. "Y'all stopped working, so I assume you're done."

Jace and Saint looked at each other. Mr. Oatley's stress seemed to be stuck at a nine. Jace wondered whether he was like this all the time, even at home.

"At least the twelve classrooms are done, right?"

Jace swallowed. "We've got a few more to go." He checked his watch. They had one more hour.

Mr. Oatley scratched the back of his neck. "Well, *that* progress ain't nothing to write home about. But I'm good and ready to eat. How about you fellas?"

Jace shrugged.

"I'm fine," said Saint.

"Well, it's either that or keep working. You got another hour before y'all can leave. We can finish this up Saturday."

They looked at each other again.

"Okay, we can eat, I guess," said Saint.

Outside, the three of them set their tools in a lock box attached to the back of the cart and climbed in.

"How's Munchies?" The local restaurant was actually called Meals, Meats, and Munchies so they could cleverly weave the three M's together on their logo, but everyone just called it Munchies. Mr. Oatley drove them there without waiting for an answer. Jace silently begged Mr. Oatley to park the cart instead of using the drive-thru. It worked.

Inside, the employees outnumbered the diners. Saint smiled at Jace, who looked away and shrugged it off before ordering a spicy chicken sandwich meal with a Dr. Pepper. Saint got two small hamburgers and a water. They selected a table and listened to Mr. Oatley argue loudly with the cashier about the medium shake being on sale at a lower price than the small.

Mr. Oatley finally joined them with iced tea, three orders of chicken nuggets, and a large chocolate chip cookie.

"No milkshake?" asked Jace.

"Nope. I don't do milk." He looked at Jace. "The chicken here ain't *that* spicy, son."

Jace blinked. Saint smiled again.

"You left your dang glasses on," Oatley hollered.

Jace quickly took the bulky wrap-around safety glasses off his head and set them on the table. "Thanks." He glared at Saint, who smirked and unwrapped one of his hamburgers, the other he placed on his lap.

The only noise at the table was the slurp of Oatley's iced tea and the scratch of breaded chicken on cardboard. Finally, Mr. Oatley popped the last nugget in his mouth, brushed his hands together and stood. "Well, y'all want a ride back anywhere?"

"No," they said together.

"All right. Jace, I'll put your glasses away for you. See y'all Saturday." He grabbed the glasses and stumped out the door.

Outside, while Jace waited to see which route Saint would take so that he could go the opposite direction, he checked his phone. Rob had been texting.

The next operation is underway. Minor change in strategy.

Jace zoomed in on a picture Rob had sent. It was a hand-drawn poster.

Wanted: New Zero Supremacists.
Zero Supremacy is in a crisis and needs your help. We are losing members! Once they see what a sham our organization is, they abandon us. Show your blind support for our dubious causes and sign up today!

Jace grinned.

Must have: a warped sense of justice. A misunderstanding of the truth. Little to no sense of humor or honor. No regard for human life. A generally cowardly nature is preferred. Hurry, positions are filling fast.

It had a drawing of Uncle Sam pointing at the reader and carrying a baseball bat.

Jace walked north on the sidewalk and called Rob.

"What do you think?" Rob answered.

"Quality stuff. Just going to post these everywhere?"

"*Everywhere.* All along the street. And long before the Zeroes get there this time."

Jace sighed. Saint was still visible, walking across the grass. He looked like a twelve-year-old kid from that distance, hands in his large pockets, dipping with each long stride, appearing very different from the arrogant jerk he really was.

"Want to add a photo of an actual Zero to the poster?" Jace asked. "I'm looking at one right now."

Jace recounted his depressing afternoon and recited all the insults he could remember.

"Wow! And you have to spend another twenty hours with him?"

"Thirty-five," Jace groaned.

"Dude! If they tried to make me do that, I'd literally drop out of college. I mean it."

"I know."

"Maybe we can use your situation there for an operation sometime. Later, though. So, you're going to help us with these posters, right? India's definitely not coming. I think it freaked her out when Eli got hurt. We could *really* use your help."

Jace frowned. "Is this really helping Gina, though? Do you think it might just make the Zeroes angry? Angrier, I mean?"

"I don't care *what* the Zeroes do about it. I'm just speaking the truth. *Someone* needs to stand up to them, Jace, you know that. The mayor isn't serious about it. The officers are told to sit back and let them get away with all kinds of stuff. Even here at Cale."

"I know."

"The trial is in a few weeks," Rob said.

Jace frowned as he walked, his phone to his ear. He wanted to help with the well-deserved harassment of the Zeroes. Especially now, after his miserable day with Saint. He thought of Mari, though, and what she'd say if she knew Jace hung posters like that. After their big talk, and the test, and that meeting...

Jace cleared his throat. "I think I'll have to sit this one out. I've got something else going on."

The phone went silent for a moment. "I haven't even told you what day we're doing it, genius."

Jace tipped his head back and winced.

There was a tense silence finally broken by Rob. "You need to shoot straight with me, dude. If you don't want to come, man up and say it."

Rob ended the call abruptly, leaving Jace standing on the sidewalk with a dead phone and a sinking stomach.

CHAPTER EIGHTEEN

OKLAHOMA WAS BEATING them twenty-three to zero as the second quarter ended at Saturday night's football game. Nobody was surprised. But neither the score, the sparse attendance, nor the threatening clouds could dampen the spirits of the marching band. They rivaled the cheerleaders and Cale's ranch hand mascot as they danced and swayed in the stands.

Jace was not in marching band—his scholarship didn't require him to be—but he sat in the row behind to be near his friends. As the band left the stands to prepare for their halftime field show, they left a large, empty square.

It was so quiet that Jace heard his phone vibrate in his pocket. Mari had texted.

Good luck on your field show!

Thanks! Also relevant: I'm not in marching band.

That's pretty obvious.

Jace scanned the seats behind him, and found Mari sitting about ten rows up with T.J., Amber, and Dylan. She wore a green Cale baseball cap, sunglasses, and a black jacket. She gave him a little wave.

He walked up the stairs. "You're smart," he said. "Much better view of a marching band show up here."

"Of course!" said T.J. with a grin. "That's why we chose these seats. Come sit with us."

Jace sat next to Mari on the end.

"Hey man. I thought you were in the band," Dylan said. He lifted his hat, his thick hair giving Jace the quick impression of a rooster, then settled it back on his head.

"Not the marching band," Jace replied. "If you want to hear me play, you'd have to come to a concert." He immediately regretted saying this. "I didn't mean I think you should come to one of our concerts."

"No, no, that sounds fun," Dylan said unconvincingly. "Let us know."

"Will do," Jace replied, with no intention of ever doing so.

They watched the band weave together on the field.

"I don't know how they do it," Mari said. "Not falling over or running into each other."

"Oh, they fall over," Jace assured her. "My friend Mason played bass drum in a parade and stepped in a pothole. He broke his ankle. They had to stop the parade and everything."

Mari covered her head with her hands. "Oh, no!" Then she bumped her shoulder with Jace's and asked, "So, how was your first week of community service?"

Jace had spent another five hours working earlier that day. However, after realizing how little they had gotten done on Thursday, Mr. Oatley had insisted on working closely with them. That wasn't pleasant, but neither was time alone with Saint.

"You'll never guess who has to do it with me," said Jace.

Mari thought for a moment. "Professor Adelson!"

Jace laughed. "That *would* be a plot twist. Nope. It was a Zero."

"I see. One that you can hardly hold a conversation with?"

"Yup. Aren't they're *all* like that?"

Mari turned her head. "If you think they're all the same, Jace, then you haven't been paying enough attention."

"Hmm. I'll watch out for those *good* Zeroes, I guess." Jace studied her. "Do they call everyone a racist Nazi, or am I just special?"

She laughed and gestured to her friends. "Each one of us has had that honorary title yelled at us many times."

She lowered her voice. "I hate that the Brigade has to meet in secret. But it's *so* nice not having constant interruptions."

"I think it's cool that you invite new people like me."

"We *have* to. The rest of us will all be graduated in a few years. I've only got a year and a half left myself. At the start of the semester, we decided that each of us regulars would get one new person to bring to our meetings. A freshman or sophomore to go through the dojo lessons and everything."

"And you picked me. That's cool. I was the obvious choice, though." He smiled.

"You mean, you have the most room to grow?" She nudged him with her elbow.

"I'll try not to disappoint, but I'm not sure I'll be a lifetime member."

She smiled at him. "Sure. Just come to a few more meetings and see what you think."

The band filed back into their stadium seats as the third quarter began. Cale surprised Oklahoma by returning the kickoff all the way into the end zone. Everyone sprang to their feet with ear-splitting cheers. Mari clapped and surprised Jace with a brief, tight hug.

They all knew that this might be the only touchdown celebration today, and they made it count. The traditional victory chant of "Eat Your Kale!" roared impressively from the half-filled stands. It went on for a few minutes before the fans slowly took their seats, resigned to their impending loss.

"Hey, I have a question for you," Jace said. "All that artwork in the Bathwater room. Does it all mean something?"

"Yup. Each year the senior class makes a painting or something to contribute."

"Cool. I saw one with a football player walking off the field."

"Oh yeah. That's one of my favorites."

"So, what is that one supposed to symbolize?"

The sun slipped behind a cloud and Mari took off her sunglasses.

"From up here," she said, "try to look at the field with fresh eyes. Pretend you're not rooting for either team. You're not even familiar with sports at all. What do you see?"

Jace scanned Oklahoma's red helmets lined up against Cale's green ones. "Maybe I'd wonder what the difference is between the two teams. And how people decide which one to cheer for."

"Good. Nearly everyone here identifies with one team or the other. You can tell by how the fans dress. The coaches and the players study the other team, find their weakness. It's all about the team and winning. The cheerleaders, the band, everything."

"Yup, that sounds like football."

"Now imagine if the goal of it all wasn't to *compete* against each other but to *build* something together."

Jace squinted. "The teams? Build something together? Like a house or something?"

"Sure. Or anything, really. If that's the goal, doesn't it look a little silly to be fighting and cheering here in the stadium?"

He rubbed his chin. "I guess it would."

"That's how I see society sometimes," she said. "When the talking heads are arguing with each other on the news, does it feel productive? Like we're building anything?"

Jace shook his head. "So, the guys yelling at each other on TV are the players on the field?"

She nodded. "And the TV viewers are us here in the stands. We've picked our team already, and we're cheering for them and booing the other side. They're usually talking about important things, but when everyone separates into teams like this, we don't *really* listen to the other side, you know? We're usually just trying to win."

"Hm," he said, still thinking. "What do we do about it?"

"When it starts to feel unproductive?" Mari shrugged. "Just stop playing."

It started to drizzle. Dylan popped open an umbrella, huddling under a blanket with Amber. Mari pulled out her umbrella, too, and Jace held it between them. Mari scooted closer. He smiled to himself, hardly noticing Oklahoma's diving catch, putting the score at thirty-seven to six.

"So, that's why the football player in the painting is removing his jersey. He's choosing not to play the game."

"You're doing so well today!"

"The coach wouldn't like that, if one of his players walks off."

"Nobody's happy," she said. "The coaches, the players, fans, the media in the press box. There is a lot of pressure to play the game. But if you find that playing doesn't make things any better, and might even make it worse, why should you keep going?"

"You're not saying we shouldn't participate in politics at all, though, right?" he asked. "And never be divided? I mean, should we have never fought the Civil War?"

"There *is* a way to do party politics that's productive, and there *are* important battles to fight. Pay attention and I think you'll start to see the difference between that and the silly team games."

The rain intensified and the sound of it hitting the umbrella drowned out the game. The band had stopped playing and were trying to keep their instruments dry.

Jace imagined the Cale quarterback walking off the field in the middle of the game. "If the players quit, it would kind of take the fun out of football." He winked at Mari.

"It's just a metaphor," she said, leaning slightly closer. "I love football."

Most of the fans left as the rain made clear its intentions of staying the weekend.

Jace, however, wouldn't have moved for a hurricane.

CHAPTER NINETEEN

T.J. WELCOMED everyone to Monday's Bathwater meeting. Mari had a history lecture she couldn't miss. It felt strange to Jace, being there without her. Not that everyone wasn't welcoming, but still... And it didn't help that Eli and Rob were conducting their latest operation right then, either. He forced the awkwardness and guilt from his mind and watched as Kendric typed on his laptop, revealing today's topic. *If I Ran the Diversity Department.*

"We were going to discuss the military today," T.J. said. "But we heard from some Bathwater fans who saw our fliers about race in America. They wanted us to do a meeting on better ways to approach diversity here."

He had Kendric and Amber take the front two seats. "I know Kendric was up here last week, but he seems to be the most passionate about this subject."

"Plus," said Kendric, "it's apparently easier to talk about this stuff if you're a person of color."

Amber laughed. "It *was* nice having Kendric there with those fliers. Some people don't want to hear about this from a white girl."

Jace recalled Kendric's views on race from the cupcake table, views he didn't expect from a black person. He sipped from the cream soda he had gotten from the fridge. This was going to be interesting.

"All right," T.J. said. "We all know that diversity is a big deal at Cale University. We have mandatory lectures on microagressions, cultural appropriation, and white privilege. So, what's the bathwater that they're throwing out here?"

Amber raised her hand. "Easy. It's racism and prejudice. Good riddance."

"Great. And what's a baby they might be throwing out along with it?"

"Unity," said Kendric. "The diversity department has fine people, but their approach is dividing us."

They waited as Dylan put this on the screen projected behind them.

"Perfect," said T.J. as he sat between them. "Go."

"Kendric," said Amber. "I like unity, too. But what do you mean by it? Like, not caring about skin color?"

"Pretty much."

"My mom has a beautiful black friend who is always saying that she doesn't want people to be colorblind. She wants them to see her, and her color, and her history. All of it."

"Ah. I didn't say colorblind. Yes, let's understand and learn about our friends. But I want a world where color isn't a factor we use to *select* our friends."

"When I hear what you're saying to me, it sounds like we have the same goals," said Amber. "So how does the diversity department divide us, then?"

"It's not all bad, of course. But look at their focus. They're always highlighting our differences. They show ways we should be offended by each other. Even when no offense is meant, and often when no offense would even be taken if we weren't taught to think that way. I mean, how do you feel after those seminars? My friends and I have felt *less* likely to go make a friend from another race. Either because we're afraid we'll offend them, or because we feel a little resentful of other races because of things that were brought up at the seminar. That doesn't feel like racial progress."

"I can see that. But what's the alternative? Never talking about those things? For me, I want to do all I can to help myself and others stay far away from anything that's racist at all. And how can we do that if we don't talk about it?"

"Sure, we should talk about it. But it's the constant dwelling on things that are difficult to change that's the problem."

Amber tucked her blond hair behind her ears and tilted her head. "Interesting. Because it's difficult to change, we shouldn't try?"

Kendric smiled. He put his hand to his mouth for a moment. "Okay. Has anyone here had microbiology?"

Nobody raised their hands.

"Well, do you remember in grade school where you learned about microbes and bacteria? You saw pictures of them under a microscope and they looked like giant monsters?"

Heads nodded. "I had the creepy crawlies for a week!" said Danica.

"What if your school decided to revisit that section once a week. And they put up posters in the hallways, reminding you that those bugs are around you all the time and there's nothing you can do about it."

Amber nodded.

"I don't know about you," Kendric said, "but I'd probably go all OCD and spend my afternoons scrubbing my hands and arms while my friends from other schools are out playing."

He leaned back in his chair. "That's how I view the Cale approach to diversity. We start seeing everything through race-colored glasses, watching for things to be offended about and keeping the worst parts of our history constantly in mind. They tell some of us that because of our skin color we're an oppressor, and we'll always be one no matter what we do. And they tell others of us that we're forever a victim. Is that an empowering message? I think it distracts us from friendships and life opportunities that are right in front of us."

Amber looked at the ceiling. "It's a bit counterintuitive. You're saying that if we talk about racism less, then we'll be less racist."

"Is Cale's diversity department really that essential? We've already come a long way and we're moving ahead every day—or at least we would be if little things weren't blown up into monsters every day. If there was a racist person, or law, or school policy, don't you think we'd all unite against it, whether or not the diversity guys are here?"

Amber agreed. T.J. invited questions from the rest.

Jace hesitantly raised his hand. "In high school, they basically told us that being white makes you a racist. That you're part of a system of power or something like that."

Kendric switched seats, moving to the empty one next to Jace. He put his arm around the back of Jace's chair and winked at T.J.

"Jace, do you believe that one race of human beings is superior to another?"

"No."

Kendric held out his hand, and Jace shook it. "Congratulations, my friend. You are not a racist."

Jace smiled. "I'm relieved to hear *that!*" He was kidding. Sort of. Only now, after hearing a black man tell him he wasn't racist, did he realize the worry that such a small statement made years ago had given him. He wondered if his little brother and sisters could have been labelled a racist, too. Maybe even in elementary school. He shook his head as he thought of the burden society was asking little kids to bear. Just for their skin color.

Kendric became serious. "The next time someone says you're racist simply because you're white, you tell them Kendric says they need to stop being lazy. They need to pick a different word or invent a new one. Sure, we can talk about systems and power and all of that. But the color of your skin or the place where you live doesn't make you a racist. That word means something else. It's ugly. And it's real. I've experienced it. To be racist is a personal choice. Not a group identity."

A few in the audience couldn't contain brief applause, and Kendric resumed his position at the front.

"What about when they say the *system* is racist?" continued Jace.

"Which system?"

Jace shrugged.

"There are a hundred systems in America. Jace, if you have a cavity in a tooth, you fix the tooth, right? Or do you tell the dentist to just pull all your teeth and go with dentures?"

"I hate the dentist. Just one at a time is fine."

"There are some systems I think we should take a hard look at.

Prison reform. I'm not a fan of stop-and-frisk policies. A few things in education rub me the wrong way.

"When they say *the* system is racist, though, that's clearly an over-simplification. Some want you to believe that the Founding Fathers and the Constitution and the flag are all part of a structure that was built to only serve white people, and that we need to dump the entire thing and start over. If you ask me, that's the worst idea ever. We're not perfect people, but the founding ideals of this country are sound, even if we still haven't achieved them all."

"There are quite a few things in America's past to be ashamed of," said Dylan thoughtfully. "We *should* be ashamed of some of them. But our country is like a family, right? My own family has issues, but I'm not going to blow up my house, disown my parents, and find somewhere new to live. We have our rough times, but we stick together as we try to fix what's wrong, and make things better."

Kendric gave Dylan a nod. "America is a grand, glorious tree. There is some pruning and grafting to be done, and lots of us are up in the tree working on it. And that's great. It's the guys standing at the base with chainsaws that are scaring me."

Amber nodded, arms folded. "I agree with that. And since we're talking about getting our terms and definitions straight, one thing that bothers me is what they call white privilege."

"What would you call it?" asked T.J.

"Well, if you read the essay about white privilege, it's a bunch of things, actually. It describes how, if you're white, you can move around your community comfortably, count on seeing your race on television, that sort of thing. But there's not much there that's inherently *white*. You know? I think what they're describing is *majority* privilege."

Kendric smiled and nodded.

"My friend is white and was born in Japan," she continued. "Being a racial minority there, she experienced a lot of the same kinds of things that are mentioned in the essay. Japanese people confused her with other white girls that she doesn't look like at all. They always asked where she was from because she didn't look like them. They wanted to touch her blond hair. Nearly everyone on local TV was of a race different than hers. That sort of thing. So, a lot of the white privilege theory isn't *wrong,* I just think it's wrongly *named.*"

"We're in America, though," said Danica. "Why not just call it white privilege here?"

"It's because it's something that's human, not just white. The more we attach things to a race, the more harmful I think it is. Whiteness, blackness. It's divisive. Like Kendric is saying." She turned to him. "Kendric, you said you've experienced racism. Do you mind sharing?"

Kendric paused, shifted his jaw, and nodded. "When I was ten, my family stayed with friends in a Montana condo complex for a week in the summer. Being the only black kids at the pool, my brothers and I were told more than once that the pool was only for kids who lived there, even though some of the other white kids were visitors, too." He looked at Danica, who gave him a knowing, sympathetic nod.

"Wow, that sucks," said Dylan.

"Now you might be thinking, it was thoughtless, but they probably didn't mean anything racist by it. After all, it's natural to notice someone new when they look very different from the rest." He shook a finger. "And I agree."

"So, you're saying it wasn't racist, man?" asked Dylan. He was hunched forward, eyebrows knit in concern for his friend.

"The pool was the thing that got my attention—I was all self-conscious about my color for a while—but the racist thing happened a few days later. I caught my parents talking, all upset. Wouldn't tell me why, but I saw my mom put a piece of paper in her suitcase. I got it out when the adults went out to eat. Some lady in the complex wrote that we weren't welcome. She'd gone to all this work to find a place without black people, and now here we were."

Amber closed her eyes and shook her head.

Jace's mouth dropped open. "Woah."

"Turned out she was causing a lot of other problems for people there. Just about everyone else we saw on our trip was super nice. But yeah, when you get a note like that, you remember it."

There was a somber pause.

"Well, that just brought the meeting to a halt, didn't it?" Kendric slapped his thigh, straightened, and smiled. "Sorry, guys. Who else wants to say something?"

Dylan gave him a nod. "I was just thinking about how you didn't call it racism when they noticed you at the pool. I think I agree. Society is pretty quick to assume racism everywhere, even though hardly any of us actually knows a racist person. We immediately jump to conclusions of racism when we see two people arguing, just because one is black and one is white. Some people are just jerks to everyone, no matter the color."

Kendric said, "Yup. We're destroying the meaning of the word. Making it so broad that certain people are racist just by existing, and so narrow that supposedly only one color of people can be racist, which is completely untrue. We've taken the character and the choice of the person out of it entirely."

T.J. turned to Amber and Kendric. "You guys still haven't told us what you would change about the diversity department." T.J. winked. "Mostly, I've just heard Kendric complaining about it."

Amber shrugged. "I think the seminars and guest speakers are still valuable. I, personally, think it's a good thing to be aware of how people might feel who are different than me."

"I'm with you there," said Kendric, "but I think with all their meetings and workshops, they're still missing the main event. Here's what I'd do." He sat on the edge of his chair and held out his hands. "I wouldn't come out of the gate and accuse people of benefiting from racism or anything like that. I'd tastefully add some humor. Maybe mention some annoying things that people of all different races do and say to others. Like, asking whether black people sunburn."

Jace chuckled along with the others, curious now about the answer.

"Then I can ease into the more serious stuff. Tell some stories, like my experience with the racist lady. I'd have some of us talk at the front of the room, kind of like we're doing here tonight in a panel format. Give students some things to be aware of. Like cultural or religious things to be sensitive about. And encourage those from other cultures to be patient with the rest of us if we say the wrong thing or ask silly questions.

"I'd encourage them to watch out for each other, no matter the race.

I'd give them the benefit of the doubt that they have a good heart and want to help. I don't think I'd talk about politics. Leave that to them to figure out on their own. But the main thing is that I want them to leave feeling good. Smiling at each other as they walk out the door, not looking down or feeling resentful or guilty."

"You should do it," said T.J.

"Run the diversity department?"

"Put on a show like that. I bet it would be really popular. Call it the Unity Department."

Kendric grinned. "You know? I just might."

CHAPTER TWENTY

THEY TOOK a break and Jace wandered upstairs among the flowers, ferns, and cell phone reception. He shot Mari a text, and Rob had sent a video where he and Eli excitedly showed the result of their latest operation. *Wanted* fliers were taped to posts and windows, and some were simply strewn on the ground. Jace smiled as he imagined the face of a Zero reading one as they marched through later that night.

As he took his seat again in the basement, T.J. crouched next to him. "Hey, man. How are things?"

"Great," Jace replied. T.J.'s biceps stretched the sleeves of his T-shirt. Jace wondered whether he was flexing.

"Liking the club so far?"

"Oh yeah."

T.J. nodded. "Good. I can't wait to see what you add to the Brigade."

"I'm glad *you* feel that way." Jace glanced a few seats over.

"Amber?" T.J. chuckled. "She's always been a professional skeptic. She's suspicious of most of what *I* do. Don't worry about her."

"Okay."

"Hey, did I ever show you my favorite tattoo?"

T.J. lifted his left sleeve. A roaring lion blended into intricate patterns that simultaneously reminded Jace of ocean waves and dragon scales. Above this was the club logo. A small, simple shape of a rubber duck.

"Nice!" said Jace. "You're really into this, aren't you?"

"I guess I am," T.J. said. "College students like to get involved in causes. We all want to change the world. Fix problems left by the last generation, you know? But the more I experience, the more I think *this* is what we need right now. Really communicating with each other is how we'll get concrete, lasting solutions."

"Yeah. No matter what your cause is, this seems like the first step."

"Couldn't have said it better myself," said T.J.

"Hey, I've got one question. How do you become a member here?"

T.J. grinned. "Hey, Dylan. Jace wants to know how to be a member."

Dylan jumped up from his chair. "Mari hasn't told you? First, we all go to the pond near the visitor's center and you have to catch a duck with your bare hands."

"Only they don't like us doing that," T.J. said, "so we have to do it at night."

"Then there's the feat of bravery," Dylan said. "But if you're afraid of birds, the duck hunt counts for that, too."

Jace pursed his lips, nodded, and blinked sleepily.

"He's not buying it," said Dylan.

T.J. smiled under his beard. "We don't make a big deal about membership here. Some of the students that would come to our meetings didn't want their friends to find out. And if we pressured them to sign up, some of them might stop coming. We're just happy to have people come and talk, or just listen."

"But I *have* heard you guys talk about membership," Jace said.

"We'd love for you to finish all four dojo lessons. But after you come to a meeting or two, we'll call you a member if you like."

T.J. held up a clipboard and addressed the group. "Before anyone leaves, remember the election coming up. Here's the sign-up sheet for the fliers."

Amber grinned. "Love it!"

T.J. handed each person a yellow photocopied sheet of paper. Jace read the title aloud. "Are you up to the Pro Voter Challenge?" He dropped the flier to his lap and looked around.

"Oh, come on," said Kendric. "It's fun!"

Below the title was a cheesy black-and-white photo of a guy with a mustache and 1980s mullet peeking out of a voting booth and giving a thumbs up. On each flier was stapled a Pro Voter sticker that you were apparently supposed to put on after completing the challenge.

"This is a Bathwater tradition," said T.J. "Every election. Now that we're underground, we'll replace the Bathwater Brigade text with the duck. Any other changes?"

"We're trying to hide who made it, then?" asked Danica.

"Just making it less obvious," Amber replied. "Our friends know what the duck means."

Jace reviewed the rest of the flier. To complete the challenge, a student would have to spend at least an hour researching candidates on the ballot. *Every* candidate, no matter the party. In fact, students were required to cover up the political party the candidate belonged to while reading about them.

"Okay," Jace said. "How do we cover up the party? Like, with our thumb? It's not like we won't notice."

Amber replied. "Right. It's just trying to help us look at all the candidates with a fresh perspective. We think it's smart to be aware of which of them match your principles best, even if they're from a party that you normally wouldn't vote for."

Jace chuckled. "This is not your average campaign flier."

"One hour to review the candidates?" said Danica. "Aren't you setting the bar a little low for something as important as voting?"

"Yup," said T.J. "But we're being realistic. An hour of election research is about fifty-eight minutes longer than the average student does right now."

"Unless you count time watching political ads," said Kendric, "or at least the first few seconds before we skip them. Those things are everywhere! Isn't it crazy, the billions of dollars spent on them? Think of what would happen if more of us did a little research and kept an eye on our elected representatives. They'd have to actually keep their promises and work to represent us. And not just on election year, either."

T.J. winked at his sister. "Reminds me of Amburger cleaning her room."

Amber laughed. "So true! When I was little, I'd only jump up and work for the minute that mom or dad were walking by. Then I'd go back to my book."

Danica raised her hand. "What about a flier with advice on who you think we should vote for? Like, candidates who support Bathwater principles that most of us agree on."

T.J. gave Kendric a nod.

"Danica," said Kendric, "do you play chess?"

"A little."

"How does the game end?"

"When the king dies."

"Not quite."

Danica thought for a moment. "When the king is *captured*."

"Closer. The game ends when a king is *trapped*. Capturing or killing the king is not a part of the game. Seems like it ends just a little too early, doesn't it?"

She nodded.

"Cale students occasionally ask us who to vote for, and it would be pretty easy for a few of us to come up with some endorsements. But the actual voting booth and ballot? We never go there. It's where our game ends."

"I don't understand why, though. I think a lot of us would love advice like that from the Brigade."

Kendric picked up a red marker at the whiteboard on the side of the room. He drew a long arrow from left to right. He wrote *Principles* at the beginning of the arrow, *Policies* in the middle, and *Politicians* at the end.

He pointed to the left. "Start with your principles. Your values. Figure out what those are. Next, here in the middle, look at how we can put some of those into practice in the real world in the form of the policies you think are best. You know, the laws and programs you want to see.

"Then, once that's done, you move over here to *Politicians* at the end. Look at the candidates and party platforms to see who best represents those principles and policy ideas."

"Ah," said Danica. "That makes sense."

"If you do this backwards, it's easy to let the man or woman in office define your principles for you. And it's hard to stay consistent."

Kendric slowly paced at the front of the room. "There is an old tale of a sea captain. His crew wanted to rest from their voyage, so he sailed his ship into the calm waters of a harbor. As the crew readied the anchor, they found a great whale resting directly beneath the ship, so they couldn't drop their anchor. Eventually, they grew tired of waiting for it to leave. So, they tied the ropes around the whale instead."

"Logical," said Jace.

"The foolish crew drank and sang at the tavern. When they returned to the pier that evening, the ship was gone. The whale had pulled it far out to sea while the captain slept below deck."

Danica nodded, chin resting on her hand.

"People change," Kendric said. "They move. Anchor yourself to principles, not to politicians. Otherwise, you'll probably drift without realizing it."

"I have friends who *love* the mayor, Rosie Wells," Amber said. "They defend everything she does, even though she contradicts herself all the time. They know *who* they're voting for, but if you ask them *why*, the reason always changes."

"Is this all making sense?" T.J. asked Jace and Danica.

"Looks good," Jace said. "But I've got to be real here. I won't even finish step one before November. It's going to take me a while just to figure out what all my principles are."

"I know what you mean," said T.J. "Don't let that stop you from voting, though. Just do the best you can and keep working on it. That arrow on the board, that's not a one-time thing. Do it again and again."

Amber said, "Each time I come to one of these meetings, I change my mind on something. If I waited until I had life all figured out before I vote, I'd never do it."

"Sorry if I'm asking so many questions," said Danica, "but if you're changing your mind on things...I thought we should be anchored in the harbor of principles and not move around."

T.J. chuckled. "Oh, you can definitely move. In fact, you should. You mature, things change in your life, things change in society, you learn and understand the world and others better. All of these things affect your principles. But *you* do the moving. Steer your own ship. Don't be lazy and tie yourself to a person or political party and drift wherever they go."

"I still don't see why it would be bad if we give suggestions for who to vote for," Danica said.

"You can do that on your own," Kendric said. "But hypothetically, let's say most of the Brigade likes Rosie Wells, so we stick her name on the flier. However, once in office, she does things we didn't expect and that some people don't like. They'll remember we endorsed her, and we'd lose credibility."

"Oh."

"If you hate a politician that we've endorsed, are you going to want to come to one of our meetings?"

Amber nodded. "That's why we've had strong, loyal membership for forty years with so much diversity. That would drop fast if we got all political. We've seen that happen in other campus clubs, actually."

T.J. stood, stretching his legs. "We come to the Bathwater Brigade to forget about the teams in Washington for a while. We learn how to steer and anchor our own ship." He went to the board. "The Bathwater domain is here," he said, drawing a circle around Principles and Policies. "The politicians we each figure out on our own."

"I get it," Jace said, looking at the flier. "Sounds smart."

"Maybe," said Dylan, sitting low in his chair with arms still folded. "Maybe not."

Amber put a hand on his knee. "Dylan."

T.J. smiled slightly and nodded. "See, Jace and Danica, we don't all agree on everything here and that's fine." He turned to Dylan. "What are *your* thoughts?"

"As if you didn't know," Dylan said, forcing a smile. Danica glanced at Jace, who shrugged in return.

"It's great to be informed," Dylan said. "But I don't think we should encourage people to get too creative with their vote. Political parties are how big things get done, and they need a lot of support."

"So, even if another candidate will follow more of your principles and policies," said Danica, "you'll still vote for the party guy?"

"Sure, most of the time. Otherwise the party can risk losing a lot of influence. Especially when you throw away your vote on someone that can't win."

Kendric weighed in. "A so-called third-party candidate *can* win if enough people decide to vote for them."

"Except that it never happens," said Dylan.

"Good point." Amber shrugged.

Kendric turned. "I see it differently. If the party can always count on your vote, they don't have to listen to what you want. They're smart, and they watch votes closely. If they see that they're losing some votes to a third party, they want to find the reasons why. They'll be motivated to get a candidate that is more of what you want next time, so they'll have a better chance of winning."

"True," Jace said. "If a restaurant has lousy service but all the customers keep coming, what's going to change?"

"I see what you're saying," said Dylan. "But when you understand party influence, that's a dangerous game. Sometimes a senator gets a powerful position and it took her a long time to get the seniority for that. We can't just throw that away so easily."

Kendric shrugged. "Not sure I like the idea that I need to support elected officials decade after decade, especially when they're not lining up with my principles. I'm willing to let my party lose a race now and then to help them be better in the long term. If I just vote for the big two every time and pick the least bad candidate, then I can't be surprised when we have crap for government in twenty years."

Dylan hadn't changed his posture, his facial expression, or his mind. "While you're splitting the vote and making your party lose in the short term," he said, "the damage to the country might be too big to undo."

Jace raised his eyebrows and nodded. Both had excellent points.

T.J. leaned forward. "I get it, Dylan. Vote however you like. But this flier isn't telling people they shouldn't vote for their favorite party. Only to have eyes wide open while they do it, and to know where their principles are compared to the candidates. Do you want to call a revote on whether we hand them out this year?"

Dylan sighed and pursed his lips for a moment. "No," he said. "Go ahead."

CHAPTER TWENTY-ONE

"THIS IS THE SECOND DOJO," T.J. said, after a short break. He was wearing his headband. "Jace, Danica, you with me?"

They nodded.

"Sun Tzu says, 'If you know the enemy and know yourself, your victory will not stand in doubt.'"

From the corner, T.J. fetched what looked like a Victorian jewelry box. Ornate designs decorated the sides of the dark mahogany case, and a beautiful carving of the globe sat in relief on the lid.

"We begin by knowing yourself." T.J. carefully handed it to Danica. "This is your worldview. It's truth—as you see it."

She lifted the lid. The hinges allowed it to swing fully open. Jace stood to see inside. Red felt lined the insides, and a puzzle covered the bottom, already assembled enough to reveal a painting of a lush garden pond. Five or six pieces were missing.

"Each piece is a belief, value, experience, or opinion of yours." T.J. clasped his hands behind his back. "At a young age, you took the jumble of pieces you had collected so far in life, and you began to fit them together into your worldview. This is how you made sense of things around you, and it helped you make decisions."

Danica looked up at T.J. and smiled politely.

"Everyone else get up here," he said. They did, and he handed each of them a few puzzle pieces from his pocket. Kendric walked to Danica and held a piece out to her. She easily found its place in the puzzle and pressed it in. Amber was next. Her piece fit as well.

Dylan's puzzle piece, however, was nothing like the serene picture in her box. It was bright red and yellow. Danica held it in her hand and pursed her lips.

T.J. set a wooden cylinder on the seat next to her. "If you don't have a place for it," he said, "then you must discard it."

Danica tapped her chin. She examined the bright shapes on her new piece and the flowing greens of her nearly complete puzzle. She laughed. "I know I'm missing something."

"Do you have a place for it?"

"No." She put it in the cylinder.

"Do these dojo lessons always have to make the new people look dumb?" asked Jace.

"The lessons stick with you better this way," said Amber. Then she smirked. "Plus, it's more fun for *us*."

Kendric handed Danica another piece with strange, bright shapes, which she promptly set in the cylinder. They took turns until she had one remaining hole in her painting. T.J. held the piece out to her, and she pressed it into place.

T.J. clapped. "Great job! Your worldview is complete. How does it feel to have all the answers?"

"It feels like you're mocking me," said Danica. They chuckled.

T.J. took the box. He removed a few pieces from the middle of the puzzle and gave it to Jace. "Want to try?"

He shrugged. "Sure."

They each took turns handing him the pieces.

Amber was the first to give him a strange one. Jace held it in his hand.

"Are you going to discard it?" asked T.J.

"I want to say no," Jace replied, scanning the puzzle.

"Is there a place for it?"

Jace held the piece to T.J. "You do it."

"This is *your* worldview. Only you can control it."

Dylan lightly tapped the red felt inside the lid of the box. "Here?"

Dylan nodded.

Jace set the piece in the center of the open lid.

The rest of the puzzle went quickly, Jace setting the odd ones onto the lid instead of in the can. Everyone but T.J. took their seats.

A chair quietly appeared next to Jace. "Ooh, the puzzle!"

"Hey, Mari," T.J. said, winking. "We start at seven."

"I know that!"

Jace smiled at Mari and then looked at T.J. "So, am I done?" Jace held the open box out to him.

"What have you learned?" said T.J.

Jace chuckled nervously. "I'm not really sure. Maybe that when we have a new experience or get new information, then we should never throw it away?"

"You're close. We have a bit left to do." T.J. looked around. "Who wants to do a puzzle?"

Amber walked over, and she and Mari quickly assembled a second puzzle on the lid with the brightly-colored pieces. It was a curious picture with red, yellow, and black shapes, and the head of a zebra in the center.

"What in the world…" said Danica.

There were five random pieces still left over.

"What do I do with these?" asked Jace.

"Those?" said T.J. "Yeah, you can toss them."

Jace did. Then he looked at the box. "I've got two worldviews now."

T.J. gave a half smile. "No, still just one. But here's a lesson. We all do it like Danica sometimes. It's human nature. We feel like we've sorted life out. It's all nice and neat. We're comfortable. When we learn or experience or see something that fits our puzzle, we immediately put it into place and pat ourselves on the back. When something comes our way that *doesn't* fit our view of the world, then we're quick to throw it out and we don't give it a second thought. At least, that's the *easy* way to go through life. The lazy way."

"Thanks a lot," said Danica.

T.J. grinned. "Have you ever described an experience that you had actually witnessed, and they accuse you of lying? Just because it doesn't make sense to them?"

Dylan chuckled from his usual slouched position. "I wish I could say I haven't done that. It's embarrassing to look back and realize you have."

"Have you guys heard of an echo chamber?" asked Kendric, adjusting his glasses. "They use those when recording sound. But it's also a term to mean when you surround yourself with people and media and things that you already agree with and that don't challenge you at all. Everything you hear is an echo of what you're already thinking and saying."

"Yeah, don't do that," said T.J. "Here's the thing. You're going to read a book, or have a friend, or take a class that challenges your worldview. It might not even make sense to you at first. But just because something doesn't fit nicely into your puzzle right away, and makes you a little uncomfortable, it doesn't mean you have to immediately reject it. There are some pieces you may want to keep to the side for a while, you know? Figure it out later. It's okay to have some things inside your box that don't feel like they should belong together."

"So, if I look at the pieces long enough," Jace said, "then I might see how they fit."

"Remember the old story of the blind guys and the elephant?" T.J. asked. "Each one walked up to a part of the elephant and had a unique perspective. It seemed to be a wall, or a fan, or a snake, or a tree trunk. And they argued about it. This has happened to me so many times, where I was completely convinced of something at first. I knew I was right and the other person was wrong. Well, later I found that the truth was somewhere in the middle, as they say. There was more nuance to the situation that I had to learn. To really know yourself is to remember that there's a chance you might not have it all down yet."

"For me," said Kendric, "it was science and religion. At first, they seemed completely incompatible, but after some study and thought, I was able to nicely fit them together."

"What's a way that we can examine something in our box?" T.J. asked the group.

"You can look at the pieces differently," said Amber. "You know, by swapping variables. I did some of this today with white privilege.

Swapped out the country from America to Japan and the racial majority from white to Japanese. And if you remember, we saw many of the same privilege issues there, too."

"Oh. Right," said Jace. "We did it last week too, didn't we. About Sophia and the wedding cake."

"Swap out variables to see if the principle you're talking about still holds true," said T.J. "It can help make sure you're treating people as individuals and being fair and consistent. A fun thing to do is to take something a politician you hate is saying, and imagine a politician you *like* saying the exact same thing. And vice versa. Be honest with yourself."

Danica nodded. "We *do* throw pieces away sometimes, right?"

"Yes," said T.J. "We have to. The lesson is that we shouldn't be *too* quick to discard what doesn't immediately make sense to us. Here, let's start with something stupid. You're convinced the world is round and someone tells you it's not. What do you do with this new suggestion?"

"Toss," said Danica.

"Sure. Now, what if you believe that socialism has never worked, but someone brings evidence that it supposedly has?"

"Toss," said Jace, smiling. "No, I should probably start with a bit of research on my own and try to get a fair look at their claim. And depending on what I find, maybe like you said, I'd need to examine my beliefs and opinions and stuff. I might need to change them."

"Cool," said T.J. "And you don't suddenly have to turn your worldview upside down. But give yourself a chance to work it over. Like I said, it's okay to have a box where not everything fits perfectly all the time. You can have a few things in there that seem to contradict each other at the moment. Actually, you *should*. If you think you have everything figured out, you're doing it wrong."

Kendric raised his hand. "Have a little humility that you might not understand the whole universe just yet. And have some patience with yourself. Examine your pieces once in a while. Maybe even the ones that you're already pretty sure about and seem to fit with the others. As you learn and grow, you may find that you can fit more pieces together than you had thought possible."

"Shall we?" said T.J. Kendric nodded. With the box still on Jace's lap, they each put a hand over the puzzle on the inside of the lid, then flipped the lid over. When they opened it again, the puzzle of the zebra was now upside down, revealing a picture of another garden by the same artist as the one in the bottom of the box. T.J. and Kendric placed this back in the lid. "Those pieces weren't as out of place as you thought."

Danica smiled and nodded. "Cool."

"Except," said Jace, "I would rather have two zebra pictures instead." They laughed.

T.J. moved to the next part of the lesson. "That was how to know yourself. Now, as Sun Tzu says, how to know the enemy."

"...who isn't really your enemy," added Danica.

T.J. smiled. "Right."

He held up two objects. A metallic person like you'd see on top of a trophy, and a piece of paper cut in an outline that roughly matched the metal figure.

"This," he said, holding up the paper figure, "is a straw man."

"Actually," said Amber, "Dylan just didn't want to take the time to make it out of straw." Dylan smiled sheepishly and shrugged.

"And this is a steel man," continued T.J. "Imagine these are both as tall as you. Which would you rather fight? Which would be easier to knock over? Obviously, the straw man, right?"

"To set up a straw man," said Kendric, "just say what your opponent thinks, but put it in the worst possible light. Or, at least in the way that is easiest for you to defeat.

"Here's an extreme example. You're setting up a straw man argument if you say that anyone who wants a national border fence just hates people who look or talk differently than them. Or, if you don't want a fence, then you must hate America. Either way, you're avoiding the tough issues and just trying to make the other side look bad. And though it might feel good to get an easy win, it usually backfires."

"The steel man is what you want," T.J. said. "For that, you must understand your opponent as well as you can. And have them *know* that you understand. Be generous. And give them the benefit of the doubt. Put yourself in their shoes for a moment. Want to achieve the ultimate steel man? Listen to what they're saying and keep articulating their own position back to them until they say, 'that's right.'"

"When we remember to," said Amber, "we set this steel man out during our Bathwater meetings. When one of us does exceptionally well at representing the other side, they'll get awarded it for the night."

"What if I can't beat the steel man?" asked Jace. "Maybe I don't know enough. Or I'm not sure of myself."

"Do it anyway." T.J. smiled. "Trust me. Even if you can't defeat it, your opponent will be impressed and prepared to consider what you have to say. And *you* will be prepared to engage them like never before."

"And how do I do that?"

"That...is next week's lesson." T.J. smiled and ended the meeting.

While Jace waited for Mari to finish talking with her friends so he could walk her back to her dorm, T.J. approached. "Well?"

"Very cool. Mind-blowing, actually. For some reason I'd never heard of the worldview puzzle until last week. Now I know where it comes from."

T.J. smiled curiously. "It's just a Bathwater thing. Mari spoiled it for you?"

"No, some lady in the Administration Building mentioned it."

"Ah. Maybe she was a Bathwater member once."

Jace coughed away a laugh. "Strongly doubt it."

As they were leaving, Mari stopped in front of the whiteboard. Kendric's illustration was still there, with an arrow starting at *Principles*, passing through *Policies*, and ending at *Politicians*.

"This isn't right," she said.

She drew another arrow which began at *Principles* and pointed just above *Politicians*. She wrote *YOU* in large block letters. "We don't always have to wait for a politician to get big things done."

T.J. watched from behind. "Good fix."

141

CHAPTER TWENTY-TWO

THAT THURSDAY, Saint and Jace finished the Florence Hughes Fine Arts Building. Jace sent India a text.

Worked hard on your grandma's building. I'd say I'm part of the family now.

Mr. Oatley sent them to the Tech Ed Building next door. Their first classroom was overflowing with desks attached to chairs. Four large whiteboards filled the walls, covered in blue symbols and diagrams that Jace didn't understand. They each took a door at the opposite ends of the room.

"You're making a mess of it," Saint said, as Jace wiped the excess lubricant from a hinge.

Jace said nothing.

"Seriously. Your cloth is getting soaked."

Jace checked his watch. Two more hours to go on day three of eight. He gritted his teeth.

"Well, *you're* quiet today," said Saint.

Jace sighed. "If I say something you don't like, I'll probably get sucker punched."

"Yup," Saint said. "You never know."

"We don't have to be in the same room, you know. We can start from opposite ends of the building."

"Oh, and leave a Nazi alone in a room? How do I know you won't start setting up a concentration camp?"

Jace looked at Saint in disgust. "That's offensive on many levels." Then he turned back to the door. "And will you stop calling me that? I'm happy that you're in a Nazi-fighting club, but look around. You're on the wrong continent and about eighty years too late."

"Oh, seeds of it still remain." Saint polished the doorknob. "Let them grow, and you'll have the next Reich."

"You're crazy," said Jace, clenching the fist that was out of Saint's view. Forcing himself to relax, he swung the door wide a few times and moved to the next room.

Saint followed, starting on the second door. "So, are you going to organize a tuba blast at the next funeral you attend? Or was Stephen Hobbs just lucky?"

"Your anti-police protest wasn't a funeral service."

"Actually, it kind of was. Mourning a life lost to police brutality."

"Well, *you* have an odd way at behaving at funerals. Do you always chant and block traffic?" Jace adjusted his safety glasses. "Since you're so interested in Nazi's, that sounds more like what the Brownshirts would do than anything I've ever done."

"The brown what?"

Flustered, Jace checked his watch. One hour and fifty minutes to go. "You don't even know who the Brownshirts are? Learn your history before you call people Nazis." Jace folded his cloth and wiped down the bottom hinge.

"I know a Nazi when I see one."

"Listen to me!" yelled Jace in a sudden outburst which made Saint jump. "I'm not a Nazi!" Jace faced Saint, standing tall and breathing hard in the heavy silence.

"You made me get graphite all over the floor," Saint said without making eye contact. He began cleaning it up with a spare cloth from his tool belt.

Jace watched Saint for a moment. Then he walked to the next room and forcefully shut the heavy door behind him. The hinges squeaked loudly. He'd need more than WD-40. He angrily popped the three pins out of the hinges using a hammer and a screwdriver. "Graphite all over the floor," he muttered to himself. He found the tube of grease and applied a bead of it on one of the pins.

Saint stormed in. Midway through the swing, the door fell from the hinges and slammed onto the ground. It teetered for an eternal fraction of a second before it tipped forward, the sharp corner narrowly missing Saint's face, and crashed onto a desk.

As the echoes died away in the stunned silence, Saint's eyes narrowed. "What the...what did you *do*?"

Jace, wide-eyed, put up his hands, still holding the pins. "I was fixing it."

"You took out all three pins at *once*?" growled Saint. "What kind of idiot does that?" He quickly removed both pairs of glasses, safety and prescription, and set them on a desk.

"I didn't think you'd be walking in," Jace said, taking a step back.

"You did that on purpose!" Saint threw his tool belt it in the corner. Metal wrenches and screwdrivers scattered and clanged on the ground.

That was it. Jace was sick of being accused of being the worst kind of a person. Saint had been looking for a fight ever since they started this stupid job, and now he was going to get it. He knew he'd probably get even deeper into trouble for this, but there are times you reach the point where you simply don't care.

Saint charged. Jace had just enough time to rip off his tool belt before Saint grabbed him around the waist. Jace fell backward, the edge of a desk digging into his back as he went down. He tucked into his fall to keep his head from hitting the tile.

Saint sprawled on top of Jace. Jace grabbed Saint in a bear hug, pinning one of Saint's arms to his side. Saint beat at him with his free hand, his legs flailing about and knocking a desk onto its side. Jace's safety glasses were diagonal across his face.

"Stop it!" Saint grunted.

"You're the one attacking *me*!"

While Saint had the advantage of surprise, he did not have the skill or the body mass to compete for long. In a series of moves rehearsed during similar fights with his younger brother, Jace arched his back and flipped onto his stomach. Before Saint could reposition himself, Jace tucked his legs underneath and launched into a somersault which flung Saint off of him. Jace sprang onto Saint's back and tossed his safety glasses aside. Using all his strength, he pried Saint from the tile and turned him over. Then, tightly gripping his own wrists, Jace locked his arms under Saint's shoulder and around his neck, and ensured Saint had plenty of room to breathe.

Saint alternated between struggling and panting.

"You done?" Jace asked, after it had been at least twenty seconds since the last fruitless effort.

"No!" Saint grunted and struggled again. Jace held tightly. The only thing Saint had left in the fight now was his pride.

"Okay", Saint panted.

"You're *really* done?" Jace asked. "No sucker punches?"

"Done."

Jace scrambled off his defeated opponent and sat against the wall. After a moment, Saint propped himself upright a whiteboard's length away.

"I don't care about you or what you think," Jace said. "We're not going to agree. I just want to get this done and move on with my life." He turned to Saint. "But you've *got* to stop calling me names all the time."

Saint rubbed his head. Jace softened.

"Look. I'm sorry about the door," Jace said. "You're right, that was dumb to take out all the pins at once." Then he chuckled. "Maybe I *should* read that *Door maintenance for Nazis* book you keep talking about."

"Probably not," said Saint. "It makes you Heil Hitler at each door you service."

Jace laughed. He slowly stood, holding his back with his right hand. "That will leave a bruise." He reached out a hand to help Saint up. "Let's put the door back on before we get in trouble."

They carefully set the door on its hinges while Jace applied the grease and tapped the pins back down. There was a shallow dent in the door, but the real casualty was the desk—the metal bar had broken, and the writing surface dangled to one side.

"Cheap piece of junk," said Saint, kicking one of its legs.

"Wasn't built to handle heavy doors falling on it." Jace shook his head. "If I were building these, that's the first thing I'd test."

They swapped the desk with one near the window and put their tool belts and their glasses back on. "Weird," said Saint as they were about to leave the room. He stooped and picked something off the floor. "What's this?" He was holding a small, rectangular piece of metal.

"Give me that." Jace snatched his token out of Saint's hands.

"Easy, Gollum. What is it?"

"Something my dad gave me." Jace examined it for dents or scratches, then slipped it into his pocket.

"A thumb drive?"

"No."

"All right." Saint shrugged.

"Hey!" came a voice from down the hall.

Saint stepped into the hallway and waved at Mr. Oatley. Jace followed and shut the door behind him.

"Let's check your work, boys." Mr. Oatley opened the door and went into the room that had hosted a cage match only minutes before. Jace and Saint glanced at each other and followed.

Mr. Oatley looked the door up and down and swung it back and forth a few times. He stopped and faced the boys. "Well ain't you two slicker than a slop jar," he said. "Did y'all think I wouldn't notice?"

Saint raised his eyebrows and looked at Jace. Jace kept his face blank while his mind scrambled to come up with a defense for the dented door and the broken desk.

"This hinge has grease all over it!" Mr. Oatley yelled.

Saint quickly cleaned it up.

Oatley examined the hinge again. He gave a grudging nod of approval before turning to Jace. "You been sleeping on the job, son? Your hair is all messed up. Looked much nicer this afternoon."

"Nope," replied Jace. "Just gets that way when I'm working extra hard, I guess."

Mr. Oatley shook his head. "It's been a week and y'all still can't handle the basics. I don't have time to check every door you do! I might not have you work on door closers Saturday after all." He talked about working on door closers as if it were some big reward.

Saint shrugged. "Whatever you want."

"Whatever I..." Mr. Oatley began, and then just hung his head. He worked alongside them for another hour.

While in the next classroom, Jace looked over at Saint, who squinted as he adjusted a door latch with a screwdriver. He wondered what Saint's home had been like. Judging by his ineffective fighting style, Jace guessed he didn't have any brothers. What were his childhood friends like?

Jace frowned and went back to work.

Even though it felt like Mr. Oatley thought they were ruining his life, he surprised them by taking them to Munchies again. Jace ordered—and regretted—the fish burger. The other two ordered the same meals as last week. Jace watched as Saint put one of the two wrapped hamburgers in his lap as he sat down.

Jace and Saint listened to stories from the ranch as Mr. Oatley drew livestock brand designs on napkins and told of cattle rustlers and hog hunts.

Mr. Oatley didn't offer them a ride home. Strangely, today Jace probably would have accepted. Saint and Jace stood outside for an awkward moment before they glanced at each other, nodded, and Saint walked away.

Jace walked back to his dorm, less upright than usual. He called Rob. No answer.

Halfway up the stairs to his room, he wished he had taken the elevator. He went straight into the community bathroom, pulled up his T-shirt, and examined his lower back in the mirror. Just a little red, for now. He smirked when he saw his hair. It really did look like he'd just woken up. There was also a large, dark grease streak on his pale forehead and another one on his cheek which took him a while to scrub off.

His dorm room was empty. Jace took a long drink from his water bottle and a soy nut bar from a box on his shelf. He didn't like these nearly as much as regular granola bars, but he found that they had a considerably longer shelf life—since he made the switch, he had only seen one go missing.

He looked at his backpack and pictured the calculus homework inside.

Not tonight.

He slowly crawled onto the top bunk, lay flat on his back, and fell asleep.

CHAPTER TWENTY-THREE

HALF THE TREES in Oak Bend Park were conceding defeat to autumn, while the rest clung to the good times of summer. Orange and yellow leaves were poised to blanket the trail in a matter of weeks. Until then, mountain bikers enjoyed the clear view of the trail's contours, rocks, and roots.

It was Friday afternoon, and the motion of the pedals sent Jace's back a continuous, painful reminder of yesterday's Zero attack. However, it wasn't all bad news. A few weeks of consistent riding had paid off, his lungs and legs having gotten used to the idea. In fact, Jace had no trouble at all keeping up with Rob.

They had stopped at one of the larger jumps where a dip into a small ravine gave them instant speed, launching them halfway up the other side. Rob got several feet of air. Jace, however, was more cautious on the jumps, and he could never quite bring himself to arrive at full velocity.

After jumping a few times, they leaned their bikes against a huge tree trunk and sat facing the dirt ramp. The faint patter of falling leaves played through the air each time the breeze swelled. A rich, earthy smell resided there. A mighty and decaying trunk lay on the ground a little way down the ravine. Something scampered nearby.

"I would have hurt him," Rob said. "Bad."

Jace thought of Saint struggling on the floor. "Nah, you wouldn't have. I felt kind of sorry for him, actually. He talks tough, but he has no idea how to fight. Or even wrestle. I don't think he'll try that again."

"Your punishment is cruel and unusual, though. Having to listen to a Zero call you names, literally ten hours a week."

"Yeah, I don't know. I was mad at first. But it's clear he doesn't know what he's talking about. It's more just annoying."

"I'd give that kid a *reason* to call the police. Then maybe he'd appreciate them. Do you know what Gina's life is like right now because of fools like him?"

"No."

"She can't go out in public. Can't even tell her friends where she's staying. She's getting death threats. She's got a two-year-old daughter for heaven's sake."

Jace dropped his head. "Yeah."

"All this, and she hasn't even had her trial yet."

Jace sighed. "Did you hear anything more about your Wanted fliers?"

Rob grinned as he threw another rock, not quite hitting the other side of the ravine from his seated position. "Yup! The Zeroes are *mad*."

"What's the next operation?"

"Not sure yet. We'll probably do one next week though. We have to."

Jace nodded. "Well, just don't get caught. You might join me and Saint with campus service. Or worse."

"I don't care. You think I'll back down from defending my brothers and sisters in blue?"

Jace grinned. "Nope."

A light breeze rustled the leaves, and trunks creaked.

"You know," said Jace, "there is more than one way to defend the police. Like, more than just making fun of Zeroes. Even though that's well deserved and all."

Rob looked at Jace. "So, what would you do, then? Go talk to them? Apologize? Find common ground or something?"

"I don't know." Jace thought about it as he looked for a rock to throw. "Is that what they tell you to do at the bathtub group?"

Jace sat up straight and narrowed his eyes at Rob.

"Eli told me you've been going to those with that Mari girl."

Jace smiled. "Yeah, I've been going."

"It's fine to, like, learn about different viewpoints and all that," Rob said. "But some people just aren't worth talking to."

Jace nodded. "I get it."

"Those Zero Supremacy idiots are getting people killed."

"That's the same thing they say about cops," Jace said, almost to himself.

"Woah." Rob turned to face his friend. "Are you saying they have some good points? That the truth is in the middle or something like that?"

"No."

"Good."

Jace sighed. "I'm starting to think that talking to them might do some good, though."

"Want to bring a bullhorn at the next operation? That might work..."

"No, not all together at once. But if you can talk to them one on one, away from the noise and everything...I don't know. Maybe you could get through to them. Theoretically."

"Hey, if they want to join my side, fine by me," Rob said. "But I'm not going out of my way to listen to *them*."

Jace shrugged.

"You're scaring me, Jace," Rob said. "You can't give those guys an inch."

"You're probably right." Jace stood slowly, holding his back. "Yikes. I'm walking like Mr. Oatley now. Maybe he got in a door-related fight years ago." Jace pictured himself in fifty years, driving a speeding golf cart and yelling at students.

Rob stood, too. "Actually, I've been thinking. I kind of agree with you. I mean, going head to head with Zeroes is fun, but I don't think we're helping Gina all that much, and we're running out of time."

"You have other ideas?"

"Remember Cupcake Day? Maybe we need to do something like that, with that sort of flier. Forget about the Zeroes for a minute and go straight to the people."

Jace nodded.

"Do something like what Mari was doing, but in the city. If we can spread a message out there that counteracts what Zero Supremacy is saying, then we can help bring public opinion back to sanity in time for the trial. I think that's sort of what Mari was trying to do. Right?"

"I think that would be a great idea," said Jace.

"Do you think the bathtub people would join us?"

Jace smiled to himself as he thought of Mari and Amber. Not in a thousand years. But he didn't want to be the one to tell Rob.

"Maybe," Jace said.

"Can you ask?"

"It's not like we talk all the time."

"When will you see her next?"

"In class, I guess. Next week."

Rob nodded and stroked his chin. They mounted their bikes.

"Hey. Are you going to bring her to India's party?"

"Party?" Jace said. "Oh, that thing at her grandma's house in a few weeks?"

"Of course! It's the highlight of the year."

"I'm not even sure *I'm* supposed to go."

"You were there when she invited everyone." Rob pulled his phone from his pocket and began tapping. "Here. Let me prove it."

"Don't ask her," Jace groaned.

Moments later, Rob showed him his phone.

Jace raised his voice. "You asked if Mari could come too?" He knocked his head against a tree.

"Yup, you're both officially invited. So, are you going to ask Mari?"

"I...don't know. We've gone to meetings and class together, but we're not really like *that*, you know?"

"Do you *want* to be?"

Jace smiled. "Well, I wouldn't mind, I guess. I'm not sure if she likes me like that, though. She might even have a boyfriend."

"You don't see it, do you?"

"See what?"

"We saw you two behind us at the football game," Rob said, eyebrow raised. "She's totally into you."

Jace shrugged.

"I don't think you even have her phone number," Rob said.

"Yes, I do."

"Prove it."

Jace pulled out his phone and opened his text messages with Mari. When he held it out as proof, Rob snatched the phone and turned his back. Jace dropped his bike and lunged for his phone, feeling his back complain. Rob turned and blocked him.

Jace heard a ring, it was on speakerphone. "Hang up!" he said.

"Hi Jace," said Mari.

"Hey, uh," said Rob. "This is Rob, his friend. Jace is here. How are you on this fine day?"

"Good." She drew it out with a laugh. "Hi, guys!"

"Yes, hello," said Rob. "Anyway, my friend had his hands go numb. It happens when he rides his bike. Really sad. He wanted to call you, but he wasn't able to dial, so he asked me to."

"Oh, that *is* sad," she said, obviously not buying his story.

"It looks like his face is going numb now," Rob said, "so I better do the talking. He wants to know if you'd like to come to a party at a beach house on October the nineteenth with a bunch of friends."

"Um, let me check," Mari said. Rob grinned at Jace and briefly raised his eyebrows. Jace rolled his eyes.

"Yeah, I'm free," she said. "I think I'll talk this over with Jace though. After the numbness wears off and everything, of course."

"Right," said Rob. "Well, put it on your calendar. What's that, Jace?"

Jace glared at him, arms folded, waiting for the phone call to end.

"He's signing something to me, which is very difficult to do with numb hands. You should be proud of him. What a fighter. What's that, Jace? I see. He's wondering if you want to go to the pool tomorrow night. Oh wait. No, he wants to *play* pool with you tomorrow night. Is this acceptable?"

"Saturday? If it's after eight thirty."

"Fine, fine. He says he'll meet you at the Union Center at eight thirty-five."

"All right," she laughed. "Thanks, Rob. Bye, guys."

Staring across the ravine, Jace held out his hand. Rob gave his phone back.

"Well played," Rob said. "You're a charmer."

CHAPTER TWENTY-FOUR

MR. OATLEY WANTED to finish maintaining door closers on the Tech Ed Building on Saturday morning. The structure was more glass than brick, and Jace paused near the entrance and smiled. On the cornerstone plaque, the sun's sharp angle revealed the light impression of a rubber duck. This was his new favorite building.

Three hours in, there had been no fights and hardly any insults. There hadn't been much talking at all, in fact.

In what Mr. Oatley called a desperate move to prevent dumb mistakes, he had insisted they work closely together. This explained why Jace stood at the base of a six-foot ladder in the men's bathroom while Saint cursed and clinked his tools at the top. The door wasn't closing on its own—not ideal for a bathroom.

While Jace waited, he pulled out the metal token his dad had made him, and continuously flipped it over with one hand.

"Can't figure out how this stupid thing works," Saint grunted. He descended the ladder, wiped sweat from his nearly shaved head onto his black T-shirt, and leaned an arm in the door frame. "All right," he said, frowning at Jace's hand. "Really. What is that thing?"

"Oh. Right," Jace sighed. "It's called a token."

A guy with a beard and dark rimmed glasses squeezed by the ladder.

"Excuse me, we're working here," said Jace. "The second-floor bathroom is free."

"I don't mind," the man said, and loudly shut a stall door.

"We do," Saint mumbled. He and Jace looked at each other and stepped into the hall. "You said your dad gave it to you?"

"Yeah. He's made us kids stuff like that since we were little."

Saint moved his safety glasses to the top of his head and held out a hand. Jace looked at him doubtfully.

"Oh, come on, I'm not going to do anything to it."

Jace slowly handed it over, and Saint pretended to drop it. Jace lunged to catch it, and then grimaced as he straightened, holding his back.

"Sorry, couldn't resist," Saint said as he turned the tablet over and looked at the other side. "It's light. Plastic?"

"No, titanium. He was a machinist." Jace studied the red exit sign at the end of the hallway. "It's the last one he ever made."

"He died?"

"No. He has something called essential tremor and he can't make stuff like this anymore." Jace shook his hand to demonstrate.

Saint tapped it with his fingernail, then pulled and pushed at the ends. "So, what does it...do?" He squeezed it and pointed it at the wall as if to activate a laser pointer.

"See the grid of dots in the middle?"

Saint nodded.

"There are tiny points in some of them. If you interpret it as computer binary language, it has a message. My dad knew I was going into computers, so he researched how to encode a message into it for me."

"Not bad," Saint muttered, squinting at the grid. "Probably eight-bit characters."

"You're a computer guy too, huh?"

"Computer science major. What? I don't look like it?"

"No, you do. You look like a complete nerd."

Saint ignored Jace's dig. "What's the message?" He turned his phone's flashlight and moved it across the token.

"It's not a secret Nazi code, if that's what you're thinking."

"Just the thing a Nazi would say," Saint softly replied, eyes never leaving the token.

Jace hesitated and cleared his throat. "If it is to be, it is up to me."

Saint laughed. "Okay."

Jace chuckled. "I know. He didn't make it up. He says it's a quote by a guy named William H. Johnson." Jace sighed. "He'd say it all the time to us kids, actually. Especially when we weren't living up to our potential. Or if we wanted to buy something awesome but didn't feel like earning the money for it. He'd try to inspire us."

Saint tossed it back. "Sounds like he's a good dad."

Jace tucked the token back into his pocket. "The best."

The bearded guy left the bathroom, and Saint climbed the ladder once more. Mr. Oatley returned a few minutes later.

"Can y'all finish in an hour? I think there are just two closers left that need adjusting on this floor. I want to get going on another building today."

"Sure," said Jace.

"All right. Now just making sure, but you remember how to fix them when the rod and seal pulley bolts are weak, right?"

"Yup," Jace assured him.

"Okay. How do you do it?"

"Hmm?"

"How do you fix the door closers when the rod and seal pulley bolts are weak? You just said you knew how to do it."

Jace scratched his head. "Actually, now that you mention it, I must have forgot."

"Of course you forgot!" Mr. Oatley boomed. "I made it up! There's no such thing as rod and seal pulley bolts." Oatley had the pained expression of a man at the end of his rope. He squared off with Jace and held up both hands. Jace winced in anticipation. "Don't say you know something when you really don't," he yelled, louder than before. "You get people hurt that way."

Jace nodded. It was a valid point, actually.

"I can explain it to you, but I can't understand it for you." Mr. Oatley turned away and shuffled down the hallway, shaking his head and muttering under his breath.

Saint stepped off the ladder and moved it out of the way. The door remained open. "Hey Jace. I think I made it worse. It's stuck. See if you can move it."

Jace threw himself against it. To his horror, the heavy door swung freely. He willed it to slow, but it slammed shut, echoing through the building like a gun shot. He cringed and quickly opened the door again. Dust drifted from the ceiling lights. Ears ringing, Jace inspected the door and frame for damage, then he looked up. The closer assembly had been detached from the wall completely. Saint had his back turned, shoulders shaking in silent laughter.

Predictably, Mr. Oatley yelled something indecipherable from down the hall and hurried back to the bathroom. Jace considered hiding in a stall.

"Who did that?" Mr. Oatley bellowed, his face redder than Jace had ever seen it.

Neither spoke. Jace blinked at the ground and was about to raise a hand when Saint spoke up. "It was me. I was testing it."

Saint met Jace's eyes, then looked away.

Mr. Oatley took a few breaths. "Y'all don't need to slam the doors at forty miles an hour to test them!" He took off his cowboy hat and doubled over. "How on God's green earth did y'all ever get into college?"

"Won't happen again," said Saint.

Mr. Oatley narrowed his eyes and stared at both of them for a full ten seconds before stalking back down the hall.

Grinning, Saint climbed the ladder once more and got to work.

"All right, that was funny," Jace said.

Saint paused thoughtfully, then went back to turning his wrench. "If I'm being honest, so was your little banner and musical number at Victor Square. Mostly offensive, but a bit funny too."

Jace chuckled. He leaned against the door frame, his eyes following the grout lines of the tile on the wall. His smile slowly faded. Saint ratcheted the box onto the top of the door. The clicking noise echoed off the ceramic walls.

"Why didn't she have to kill him?" Jace asked.

"What?"

"Last week you said that Gina Lambson didn't have to kill Stephen. What did you mean, exactly?"

Saint looked down at Jace, then cranked the bolts tight and climbed down the ladder. He faced Jace while wiping his hands on a cloth. "Well, for one, they trapped him."

To Jace, trapping and arresting criminals seemed like a reasonable thing to do, but all he said was, "I'm listening."

"And if you're a black man with a cop aiming a gun at you, what other option do you have than to run?"

"Um...there was another option that I'm positive the police made very clear. To hold up his hands and get against the wall or on the ground."

"You don't think they might have shot him, anyway? Come on."

Jace stared at him. "Are you serious, Saint? Think about it. The police arrest probably tens of thousands of people each day. If the police end up shooting half of the black people that they go to arrest, we would see fresh cases on the news every five minutes. I guarantee you they aren't just shooting black people for no reason."

Saint scratched his head. "You remember the part about him being unarmed, right? There is never an excuse for shooting an unarmed person."

Jace put his hands on his belt. The cold metal of the socket wrench touched his wrist, and his thoughts turned to the steel man from the last dojo lesson. He tapped his fingers on the belt and selected his next words carefully.

"Let me make sure I understand what you mean. You're saying that you have to have a weapon in hand to be dangerous."

"To be deadly, yeah."

"And that the police shouldn't be using deadly force on suspects unless they know that the suspect also has deadly force."

Saint paused. "If they think he would use it. Yeah, that's about right."

"Okay."

Saint eyed him skeptically. "So, you're agreeing with me, now?"

"Well, here's what I think. You've seen photos of Stephen and Gina, right? He's twice her size. It seems that in a few seconds, with just his hands, he could put her in the hospital or worse."

Saint shrugged. "Maybe."

"It's not supposed to be a fair fight, like a duel or a boxing match or something like that. Gina wanted to go home to her family, and the city hired her to protect the citizens. I think it's okay that the police use a level of force a notch or two above what the criminal brings to the table. Especially when they're coming at you."

"I don't know about all that," Saint said. "Still doesn't seem right. If he was trying to get away, why didn't she just let him go?"

Jace nodded. "I'm guessing she didn't know why he was running at her. If she had stepped aside, he still might have attacked her. And it looked like he had a weapon. Plus, there's the whole part about protecting the community and getting crime off the streets. Even if he wasn't a threat to her at that moment, doesn't mean that he wouldn't have been a threat to someone else later. There was a reason they were after him in the first place, remember?"

Jace reached his hands to the top of the door frame and leaned forward, casually stretching his arms. "Actually," he continued, "I *do* kind of agree with you. Stephen Hobbs didn't have to die. But I'd say he also didn't have to *run*. And if he didn't run, he wouldn't have died."

Saint played with the ratchet in his hand. "So, you're putting the blame on him, then?"

"I used to work at a golf course," said Jace. "It's funny, sometimes I'd be making the rounds while golfers were playing, and a pair of them would be mad because the group ahead of them was so slow. I'd drive up to the slow group to see what was up, and guess what? They were mad at the group in front of *them* for the same reason. Sometimes the problem is actually way down the line, and we can't see it from where we're standing. But we blame the only person that we *do* see—Gina Lambson."

"What's your point?"

"Well, I'd say that there was a big string of events that led to his death, and some of those events were in his control. I know enough police officers to be very confident that they gave him orders. And if he had followed their orders, he'd be alive today."

Saint shook his head. "It's not that simple."

"Sure, it is. The commands they give aren't complicated. Hold up your hands, stop, get on the ground. It's common sense to know that some force is coming your way if you ignore them."

"When you're in that situation, you don't always have common sense."

Jace chuckled. "Especially if you're a criminal."

Saint paused. His voice was calm, but the muscles in his face trembled slightly. "Have you ever had handcuffs put on you, Jace?"

"Nope," he proudly replied.

"Next time you're around a pair, have a friend try putting them on you. Even if you've done nothing wrong, and everything's calm, it's the most natural thing in the world to resist. It's like instinct. There's a reason these things always seem to escalate."

Jace held out his hands. "What do you want the cops to do, then?"

Saint was quiet.

"It sounds like the whole trial is unnecessary, anyway," Jace continued. "Apparently the evidence is pretty clear. If it wasn't for people like Zero Supremacy making a big deal about it, there wouldn't even be a trial."

"If someone didn't make a big deal about it," Saint shot back, "do you think African Americans would be allowed to vote?"

This time it was Jace that was quiet.

They finished the rest of the doors in silence and waited by the front doors of the building. Mr. Oatley pulled up with the golf cart. They loaded their tools, strapped the ladder on the back, and took their usual seats.

"It's hot as the hinges of hell today," Oatley said. He grabbed his clipboard and pencil from behind his seat and crossed off a line.

"All right," he said. "We've got...what? An hour and a half? Let's get one of these small ones done."

He put the clipboard back behind him and drove north.

"Where are we going?" Saint asked.

Mr. Oatley harrumphed. "To the greenhouse."

CHAPTER TWENTY-FIVE

"LOOK," Saint said, turning a door handle repeatedly to distribute the graphite. "All I want is for people to not be victimized."

"Me, too." Jace checked his watch. They were fifteen minutes in and had already finished two of only six doors on the main floor of the greenhouse—the *only* floor, for all Saint knew. Two building entrances, an office, and two closets.

And the stairwell door.

"But I'm the one that actually cares," Saint said.

They had entered at the back and worked their way left as Mr. Oatley had taught them. "If y'all don't do it systematic," he had said, "in five minutes you'll be as confused as a goat on AstroTurf." Thankfully, this meant that the stairwell would be last.

Jace worked slowly, but he knew it wouldn't be slow enough. He thought of going home sick, but if Saint was going to land in Bathwater Grand Central, Jace would rather be there to keep an eye on him.

"Why do you think you're the only one that cares?" Jace asked.

"Let me get this straight. A bunch of us show up to support the family of an unarmed black man who got killed. And you show up and make fun of everybody. So, *you're* the one who cares about saving lives?"

Saint moved to door three.

"Hey," Jace said. "I'll go start at the other end and work back this way. We'll get done quicker."

"Why would you do that?" asked Saint. "It won't make any difference. It will just get Mr. Oatley mad when he gets back. He'll say we're doing it all cattywampus again."

Jace slumped. He had nothing.

"Well," said Saint, "you going to help?"

Jace sluggishly worked the hinges on doors three through five, using all his creativity to come up with a plan to avoid door six.

Saint tried the handle of the last door. Locked. He pulled out the large key ring Mr. Oatley had lent them. Oatley had told them that this set of keys would open nearly any door on campus, the first two on the ring being the ones that would work most of the time. And the first one did.

"Woah," Saint's voice echoed. "I thought this was just a closet."

"What?" Jace asked. "Oh, weird."

"I didn't know greenhouses had basements." Saint flipped the light switch and descended the stairs.

"I don't think we're supposed to work on that one down there," said Jace at the top, the hollow echoes distorting his voice. "Even if we are, Mr. Oatley's definitely not going to check that one."

"Are you kidding? This is awesome! You don't want to see what's down here? What if it's like a bomb shelter with food and stuff?"

Jace swallowed. "That hungry, huh?" He felt as if St. Peter had given him the key to the back door of heaven, and he was now approaching with one of Satan's minions. He was sweating.

This can't happen, Jace thought. *It just can't.* He plodded down the stairs. Saint picked up the rubber duck on the landing and drop kicked it back up the stairway. He cursed as it hit the wall halfway up and bounced back down.

Jace grabbed the key ring from Saint. "I'll get it." He tried the first two keys. The second one worked, but he pretended that it didn't. Knowing that Saint wouldn't be satisfied until he tried them all, he went through each.

"Looks like there's one door that Mr. Oatley doesn't have access to," Jace announced. "Let's go."

"Give me that." Saint took the key ring. Jace ran his hands through his hair. The door unlocked on the second try. Saint gave him a disappointed look, stepped inside, and flipped the light switch.

Jace hoped that the room would somehow be empty, with all the artwork and dojo props and filing cabinet magically gone.

"A classroom?" Saint said. "Weird."

It looked the same as when Jace had last left it except that the folding chairs were leaning up against the walls.

"All right," said Jace, "why don't we focus on the door?"

"Just a minute." Saint went to the far wall and walked along the artwork. He stopped in front of a canvas with a large, yellow rubber duck.

"Wait." Saint peered closely at the group photo below.

Jace held his breath and closed his eyes in silent prayer.

Saint began to laugh. "Wow. This is it!"

Saint quickly paced the perimeter of the room, taking in the rest of the photos and artwork.

"This is really it!" He excitedly took photos with his phone. Then he stood in the middle of the room with his arms outstretched. "Jace, do you know what this is? It's the headquarters of the Bathwater Brigade!"

Saint began tapping on his phone. Jace, who hadn't moved from the doorway since they arrived, made no move to stop him.

"Best day of my life!" Saint smiled and shook his head. "Forty hours of service? Well worth it."

Jace had no idea that Saint was capable of this much joy.

"Jace," Saint said again. "Do you have any idea where we are? Jace?"

Defeated and stone-faced, Jace stared at Saint.

Saint's thumbs slowed to a stop. "Hold on. Don't tell me you're one of them." Saint put a hand on his forehead, and he laughed. "Wow. This makes total sense, actually. I should have suspected that."

"What are you going to do?"

"Me? Nothing."

"Did you text someone?"

"Just sharing the good news about your club. Let's just say you might see a spike in membership very soon. So when is it that you guys meet?"

"You have to delete your texts," Jace said calmly.

"Can't delete a text after it's sent."

"Check your phone," said Jace. "They aren't sent. There's no reception down here."

Saint checked his phone and shrugged. "So, all I have to do is walk up those stairs."

Jace closed and locked the door. Saint took a step back, and the smugness left his expression.

"I'm not going to fight you," Jace said. "But I'm not moving from this spot until you delete those texts. I don't care if Mr. Oatley is banging down the door, or if he calls the police, or if we have to stay here all week. I'm not moving."

Jace pictured T.J. arriving Monday evening for the next Bathwater meeting and finding the newest bathwater baby holding a Zero Supremacy member hostage.

Saint dropped his hands to his sides. "All right, I can delete a few texts," he said. "No big deal."

"And you have to delete the pictures. And promise not to tell anyone or give any hints about this place. And never come back here again."

Saint narrowed his eyes. "That's a lot of demands. The terms seem lopsided. I've basically found Hitler's bunker, and I'm supposed to pretend it never happened."

Jace raised his hands high. "Hitler's bunker? Really? I...I don't know how your mind works. What have you been told about us?"

"You already know how I feel about your stunt on the roof."

"Saint. Listen to me. That was me and some other friends. Bathwater Brigade nearly banned me because of it. What I don't understand is why you are so against them. They would *invite* you Zero Supremacy guys to come to their meetings if you could manage a calm conversation instead of sabotaging everything you're not sure you agree with. The Bathwater Brigade is about the furthest thing from Hitler that I can imagine. They are a club that respectfully invites *everyone* to speak and share their ideas."

"Even racists?"

Jace raised an eyebrow. "They have a black person and a Hispanic one in their core membership."

Saint laughed. "That doesn't mean your club is not racist."

"Well, you make it sound like we're the KKK or something. Yes, I've seen race discussed here, but it's been *anti*-racist."

"You haven't gone through the archives, have you?"

Jace stood with his arms folded, leaning against the door.

"Look it up," said Saint. "April of this year."

"Gladly. Can't be worse than what you guys say about the police."

"Just see for yourself."

There was no way a Bathwater meeting took a racist turn. Still, Saint seemed so sure of himself. Jace kept his poker face but promised himself he'd look into it. Wasn't that what the Brigade taught them to do—keep an open mind and research things for themselves?

Saint unfolded a chair near him and sat, leaned back with his hands behind his head. "Does T.J. still come to your meetings?"

Jace didn't answer.

"Okay, so he does," said Saint.

How in the world did Saint know T.J.?

Saint looked at the ceiling and laughed. "Oh wow," he said. "They are going to go crazy over this."

Thirty minutes later, Jace sat in silence on the cement floor, head down, with his back to the locked door. Saint studied one of the group pictures on the wall, holding the last Mountain Dew. One by one, Saint had drained the fridge of them. He'd taken a few sips from each can, dumping the rest down the rusty drain in the middle of the cement floor and stacking them in a pyramid. Each time, he had said, "Guess I wasn't as thirsty as I thought."

"Real mature." Jace had rolled his eyes but couldn't stop him without leaving the door unattended.

"So, you said that he didn't have to run," Saint said at last, stepping to the next picture. "But he was being chased by people with guns."

"Police officers, you mean." Jace lightly rapped his knuckles on the cement. "Ever done any mountain climbing?"

Saint turned. "A little..."

"Let's say you're free soloing."

"Remind me."

"Climbing without ropes. So, you're thirty feet up this cliff. You see a snake in front of you and recognize the markings. Your friends told you that kind of snake is deadly. What do you do?"

Saint sat a few feet in front of Jace and gave him a flat smile with tired eyes. "Get away."

"That's hard to do when you're hanging on the side of a cliff. So, you try to scramble down in a frenzy and you fall. You wake up in the hospital, and the doctor tells you the snake was actually harmless."

Saint's sleepy expression remained.

"Do you get it?" said Jace. "If you exaggerate the threat and get desperate, then you can easily make things worse. Sounds like Stephen was convinced the police were going to kill him."

"They *did* kill him."

"Well, yes. But it could have been a self-fulfilling prophecy. Don't you see? Like if you start spreading rumors that there's an egg shortage and that all the stores are running out. Soon everyone goes and buys up all the eggs. Before you know it, the rumor comes true." Jace shifted and pulled his knees up to his chest. "I'm sure there are some tragic cases of it happening, but police don't really shoot people who are complying with their orders. I honestly think that if groups like Zero Supremacy weren't putting out the message that police are out killing black people, then Stephen probably wouldn't have taken his chances, running at a cop whose gun was drawn."

Jace thought he had made the perfect argument. Of course, Saint brushed it off.

"What are *you* doing to help, Jace?"

"To help what?"

"Help keep the Stephens of the world from being killed," Saint said, arms folded. "Remember Pauliston? The protests against police brutality? Were you there?"

"I didn't spray paint the city and throw rocks at police, if that's what you mean."

"I mean the peaceful ones. Did you show up? Speak out? What are you doing to help?"

"It...wasn't even in my state. And the cop was arrested and charged.

I don't think we need the entire nation to spend a week in the streets. I mean, there are a lot of causes in the world."

Saint shrugged and gave him a disappointed glance.

"Look," Jace said, feeling a little defensive, "when I see racism or police brutality happen around me in a way that I can influence, then of course I'm going to do something about it. What else do you want?"

Saint was silent.

Jace shook his head. "At least I'm not making things worse, like you Zeroes do. Look at the statistics. Police aren't out there looking to shoot black people."

"Isn't it the police that gives those statistics?" Saint asked.

"Wow, you have some trust issues, don't you? Have you ever done a ride-along with a cop?"

"A what?"

"You can hang out with them for a few hours and see what their job is like."

"No."

"You should do one. You might have a different opinion after."

"Have you ever had a black friend whose innocent dad was beaten by cops?" Saint shot back.

"No."

"You should get one. You might have a different opinion after."

Jace took a deep breath and rubbed his eyes.

Saint laid flat on his back. "I'm fine staying here overnight. But I don't want to tick off Mr. Oatley."

"You know what has to happen before you can leave this room."

"I could press charges for this."

"I don't even care."

For the third time that hour, Saint loudly popped his knuckles, going through each finger one by one.

"Will you cut that out?" Jace growled.

Saint just smiled.

"Maybe we can make a deal," Jace said, shifting positions on the cold cement floor. "I'll do all your door maintenance work. At least, when Mr. Oatley isn't with us."

Saint laughed. "Nope."

Jace frowned. "I will quit the Bathwater Brigade."

"I honestly don't care if you're a part of it or not," Saint chuckled. He stood up and wandered over to the whiteboard. He picked up a red marker. He flipped it into the air and caught it again over and over while he paced the room.

"Oh, I think I've got it," said Saint. He stopped in front of Jace. "I'll do all that stuff you said, if you do one thing for me."

"What's that?"

"Bring me to your next meeting."

Jace coughed. "Um, no."

"Didn't you say that they want lots of perspectives?" Saint grinned.

"You *do* know why they're meeting down here, right?" Jace asked. "You guys chased them here."

"I know better than you," Saint said proudly. "Well, that's the only deal I can think of." He walked to the far side of the room. "I assume you're taking the spot by the door. I'll sleep under this rubber duck painting over here."

"I can hardly get permission to bring my *friend* to one of these meetings."

"Who said anything about permission? You just have to bring me."

Jace pictured walking into the meeting with an uninvited plus-one, who just happened to be a Zero Supremacist. He imagined the faces of T.J. and Kendric. And *Mari*. He shuddered. However, the alternative was for Saint to blow the lid on everything and then they'd have a mob on their hands instead of just one.

"Okay, let me add one more thing to the deal."

"What?"

"You need to bring me to one of *your* meetings first. You know, Zero Supremacy." Jace had no desire to go, but he hoped that his demand would get Saint to back off.

Saint grinned. "Really?"

"You guys meet sometimes, too, right?"

"Most of it is online, but yeah, sometimes."

"Take me to your meeting first," Jace said, "and then I'll bring you to mine."

Saint smiled a crooked grin, making Jace uneasy. "Deal."

"Wait," Jace hesitated. "I'll come in disguise or something, so they can't tell that I'm that trombone guy. And you can't tell them it's me."

"Sure."

"Just one problem still," Jace said. He stood and squinted.

"What?"

"You said once that you didn't mind lying to a racist. And you just made a deal with someone you think is a racist."

"True." Saint's smile faded. He studied the ground for a moment, then looked at Jace. "But I'm not lying."

Jace leaned down a little and peered in Saint's eyes.

"Really," Saint said.

Surprisingly, Jace believed him. They shook hands.

"When is your next meeting?" Jace asked.

"Hopefully soon. I'll let you know."

Saint handed Jace his phone, and Jace verified that the pictures and texts had been deleted. He held the phone out of Saint's reach. "You remember what you agreed to?"

"Yes, Dad. Just give me my phone back."

Jace did. Then he stretched his arms and arched his back. "Well! Let's give this door some maintenance."

Jace worked the hinges as usual. Saint finally came over to help after setting the red marker back on the tray of the whiteboard.

Once finished, Jace stood at the open door and held out a hand, politely directing Saint through the exit and up the stairs. After Saint left, he threw the pyramid of empty Mountain Dew cans into the recycling bin and scanned the room once more with a furrowed brow. He took a determined breath and let it out slowly. Then he turned off the lights and locked the door behind.

CHAPTER TWENTY-SIX

THAT EVENING, Jace leaned forward in a padded chair in the corner of the Union Center lobby and stared at the carpet. He wondered whether to tell Mari about Saint's visit to the greenhouse. A Zero. In the headquarters of the Brigade. *Her* Brigade.

"Hey, Jace." Mari waved a hand in front of his face.

He raised his head and quickly forced a smile. Her hair was curled today. She wore blue jeans and a short-sleeve pink shirt, accented by her usual silver necklace. In that moment, he decided that there was no upside to telling her. It would only worry and disappoint everyone. He'd have to fix this on his own.

"It looks like you're inventing your own calculus theorem," she said. "Want me to leave you alone?"

"Just thinking." He stood and gestured toward the game area, feeling formal and awkward. "Well, should we go play?"

"Sure." She walked next to him. "Looks like the numbness wore off."

"What?"

"When Rob called yesterday."

"Oh. Right. Apparently, I couldn't wait for it to pass before I called." She laughed. "It sounds like there was a possibility for mistranslation with Rob in the middle. Are you sure you want to hang out with me tonight?"

"Yeah!" Jace blurted out, then immediately regretted sounding so eager. "I mean, I didn't really have anything else to do, you know?" He took a floundering breath and mentally beat himself up with a few punches to the gut and a roundhouse kick to the face. Mari looked ahead and tried to conceal a smile.

All the pool tables were taken, and about twenty people were waiting their turn.

"I love standing around as much as anyone," Jace said, "but the bowling lanes are empty. Want to switch?"

"Sure! Whatever."

"Cool. It will feel nice to sit."

"Oh yeah. How did your community service thing go today? Get in any arguments?"

"You could say that."

"I've got something I need to tell you," she said as they approached the counter.

He stopped. *She knows.*

"I've only bowled like twice in my life." She hit his arm playfully. "Oh, my gosh. Why are you looking at me so serious? I promise I'll try not to embarrass you. No guarantees, though."

He forced a weak smile.

The middle-aged woman behind the counter had gray hair bundled beneath a baseball cap. She handed them stiff shoes that flaunted about six shades of brown and assigned them a lane in the middle.

"So Jace," Mari said as they laced their shoes. "Tell me about your family. Any brothers or sisters?"

"Yup. I'm the oldest. I have a little brother and two little sisters. All in Kansas."

"What are their names?"

"Parker, Mindy, and Samantha. You?"

"Two brothers. One older, and one younger. Mateo and Lucho. I grew up in Amarillo. My parents and Lucho live in San Antonio now, and Mateo builds homes in Dallas."

Jace pictured two muscular men scowling at him for bowling with their sister. "Awesome. What does your dad do?"

"He runs an auto mechanic shop," she said as she set up the game at the computer.

"Does *everyone* call you Mari?"

"My parents call me Mariana."

"I like it," Jace said.

"It has a few meanings. It has ties to the Roman god of war. And in Hebrew, it means rebellious."

"Sounds like you."

She smiled. "How about *your* name?"

He shrugged. "Short for Jason."

"It's got to mean *something*." She pulled out her phone and moved her thumbs over the screen. "Looks like it means *healer*."

"You're the rebel warrior, and I'm the healer." Jace smiled. "Great. So, I bring you medicine after you've been injured on the battlefield."

"Hey," Mari said, earnestly. "Don't underestimate healing. You can be a physician that mends the rifts in society, helping a broken nation move forward together."

Jace narrowed his eyes, nodding. "Still doesn't sound as exciting."

"Sometimes you need just as much courage to do that as to fight. Wouldn't you call Gandhi a healer? Dr. King? Jesus?"

"I guess so."

"But they were also rebels. Society didn't know what to do with them. Their lives were anything but boring."

"True." He grimaced. "I guess they *were* all assassinated."

She winked at him. "There you go. All the excitement you could wish for." Then she turned serious. "I get asked why the Bathwater Brigade attracts so much hate, especially since some students find our club to be the most boring on campus. I mean, all we do is sit around and talk! But when we bring the people together that society wants to stay divided, tremendous things happen. There are people in this world that lose power when that occurs. *Those* are the ones who don't like the healers."

His mind turned to Saint and the greenhouse. Today he felt less like Jesus and more like an unwitting Judas. But he liked how she built him up and praised him in ways he didn't always think he deserved. It made him want to do better.

"Let's get some points on the board!" he said. "Looks like you're first. You said you're a pro, right? I'm expecting big things from you, rebel warrior Mari."

She rolled her eyes and picked up her pink-and-orange-swirled bowling ball—the ugliest one she could find, she'd said—and squared herself in front of the lane. She held the ball to her side and went for the pins at a run. She crossed the line, took a few steps onto the lane, then her feet slipped out from under her like some cartoon character on a banana peel, and she sprawled onto her backside. The ball went directly into the gutter and slowly rolled toward the pins. She leaned forward, her head in her hands and her shoulders shaking.

Jace sprang from his seat and hurried over to help her up. It only took one step on the slippery lane for him to join her on the floor, catching himself with his left arm. Mari took one look at Jace, and her silent laughter turned into uncontrollable shrieks. Jace laughed, too, as he cautiously stood and offered Mari his hands. She grabbed them, hauled herself upright, and hugged his midsection tightly as they walked off the lane.

As they returned to their seats, a grumpy voice crackled over the loudspeaker: "Do not step onto the lane."

Jace turned to the woman behind the desk and gave her a thumbs up. "Thanks for the info." Then he turned back to Mari and folded his arms. "I don't think you're being honest with me. You claimed you've been bowling before. But I think this is actually your first time."

She bit her bottom lip to stop from smiling. "No! I swear I've been before. I thought you were supposed to walk right up to the arrows. I must have remembered wrong."

He raised an eyebrow at her. "If you've been before, then you also know that you still have one more ball to bowl."

"Right!" She stood and lifted her ugly ball again. "I can only improve from here." She sent the ball careening down the lane and jumped and clapped when she knocked down three pins.

"Woo-hoo," said Jace dryly. "You're on the board."

His first round netted six and then three. She gave him a high five.

By the end of the game, Jace was eighty-six and Mari forty-one. They returned their brown shoes, and the woman handed Jace a half sheet of paper with their bowling score.

Jace bought ice cream for the both of them on their way out of the Union Center. He got his usual cookie dough, and she ordered chocolate brownie. She walked close to him.

"Should we burn this?" Jace asked, holding up their scores. The wind had picked up a little, and the curls in her hair caught the breeze as they strolled along the sidewalk.

"Actually, I'd like to keep it if that's okay with you."

He handed it to her with a groan. "Just don't blackmail me. We shouldn't have used our real names. Those scores are awful."

Jace's phone buzzed. He pulled it out and saw it was a text from Rob.

What did she say?

Jace winced. This was not the conversation he wanted to have right now. But since he couldn't think of a time that he *would* ever want to have it...

"So Mari," he said. "You know how my friend Rob is trying to get the truth out there, about the Gina Lambson trial?"

"You mean, how he's fighting the Zeroes?"

Jace smiled sheepishly. "Yeah, I guess so. Well, what if he changes his approach a little, and we all team up together? Go hand out fliers or something in town?"

Mari stopped walking. "Rob wants the Brigade to team up with him out in the city?"

Jace shrugged. "Maybe."

Mari laughed. And when she kept on laughing, Jace cleared his throat.

She pulled herself together. "Where do I even begin? I think you've seen that we're picky about the alliances we make and the things we get involved in. Especially right now. I mean, I could run it by the others, but I'm afraid you'll get the same reaction with them as you did with me."

Jace sighed. "Yeah. That's what I told him, but he wanted me to ask anyway." He quickly texted Rob.

She's leaning no.

Will she let us use that flier, then? The one about race?

Jace rolled his eyes, but asked Mari anyway.

"No, sorry," she said. "I like the direction he's going, but we can't let him use our flier. One of the rules we have to follow is that club materials can only be handed out on campus. He'll have to make his own."

Can't use the flier. Let's talk later.

Mari finished her cone and wiped her hands. "I just don't think he's Brigade material yet, you know? He's not like you."

"Rob has some great qualities that I probably never will, though. He's the kind of guy who gets more upset when someone else is cut off on the freeway than when he is himself. He's really protective of other people."

"I believe it."

"When we were about nine years old, a child abuser had killed a police officer in a town near ours. Rob wanted to stand at the side of the road during the funeral procession and hold up a flag. He invited me to come with him. The procession was miles long and it snarled traffic. They were completely stopped for about forty-five minutes. I lost interest after ten and wandered around. Rob, though, held his position the entire time."

"Wow," she chuckled. "Pretty impressive for a nine-year-old."

"Yeah. After about thirty minutes, a police officer in the car stuck in front of us stepped out, squared up in front of Rob, and saluted him."

Mari patted Jace lightly on the back. "That is so cool. He must be a great friend. Both of you are."

They strolled toward her dorm. A dry leaf occasionally brushed across the sidewalk ahead of them.

"You know it's not that I think there's anything wrong with him, right?" she said. "He's fine the way he is. It's just...the Bathwater Brigade is doing something that's unique. And a lot of good people just don't get it."

"Would you have said that about me a few weeks ago?"

Mari grinned. "Probably. It's different with you, though. You came to *me*. You wanted to learn. If he wants to learn sometime, let's talk. Maybe you can work on him."

When they reached Miller Hall, they talked for a while longer, discussing their favorite movies.

"Guess I'll see you Monday," Jace said. "Excited to see what the third dojo lesson is all about. Engaging the opponent, right?"

"My favorite one!"

He looked at her. She looked at him. "Well," she said, shuffling her feet.

"Yeah." He reached out, wondering if he was going to get another brush off, but she stepped into his arms for a quick hug.

"Thanks," she beamed as she backed away. "I had a good time."

"Me, too."

She moved toward the doors, then turned back. "Bye." She slipped inside.

Not even Saint's upcoming appearance in the greenhouse basement —which Jace had completely forgotten about until he was halfway home —could keep the smile from his face.

He checked his phone. One more text from Rob.

Hope your evening with Mari went well. Looks like mine was a bust.

Jace chuckled.

You were a nice third wheel tonight. Next time you want something from the Bathwater Brigade, go date one of them yourself.

CHAPTER TWENTY-SEVEN

JACE HAD ALWAYS HATED MONDAYS—THE shock of the alarm clock after two days of sleeping in, and the hopelessness of five days of school ahead. Lately, though, Mondays had been rising in the rankings. They were the days he spent the most time with Mari.

Near the end of botany, Mari slipped him a note written on ruled paper and whispered, "They wanted me to give this to you. Sorry."

Jace looked at the paper.

OFFICIAL CALE ADMINISTRATION

Jace Kartchner,

We have learned of the bowling score that has been attributed to you from a game played on September 29th. We join with all Cale students and faculty in shock and embarrassment at this substandard performance.

We have decided to extend your campus service until the end of the semester. Mr. Oatley has been notified. He began yelling once he was told, and we can only assume that he is ecstatic.

Thank you for your cooperation in this sad matter.

It had a bunch of scribbles at the bottom, apparently signed by fifteen people, all with the same handwriting.

"How did they find out my score?" Jace had whispered back.

"All bowling scores are reported to school administration. You didn't know? It's stated clearly on your admission forms."

Jace suppressed a smile. "Did they give you one of these, too? Your score was even worse."

"I think they expected more of you."

Jace had read the note, chuckling to himself, a few more times that day.

Now approaching the greenhouse, he was relieved to see a complete absence of red T-shirts and hoodies. He had never told Saint the day or time of the Bathwater meetings, of course, but it wouldn't have shocked Jace to see him there with a few dozen friends anyway.

The usual group was there in the basement, but they were gathered around the whiteboard. It was quiet. T.J. motioned for him to join them. In the bottom right corner of the board was a message in red: "T.J.—just wanted to say hi." Below it was a circle with a line through it. Zero.

Jace stiffened.

"They know," T.J. said, nodding.

"How?" said Amber. "There are like three keys to this room. You have one, and then there's Wayne and the greenhouse guy. Have you asked them about this?"

"Not yet."

"Well, at least they're not here *now*," said Kendric.

"They could show up any time," sighed T.J.

"I'm surprised that they didn't trash all our stuff," said Kendric.

"Me too," said T.J.

"What should we do?" asked Mari.

T.J. lowered his head for a moment. Then he squared his shoulders. "Start the meeting."

"What if they show up?"

T.J. held up his cell phone. "Just record whatever happens. We have a right to be here."

"Do you mean you'll fight them?" asked Danica.

"No. But I won't keep running, either. They'll have to do more than write a love note on the board to get to us."

The core members voted on it and agreed with T.J.

"Should we erase the note?" Amber asked.

T.J. paused, then smiled. "No, let's leave it. It will keep us on our toes."

"I wonder how they found out," Kendric said.

Jace turned away from the board and tripped over the metal chairs. He went all the way to the cement floor.

"Are you ok?" said Danica.

Jace jumped up and fixed the chairs. "Yup. Thanks."

Kendric looked at Mari, holding in a laugh.

Jace didn't even smile as they took their seats.

"Danica has to leave early, so we're entering the dojo first today," T.J. said, tying his headband. "Today's lesson is on engagement. And not the romantic kind," he said with a smirk. "Unless...Amber? Dylan? This is probably as good a time as any for an announcement—if you have one."

Dylan shifted uncomfortably and let go of Amber's hand.

"Or a proposal," T.J. added. He stood motionless, watching Dylan and his sister expectantly.

Amber glared at him. "T.J.!" she growled through clenched teeth.

T.J. suppressed a laugh. "Not today, I guess."

Jace and Mari exchanged a grin.

T.J. turned serious. "You have learned about your opponent and yourself. You have surprised them, showing you don't follow the traditional rules for what to think. And today, we learn the best way to meet them on the field."

He retrieved an old, brown book from the corner.

"We've gained valuable insight from *The Art of War*," he said, "but let's move to something newer. Have either of you read Benjamin Franklin's autobiography?"

"You mean something *older*, right?" asked Jace. "Wasn't that Ben Franklin book written in the eighteen hundreds?"

"Seventeen hundreds," T.J. replied. "And how should I put this? *The Art of War* was created during the Old Testament."

"Really?" asked Jace, wide-eyed. He looked at Mari. She raised her eyebrows and nodded.

T.J. continued. "In chapter nine, Ben wrote about trying to improve himself. A friend told him once that he was proud, overconfident, and overbearing when talking to people."

"Ouch," Danica chuckled.

"He was crazy smart," added Amber, "so he probably *was* right a lot of the time, even if he was a bit of a jerk about it."

"Yes," said T.J. "But he discovered some ways of engaging with people that helped him get much further with them. He convinced people of his ideas about new institutions, and he had a lot of influence. They admitted they were wrong more easily. And if he discovered *he* was wrong about something, that situation was a lot easier to handle. He wasn't as mortified, as he called it."

Mari said, "I'd bet a thousand dollars that he wouldn't have found himself at the Constitutional Convention if he hadn't learned these tricks."

"Franklin made it a rule to 'forbear all direct contradiction to the sentiments of others'. What does that mean?"

"Don't say 'you're wrong,'" answered Danica.

"Correct. And he also forbears 'all positive assertion of my own.'"

"Don't say 'I'm right'?"

"Correct again. He even tried not to use words like 'certainly' and 'undoubtedly.'"

"But what if I actually *am* right," said Jace, "and I'm sure of it?"

"Let's find out. Here, read this bit." T.J. handed Jace the book, pointing to a highlighted section in the middle.

Jace read aloud. "'I adopted, instead of them, *I conceive, I apprehend,* or *I imagine* a thing to be so; or it *so appears to me at present.*'"

"Okay," Jace said. "You can still claim you're right, but just say it differently."

"Yup," said T.J. "When you talk this way, you don't sound as sure of yourself, and it helps the other person relax and think about your point instead of focusing so much on defending their own positions."

"Oh, I get it," said Danica. "If you tone down your confidence, and you're just saying that this is how it looks to me right now and why, then it's a lot easier to say 'oops, I was wrong' later."

Jace raised his hand. "So, what if the other person is right?" he asked. "Can I say, '*you're* right'?"

"Of course," said T.J. "In fact, the more you can validate them on the points that they have right, the more they'll listen to the points *you* are trying to make."

"'Agree with thine adversary quickly, whiles thou art in the way with him,'" said Kendric. "Matthew five, twenty-five."

"Depending on who you're talking to, though," said Amber, "sometimes it's difficult to find *anything* to validate."

Dylan laughed. "True. But you can always find something."

T.J. nodded. "Mr. Franklin wrote that if a person said something he thought was wrong, he wouldn't come right out and say that. Instead, he'd say something like, 'That's correct some of the time, but in this case it looks different to me.'"

"This is powerful stuff," Amber said. "Once you're good at it, it makes all the difference when you talk to people."

"Ben said that he had to force it at first," said T.J. "But practice made it easy." He stood. "So, let's practice!"

Two at a time, the Bathwater Brigade and the two newcomers stood and demonstrated the wrong way to disagree, with creative insults and overconfidence.

"Only a fumbling flidget would believe that!" Kendric said to T.J.

When Dylan asked Jace if there was a chance he could be wrong, all Jace did was laugh disdainfully, which made everyone else laugh, too.

Next, they attempted to rehearse the Benjamin Franklin method, but they all kept bursting into giggles. Finally Kendric said, "I think we've got it."

"Does anyone have something to add?" asked T.J.

"Listen to them," said Amber. "Actually do it. When we argue with people, sometimes we're just thinking of what we'll say next instead of listening. And they can tell when you're doing it, even if you think you're good at hiding it. If you want them to listen to *you*, then you should do the same and show them how it's done."

"Good. Anyone else?"

"If they trip you up and you're not that sure of yourself," said Mari, "don't just make stuff up. Be real with them and say something like, 'I hadn't considered that before. I need to do some more research.' Then, if you continue the discussion later, they will be a lot more open to your point of view."

Jace laughed. "At first, I thought we were learning Jedi mind tricks to get what we want." The others chuckled. "But it seems like we want our opponent to learn and practice this same stuff."

T.J. smiled wide and nodded. "You're catching the vision, my friend." He pointed at Jace and Danica, then at two spots in front of him on the floor. "Now, Yukyusha."

"That means 'students'," Mari said. She gave Jace a pat on the back.

They stood in front of T.J. as he reached into his large canvas bag in the corner and retrieved a rug and four grocery sacks. He dumped the contents of each sack into its own pile on the rug, which he had laid over the bare concrete floor. Two piles in front of Danica, and two in front of Jace. Among the seemingly random objects were wooden blocks, balls, string, flat sheets of cardboard, metal coat hangers, towels, a hat, books, and, naturally, a few rubber ducks. Jace studied the objects. Both his and Danica's sets of piles seemed identical.

T.J. held up a simple toy car. "We build bridges here, right? You will make a literal bridge that this car can drive across. It must be at least four feet long and the car has to be at least twelve inches above the floor at all times."

He gestured toward the piles in front of them. "You will select half of the objects in front of you that seem most helpful, and then you will have three minutes to build it. I recommend building the bridge just off the rug, so it stands up easier." Jace and Danica glanced at each other with grins and wide eyes. Danica pushed her long black braids behind her as she leaned over. "Ready? Go!"

Danica put her arms around the pile on the left and moved it out of the way. Then she held up the longer pieces in the pile on the right, judging which of them were at least twelve inches.

Jace picked through the pieces in each pile. He went with the pile on the left. He selected three wooden blocks that each had to be at least a foot long. He stood them on end, as far apart as he dared. He placed two books on top.

He checked on his competition. Danica was doing something similar, but with books for the vertical posts and sheets of cardboard for the horizontal planks. Jace found little that remained in his pile that was useful.

Someone shouted a cheer of encouragement for Danica. Then another one for Jace, which was distinctly less enthusiastic, and which invited laughter.

"Stop!" T.J. said. "Okay, let's see how you did."

Danica grinned sheepishly. Jace shook a victorious fist in the air, even though his bridge was at most two feet long.

Kendric mimicked Jace's "sad trombone" from the Zero Supremacy protest. "Bwah bwah bwaaaaah." Jace's smile faded. "Oops," Kendric said. "Too soon."

T.J. scratched the back of his head. "Oof. I think these are the worst bridges we've ever had. Well, thanks for playing." He knocked them over and pushed the materials back into the piles. "Anyone else for a try?"

A few hands went up. "Kendric, Amber, come on up."

Jace took his seat and shrugged at Mari.

"It's easy," she whispered. "You'll feel stupid in a minute."

"I already do."

"Step one," T.J. said. "Select your materials."

Amber picked out the blocks from the pile on the left, the cardboard from the right, and the books from both piles. Kendric did the same.

"But...you can do that?" said Danica.

"Why not?" said T.J. "We said to take half the materials in front of you. You only *assumed* that you had to keep the piles separated."

Jace slapped his forehead.

At "Go!", Amber set the books upright as vertical posts, opening them a little for stability.

Jace whispered, "I still don't think there is enough to make four feet." Mari's grin widened.

Kendric brought his books to Amber's bridge and set them up. They combined their cardboard and wooden blocks for the planks. It was easily over four feet long.

Jace shook his head. "We're dummies," he said to Danica.

"Very nice," T.J. said. "Only thirty seconds." Kendric and Amber took their seats while T.J. sat cross-legged next to the bridge and rolled his toy car over it.

"You look like a bearded five-year-old," Dylan said. T.J. winked at him.

"In my defense," said Jace, "I didn't know we could combine our bridges."

"I was focused on having my bridge longer than Jace's," said Danica. "It didn't occur to me that maybe this wasn't a competition."

"Yup," said T.J. "Don't worry, most of us did exactly the same as you." He stood. "Did you learn something?"

"Yeah." Jace paused. "I don't think I'm ready to describe it, though."

T.J. laughed. "No problem. Do you know the word *nuance*?"

"Sure," Danica said. "It's, like, seeing a small difference."

"Awareness of nuance is one of the best traits you can have. The two piles of materials in front of you? That is the world presenting us with oversimplified options. Package deals. Sort of like the cable channels your parents have. To get the one channel you want, they make you buy sixty others that you *don't* want."

"An example?" Jace asked.

"Sure. How about guns? If you believe that we should have gun control, society will tell you that you fit into this pile with all these other beliefs. About capitalism, abortion, gay rights, climate change, all of that."

Danica nodded.

"And if you think we should be free to bear arms," he continued, "then they will say you belong in this other pile and have to believe all these other things."

"So, we need to break out of that somehow?" asked Danica.

"Yes. And it's the easiest thing in the world—as simple as Amber and Kendric showed you right here. Just ignore the packages. The boundaries. Society goes way overboard in linking beliefs together into massive packages." T.J. crouched in front of them. "The secret is that the world of beliefs is way more a la carte than you think."

"What if my beliefs *do* happen to fit into one of those packages?" she asked.

"No problem at all," T.J. said. "Just don't let the package define *you*. And don't expect others to cram all their experiences and ideas into one of those piles, either." T.J. stood. "Any examples of people not following their stereotypes?"

"Democrats supporting guns."

"Hispanics for a border wall."

"Atheist groups against abortion."

"Those exist?" whispered Jace. Mari nodded.

"Gay Republicans."

"Tattooed club presidents." They all laughed.

"See how silly it is to think that those things don't—or shouldn't— exist?" T.J. asked.

"Awesome," said Jace. "What about the part where Amber and Kendric worked together on the bridge?"

"Similar lesson."

"Is it to find common ground together?"

T.J. clapped. "Nailed it. Often ignored, the fabled Common Ground is indisputably the best land on which to build lasting foundations."

Kendric raised his hand. "Personally, I'd put Jesus Christ a rung higher than that. But I get you."

"Noted," T.J. said with a smile.

"Politics, media, stuff like that," Mari said. "Oh, they divide us, whether or not they intend to. They highlight our differences instead of our commonalities. They make us angry or afraid to even *talk* with the other side. They make us think we're far more different than we really are. I guess it helps them get reelected or higher ratings, but it really holds us back."

"To me," said T.J., "it's stupid to allow ourselves to be divided like that. So many missed opportunities. Sure, we don't all see the world or its solutions in exactly the same way. But think of what can happen if we just come together, set our differences aside, and use the tools we have."

"Just pretend we don't disagree anymore?" Danica asked.

Kendric held up a finger. "He said to set differences *aside* for a moment—not to bury them or pretend they don't exist. Look for what you can do that doesn't involve those differences, and all sides will get at least eighty percent of what they want. You'll shock the world at what you can accomplish."

"Well said," remarked T.J. "Just ignore the dotted lines that everyone is drawing around you. And go explore together."

CHAPTER TWENTY-EIGHT

DANICA LEFT and the group set up for the day's discussion.

"I still can't believe it," Mari said. She leaned forward in her chair and gazed at the whiteboard.

"Maybe someone here wrote it as a joke," Jace said.

"No. T.J. was the last one out last week, and the first one in today. He's the only one of us with a key."

"Oh. What's the worst that could happen, we find a new place to meet?"

"We're pretty much out of options." She glanced around the room and sighed. "The Bathwater Brigade has been going for over forty years. Look at all those photos. That's Danica's mom over there. Twenty-five years ago. I wish you could have met last year's Bathwater seniors." She shook her head. "We won't let the flame die on our watch. The thing that's confusing is why there isn't a crowd of Zero Supremacists here right now. They've been hunting us."

"It could get scary if there were a bunch of them in the stairwell," Jace said. "The only exit."

"They haven't gotten very violent with us directly. But you're right. We couldn't even call 911 from down here."

"So how do they know T.J.?"

"He used to be one of them. When he was a freshman."

Jace stared at her. "Woah."

"It's a cool story, actually." Her eyes lit up. "He was on his way to a protest about climate change, got a flat tire, and realized he didn't have a car jack. Another student, who happened to be a Brigade member, stopped to help. They got talking. T.J. liked how the other guy listened, and was super friendly. He told T.J. they'd had a meeting that touched on the same topic as the protest just two weeks before, and that he should look it up on the website. He came to a few meetings, and he was hooked! He eventually brought Amber along, too."

"I would never have guessed he used to be a Zero."

"Want to hear something crazy? He still believes a lot of the same things that the Zeroes do."

Jace chuckled. "What? How is that possible?"

"I know. The main thing he changed was his tactics. He saw the value in listening, thinking, and talking in the ways that Bathwater teaches. For two years he's been one of our biggest supporters. I mean, obviously. He's the president."

"Hm. Well, I hope nothing else happens with the Zeroes. I'll do what I can."

Mari frowned. "What do you mean? What could *you* do?"

Jace held up his hands and cleared his throat. "I don't know. If I see something that I can do, sometime, then I'll try to do it. I guess."

She eyed him curiously. "Thanks for that."

T.J. started the Bathwater discussion. Health care. Specifically, about government getting more involved with it.

Mari and a visiting Bathwater member named Hunter took the two seats at the front. Hunter wore cowboy boots and had thick brown hair, the shape of which indicated the recent removal of his hat. He spoke slowly, with a native Texas drawl.

"All right. What's the bathwater being thrown out when we involve more government?" asked T.J.

Hunter spoke. "People not having access to health care."

"And what's a baby being thrown out with the bathwater?"

"Free market forces are being crowded out," Mari said, "and health care will eventually be worse for everyone because of it."

"Interesting." T.J. sported his usual smile in anticipation of what was to come. "Okay, let's do it."

"I guess I'll start," Hunter said, shifting in his seat. "So, this is fairly simple. Health care is super expensive and getting even worse. Lots of people don't have the money to pay for it. Seems like a good thing to have programs that help." Many in the room nodded. Including Mari.

T.J. turned to her. "Well? How is helping people going to make health care worse for everyone?"

Mari laughed. "You make it sound like I don't like to help people. My stance is not that we shouldn't help, but that doing it through government comes with a list of negative consequences."

Hunter folded his arms, sat low in his chair, and gave her a nod.

"The more we involve the government," she said, "the more we crowd out the private sector. The free market is the secret ingredient that has given us the explosion of quality and inexpensive health care we've seen over the past hundred years. Let's think hard before we mess with the formula."

This reminded Jace of her argument with Professor Adelson, about the Planet Survival Accord. Huge, well-intended government programs are hitting the brakes on the very thing that is doing the most to help.

"I don't really care how it happens," said Hunter. "Maybe they get money to pay for it, or we pass some laws that make medicine companies sell it to them cheaper. We can pick the way that doesn't hurt the free market very much."

"The problem is," said Mari, "it doesn't matter how it happens. It's like a law of nature. If the government steps in to connect someone with something they couldn't otherwise afford, then it steps on the toes of the free market. To think that we can have a government so big that it gives us all the health care we need, and at the same time have an army of strong entrepreneurs? Well, it's like believing in a perpetual motion machine. Believe me, my brothers tried to build one of those when we were kids. Spoiler alert—they're impossible."

Hunter laughed. "Fair enough. But how does giving money to a poor guy hurt the free market? Seems like it would help. Think about it. When the poor guy goes to buy the medicine, doesn't he give the money to a private company?"

"But you have to think of the full ecosystem. Where does a government's money come from?"

"Us, I guess. Taxes."

"Yup. Let's say I'm the government, and I take a hundred dollars from Jace and give it to poor Amber over there so she can get her medicine. Jace, do you have a hundred-dollar bill for illustration?" He shook his head and smiled.

"Watch what happens," said Mari. "Yes, Amber just got her medicine. But haven't I made it harder for Jace to afford that same medicine that I'm giving Amber for free?"

"Yeah," sand Hunter after a pause.

"Kendric, let's say you're the company that made the medicine. Now you have to raise your prices."

"Woah," said Hunter. "Why does he have to do that?"

"Businesses pay taxes, too. The government took money from them to help T.J. buy the medicine this time. So now the company needs to adjust its prices higher to stay profitable. In fact, workers of all companies have a slightly higher cost of living now that prices for that medicine are higher. So, Kendric should probably give some raises to make up for it. Now the price of the drug goes up just a little more. Are you beginning to see some negative side effects here?"

"Only if profit is all you care about. We're talking about helping the poor, not the businesses, right?"

Mari smiled. "But you can't split them up like that. They aren't two separate things, they're two sides of the same coin. Profitable businesses give raises and hire more people. Isn't that fighting poverty right there? Also, it's not the government that is creating the vast majority of new medicines and surgeries for the world. It's private business. And they do it partly by reinvesting the profits that they earned. Take away more of the profit, and we start to see fewer great new products out there."

Hunter nodded.

"The cool thing is that if you have *two* profitable companies that make a similar product, they compete against each other to make it better and cheaper in hopes that you'll buy their product and not the other guy's. Just as prices started to spiral upward as the government got involved, free-market competition gets prices to spiral downward. If I'm a poor person, I very much want companies to be profitable."

Jace sat forward in his chair, elbows on his knees. He had never heard it explained this way before. Mari was making sense. But he thought of his dad, barely able to work because of his tremors. He needed some of that government help to keep the family and the business going. And it looked like Mari wanted to pull the plug on it.

"I get that there are some downsides," said Hunter. He sat low in his chair and put one leg out, his boot pointing to the ceiling. "What if we just make a law that a company can't charge too much?"

"Ah," said Mari. "Now you're messing with nature again."

"Nature?"

"Supply and demand, prices and wages. Free market competition between companies. The more we can leave these things to 'we the people' to handle, the more we get better and cheaper things. The free market is the only sustainable way to give the poor a higher standard of living. And you don't need a set of laws or a government bureau to make that happen. It just happens on its own, like how nature purifies water from the ocean and sends it past us in rivers without us having to do anything."

Mari sat on the edge of her seat, gesturing with her hands for emphasis as she spoke. Dylan raised his eyebrows at Jace and nodded his head toward Mari. Jace nodded in return. He'd hate to run against her in an election.

"It might sound heartless at first," Mari said, "but would you rather have a life-saving drug that is expensive for a while? Or none of that drug, expensive or cheap, because the government has squashed the businesses that develop it? Unfortunately, sometimes that's our choice."

Hunter crossed one boot over the other. "Doesn't seem right for it to be expensive, though. Especially if it's life-saving."

"Ah," Mari said with a smile, "that's an excellent example of a false dilemma fallacy—in this case, that either poor people have to go without the life-saving drug or that government has to step in and help. There are other ways that expensive drugs can get into the hands of the poor without involving government programs. Private health insurance is huge. And charity work, stuff like that."

Jace shifted uncomfortably in his seat. This discussion about policies that would affect real people seemed too academic. Could charity really make up the difference for his dad? He was doubtful.

"You're saying that government-run research facilities couldn't come up with the same drugs?" Hunter asked.

"With the free market, people and companies are investing their *own* money, and bear all the risk. We get much better results that way, and without having to tax anyone."

Jace fidgeted absent-mindedly with his titanium token, and looked around at the others, who were watching, calmly and intently. His face felt hot, and he kept checking his watch.

"Are you including things like Medicare and Medicaid in these government programs that you're talking about?" asked Hunter.

"Yes. Government is great and even necessary for some things. But as far as providing health care to its citizens, it's like my four-year-old cousin who tries to help with the dishes. He has a great heart and wants to help, but he just ends up making things worse."

Jace imagined Mari holding his dad's medication just out of reach. If you have the power to help someone who needs it right now, why wouldn't you? He spoke up. "Do you know how selfish this sounds?"

All heads in the room turned to him. He tried to hide the tremble in his voice. "What do you tell the people that need help *now*? Too bad, you should have planned better so you could afford giant medical bills. Have a nice life, whatever's left of it."

An awkward silence followed. Mari looked at Jace, her mouth open.

T.J. sat forward in his chair. "Good question, Jace. Do either of you have ideas on how to help the poor in a way that maybe doesn't hurt the free market?"

Mari spoke slowly, her eyes still on Jace. "Besides insurance? Like I was saying, there is philanthropy. You know, people and churches and organizations that donate to help people with basic needs like health care. Doctors often donate their time—"

"And you think they are better than government at helping people," Hunter said.

"Yes. Definitely."

Jace's hands tightened into fists, his nails digging crescents into his palms. "So, if we stop Medicare and Medicaid and all the rest, then regular people and churches will start paying for our expensive medications and surgeries?"

"They already do some of that," said Mari. "And I have some ideas on how that could grow. Especially since good people would have more of their own money as the government stops taking so much of it. See, it's the same money that helps people—I'm simply making the case for private citizens to be the ones in charge of administering it."

Jace abruptly stood, his metal chair scraping backward across the cement floor. "I've got to go." The room was silent as the door closed behind him.

CHAPTER TWENTY-NINE

AS SOON AS Jace came into the band room, Dr. Kline approached him.

"May I see you for a moment?"

"Sure." Jace, who felt he had been playing better lately, was suddenly nervous. Kline held the door open for him as they entered his office. Plaques and awards covered the brown, carpeted walls.

Kline motioned for Jace to have a seat, then circled the desk and dropped into the large leather chair behind it. "I understand your weekends have been busy."

"Not all that busy," Jace said. "Think I should do some extra practicing?"

"That *would* be nice," Kline replied with a brief, forced smile. "I'm talking about your campus service, however."

"Oh. Yeah, I'm about halfway done."

"I know about the event that led to it."

"Oh." Jace cleared his throat. "An error in judgment. Learned my lesson."

"How do you think that reflects on our band?"

"Hm? Well, I guess I don't see a connection..."

"Three Cale band members disrupting a vigil, and one of them even using their band instrument to do it."

Calling it a vigil was quite a stretch, but it didn't feel like the time to argue.

A letter sat on the desk. Jace recognized the large, swooping signature of Janet Thompson at the bottom. Kline noticed Jace's glance and quickly flipped it upside-down. He leaned forward and looked at Jace over his glasses. "I'll make this short. I know why you were there."

"You do?"

"The Bathwater Brigade."

Jace swallowed.

"A security officer reported that you were part of the Bathwater Band. It wasn't difficult to make the connection."

Jace recalled their operation, mentioning to Eli that they should be called the Bathwater Band. Did Eli repeat it to the security officer? He couldn't remember.

"You know about the Bathwater Brigade?" Jace asked.

"Yes, and it doesn't surprise me at all that they had you disturb that vigil. I'm disappointed that you brought Eli and Robert into this, that you hurt the name of the university, and that you tarnished the image of our band."

Jace bristled at the unfair attack. "Hang on. I think we're connecting too many dots here. Bathwater didn't put me up to it."

"They *inspired* you to do it, then."

"No. It was just our own idea. And if I thought this could have affected the band, I definitely wouldn't have done it. It's probably time for me to apologize."

"The Bathwater Brigade is not one of our finer associations at Cale. It doesn't reflect our values. I've heard them question things as basic as social justice."

Jace raised his eyebrows and blinked.

"I can't stop you from being a member of a legal campus organization. And your place in the band is not in question."

Jace nodded.

"However, there are standards of behavior required of band scholarship recipients. After a great deal of consideration, it's been decided that in order for you to keep your scholarship, you must leave the Brigade."

"Wow." Jace leaned back in his seat. "Is there some kind of appeal process?"

"Yes, but it will be a waste of your time. Have I gotten any of the major facts wrong?"

"Just that the Bathwater Brigade inspired us to do it."

Kline smiled condescendingly and stood. "Let me know by the end of the week what you would like to do."

"Okay."

Jace left the office and slumped in his chair at the back of the band. After his experience at the last Bathwater meeting, he wasn't so much upset about leaving the club as he was angry that Dr. Kline was telling him what to do.

He pulled out his phone and reviewed his texts with Mari from the past few days.

Not answering your phone?

Sorry. Was busy. I'll call you back later.

Didn't see you at class today. Just remember, if your grade drops, Adelson wins! :)

Ha. True.

Okay, it's been a few days. Can we talk?

Jace sighed. Things had been left in limbo for long enough. He texted a reply.

Okay. You busy tonight? Maybe you could let me know what I missed in botany.

Jace began assembling his trombone when something flicked his ear. He turned to see Rob holding his drumsticks.

"You have that same look when you'd find out your mom was making fish soup for dinner. What's up, man?"

"Kline wants to take away my scholarship."

Rob grabbed the chair next to Jace, turned it around, and sat with his arms resting on the back. He lowered his voice.

"I thought you'd been playing better lately."

"It's about the Bathwater thing. He wants me to quit the club or lose the scholarship."

"Weird. I didn't think a school could do that, but okay. What are you going to do? You already know that I think Bathwater is avoiding the real battles."

Trombone ready to go, Jace lightly kicked the case under his chair. "I'm not sure what I want to do."

"So, what happens if you lose your scholarship? Do you have other options?"

"My parents are already paying all they can," Jace replied. "And they really don't want me taking out more loans. I don't want to either."

"Yeah. So, it would almost be like you're paying a bunch of money to be in that club. Talk about a steep membership fee! How much do you want to pay to go to meetings where you learn how to appease anti-cop Zero Supremacists?"

Jace chuckled. "It's not like that. They definitely don't side with the Zeroes. But yeah, a couple thousand dollars just to join a club. I don't know. If I quit the band, though, I'd have the added benefit of not having to listen to your awful drumming. Might be worth it."

Howard, the first-chair trombonist, walked up to Rob and stopped. "You're in my seat."

Rob leaned in from behind as Dr. Kline stepped onto the stand. "What do you think about Mari? Is she still going to be into you if you quit her club?"

"I really don't know."

Jace was deep in thought for most of the rehearsal. He studied the ceiling tiles, how the last line of the grid didn't align perfectly with the high wall. He wondered which was straight, or if neither were. Dr. Kline's instructions were white noise. Jace used Howard's movement in his peripheral vision as his cue when it was time to play or switch music.

As Jace put the instrument away at the end of rehearsal, Dr. Kline appeared behind him. He put a hand on Jace's shoulder, leaned over, and almost whispered, "I noticed that you were distracted during rehearsal. I wondered if you had decided already?"

Jace nodded. "I'll keep the scholarship."

Kline smiled and patted his shoulder. "Excellent choice."

CHAPTER THIRTY

THAT EVENING, Jace parked his car in front of Mari's dormitory and waited to have the conversation he had been dreading ever since telling Kline his decision. Mari wasn't outside yet, so he scrolled through his phone. He stopped at a video of a woman being interviewed by some local news station.

It was Deborah Hobbs, the mother of the black man Officer Davis had shot. A man, probably her husband, stood beside her.

Jace tilted his seat back and watched.

"Have you viewed the bodycam footage?" asked the interviewer.

Deborah shook her head. "But I've had it described to me."

"What strikes you the most?"

She paused and frowned. "I think Stephen was scared. The officers' actions sounded very...draconian to me. Very forceful."

"You believe they should have taken a softer approach?" said the interviewer.

"With my Stephen? Yes. I think the yelling and the ferocity they came at him with...his survival instincts just took over."

Jace put the phone down. "It's not like the officer has time to get to know the criminal first," he muttered. He and Rob had discussed police tactics many times over the years. They *have* to be dominant and force-ful. He sighed and glanced at the front doors. Still no Mari.

Hands behind his head, he tapped his foot on the brake pedal and stared at the roof of his car. He frowned and stopped tapping his foot. Then he leaned forward and typed into his phone: *how to create a website.*

Their drive to Oak Bend was a quiet one. Noticeably more leaves had fallen since he was there last. Side by side, they walked slowly up the main path.

"This is so beautiful," Mari gasped as she pointed out the colorful primrose and occasional snapdragons visible from the path. Jace had never noticed these before. Mari was always pointing out a fresh perspective.

"So, can we talk about it?" she finally asked.

Jace cleared his throat uncomfortably. "I guess I should apologize for kind of being a jerk at the meeting."

"You know someone that relies on government for health care, don't you."

"How did you know?"

"It was obvious. You've been pretty matter-of-fact in the other meet-ings. Tell me about them."

Jace cleared his throat and put his hands in his pockets as he walked. "It's my dad. He's a machinist. Or *was* a machinist. He's got what they call essential tremors. His hands shake when he tries to use them."

"Oh."

"Some expensive treatments helped, but he still isn't able to work."

"That's awful." Mari put a hand on his arm.

"He still has a business. A few guys do the machinist work, and he does the sales and business stuff. My mom helps. They don't make as much money, but it's working. For now."

"I'm guessing some government help has come in handy," said Mari.

"You don't like governments very much, do you?" Jace smiled.

"I wouldn't say that!" said Mari. "We need it. Government workers are people, too. Good people. But a lot of what we ask the government to do is just not a good idea, wasting our money and nibbling away at our freedoms. It's using the wrong tool for the job, like chopping firewood with a butter knife."

"And charity is one of the things the government shouldn't be doing?"

"Doesn't it seem shady to take someone's money and give it to their neighbor?"

Jace grinned. "Well, if *I* did that, sure."

"So, what makes it okay if you ask someone else to do it for you? I mean, isn't that what happens when our elected officials take someone else's money and give it to their neighbor? Why not leave it to everyone to give and help where they can, in a more personal way? When we do that, I believe we're more creative and compassionate. Each dollar goes further, and we help people improve their own lives where they can, instead of mostly just handing them stuff. And the people who are being helped tend to be more resourceful with personal charity instead of acting wasteful or entitled when the help comes from a faceless, impersonal, massive government. That's just human nature."

"Okay...but a lot of people are going to be selfish and not give. Isn't that a problem?"

"I don't know. Is it?"

Jace shrugged.

"Lots of people make choices that disappoint me." Then she grinned at him. "Are you saying you won't help your neighbor unless all the people on your street help the same amount?"

Jace tried to hide a smile. "Well, no..."

"I think we'll do fine. Americans are the most giving people on Earth."

"How can you know that?"

"The World Giving Index. Look it up if you want. It's pretty cool. The point is that if we cut back on government programs, people would have even more resources to help others in more effective ways."

"Charity versus taxes, huh?"

"Yup. One is given freely, and the other is taken. I mean, if you don't pay your taxes...bad things happen."

Jace kicked a rock into the grass. "I guess *helping* and *giving* don't seem to be the right words if we'll put you in jail when you don't participate."

"Great point!" she laughed. "And you know, Jace, you might say that giving to your neighbor is selfish, too. It helps create a world the giver wants to live in."

The trail went through a clearing. The evening sun slanted through the trees behind them, and Jace turned his baseball cap to shade the back of his neck.

"I think there's something else I need to make sure you understand," Mari said. "You know that I'm not saying we need to take away all the government health care programs immediately, right?"

"You're not?"

"Of course not. I'm actually pretty reasonable." She playfully bumped into him, knocking him off his balance. "We've been building those welfare programs for like fifty years. So, we're all standing on that giant, old government platform now. I don't think simply knocking down the pillars holding everything up would be very smart."

Jace nodded.

"We need to get people off it first, so they can build their own platforms. We need to build a staircase before we do any deconstruction. Nice and orderly."

"Metaphorically speaking, wouldn't it be easier to have everyone walk back down the stairs they used to get up there in the first place?"

"But I don't see this as going backward from where we came. I want to put more power into the hands of the people to go into an exciting new future. Millions of regular people. Patients, employees, CEOs, and doctors making their own personal decisions. Better health care, new cures and procedures we haven't even thought of, lower costs, all of that. Seems like a brand-new staircase ahead of us is appropriate."

"Or an escalator, even."

Mari winked. "With the obesity epidemic going on, I think we can take the stairs."

They walked in silence around a bend. She looked down at the path. It was getting steeper, and their steps slower. "I'm sorry. I can see how it could have felt like an attack on your dad the other night."

Jace sighed. "You know what? I think he probably agrees with you."

"Really?"

"Yeah." He chuckled. "He hates it when government wastes our tax dollars. They spent millions to remodel the library in our town. He called it the book palace. He was so mad, he couldn't even look at it when we'd drive by. We finally got him to come to my sister's piano recital there, but you could tell he wasn't happy about it."

Mari grinned. "Sounds like a cool guy." Her smile faded and she looked at him with sincere compassion. "I hope he gets better."

"Me, too."

They reached the overpass and stood in the shade of the tall concrete wall. Mari took in the view and sighed. "It's beautiful up here. Nature gives us so many lessons to live by."

Jace glanced over. He could tell her gears were turning as she looked out over the soil and the trees and the birds. She seemed to always be thinking. Learning. Connecting things in her mind.

He smiled a little. "I'd like to eventually hear some of your nature lessons. But sometimes you can just enjoy life, too."

She laughed. "I'm sorry. Get me going on certain topics, and I'll talk forever."

"I probably can't talk about any of those things for more than two minutes," lamented Jace.

"What? You're having intelligent conversations already! You don't have to be an expert on anything. Start with what you know and ask honest questions about what you don't."

"Easy for you to say. I bet you've always been good at it."

"I've had my own incidents that I'm not proud of," Mari said, soberly. "Once at a family party I really blew up at a cousin about abortion. I still believe in what I said, but I regret how I went about it." She nodded at him. "You'll get better at it. Just don't give up. Don't be afraid of saying something dumb. Jump into the conversation. You have more insight than you think. Besides, you can't get too down on yourself. You're not even done with the dojo lessons yet!"

Jace took off his hat and ran his fingers through his hair. He looked away. "About that..."

Mari blinked, still smiling. "What is it?"

"I'm not coming to any more meetings." The pitch of his voice rose with every word. By the end, his statement sounded more like a question.

Mari winced, as if the words had physical force behind them. His heart ached for her, hating that he was the cause of it.

"I can explain," he said.

She cleared her throat and forced a smile. "No need." She folded her arms and kept her gaze resolutely forward. "It's pretty up here."

"Look. I've learned a lot of useful stuff. But I think I'll be fine now. Maybe you can even let me know what happens at the meetings."

Mari sighed. "What about us? The group? This isn't just about you, Jace. We need people like you to help." She wouldn't look at him.

Jace held out his hands, exasperated. "What is the Bathwater Brigade *doing*, really? I mean, Dylan kind of had a point. Washington is where things change. It feels like we're not really doing anything." Even as he said it, Jace knew he didn't mean it.

She was motionless, and then turned her head and fixed her gaze on him.

"Tell me, Jace. Have you ever been outside of the United States?"

"I've been to Hawaii," he offered.

"Have you spent a weekend with relatives who literally live off five dollars a day?"

"No."

"How much time did you spend this week hauling water, or hand-washing your clothes?"

He shrugged.

"Or let's say you're one of the wealthy ones and have a run-down apartment and an old laptop, and you hear someone in the hallway at night. Does your heart jump into your throat because your blog criticizes your government?"

Jace looked down and said nothing.

Her eyes flashed. "You have no idea what you have, Jace."

"I know we're pretty lucky here in America. We have a lot. What does that have to do with anything?"

"You were lucky to have been born here, that's true. But American life isn't great because of luck. We made a discovery greater even than electricity. We discovered some principles. A set of ideas that set the stage for the freedom, happiness, and prosperity that you take for granted and that many of the poor and huddled masses of the world desperately crave. Tell me, Jace, how would you help those poor people?"

"I don't know," Jace said, increasingly annoyed. "Send them help, donations and stuff."

"That's good. But that only takes the edge off their suffering. What else?"

"Um, allow them to immigrate to America?"

"That's important, too. But as a strategy to solve world poverty and corruption? That's like trying to pile all the guests from the Titanic into one lifeboat."

Jace shrugged. "What else, then?"

"You show them how it's done, Jace. It might sound cheesy, but you become a beacon for freedom in the world. Show them what a free country really looks like. Inspire them. Give them a place to visit to see it done right. And when they return to their homeland, they'll tell stories of what they saw. Regular people living and breathing free air, creating something wonderful."

"So, we just do our thing and that will help other countries."

"Yes!" said Mari. "America has exports of food, and manufacturing, and technology that are raising the standard of living across the globe. But that's not our *best* export. The most important thing we can do is to give away the recipe. Show them how they can do it, too. This has been going on for two hundred years, Jace, and it has been working. Our government, and people, and Constitution used to be the marvel of the world. Other nations tried to emulate it."

She now looked more passionate than angry.

Jace removed his hat and scratched his head. "So, we help the world just by being ourselves. It sounds too easy."

"It *is* easy. But we're not *doing* it. We're forgetting who we are. Have you seen movies where the old hero is washed up, drunk, and disillusioned? They seek him out, remind him of his past, and show him that the world needs to be saved again. They need *him* again."

"Sure."

"America is that old hero. We're forgetting what made her remarkable. We're throwing out the old principles simply because they're old. Or because somebody misunderstands, or says that they're racist. Or greedy. Or anything else. We've forgotten what it means—what can happen—when you just let a person be free. Little by little, we've chipped away at it with a thousand ideas from people trying to be helpful. Yes, like too much government involvement in health care."

Jace frowned and nodded.

"Take botany. The more we understand the nature around us, the more we're able to use it and take care of it. Right? The Constitution is a nature book, too. About *human* nature. The authors knew how power slowly corrupts us if it's concentrated—you know, not spread out among the states and the communities. They knew about greed. How government is fire—useful, but dangerous if not controlled. And how a thousand individuals are almost always better at solving a problem than a central government.

"Some governments in the world fight against human nature, or pretend that it doesn't exist. But the Founders set ours up seeing human nature for what it is—its flaws *and* its strengths. In the same way that you can build an airplane once you understand the principles of flight, our nation has soared for centuries. Far higher and further than even the Founders probably could have predicted. But our generation was born mid-flight, and we are forgetting what makes it fly."

Jace swallowed.

"Why am I in this little club?" she asked. "I want to help my family in Guatemala and the five million other families just like them. From where I stand, it appears the most powerful way I can help is just to remind America who she is."

Jace felt she was right. But he pushed back anyway. "How many people think like you? This isn't a very popular opinion right now."

"It's more popular than you think. Don't assume the loudest voices are the majority."

Jace shrugged. "The majority might be shrinking."

"Shouldn't that be all the more reason to talk about it?"

"I'm not saying we shouldn't," he said, thoughtfully. He paused, not knowing how to phrase his next question. "But how much effort do you put into a lost cause?"

She lowered her voice. "Lost cause? How dark do you want to go here?"

He shrugged again, unsure of what she meant.

"Do you think I don't see the problems? We're ignoring our founding ideals, and instead we're fixating on the faults of those who set them up. We're torching our own history. We're in the streets demanding that power be given to the people, not realizing that what we're asking for will take individual power *away*. We're stoking the flames of division and burning down everything that unites us. America has left her diamonds in a tub of what appears to be nothing but dirty bathwater. She's carrying it to the window, about to make a catastrophic mistake that the world will mourn for generations."

A lump formed in Jace's throat as he put his hands in his pockets.

"Yes, the days keep getting shorter and colder, and it looks like America might have a hard winter ahead of her. I don't know what scenes are going to play out, but I do know that spring will come eventually. I want to tell my grandkids that I kept my head—and my heart—about me, and planted seeds of freedom where I could. Even if that one conversation with my grandkids is the only hope I have, Jace, it's not a lost cause. Not to me."

Jace suddenly felt ashamed that she needed to talk to him about the virtues of standing for something. A daughter of immigrants, Mari was the most powerful American freedom fighter that he had ever met.

He sank onto a large, flat rock and dropped his head in his hands. "I'm tired of disappointing everyone!" Then he sighed. "Sorry. I just don't know what to do."

Mari looked shocked at his outburst. When she recovered, she said, "Look. If you don't want to be in the Bathwater Brigade, I don't want you to be. I don't think you're a jerk. I'm just disappointed."

He clenched his fists and looked up at Mari. "I want to be in it. But I can't."

"Why not?"

"Dr. Kline will take away my scholarship."

"You have a band scholarship?" She sat beside him.

"Why does everyone sound surprised?" he said. "Yes. Half tuition. It's not huge, but it's the only way I was able to come here."

"Well, you could have mentioned this five minutes ago!" Mari paused for a moment. "Why would a band teacher care what club his students belong to?"

Jace explained the supposed connection with the musical Zero Supremacy operation. "I honestly thought you wouldn't want me in the Brigade anyway. Not just because I got mad and left the other day. But it's my fault the university apparently thinks you guys were behind that prank now."

"Jace, look at me." She gave him her trademark calm, intense gaze. "We really do want you there." She looked to the side for a moment. "*I* want you there. Not just to try to get you to see things my way. I love it when we talk. I like your thoughts. Your perspective and your questions. You're different, Jace, and I've seen you grow since I met you. I grow, too, by spending time with you."

Jace didn't know what to say.

Mari stood. "What if we figure out the money thing together? Some of us could even pitch in, maybe."

Jace stood, too. "That means a lot. But no. I won't accept money from you guys."

"Have you looked at other scholarships?"

"My grades weren't awesome in high school."

"You'd be surprised what's out there. If you're determined, I'm sure you can find a way."

Jace shrugged.

"Is your band conductor guy really going to know if you're coming to meetings?" she said.

"I don't think he could know. But with my luck, it would backfire like everything else, and I'd somehow lose more than the scholarship."

She sighed, then placed a hand on his back. "All right, I'm not mad at you. I can see the reasons behind the decisions you're making."

"I really do want to hear about what happens in your meetings, though. More than just looking up the transcripts." Jace cleared his throat. "Maybe you could, you know, update me now and then. I mean, if you're okay with that."

She smiled. "I am."

CHAPTER THIRTY-ONE

THURSDAY AFTERNOON, Mr. Oatley flipped through the papers on a clipboard that was nearly black from oil and grease smudges. Jace and Saint waited.

"Mr. Oatley?" Saint said.

He looked up at them. "You still here? Y'all are going to the Union Center today like I told you."

Jace frowned. He hadn't told them. Saint looked just as confused.

"Are you lost? Broken legs? Do y'all need me to drive you there or something?"

"No."

He went back to his clipboard. Jace and Saint glanced at each other, picked up their tool belts, and left the Maintenance Building.

"How did your Bathwater meeting go?" Saint asked.

Careful to keep as much information from Saint as possible, Jace said, "Well, if we had a meeting, it would have gone just fine."

Saint smirked. "T.J. get my note?"

Jace sighed. "Yeah, he saw it."

There was a little silence, broken only by the sound of their shoes on the pavement. Then Jace said, "I quit the Brigade, by the way."

"Woah. My note made you quit?"

"Nah. Just figured it wasn't my thing."

"Interesting."

Jace entered the front door of the Union Center, making no effort to hold it open for Saint behind him. It was busy. And loud. Thursday afternoon seemed to be the Friday night of Cale University. Nearly all the week's classes were over.

Jace was instantly self-conscious in his old clothes and tool belt.

"Let's start upstairs," said Saint. Jace nodded.

They climbed the stairs. The first door on their left was a large, empty ballroom with five sets of doors on the perimeter. Their steps echoed inside.

Saint got out his gloves and graphite powder. "It's Monday night."

Jace froze, crouched at the base of a door. "What's Monday night?"

"The next Zero Supremacy meeting. We're going to plan some stuff."

"Oh. Well, have fun."

Saint chuckled. "You're coming."

"What?" Jace stood.

"Can't you remember anything past yesterday? You're coming with me to this meeting and then you're going to bring me to yours. Unless the deal's off, of course. But if it's off, and if I don't see you at the Zero meeting Monday, I'm making a big announcement there."

Jace hesitated. "I can't bring you because I can't go to any more Bathwater meetings."

Saint laughed. "You got kicked out? What did you do, serenade them with your trombone?"

"Look. It's about Victor Square. The band will take away my scholarship if I'm in the Bathwater Brigade."

"How would they know if you go to one more meeting?"

Jace shrugged. "I really need that scholarship, Saint. Without it, I wouldn't be in college."

"You mean if you get caught at a Bathwater meeting then they'll kick you out of school?"

"Pretty much."

"One less white supremacist at Cale. I like the sound of that." Saint shrugged. "Well, enrolled or not, I don't care much either way. You might as well tell them to find about fifty more chairs for their next meeting. Don't worry, we'll figure out when it is."

"Okay, fine." Jace turned back to the door. "Deal's still on."

Jace stewed in silence until they finished the ballroom. Next, they found an unlocked conference room and got to work.

"I'm barely here, too," said Saint as he tested a door handle.

"What?"

"I'm the first to go to college in my family. Lots of pressure to finish. I know how it is not to be the richest kid on campus. I guess you could say I'm one of those starving students." Saint shrugged. "Guys like us work harder, right? We have to."

"True," said Jace. "So how close are you to being done?"

"Graduate in a year. If it all works out." Saint removed his toolbelt, grabbing a bottle of water from one of its pockets, and sat in a padded chair next to the long, wooden table in the middle of the room.

"And after that?"

"I'll be coding software, probably in the Fort Worth area. I don't know."

Jace sat in a chair opposite Saint and thoughtfully rubbed his chin.

"What?"

"I could use help on something, actually," Jace said.

"From me?"

"I'm trying to build a website. And you're a lot further along in computer science than I am."

"Nah," Saint said, standing up. "Thanks for the offer, though."

"It's about police brutality."

Saint stopped and turned. "What do you mean?"

"Well, if Stephen Hobbs knew what to expect from the police, don't you think he'd be alive today?"

Saint narrowed his eyes.

"Think about it. In those ten minutes that night, he made a series of choices. And with each one, the police were trained to respond in a way that escalated things. Especially at the end, when he grabbed what turned out to be his cell phone and ran at Officer Lambson. Things might have ended differently if he knew that running at her like that would cause her to shoot."

"If she was following her training, then their policies are off-the-charts horrendous."

"I know you're not a fan of their policies. But set that aside for a second. If Stephen knew what Gina was trained to do, then he could have made better decisions for himself in that moment."

"What. Do you think he was stupid?"

"No." Jace leaned forward and pointed at Saint across the table. "I think he was *panicked*."

Saint dropped back into his chair.

"You said it yourself, Saint. You don't always have common sense in that situation. Like what you said about handcuffs. It's instinct to resist, and maybe to run, even if you aren't really meaning to. Right now, in this room, things are calm enough for us to make rational decisions. But imagine the chase, and then the standoff. You don't have time to think."

Saint slowly nodded. "It would be pretty easy to freak out."

Jace shifted. "But only one of them did. Gina acted deliberately."

Saint shrugged. "Yeah, she was a cop."

"It was an intense situation for her, too. But she was *trained*."

"So?"

"She had rehearsed this situation a hundred times before. Her training took over and she wasn't ruled by her emotions. I want the same for the Stephens of the world so that they can stay alive to sort it out with the judge."

"So it's a website telling people to obey the police? *That's* going to be popular."

Jace chuckled. "It will show how to interact with cops safely. Help get it drilled in our heads before we're in the situation and tempted to panic. I really think the more people I can get to spend time at this website, the safer our communities will be."

"What's it called?"

"I don't know yet. All the good domain names are taken."

"Is this a pro-cop site, then?"

"Nope. I mean, having the community more educated about their job will help cops be safer. But you could say it's neutral. Meant to help everyone, including criminals—suspects, I mean."

Saint nodded in thought, looking down at the table. "Have you heard of 'the talk' that black parents have with their kids, Jace?"

"No."

"It's the same kind of thing, in a way. They let their kids know that the police will probably target them at some point in life, and they tell them how to act to stay safe."

"Oh. That's...kind of sad. I had no idea. I'm not sure that police are always going around targeting black people—"

"I *know* that's what you think, Jace," Saint said, rubbing his face. "But trust me, it's definitely a thing, at least in some parts of the country."

Jace took a deep breath. "The other day you asked me what I'm doing to help. Well, this is it."

Saint blinked slowly. "What do you need help on? Specifically."

Jace scooted up to the table. "I want to be able to show visitors which law enforcement precinct they're in. I'm using this website builder tool, but apparently I need some custom coding to get their approximate location."

Saint rested his chin on his hand. "Browsers support that natively."

"Oh. Cool," said Jace. "And I need a database to put all the Texas precincts into."

"You'd better set up the schema in third normal form or you'll be hating life."

"Don't know what that means."

Saint stood. "Let's swing by the computer lab once we're done."

Jace nodded and gathered his tools from the floor, hiding a grin.

Saint sighed. "Just more work I'm not getting paid for." He tightened the screw underneath the door handle.

"At least we're more than halfway done with this," said Jace. "One more week, and you won't have to spend time with Nazis anymore."

"So, you're admitting it, now?"

"Nah, I mean the Munchie's employees. You can just tell."

Saint shook his head and smiled.

CHAPTER THIRTY-TWO

FRIDAY AFTERNOON, Jace and Eli worked on calculus homework together in the empty, unlocked dorm next to Jace's. Rob texted and invited them to go see a movie. They slammed their math books shut and met him at the Good Times Theater just west of campus.

They ended up watching *Little Mutt*, the latest animated flick about a boy and his dog. Children and reluctant parents streamed into the theater.

The big comedic moments were mostly comprised of people or animals either falling down, being hit in the face, or passing gas. The little kids roared with laughter and the parents checked their phones. Jace and Eli exchanged glances and slid down in their seats. Rob, however, laughed out loud and ate handfuls of popcorn.

They emerged from the theater into the afternoon sun, the only ones in their age group by a wide margin. "We never speak of this," Jace said to the others.

As they walked back to Stoddard Hall, Jace told them of his meeting with Dr. Kline.

"So, what did you decide?" Eli asked.

"You mean whether to keep my scholarship or stay in the Brigade?"

"Yeah."

Jace looked at Eli with raised eyebrows. "What do you think? I kept the scholarship."

"Oh. Darn."

The light changed, and they crossed the street.

"Does this mean there could be an opening for me?" Eli asked.

"You *want* to join?" said Rob.

Jace imagined Eli and Mari walking to meetings, having deep moonlit discussions about life and fixing the world's problems together. He cleared his throat. "I don't think so. I could ask someone, though."

Rob talked about his plans for the next operation. He'd ignore the Zeroes, as difficult as that was for him, and go directly to the public.

"I might be able to help this time," Jace said. He didn't think Mari would have a problem with the fliers Rob was planning to hand out. And he didn't know if that even mattered anymore. They hadn't talked since their hike last week.

As they turned the corner near the science building, Jace recognized Kendric and Danica, standing on each side of the wide sidewalk. Amber was in the middle. They offered sheets of paper to students as they walked by.

When Amber saw Jace, she turned away slightly and stepped out of his path. Jace and Eli found themselves walking directly up to Danica. She smiled and handed each of them a flier.

"Hello, Jace!" she said brightly. They stopped.

"Pro Voter," Eli read aloud. "What's this?"

"You could just read the paper," Jace said, turning to give Kendric a nod.

"You want me to be a professional voter?" asked Eli.

"No," laughed Danica. "That sounds illegal."

Eli stared at the flier, confused. "I'm supposed to look at all the candidates?" He put the flier down to his side. "What are you? Democrats? Republicans?"

"We just want everyone to be aware of all the candidates. It's an important civic duty, and we think it's smart to know the full choice in front of you."

Rob stood to the side and studied the flier.

"All right," Eli said. "So, if I do it, what do I get?"

"A sticker," she said.

"You already gave me one. It's stapled right here."

"Then you get permission to wear it."

"Oh."

"I'll let you two work this out," said Jace, patting Eli on the back. He wondered how long it would take him to discover that he was talking to a member of the Bathwater Brigade.

Rob put a hand on Jace's shoulder. "Hey. You're positive Bathwater won't let us borrow one of their fliers? The one they had at the cupcake table? That's pretty close to the flier I want to use in the next operation, and it would save me a ton of time."

Jace shook his head. "They won't go for it. I'm positive. Sorry, man."

Rob nodded and looked back at the Pro Voter flier.

"What's up, loser?" Kendric said, swiping the sweat off his brow. He greeted Jace with a handclasp and a smile.

"Just getting back from a movie." Jace put his hands in his pockets.

"Yeah? Which one?"

"Doesn't matter," Jace said. "So it looks like you guys have been here a while."

"Yup." Kendric held up his stack of fliers. "This morning I had double."

"Nice."

Someone grabbed Jace from behind and put him in a soft headlock. "So, uh, Mari says you're not that into us anymore."

Jace pulled free and turned to see Dylan. "Oh. Hey."

"Yeah," Kendric said. "So what's this about leaving the Brigade, man?"

"She told you, huh? But you haven't even held a meeting since."

"Group chat," he said. "The core is pretty tight. She told us not to give you a hard time about it though."

"Oh."

"You're lucky she said that, too. You'd be flat on the sidewalk right now." Kendric's expression was dead serious. Then he laughed. "I'm kidding, man! Lighten up."

Jace turned to Dylan. "I thought you wouldn't be here since you're not a big fan of these fliers."

Dylan rolled his eyes. "I was just walking by." He looked at the flier Jace held. "We'd be a lot smarter if that title said Weaver for Congress."

Jace had seen a few commercials for the Texas senator, but other than that, he knew almost nothing about the man.

"You mean, if we campaigned for him?"

Dylan nodded. "Ever heard of having friends in high places? Comes in handy." He looked to his left. "Oh. Hey, Rob." Rob looked up and smiled.

"Good memory," said Jace.

"Actually," said Dylan, "we have Criminal Justice together."

Rob nodded. "Easiest class I've ever had. And I'm including elementary school here."

"Not surprised," said Jace. "That's your thing."

"No. You don't understand. All we have is like six small tests for the semester. And Farnsworth gives us all the answers first. We could probably pass the class investing a total of two hours."

Dylan laughed. "So true." He gestured to the flier. "But Weaver, man."

Kendric moved close to Jace and chuckled. "Dylan doesn't quite get it. The Brigade is all about coming together. For Bathwater, party politics is like a dirt bike. Ride it all you want outside, but you don't bring it in the house."

"Yeah," agreed Jace. "You don't want to turn some people off and limit your membership because of your politics."

"Oh, it's more than that," said Kendric. "Here, think about this for a minute. If you get your guy in office for a few years, he might do what you want for a while, and put policies and laws in place that you like. But when the next guy gets in from the other party, he will probably undo all that."

"What's the alternative, though?"

"Go for something much more sustainable, look for things that a vast majority of us can agree on. It's what we *do* as the Bathwater Brigade. Pick things apart to find the actual points of disagreement and set those aside for later. Come together on the common ground that's left. If you can get broad support like that, we can have good policies that are here to stay."

Eli was still talking with Danica. They were smiling. Jace watched as Amber handed fliers to most who walked by. Only a few stopped to chat.

"This doesn't seem as exciting as the race celebration thing you guys had a few weeks back."

"We've had a few interesting discussions, though," Kendric said. "This one dude. He was obsessed with the presidential election. He kept asking who I'm going to vote for. I didn't tell him because, well, I'm representing Bathwater here. But I told him, like, it really shouldn't matter all that much who the president is."

"What do you mean?"

"That's what *he* said!" replied Kendric. "Well, look. Here's how I see it. The president didn't used to have this much power. Washington, D.C., too. When this country began, we had a national government to do only a few basic things to keep us together as a country. State and community government solved most problems, if government got involved at all, which still wasn't very often. There was so little to do, members of Congress used to live in their own states for most of the time, and they met in Washington just once a year to get some business done."

"Woah. That's hard to imagine now," Jace said. "I'm guessing that you think government worked better back then than it does today."

Kendric laughed. "Yup! And here's why. Let's say you have some kids in the community who want to sweep floors after school, and they'll do it for cheaper than minimum wage. Business owners are cool with the idea, but they have to follow the law, and can't afford to pay them minimum wage. Even though the kids and the employers are willing, the minimum wage law says, nope! Can't do it. This actually happened to me. So, what could someone like me do to get that law changed?"

"I don't know," said Jace. "Get your friends and family together. Pass out fliers. Have meetings at the library."

"Sure, if the minimum wage were decided at the community level. The problem is, there is a *national* minimum wage law. I don't have friends and family in all fifty states to help me out, or millions of dollars for commercials. How empowered do I feel right now?"

Jace chuckled.

"*That's* why I want things decided at the community level. It literally puts power in the hands of the people. And that's why I don't think it should matter all that much who the president is. Washington, D.C. shouldn't be in charge of so much."

A smattering of applause took Jace by surprise. Some students had gathered behind to listen. Jace clapped Kendric on the back. "You tell them, man. I've got to get going."

Kendric started answering questions, and Jace stepped to the side. He caught Eli's glance and motioned 'let's go' with his head. Eli finished up with Danica and joined him.

"Where's Rob?" Jace asked as they walked away.

"He said he had to go to the library. I think that other guy went with him."

"Dylan?"

Eli shrugged. "They were talking about the Zeroes." He marched quickly next to Jace, his head high.

"Did you get the Pro Voter thing figured out?" Jace asked with a smile. "You look inspired."

"Yeah. Did you know she's in the Bathwater Brigade?"

"Yup. She goes to all the meetings."

"I got her phone number."

"Nice! She's cool. What did you guys talk about?"

"Just voting. And a party she went to."

"What kind of party?"

"They played a game called 'Don't You Dare' and one of the dares was to pass your wallet around the room."

"Fascinating," Jace said dryly.

"She had some friends with her that she trusted. But there were a lot of people at the party that she didn't know. And people were coming in and out of the party all the time."

They crossed into the shade of some trees.

"So, did she pass her wallet around?"

"It doesn't matter."

"What?"

"It was an analogy."

"Of course," Jace laughed. "Get used to those."

"She made the point that you want to be careful how much power you give an elected official, because you don't know the person who comes next. She knew and trusted the friend next to her, but not the people on the other side of the room. She says that when someone is in office that we like, then we're tempted to make them in charge of lots of things."

"And the flip side," said Jace, "is that when we vote the next person in, we might not like them as much, and we'll regret that we put them in charge of so much."

"Yup!" said Eli. "She's pretty smart."

"You mean she's pretty and smart?" He wasn't certain, but Jace thought Eli's tan face just blushed a little.

"Sure."

Jace smiled. Welcome to the Bathwater Brigade.

CHAPTER THIRTY-THREE

IN THE MUNCHIE'S parking lot, Saint handed Jace his over-sized red hoodie with the Zero Supremacy logo. It was Monday, 7:30 P.M.

"You don't think anyone will recognize me?" Jace asked.

"Leave your trombone in the car, and you should be fine."

Jace didn't smile.

"Stay at the back of the room," Saint said. "I'll be near the front. Just ignore me. If my friends find out about this, it will be worse for me than for you."

Jace had considered wearing some sort of vest or armor under his shirt, just in case. But he had no idea how to find those kinds of things.

"Should I leave early?" asked Jace.

Saint shrugged. "If you want. Isn't the Bathwater Brigade supposed to be all open-minded, though? Maybe you should stick around and learn something."

They drove separately to the Boar Tusk Coffeehouse, two miles north of Cale.

The wooden floors creaked inside, and a girl with a knit cap, no makeup, and no expression worked the cash register. There was a room to the side which seemed bigger than the rest of the building combined. A framed newspaper article on the wall explained that the whole building was once a Baptist church. Zero Supremacy met in what used to be the chapel.

Jace stood at the back of the shop, hood over his head, like he was deciding what to order. It was nearly eight. People wearing mostly black and red streamed through the shop and into the meeting room, some purchasing coffee first.

Jace glanced toward the doorway and fidgeted with the token in his pocket. He imagined the worst-case scenario and what life would be like without him. Adam would be pleased to have more room in the dorm. Dr. Kline would probably celebrate. Rob and Eli would move on with their lives. And Mari...

Jace checked his phone. Mari had texted during his drive.

About to enter the dojo. So, I know you can't do anything about it, but I'm kinda sad you're not here.

The murmur in the old chapel grew. The stream of Zeroes going in had slowed to a trickle. Clutching his token, he walked in.

Jace avoided eye contact. Though there were some seats in the middle, he opted to stand near the exit with his back to the wall.

He scanned the room. There were about seventy-five people there. It was close to an even split between white and Hispanic, and a handful were black or another race. Some had hoods up like Jace. A few had gray hair, and a couple of grade-school kids were with a parent, but most seemed to be in their twenties and thirties. Jace thought he recognized a few from campus.

A few Zeroes were stoic and kept to themselves, but mostly there were handshakes, laughs, and arms around shoulders. This took him by surprise somehow. He had pictured a scene with angry chants and fists in the air. Maybe that would come later.

Saint was in the second row from the front, speaking with a guy next to him.

Like the greenhouse basement, this room had artwork, too. A framed photo of a lady who he thought was probably Harriet Tubman hung on the opposite wall, next to one of Rosa Parks. There was a black-and-white photo of a police beating, and a framed poster that looked like

World War II propaganda with its bold, solid shapes and stark shadows. It was of a man in some kind of uniform staking a red flag into the ground, and the words on it were in a language Jace didn't recognize.

Standing next to the propaganda poster was a man in jeans and a black sweatshirt, a little overweight, with dark, short hair and a black beard. He was looking directly back at Jace.

Jace immediately looked down and away, and then to the front of the room. He waited a few moments. Then, painfully self-conscious, he stole one more glance, hoping to discover he wasn't still the object of the man's attention.

The man was still watching.

Jace straightened from his lean against the wall. The man shifted. Jace again turned to face the front of the room, but all his thoughts were on the man in the sweatshirt.

The meeting began. A young, short woman with giant glasses approached the podium and introduced herself as Paladin. She wore red lipstick and a brown business suit over a white top. Her hair was short, stylish, and a light blond that was nearly white. She looked just like the girl in the video Rob had showed him over sweet rolls all those weeks ago.

Paladin welcomed everyone to the Zero Supremacy meeting. She asked any newcomers to raise their hand. Jace focused on the wall behind her, barely breathing. Five took her up on the offer and introduced themselves.

Paladin continued. "We begin our meetings by reviewing why we're here," she said. "Hate, misogyny, racism, and bigotry are never defeated. But they change forms and faces, when forced to."

There were some nods, and a few mouthed the words along with her.

"The defeat of Nazi Germany, the Emancipation Proclamation, and women's right to vote. When the rest of the world takes a victory lap, *we* are on the hunt. We expose the new manifestations of hate and shout them down. We use violence only when violence is imminent. The world may never be clean, but we fight for the beauty that we still have, and keep corruption and injustice in check."

More nods, a smattering of applause, and a few audible "yeah's."

"We must have zero white supremacy. Zero gender supremacy. Zero economic supremacy." She raised her eyes and her voice. "Zero Supremacy!"

Stronger applause.

Jace looked to his right. The man that had been watching him had gone. Jace wanted to slip out the door and back to Cale, but something stopped him.

During the next part of the meeting, Paladin introduced a guy who she called Rogue. He was about Jace's age, a little taller and thinner. He read from a binder and recounted some historical events. He described the treatment of the Jews in Europe. Something called ghettoization, where they had forced Jews to live in a certain area, in horrible, crowded conditions. Not just during the Third Reich, but in the centuries before that, too. Jace had only a vague understanding of these ghettos.

Rogue then read a story of three families of color living in urban Dallas today. He described their poverty and compared this to three white families who lived in one of the wealthy suburbs. He never said it directly, but he seemed to imply that the same ghettoization was happening today. This kind of presentation appeared to be a regular segment of their meetings.

Next, Paladin pulled out a notebook and announced some upcoming events that they had the "opportunity to affect".

First on the list was the Gina Lambson trial. It was nearly over, and the jury was expected to start deliberations within days. Paladin urged them not to lose energy, though. They had a major rally planned for Saturday, and she asked them to watch for texts and emails to know when news cameras would be at the court building. They wanted everyone to show up for as much visibility as possible.

There were other events, too. A New Brig city council meeting was scheduled for the next day, and the agenda included something to do with the homeless. An old guy in the audience tried to convince everyone to come protest animal cruelty at a hog farm.

"What about Bathwater?" someone yelled from the back.

Jace froze, barely breathing.

"I'm not sure," said Paladin into the microphone. "Have they been active lately?"

A muscular man held up one of the Pro Voter fliers, with the sticker and everything. "They handed these out last week."

"Kill them all!" someone yelled to some laughter.

"Shut up," said someone else, followed by brief, scattered clapping.

Jace raised an eyebrow. It appeared they didn't all have the same level of vitriol toward the Brigade.

Paladin cleared her throat, ignoring the comments. "Anyone know of any future Bathwater events?"

No one answered.

Saint was half turned in his seat with his hand to his chin. He glanced back at Jace and raised his hand.

Heart pounding, Jace drew his left hand out of his pocket, ready to grab the door handle. He hoped his car was fast enough to reach the greenhouse first, so he could sound the alarm.

"I hear there is a rally for Senator Grassley," Saint said.

"Is that next week?" said Paladin. "Raise your hand if you're willing to help organize this."

Jace nearly collapsed. Saint smiled a little and glanced once more in Jace's direction. Relief and annoyance surged through Jace, and he put his hand back into his pocket.

Next, Paladin invited anyone to come up to the front and to speak what was on their mind.

A girl that looked about twelve talked about how she feared for her future. A burly guy with a beanie gave some inspiring words, became emotional, and encouraged his friends not to give up when it gets hard. A girl Jace's age explained how she was fighting for her friends, even though some of them didn't see the problems right there in front of them.

These people really believe in this, Jace thought. *They're convinced they're doing the right thing.* It surprised him, but he didn't know why. What else did he expect? It was genuinely compelling, seeing some of the theory behind Saint's thinking. And seeing Zeroes not so much as criminals at the moment, but...day-to-day people who didn't agree on everything.

As soon as the meeting ended and the Zeroes began to stand from their seats, Jace left the room and speed-walked to his car. He imagined someone running up behind him. He glanced over his shoulder.

No, there *was* someone running up behind him. "Hey!" The bearded man who had been watching Jace was closing the gap.

"Hi," said Jace, clearing his throat. His heart pounded, and he walked faster. He decided to go to the other side of his car, and try to keep it between him and the man at all times. Nearly there, Jace fumbled with his keys as the man caught up to him. Jace put his hand on the door handle.

"Hey," the man said. "I'm Scamp. Looks like you're new here." Scamp didn't smile, but he seemed to be genuine.

"Oh," said Jace. "Yeah, I'm kind of shy. Didn't want to introduce myself."

"No problem. So how did you find out about the meeting?"

Jace pretended to have something in his throat and coughed a few times, buying time to think.

"Sorry," Jace said. "I'm from the San Antonio chapter and new to the area. They told me to come here." He had no idea whether there was a chapter in San Antonio.

Scamp studied him for a moment. Then he held out his hand. "Glad to have you. What do we call you?"

Every Zero seemed to have a sort of nickname, probably so it would be harder for law enforcement to track them down. Jace said the first word that came to mind. "Duck." He immediately screamed inside his head. Except for 'bathwater', it was the worst word he could have chosen.

"Duck," Scamp repeated, looking slightly amused. "Great. Did the clipboard get passed to you so we have your info?"

"Yup," Jace lied.

"Cool. See you in two weeks, man."

Jace drove away, trying not to speed. He parked at his dorm, pulled the hoodie off, and arched his back as he stuffed it under the driver's seat from behind. He hurried inside and collapsed in his chair. His roommate, Adam, was gone. Jace picked up the note he had left on his desk before leaving for the Zero meeting. It was the address of the Boar Tusk Coffeehouse, just in case anything happened to him.

Jace thought of the meeting. In a way, it had been exactly what he'd expected. But then, in other ways, not at all. He'd need to sort this all out in his mind—but not tonight. The Brigade was safe for now, and that was the important thing. He crumpled the note and threw it in the trash can.

CHAPTER THIRTY-FOUR

OVER THE NEXT FEW DAYS, Jace hurried through his homework and trombone practice, and spent as much time as he could working on his website. He began writing the content for each page and agonized over colors and themes. Saint had helped for about an hour the day Jace had asked for it, but hadn't offered since.

Jace had correctly predicted that Eli would attend the next Bathwater Brigade meeting. Kendric had given Danica the okay to invite him. At rehearsal, Eli was beaming.

In botany, Jace and Mari still sat near each other and exchanged the usual sarcastic comments about Professor Adelson. She still smiled at him, but her eyes had lost some of their spark. And, since their relationship had taken what felt like a step backward, Jace didn't know if she was still coming to the beach party that India's grandma was hosting in a few weeks. Even worse, Bathwater topics didn't come up in conversation at all, which made Jace a little sad. He liked how she had challenged him in the weeks before, making him think about new things. Actually, she had made him think in entirely new *ways*. He felt that he had lived in two dimensions all his life and had just now entered the third. Like when he spent the summer in the Colorado mountains, after growing up on the Kansas plains. He'd left behind the simple landscape of long, straight roads with fields on either side.

In Colorado, he had spent his mornings gazing at cliffs, the rising forests, and a snow-capped peak from his cousin's bedroom window while the others still slept. The mountain was like a large, flat facade in the afternoon, but the light at dusk highlighted the canyons and ridges, reminding Jace that the mountain was an object in this world, just as real and complex as he was.

Jace didn't speak with Saint again until Thursday at their second-to-last day of campus service—not that anyone was counting. As he approached the Maintenance Building, he found Saint sitting outside, his back to the wall.

"You gave me a freaking heart attack," Jace said.

Saint laughed. "You mean when they asked if anyone had Bathwater news? Come on. I couldn't help it."

"And then Scamp. Did you send him to talk to me?"

Saint sat up from the wall, his smile fading. "You talked to Scamp?"

"He followed me out to my car."

"No, I didn't send him. What did he say?"

"Just welcomed me to the club, basically."

Saint laughed again. "You're a Zero now!"

Jace shuddered.

"So?" Saint stood. "When is the big Bathwater meeting?"

"Are you free next Wednesday?" This was the wrong day, of course, but Jace wasn't about to trust the Bathwater Brigade to a Zero without a little more proof.

Saint slapped his forehead. "What? You mean you met yesterday? You meet once a week still, right? Why didn't you tell me?"

Jace shrugged. "This is the first time we've spoken since then."

Saint gave Jace a dirty look. "Okay. What time?"

"5:30. Let's meet at Munchies."

"Why not at the greenhouse?"

"Fine."

"What are y'all doing at the greenhouse?" Mr. Oatley had unlocked and opened the door just as Jace finished speaking.

"Botany homework," Jace said.

"Getting your degree in agriculture?" Mr. Oatley looked interested.

"Not really. It's a required class."

His face fell. "Oh. Sounds about right. Nobody wants to learn about the land these days. They all want to sit at a desk."

"Can you blame us?" asked Saint. "There's no air conditioning out on the ranch."

Mr. Oatley didn't think that was funny.

Jace muttered an awkward apology for his career choice. "Sorry."

"No need to apologize to me," Mr. Oatley said, shaking his head. "I'm worried about all you city types, raised on concrete. There are things you learn under the blue sky, working with animals and the earth, that you just can't learn from a computer."

Jace had done some summer work in Kansas on his uncle's farm. He didn't want to do that for the rest of his life, but a little part of him was sad that he would miss out on some lessons that maybe you couldn't get any other way.

"Well, come on in and get your assignment," Mr. Oatley said. "Y'all seem to be hanging out more often than Mama's washing."

It occurred to Jace that for all the hassle and frustration of service with Saint and Mr. Oatley, he just might miss it.

They went to the oldest building on campus, called the Hamblin House. It had a gray stone exterior and a complicated, high-pitched roof. The interior doors were high and narrow with windows near the top. Jace wasn't sure what the building's original purpose was, but now it looked like a museum, and was used to host receptions and events that Jace would never be invited to. It smelled like old wood and reminded Jace of his great-grandma's house. The floors creaked, and the old glass within the doors rattled each time the door closed. Everything seemed fragile, and Jace took extra care.

At the top of a wooden stairway, Jace noticed a large display on the wall under a sign that read *Financial Aid*. He slowed and glanced at Saint across the hall. Jace casually thumbed through forms and pamphlets for grants, loans, and scholarships.

Saint popped a pin from the middle hinge of a painted white door with his hammer. "You noticed there are more of us than there are of you, right?"

"What's that?" Jace asked. He folded some pamphlets into his pocket.

"We had over a hundred people there on Monday."

Jace squinted. "More like seventy-five. But what makes you think that's more than come to ours?"

Saint cocked his head to the side. "Really? I counted twenty-seven chairs in the greenhouse basement. Total."

"We sit two or three to a seat," Jace said. "Laps, you know. We're a close bunch." Jace started on the door at Saint's right.

Saint chuckled as he greased the pin.

"We used to have a lot more coming to our meetings," said Jace. "There are a lot of supporters that aren't coming out right now. And you know the reason why."

It struck Jace at that moment that he had begun saying "we" when referring to the Bathwater Brigade—now that he had officially left it.

They moved upstairs.

"Instead of arguing which club has more members," said Jace, "what if we compare them a different way?"

Saint glanced up at Jace briefly as he spread out his white cloth beneath an open door to protect the elegant carpet.

"Both clubs care about justice and helping the poor," Jace said.

Saint paused, then smiled and continued his work. "You're saying that Zero Supremacy and Bathwater have the same goals or something?"

"Not at the surface level," replied Jace. "Your surface goal is to disrupt things you think are harmful, and ours is to look for solutions by talking to people who disagree with us."

"Okay."

"I think you guys go about it the wrong way and get most people mad at you instead of wanting to join with you. But at a deeper level, we are both trying to solve some of the same problems."

"Don't know about that," Saint said as he worked a door handle.

Jace shrugged. "I could be wrong. But that's how I see it." Then he added, "I actually agree with some of what I heard on Monday."

Saint squinted at the hinge he was scrubbing.

At Munchies that evening, Jace basked in the air-conditioned dining area. The upper floor of the Hamblin House had been very warm, and Jace had once again soaked through his shirt.

"I don't think I've told you boys," Mr. Oatley said, "but I'm going in for surgery tomorrow."

Saint nodded, and Jace mumbled something like, "That's not fun."

"Hernia. Guess I've been working too hard for a man that's pushing forty."

Or eighty?

"Are you supposed to be eating, then?" asked Saint.

Mr. Oatley bit into a chicken nugget. "This is my last meal."

Jace raised his eyebrows at Saint. What a meal.

"So, looks like we need to wait awhile before we can finish up," Mr. Oatley said. "I'll be in a hospital bed Saturday."

Saint sat up and glanced at Jace. "We just have one more session. Can't we just get it done this week?"

The old man shook his head. "Nah. They won't let y'all count the time unless I'm here with you. I don't blame them. Put you two on the job without supervision, and they'd either find y'all asleep somewhere, or you'd find a way to make the building collapse on top of you."

The boys didn't hide the disappointment on their faces.

Mr. Oatley pointed a nugget at them. "Now believe me, nobody wants this all to be done more than I do. But trying to change the situation is just hollering down a well." He softened.

"You know, y'all probably could have handled it. Seems y'all are starting to get just a bit of horse sense."

"So what day can we finish up?" Jace asked.

"As soon as I can get my boots back on. They say a few weeks. I'll let y'all know. Now, I can't remember if I have your phone numbers, so write them down on this here napkin." When they finished, he stuffed it into his shirt pocket.

Jace put his elbows on the table and ran his hands through his hair.

Saint would be a rock in his shoe a little longer. He looked up to see Saint, sitting back in his seat with his arms folded, looking back at him.

Jace was looking forward to having a break from walking a tightrope around Saint. The visit he owed him to the Bathwater Brigade, however, was something he was *not* looking forward to. Then, like Saint knew what he was thinking, the Zero's scowl slowly turned into a smirk.

CHAPTER THIRTY-FIVE

ON WEDNESDAY, Jace waited near the greenhouse for Saint. His shoulders pressed against the rough bark of a tree while he tried not to fidget. When Saint arrived, the greenhouse doors were locked, and there were no Brigade members anywhere. He noticed Jace and walked over to him. "There's no Bathwater meeting today, is there," he said. To say that the Zero was unhappy was a massive understatement.

Jace chuckled nervously. "I had to make sure you weren't going to bring a hoard of Zeroes with you." He swallowed. "Congratulations. You passed the test."

Saint set his jaw and pulled out his phone. "I'm calling Paladin right now."

"It's Monday." Jace stood straight and held up his hands. "Seven o'clock. Honest."

Jace had run out of ideas on how to avoid the disastrous crossing of the Bathwater Brigade and Zero Supremacy. Everything he'd thought of —including telling Mari about it—wouldn't make it any better. Over and over, he imagined the looks on his friends' faces as he introduced the not-so-friendly neighborhood Zero to them.

Maybe Jace could just stay home and let Saint show up on his own.

That couldn't be any worse, could it? Jace likely wouldn't be feeling well on Monday evening, anyway. He'd think of something.

Saint studied him for a minute. "Monday? For sure?" When Jace nodded, he tucked his phone back into his pocket. "Well, I guess that means I can hit the press conference tonight."

"What press conference?"

"The police department is supposed to announce some more policy changes. You're following the news, right? They had a dog in the yard behind Hobbs, coming at a full run."

"Yeah, I heard that. Behind the fence, was it?"

"The cops should have called off the dog if it wasn't needed. Stephen was already cornered."

"She had no idea that the K-9 unit was on the scene, and with those factory fans she couldn't have even heard it bark."

"So she says."

Jace chuckled and shook his head. "You think she's lying then, huh?"

"Sure. She's looking at prison."

Jace frowned. It was true, people had lied for a lot less. Even if he didn't think she was lying, maybe it wasn't so surprising that others did.

Saint shoved his hands in his pockets. "So, we know why Stephen ran now. Sic a German Shepherd on a guy who is deathly afraid of dogs and guess what? He might run."

"Maybe. We'll never know for sure if that's the reason he ran." Jace leaned against the tree again and folded his arms. "But here's how it looks to me right now. Whether he ran because of the dog, or because he's been hearing the message that cops are going to shoot him anyway, it doesn't change the fact that he still wouldn't have been hurt if he had just laid down and not moved."

Saint scoffed. "The attack dog is just going to stop if you're not moving?"

"Yes. That's what they're trained to do. My friend's dad is a cop. They used to invite me to demonstrations. If you're on the ground and not moving, they don't attack."

Saint shrugged. "I still don't blame him for running, though."

"The media could do so much good here. Just report police shootings more accurately—and not just when the officer is white and the suspect is not. And maybe even help educate us on what to do if we're in a confrontation with police. You know?"

"Sounds like you're promoting your website. You need to work on that sales pitch."

Jace smiled. "It's been on my mind."

Saint looked like he was about to say something, but changed his mind.

Jace removed his hat and shaped the rim with his hands. "Your Zero friends coming with you?"

"To the city council meeting?"

"Yeah."

"Not today. At least not for a protest. We only go to ones that are worth risking getting arrested for. Why?"

Jace looked up. "Mind if I join you?"

Saint looked at Jace quizzically. "You want to come? Why?"

Jace shrugged. "I don't know. To learn, I guess. Show support for trying to get better policies."

"Oh." It was Saint's turn to shrug. "Yeah, I guess we can both go. It's probably going to be boring."

Jace chuckled. "Not nearly as boring as a Bathwater meeting." He glanced at Saint, hoping that would change his mind about going to one.

"Nice try. Come on, I'm parked right over there."

They walked through the grass toward a beat-up Jeep. Saint looked straight ahead with his usual serious expression. "You know you're in way over your head, don't you?"

"You mean, the website?" said Jace.

"Yup."

"I thought it was going pretty well."

Saint chuckled. "The click-and-drag tool you're using isn't going to cut it. With what you're trying to do, you need to move to a real development platform."

"Oh." Jace sighed. "Maybe I'll have to make it my senior project."

Saint glanced over. "Or...you could get some more help."

Jace perked up. "You would?"

"I can handle the coding. At least most of it. But you also need a designer. And that's not me."

"I've been playing with the themes. I think it looks pretty good."

"No, it doesn't," chuckled Saint.

"You've been logging on?"

"Yeah. Now and then. But I shouldn't. Your progress is depressing. Anyway, my friend Transcendence would do it."

Jace raised an eyebrow. "Transcendence? Really? Is this a guy or girl?"

"Girl. She's really good. And your content isn't bad so far, but the organization is a little scattered. And it looks like you need another English class. I have someone else in mind for that part. And you've got a mountain of data entry ahead of you."

Jace stopped. "Are these Zeroes?"

Saint nodded.

"Why would they help a Bathwater Brigade guy?"

Saint laughed. "They wouldn't. That's why I didn't tell them about you."

"You've already talked about it, then?"

"They think it's all my idea. We talked about it at that meeting, after you ran away like a scared kitten. Anyway, I asked if anyone was interested in helping."

They resumed their walk to the parking lot, slower this time.

"And they all jumped up to help?"

"No, a lot of them didn't want anything to do with it. They saw that it could help the police, too. But some of them were interested. Not just in helping arrests be safer for everyone but they liked the idea of having an easy way to look at policies, and to pick out the bad ones we want to have changed." Saint looked at him. "You going to faint? Zero Supremacy isn't just about protests, Jace."

When they reached the Jeep, Jace paused. "I like the direction here, but I have one more question. What do *I* do?"

"Besides helping me with the coding? This is still your thing. You get to direct it and come up with the content. Unless you have a stupid idea, and then I'll override you. You'll probably have to get used to that, actually. And let me be the one to deal with the others. But you're the man with the vision." Saint cleared his throat. "And I think it's a solid one."

Jace smiled satisfactorily as they climbed into the Jeep. "So what's next?"

"I'll let you know when the new environment is ready. I'm thinking we'll start with a Django backend."

Saint noisily shifted the Jeep into reverse, and they jerked out of the parking spot. "You really are an idiot, Jace," he said.

"What for?"

"If I wanted to bring other Zeroes with me tonight, I would have had them come about thirty minutes after me."

Jace cleared his throat, gripped the handle above the door, and tried not to smile.

CHAPTER THIRTY-SIX

THE NEXT MORNING, Jace met Rob, India, and Eli on the grass across the street from the courthouse. Rob had texted Jace last night to say that the trial was over. Now they waited with about two hundred other people for the verdict to be announced. Jace couldn't remember the last time he'd seen Rob in long pants.

There were no Zeroes, at least, none in the official red shirts. Maybe their leaders were waiting to see if they should work them up into an angry mob or a celebratory one. Or maybe they'd just given up since the facts of the case had all fallen on Gina's side.

"What are those?" Jace asked.

Rob held a stack of paper to his side. He and Eli exchanged glances.

Jace took one. It was the flier from the cupcake table—with some modifications. "Rob? I told you Mari said no, right?"

"Don't worry," Rob said. "It's not the same flier anymore. We changed it. I even had some help."

Instead of *America and Race*, the title was now *Cops aren't Racist*. Someone had cut strips of paper to replace portions of the text and then made photocopies. The fonts didn't match. Rob had inserted race statistics about police interactions and included some of the other points he had made that day, such as whites being lynched, and the first American slave owner being a black man.

Jace held the flier to his side, annoyed. "I guess it's not the same flier, but...feels kind of lazy."

Eli smiled. "These did some good, I think. We handed out a lot of them."

A man standing next to them looked up from his phone and threw his fist into the air. "Acquitted!"

Cheers erupted. India jumped and hugged Rob. He smiled wide—not his usual easy grin, but a look of deep satisfaction. Eli and Jace congratulated each other and slapped Rob on the back. After a minute, the noise died down again.

"What do we do now?" asked Eli.

"One thing left," said Rob. "We wait for her to come out. For a lot of us, this is our only chance to show her we've got her back."

Rob texted his family the news, and then watched the courthouse, tapping a rhythm on his pant leg. Occasionally, the horn of a passing car lightly honked, and some people in the crowd would cheer and wave back.

One car, however, slowed down. Someone in the back yelled, "She's a racist!" through an open window before the car peeled away.

"This isn't Pauliston!" someone yelled at the retreating vehicle. "Read the facts!"

Jace's phone buzzed. It was Mari. He cleared his throat. "Hey."

"Jace, do you have a minute?"

"Sure." He covered his other ear and walked a few paces away from the noise. "Just out here waiting for Gina Lambson."

"You're there at the courthouse? How is it going?"

"Acquitted."

"Wonderful! I thought that's how it would turn out."

"So what's up?" Jace asked.

"Well, I'm here with Amber. She's a little upset."

"About me?"

"No, no. Nothing like that."

"Good. How can I help?"

"You know she's on the gymnastics team, right?" Mari said. "In the off season, they teach gymnastics to kids. Well, the person in charge is telling Amber that she can't teach."

Jace had absolutely no idea why she was telling him this. "Okay..." he trailed off.

"Amber doesn't have a clue why. She asked a lot of questions, and the only thing she could find out is that an administrator named Janet Thompson has something to do with it. So, here's our question. Is that the same woman that had you do campus service? The one you thought didn't like the Bathwater Brigade?"

Jace shook his head and groaned. "Yeah, that's her. She sent my band director a letter, and that's when he decided to put my scholarship in question."

"Do you know what the letter said?"

"No idea. I just assumed she let all my professors know that I was doing campus service. Strange that she would mention the Bathwater connection in the letter, come to think of it."

It sounded like Mari was talking to Amber.

"Wait," Jace said. "You think she's going after Amber just because she's in the Brigade?"

"I mean, Kendric had something weird like this happen too, at the end of last semester." She sighed. "But no, I don't think it's connected. That would be crazy and administrators wouldn't do that. It's probably just a coincidence. Thanks, Jace."

He put his phone away and walked back to his friends, his brows drawn together. Was Janet actually going after them? Who would be next? His glance met Eli's, and Jace's expression changed to a friendly smile.

"Are we done fighting Zeroes, now?" asked Eli.

Rob shook his head. "I'm just getting started. You guys don't have to join me if you don't want to."

India scrunched up her nose. "Give me a few days to think about it."

"What else is there to do?" asked Jace. "It's not like they will keep harassing Gina. Didn't you say she's leaving the state?"

"Jace," said Rob. "She's leaving the state *because* Zero Supremacy is harassing her. It will probably get even worse now."

"Oh."

"I feel so bad for her," said India.

Rob shook his head. "Let's just hope the Hobbs family doesn't bring a civil lawsuit."

"Is it partly revenge, then?" asked Eli. "You going after the Zeroes some more?"

"Guys, think about it," Rob said. "Zero Supremacy is growing. They aren't going to stop. They'll find something else to riot about and end up fighting the police again in the streets."

Eli nodded. "You're right. This was just one battle in the war. I'm in."

Jace wondered whether Danica knew of Eli's pastime as a Zero fighter. He sighed. "I'm just not interested in fighting with the Zeroes."

"Don't blame you," said Rob, with a touch of sarcasm. "Some people are just scared."

"It's not that I'm afraid to stand up to them," Jace said. "I just think there are better ways to go about it."

"By ignoring them?" Rob shook his head. "We can't. They're dangerous and getting more powerful."

"You could just let the police deal with them," said India.

"When I'm a sergeant," said Rob, "I'll change tactics. But I'm not part of the force yet, so I have to use the tools I have right now."

"Rob, look" said Jace. "They're growing because of the ideas they have. I'm just saying I think we need to take on the ideas instead of the people."

"I thought that's what we were doing."

The crowd hushed. Jace looked to the courthouse. Three security guards exited the front door. Then, at their signal, four men and three women in business suits followed and descended the steps. One of the women wore a gray suit. She was tall, and her blond hair was pinned back. Jace recognized her from the photos in the news.

"There she is," someone whispered. Every eye was on Gina Lambson. News cameras and still photographers followed her. The crowd was silent.

Gina stopped and faced the crowd. Jace was too far away to see her expression, but he didn't sense jubilation. She slowly turned, taking in the crowd across the street. She didn't wave or call out, but somehow he knew that she was thanking them for their support.

Jace glanced at Rob. He stood at attention, his feet square, arms straight at his side, and his jaw firm. He had removed his sunglasses. Jace had imagined there would be cheers or, at the very least, some waves. But this quiet reverence for one of New Brig's civil servants was far more powerful. He blinked away a tear.

Gina gave a subtle nod, and the clack of her high heels echoed as the group continued to a pair of SUVs waiting at the side of the courthouse. After the vehicles left, the crowd began to break up.

"She was a victim, too," said India softly.

Rob's gaze remained where the vehicles had been. "That. Right there. *That* was worth all of it."

CHAPTER THIRTY-SEVEN

ON THE DAY of the beach party, Jace met Rob and India in the parking lot and drove together to Stoddard Hall. Mari sat on the steps of her dorm next to a small bag and a square pan of seven-layer dip. She wore a floral sun dress and a straw-colored summer hat. Her elbows were propped on her knees, and her chin rested lightly on her fists. If Jace had been alone, he would have let out a low whistle.

She smiled and waved to Rob and India in the back seat as Jace put the car in park and stepped out.

"Hey." Jace returned the smile. "Still good with coming?"

She turned her head, her eyes barely visible beneath the brim of her hat, and smiled. "Stop worrying, Jace. I wouldn't be here if I wasn't." She stood and handed Jace her bag and then walked to the car. "Hi guys." She slid into the front seat with the dip on her lap, while Jace put her bag in the trunk.

India and Mari complimented each other on their hair and outfits while Jace started the car and left campus.

They stopped at Bale's Grocery Store on their way out of town. Jace grabbed chips to go with Mari's dip. Mari insisted on buying flowers for Mrs. Hughes, and Rob bought a large soda for the road.

Back on the highway, Rob said, "Hey, Jace. Did you check the milk for freshness?"

Jace looked in the rear-view mirror and grinned.

Mari turned and exchanged looks with India.

Rob chuckled. "We used to take a gallon of milk at Mr. Muller's store and stash it behind stuff that isn't bought very often. Then, a few days later, after the milk had separated and it was completely disgusting, we'd come back and return it to the refrigerated section with the rest of the milk. We'd hang out and watch the reaction of the shoppers. They'd just stare, wondering why the grocery store thought to put out a jug of milk that bad."

"That's awful!" Mari said.

"It's like stealing," said India.

"I think the word you're looking for is 'hilarious'," said Rob. "We never took anything. Besides, Mr. Muller could afford to lose a few gallons of milk. You should have seen his Porsche."

"I see," said Mari. She turned, folded her arms, and glared at the white painted fences lining the road.

Jace looked at Rob in the rear-view mirror. Rob raised his eyebrows and whistled silently.

"Did you work at a grocery store or something?" Jace said to Mari.

"No, I'm fine," she said. "Just touched a nerve, I guess."

India nudged Rob, who shrugged and muttered, "Sorry."

Mari chuckled. "No, you're good. It's about my aunt."

"Tell us about her," said India.

Mari turned sideways in her seat. "Her name is Yanira, but everyone calls her Yanni. She immigrated with her dad from Guatemala as a little girl. They were dirt poor, but she worked hard at school and earned money at a day care center. Eventually got her fashion degree."

"That's great," said India.

"She *adored* clothes, and she loved movies. She wanted to make costumes, so she got a job at a movie studio."

"Have I seen her costumes in any movies?" asked Rob.

"I guarantee it," Mari said. "She mostly made dresses and women's costumes, though."

"Oh."

"Anyway, instead of buying a nice car and going out with her friends every night, she saved up her money for a few years and started her own business from her apartment. She spent every weekend at garage sales looking for cool, old things to wear. I *loved* looking through the racks that were crowded into her living room, and sometimes she'd let me try something on."

"That is so fun," said India.

"She put almost all of the profits back into the business, hired a few seamstresses looking for work, and eventually grew it into a large company. Even the big studios started using her. Remember the movie *Queen of Prussia*? It won lots of awards." Mari showed them a photo on her phone of her younger self in a long gown with deep blues and purples and shimmering gold.

"Wow!" said India. Jace was enjoying the story but wondered how on earth this would tie into grocery store milk.

"She treated her employees really well. They loved her. And she paid them more than they would get at the studios."

"Classic success story," said Rob. "Awesome."

"Well, sort of. A few employees became combative, and they demanded raises and extra benefits. They had no idea how hard she worked for them. They convinced others that they were being taken advantage of, and that since my Aunt Yanni had finally bought a nice house, it was supposedly this huge injustice—that the employees were doing the real work, and she was just taking all the profits for herself. It was just so crazy having someone come along saying they knew what to do with her own profit better than she did. In some ways, many of them began to treat her badly just because she had become a little wealthy."

And there it was. Jace looked at Rob in the mirror. Rob grimaced.

"Ugh," said India. "She didn't *take* the money—she *earned* it. And it's not like anyone was forcing them to work there. They could start their own business and run it however they like."

"Exactly!" Mari held a palm up. "She even offered free classes after work on how to start a business. There were only a few people who attended. And even then, most would stop coming after they saw how much sacrifice and risk it takes."

"I'm not doing that," said Rob. "I'll stick with a paycheck."

"She tried to keep them happy, but they kept demanding more. They lost the team feeling, and she couldn't figure out how to get it back. She eventually sold the business she loved."

"That's so sad," said India.

Jace shook his head. "What can you do?"

"I did something," Mari said.

"Of course, you did."

"I looked up some email addresses of her top employees and sent them a long email. Didn't do any good, of course. But I asked them to tell me precisely when their boss changed from good to bad."

"What do you mean?" asked Jace.

Mari shifted in her seat. "She's a poor immigrant girl from Guatemala. She comes here and works hard. We're all rooting for her, right?"

They nodded.

"But years later, some people seem to hate her. Was it because she became successful and finally bought some nice things? I mean, I'm looking at the timeline, wondering when she supposedly turned into someone we shouldn't like, someone we should stop cheering for."

Jace nodded. "It seems like the poor would be worse off if we didn't have rich people around. Someone to build and hire and invest."

"Why does that person have to be loaded, though?" asked Rob.

"Think about what you just said, Rob. Investing and hiring takes money. By definition."

"I know that. But I guess...it seems weird to tell a poor guy he has to have a rich guy around. You know? Why can't a poor person make the world awesome, too?"

Mari looked at Rob and smiled. "First of all, of *course* poor people make the world great. You don't have to be rich to have an amazing life or to make an impact. Some of the most influential figures in history were never rich at any point in their lives, and some never even escaped poverty."

Rob nodded.

"But were you asleep during the story of my aunt? She was penniless at first, and she did all of those things—invested, built a business, and hired people. And her story isn't special. Poor people become rich all the time. Especially in America."

Mari faced forward again and rested her head back on her seat. "Some people hate the rich, and others tolerate them. But from what I've seen, we just might want to thank them."

There was silence except for the drone of the engine. Jace made a mental note: when Mari's around, don't boast of pranks that cost people money—even rich people. He sighed, knowing he wouldn't be pulling those kinds of pranks anymore, either. He looked at Rob in the rear-view mirror, who was apparently thinking the same thing.

"All right," said Rob reluctantly. "I'll send Mr. Muller twenty bucks for the milk."

The others laughed.

"Together we'll make it forty," said Jace. Mari patted his arm.

They arrived at India's grandma's house as the sun started its downward turn in the sky. Light sand collected at the edges of the winding drive-way. Black iron fixtures and railings adorned tall, white stucco walls. Well-kept lawns covered the grounds, and fresh mulch and trim rose bushes proudly guarded the perimeter. The roof line of the entryway was reminiscent of the Alamo.

India opened the door without knocking and invited them inside. "You can keep your shoes on."

As majestic as it was on the outside, Jace's jaw dropped when they went in, and he suddenly felt small. Huge ornate rugs covered dark hardwood floors. Blue-gray walls rose at least sixteen feet to meet the white ceiling. Clear glass walled the entire south side. In what appeared to be the central area of the house, wide steps like risers surrounded couches and chairs which circled a ten-foot grand piano.

"Woah." Mari stood at the window. They were about fifty feet higher and one hundred yards from the shore. Jace would have been satisfied if today's plans were nothing more than sitting at the great windows and watching the ocean waves.

Jace leaned over to Mari. "Thought it would be bigger," he whispered. "Good starter home, I guess."

"India!" A thin, old woman whirled in and embraced her granddaughter. She had long, wispy white hair. The evidence of a lifetime of smiles was evident in the wrinkles on her kind, soft face. Hoops looped through both ears, rings decorated both hands, and she wore multiple necklaces and bracelets.

Mrs. Hughes put her hands on India's shoulders. "So glad to see you, hon. Who are your friends?"

India introduced each of them and made special mention of the band instrument that Jace played. Mrs. Hughes apparently knew Rob well and gave him a hug.

"I've worked on your building," Jace offered. "It's very nice." Mrs. Hughes raised her eyebrows in question. "The fine arts one at Cale University," Jace added.

"Oh yes, that one. Construction work?"

"No. Well, kind of." He cleared his throat. "Door maintenance."

She expressed genuine gratitude for his work. Jace wished he hadn't mentioned it.

"I'm happy to meet you all," said Mrs. Hughes. "The others are out back already." The way she said "out back" made it sound like they were in the yard on the swing set instead of at a private beach on the Gulf of Mexico.

"Come on," said India. The friends followed her through a long hallway, down a staircase, and out the back door.

The cool ocean breeze and the sound of the waves sent a shot of anticipation through Jace. Eli and Danica were there, along with six others, all friends from band.

Rob and India walked down to the shore and splashed each other as the water swirled around their ankles. Jace and Mari sat in Adirondack chairs higher on the beach under some umbrellas. Jace teasingly challenged Mari to come up with a beach-related Bathwater analogy on the spot. She delivered, of course.

They sat for a while and listened to the waves and the seagulls. Mari leaned back in her chair, her hands folded on her midsection. Strands of hair danced over her cheek and neck.

"You're not coming back, are you?"

Jace sighed and watched a pelican glide high above the shoreline. "I'd like to." He breathed in the salty sea air. "I really would."

"Have you looked at other scholarships? Grants?"

"Yeah. Nothing promising."

She studied him from behind her sunglasses. Then she turned her head and tucked her hair behind her ears. Jace considered telling Mari about Saint's upcoming visit—he didn't like keeping secrets—but he decided against it. Why ruin the party? Instead, he simply said, "You might see me there sooner than you think."

"It's dangerous to set you out into the world before you've had the last dojo lesson," Mari said. A corner of her mouth lifted.

"Don't you watch movies?" said Jace. "The hero *never* completes the training. They get about seventy-five percent done, and that's apparently enough to save the world."

"I guess you don't need it, then, Spider-Man."

"Well, I bet Kline would be okay if I had a tutor."

"I might be able to arrange for one." Then she grinned. "I'll see if Dylan has an opening."

CHAPTER THIRTY-EIGHT

ONCE EVERYONE HAD ARRIVED, Mrs. Hughes gathered everyone into the great room. The guests sat on the surrounding furniture. Leaning on her grand piano, she announced that it was tradition to have some live music before dinner. Performed by them.

Mari's eyes grew wide. "Jace," she whispered, "I don't..."

India leaned over and whispered, "You don't have to do anything." Mari looked relieved.

Jace noticed cases of musical instruments in the corner, including a trombone. Maybe he could play something after all? Or maybe he'd just take India up on her offer not to perform.

At India's request, Mrs. Hughes launched into the Bumblebee Boogie on the piano with frenzied precision. She beamed as she bowed to the cheers that followed.

A few others played songs on the piano, and India of course played her clarinet. An impromptu quartet played Fantasia in G Major, which Mrs. Hughes happened to have the music for. The soft strains filled the home with a sweet inspiration to greatness. Jace's skin tingled like it always did when the music became greater than the sum of its notes. He glanced at Mari. She held a hand to her chest, the song clearly affecting her as well. There was a beat of silence when the music ended, then everyone jumped to their feet and gave the players a standing ovation.

Rob insisted that Jace play something and brought the trombone to him.

"You know I don't sight-read music very well," Jace whispered as he reluctantly assembled the instrument.

"I think there's something you *can* play," Rob said, flicking his eyebrows. "You know the one."

"Do it!" whispered Mari.

"All right," Jace said. Mari patted him on the back as he stood. "This is called *Road to Hell*. It's from the musical *Hadestown*."

Mrs. Hughes shifted and tilted her head.

Jace winked at Mari and began playing a fast-paced, bluesy tune while Rob slapped the risers with his palm and fist to the beat. Soon, the rest were swaying and clapping.

After listening for a few bars, Mrs. Hughes took her place at the grand piano. She added an improvised accompaniment—a mix of rock and ragtime. Jace closed his eyes, losing himself in the music.

At his signal, they landed a big final chord together. To the applause of everyone, Jace bowed and gestured to Rob and Mrs. Hughes. Then he took his seat next to Mari.

She shifted closer, put an arm around his back, and gave him a squeeze. "That was amazing!" Jace smiled and turned back to watch the next performance, but he felt her thoughtful gaze linger on him, and he wondered what she was thinking.

Young men with white aprons served a steak dinner on the outdoor patio. The sun had set, and strands of globe lights crisscrossed above them, casting a warm, dim light. Even more than the conversation, Jace relished the lulls where he could hear the rolling waves.

"India has been telling me about this club you have at Cale," said Mrs. Hughes. "The Bathwater Brigand, was it?"

"Brigade," India said.

"That's right. Which of you are associated with this club?"

Mari raised her hand, followed by Jace, Danica, and Eli.

"Wonderful. I want to make sure I understand. What would you say the goal of this group is, exactly?"

Danica explained the connection to throwing the baby out with the bathwater.

Mrs. Hughes frowned.

"Think of driving a car on the freeway," Mari said. "You notice you're not in the lane you want to be in, and you want to change. If you crank the wheel too hard, you could roll the car."

"I see," said Mrs. Hughes. "And you are okay with the car changing lanes, but you want to make sure it happens mindfully and safely." She folded her hands together and gazed at the roofline behind Mari. "Interesting."

"We meet every week," offered Eli. "We even have a soda fridge."

Mrs. Hughes took a sip of wine and tapped her glass with her finger. "I have a question for you. India might have mentioned that I've been a leading feminist for longer than twice your lifetimes. I invite you to give this the Bathwater treatment. Point out the baby, if you will, being thrown out. The dangers of feminism."

There was an awkward silence. Mari finally spoke. "Yes. I think there are some pitfalls to be careful of."

"Actually," Mrs. Hughes interrupted, "I would like to hear from the white male among your group here tonight, if that's all right. Jace the trombonist, please."

Jace cleared his throat. "Feminism."

"Yes."

Still holding his fork and steak knife, he glanced at Mari. Her eyes seemed to plead with him, but what she wanted, he had absolutely no clue. No matter what happened next, he was sure he'd get a lecture from her later.

"One of the pitfalls," he hedged again.

Mrs. Hughes nodded.

Jace looked at his fork, which held a large piece of steak. He put it in his mouth and began to chew, hoping the conversation would move on, but only the distant ocean waves broke the silence. He glanced up. All eyes were on him. He forced himself to swallow his bite.

His mind raced. He literally had nothing. This simply wasn't a topic that he had ever paid much attention to. Definitely not enough to make a spur-of-the-moment presentation to a leading feminist. He tried to think of news stories, high school classes, overheard conversations...anything. Maybe he could bring up the pay gap. Or how he didn't think labeling masculinity as toxic was fair. Was abortion fair game?

Glancing at Mari again, his mind went back to their hike, when she had assured him that he could have an intelligent conversation. He only had to start with what he knew.

What do you know about feminism, Jace? he thought to himself. *What do you* really *know?*

Jace finally cleared his throat. Mrs. Hughes raised an eyebrow.

"I have a pitfall for you."

Mari looked up.

"Yes?" said Mrs. Hughes, smiling a little. She put her elbows on the table and gazed intently at him.

"We can't afford to lose respect. And equality."

"For women?" Mrs. Hughes looked confused.

"Yes."

She laughed. "I think you have it backwards, Jace. Gaining respect for women is the whole point of the movement."

"Just hear me out," he said.

Mrs. Hughes nodded.

Jace took a steadying breath. "Let me tell you a little about my mom. She would read and sing to me, my brother, and my two sisters. She was gentle most of the time, but stern when she needed to be."

Mrs. Hughes' smile softened.

"She had a career. Still does. She's a proud junior high vice principal. Her career was important to her, but she chose me—us—over that for a while.

"Some would say that a stay-at-home mom is a maid of the house. But she wasn't the maid. She was the queen. Regal, commanding, and feminine." Jace looked Mrs. Hughes in the eye. "Some would say she stayed home because her husband demanded it of her. But she didn't. She made a brave, intentional sacrifice for us.

"She had coworkers and friends who made career and family choices that were very different than hers. I never heard her speak down to them or bad about them. She supported their right to choose whatever path they felt was best."

Jace pointed his finger on the white tablecloth. "But this is what I mean by respect and equality. When she announced that she was planning to focus on motherhood for a while, most of her coworkers said she was throwing her career away. They ridiculed her, actually."

Jace leaned back in his seat. "So, I guess, like pretty much everyone else, I want women to have all the opportunities in the world. Let's go ahead and throw out the dirty bathwater of discrimination and harmful stereotypes and all that. But I hope we can still respect *all* choices women make for themselves. Even if it's not the popular one." He shrugged, and added, "At least, that's how it seems to me, at the moment."

Mrs. Hughes smiled and stood. She walked around the table to Jace and embraced him. "Your mom shaped an amazing young man."

Mari smiled and mouthed "good job," her eyes misty. She leaned over moments later and whispered, "I noticed your Benjamin Franklin moment at the end. Nice touch!"

It was after ten o'clock when they finally drove away. Mrs. Hughes had thanked them for coming and had given each guest a parting gift—a metronome and some chocolates.

Mari examined the metronome box after clicking her seat belt. "Can you use two of these?" she asked Jace.

"Actually, what if I put a bow on it and set it on Dr. Kline's desk?" He grinned. "I'll forge a note from the orchestra director saying that Kline should work on his rhythm."

Rob yawned. "I have to say, the food was great, but my favorite part was Jace's touching tribute to his mother."

"Shut up, Rob."

He snickered. "I thought you were going to keep on chewing until it was time to leave."

India giggled.

Mari shook her head. "Could you have done better in that situation, Rob?"

"Hey, I'm not a bathwater guy," Rob said. "I prefer showers, actually."

No one spoke for a long time. Mari tilted her seat back and closed her eyes. Traffic was sparse, and the surroundings were pitch black other than the highway's reflectors and bright yellow and white stripes on the road. Jace looked in the rear-view mirror. India's face reflected the glow from her phone. Rob was asleep, head against the window with his mouth wide open.

Between glances at the road, Jace found a dry, folded beach towel and carefully draped it across Mari. She snuggled into it. He smiled.

"I hope you change your mind about the Brigade," Mari said sleepily. Her voice drifted off. "We need you."

Jace sighed. He quietly pulled earphones from his glove compartment, started *Road to Hell* on his phone, and tapped his finger on the steering wheel to the beat as they sped back toward New Brig.

CHAPTER THIRTY-NINE

IT WAS NEARLY 1 A.M. when Jace turned off the highway toward Cale. India and Rob began to gather their things in the back seat.

They dropped India off at an old house near campus where she lived with five roommates. When they stopped at Mari's dorm, Jace helped her get her things from the trunk and walked her to the door where she gave him a quick, sleepy hug.

Exhaustion pressed down on Jace as he drove to the parking lot in front of his dorm. He pulled in next to Rob's car. A tree swayed in the breeze, and the nearby lamppost cast fluid shadows on the hood of the car.

"You have everything?" Jace asked.

"I think so." Rob gathered his duffel bag and earphones from the back seat. "Let's see. Remind me. Is this mine or yours?"

Jace turned to see Rob holding Saint's Zero Supremacy hoodie. A burning intensity flared in Rob's eyes as he stared back.

Jace gave a nervous smile and held up a finger. He opened his mouth, but no words came. He faced forward, turned off the car, and let out a deep breath.

"Jace." Rob threw the hoodie onto the floor. "What the—"

"So, you remember that Saint guy?"

Rob glared at Jace through the rear-view mirror.

"Anyway, he found out about the Bathwater Brigade. They're meeting underground, you know? Because of the Zeroes."

"So?" Impatience was ripe in his voice.

"The only way I could keep him from bringing a mob to a Bathwater meeting was if I brought him to one. Well, that would have been a disaster too. I've already caused so much trouble for those guys. I wanted to buy some time so I could figure out a way to get him to back off completely."

Rob mockingly gestured outward. "So...logically, you became a Zero Supremacist."

"No! Of course not. I'm not one of them. I just went to one of their meetings."

Rob folded his arms. "And picked up a souvenir at the merch table."

"It's not mine, Rob. I borrowed it so they wouldn't recognize me as the trombone guy from the operation."

Rob leaned forward and shook his head. "How could you do that, Jace? Do you know what would happen if I told my family that I've been hanging around a guy who goes to Zero Supremacy meetings and wears a matching hoodie? Not to mention their shock to find out it was *Jace*!"

Jace stared at the dashboard and frowned. "Zeroes have a lot of the same goals as you."

After a pause, Rob threw the hoodie down on the seat as he left the vehicle and slammed the door behind. Jace clapped his hand on his forehead and scrubbed it down his face. He jumped from the car and followed after his friend.

"Rob. Hang on."

Rob stopped. "Jace! Listen to yourself. Were you there at Victor square? Did you hear them? They are *one hundred percent* against people like us. Well, people like me and my brother and my dad. We're the ones who suit up and risk our lives. For them. The cops at these rallies aren't just there to keep property and other people safe from the Zeroes. They're there to protect the Zeroes, too. Their constitutional right to protest."

Rob's volume rose. "They want us dead! Didn't you hear them? And now you're hanging out with them! And it's not just that you're spending time with someone who happens to be a Zero—you're actually going to their meetings! And dressing like them!" He dropped his duffel bag and took a calming breath. "Jace, I would never do something like this to you."

"I get it. I really do. But you're looking at the surface. Yeah, they're way off base on a lot of it. But look at their deeper goal. They want people to be safe and happy. People like Stephen Hobbs and his family."

"How do you know that's their goal?" asked Rob. "Maybe that's part of it, but all they talk about is that they want to get rid of the police."

Jace cleared his throat. "That's fair. And I don't know all of them—"

"Just wait," Rob snapped. "Looks like you will by the end of the semester."

"Hang on. I only got to know one of them. Maybe the leaders and the others really are anti-police at their core. But all Saint wants is justice. He wants his black friends to be safe. Yes, he's buying into the crap that the police are the problem, but I honestly believe he's rethinking that right now. He said something at the press conference—"

Rob shook his head. "What press conference?"

Jace shrugged. "The New Brig police were announcing some things that went wrong with Hobbs."

"So, you went to another meeting that was anti-police with a Zero Supremacist."

"Not anti-police. The police were the ones talking."

"Whatever. And you went there with a Zero. So that he wouldn't come to a Bathwater meeting or something?"

"Well, no." Jace looked down. "He was going and I kind of invited myself along."

"Wow." Rob laughed disdainfully. "You're all in, aren't you? This is going way beyond tolerating some piece of crap at community service."

"We don't always have to pick a side, Rob. A team. I'm not siding with them."

"And you're clearly not siding with me."

"Yes, I am!" Jace stammered. "I've got your back. I'm pro-police, Rob. For the most part. You can agree with one thing that someone says without joining their team."

Rob folded his arms again. "Do you think Gina should have shot Stephen Hobbs?"

Jace hesitated. "At the moment that he was charging her—"

"It's a yes or no question."

"Well, it's actually not," said Jace. "Hear me out."

"Yes, it is!" yelled Rob. "I can't believe this."

Rob pulled his wallet from his pocket.

"What are you doing?" asked Jace.

"Here." Rob held up a twenty-dollar bill. "This is for the gas."

"Isn't that for Mr. Muller's milk?" Jace asked, trying to lighten the mood. When Rob didn't smile, Jace sighed. "You don't need to pay me for gas."

Rob held it out forcefully, and Jace reluctantly accepted. Then Rob held up another one. "And this is for driving." Rob pushed the bill into Jace's hand, picked up his bag, and stomped past his car.

"You're *walking* home, then?" asked Jace.

Rob didn't answer.

"You may not know this," Jace called out, "but friends don't pay each other for driving."

Rob walked on. "You're right," he shouted back. "They don't."

A lump settled in Jace's throat. He crumpled the bills in his fist, got back into the driver's seat, and slammed the door. He pounded the passenger seat twice with his fist, and then allowed his breathing to calm.

Jace opened the glove compartment and quietly flipped through the stack of papers inside. He stopped at a photograph, its corner torn, edges bent. Two boys stood with bike helmets askew, heads high, squinting in the sun. Each had an arm around the shoulder of the other with smiles as wide as Kansas.

He studied the photo for a time, and then dropped it to his lap. Jace stared at the tree's bare branches waving gracefully in the gentle breeze, and the corners of his mouth quivered downward. His mind drifted through a decade of memories as he watched a few of the remaining leaves tug loose and spin free into the night.

CHAPTER FORTY

"JACE."

He opened an eye to a sunlit dorm room. Sunday morning.

"Look at this," said Adam.

Jace groaned. "Another pro wrestling meme?"

"Oh, no. *You're* the star this time."

Jace leaned down from the top bunk and accepted Adam's phone. It was a news story from PAN 8 Houston. The headline read *White Students Crash Funeral of Black Man.*

"What funeral?" Jace asked, hoping he didn't already know.

"Just watch."

Jace tapped the video. It showed people outside, standing around. There were two pops like gunshots, and the camera panned up to a banner on the side of a building, confetti in the air.

Jace didn't recall the local station picking up the story. He paused the video, handed it back to Adam, and rolled over in bed. "Old news."

"It ran yesterday. My cousin lives in Victoria and she saw it. Since it mentions Cale, she asked if I knew anybody in the video. At the end it shows you sitting with some guy with blood on his face."

Jace sat up in bed. "All right. Don't spread it around." He jumped from the bunk and checked his phone. Two missed calls and a text, all from Mari.

Jace. Call me.

He slipped shoes onto his bare feet, hurried outside, and called. "Jace?"

"Hey Mari." He hoped she had called to chat about the beach party.

"Oh, Jace. You thought this would all be over after campus service."

He laughed nervously as he strolled around the back of the dorm building.

"Let me give you a link," she said.

Jace sighed. "I've seen it. Channel 8."

"Houston?"

"Yeah."

"No," Mari said. "This is a Dallas station."

Jace cleared his throat. "Two of them? Why would the news be picking this up? And so late. It wasn't that big a deal."

"Have you watched the video?" Mari asked.

"Some of it."

"Watch the entire thing."

"All right. I'll call you back."

Jace leaned against the shady side of the building and found the Houston story on his phone. The video began with two news anchors. One said that shocking video had emerged of white college students mocking a service put on for a black man who had been killed by a police officer. The other nodded, concerned. "Make up your mind," Jace muttered. "Was it a funeral or a service?"

Further down the page, Jace tapped a link to the full video, four minutes long.

It began with Stephen Hobbs' mother speaking. "My son wanted what was best for everyone, not just for him."

The video then cut to the banner, and the confetti floating down. The words on the banner had been blurred out, as if it had stated something offensive. Only the drawing of the handshake was clearly visible.

"What?" Jace straightened. "That's not how it happened! We didn't interrupt her speech. She didn't speak until later. Oh, crap."

It cut back to the mom. "We're going to honor him by making things better for everyone. We're going to cause change. My son was not perfect. But he was good."

Then Jace's sad trombone was heard.

Jace ran his fingers through his I-just-woke-up hair. "Are you serious?" he yelled.

Someone whose life wasn't imploding banged their fist against the window next to him, accompanied by a muffled, "shut up!"

Slowly walking away, he watched to the end. Jace and Eli appeared, sitting on the edge of the big cement planter box, and talking with the security guard. Eli held a cloth to his temple, and Jace was relieved to see that his hat covered most of his face. He was surprised that Adam had known it was him, actually.

Jace winced. "Please don't say it. Please don't say it." Then he watched as Eli very clearly stated, "We're the Bathwater Band." Jace groaned. He called Mari.

"Hi."

"I'm sorry. About what Eli said, about all of it. Maybe I can give the stations a call and tell them the Zeroes edited it to make us look bad. I have video somewhere that I can send them. And I can tell them that this had nothing to do with the Bathwater Brigade."

Mari said nothing.

"That was crap." Jace put a hand to his forehead. "They didn't show the chants, the anger against the police. Just a quiet eulogy."

"I'd like to see what T.J. thinks."

He could hear Mari typing.

"Still there?" he asked.

"Um, Jace? The story just got picked up by the Simmons Weekly."

"You mean..."

"It's gone national."

Jace only blinked.

"I'm calling T.J." She hung up.

Jace leaned on the white downspout on the corner of the building.

He looked at the account that posted the video. *ZeroSupremacyHouston.* "Of course."

He clenched his fist.

"Saint."

CHAPTER FORTY-ONE

JACE CONSTANTLY CHECKED his laptop that day. The views surpassed 250,000, and the search results for "Cale students black funeral" steadily grew.

Eli had sent a group message to Jace and Rob. He linked to one of the stories, and all three of them complained about the edited video and the skewed reporting. Jace and Rob never addressed each other directly.

Jace tried to focus on porting over the website content to the new location Saint and his friends had built. It had been going slower than he had hoped. In fact, he was beginning to wonder if Saint was simply keeping Jace preoccupied with the website while Zero Supremacy worked to take down the Bathwater Brigade. Or he was taking over the project in order to sabotage the whole thing, or turn it into the opposite of what Jace wanted. Jace didn't have it all worked out in his mind yet, but he knew Saint had to be involved, and that he had been played.

Monday evening, Jace leaned against the brick wall of the geology building. A treeless lawn sprawled to the west, which gave a wide panorama of the pink and orange clouds, and a prime view of the greenhouse entrance.

He watched as T.J. unlocked the door and went inside, a case of Mountain Dew on his shoulder. Jace shifted his weight but remained where he was.

Dylan and Amber entered the greenhouse next.

Jace was sick about what might happen to the Brigade, and he knew Mari was worried, too. She'd given abrupt replies to his texts, and that day in class, she'd been friendly but distracted.

Whispers and glances had seemed to follow Jace all over campus. Twice he'd been asked whether he was the one in the video. They had listened to his honest reply but had no interest in hearing his explanation.

The calculus professor even began the class with a short, vague speech against racism and invited anyone who felt the need to hate or mock others to leave campus. Jace had simply looked down at his notebook.

He was glad that so far, he hadn't heard from his family about it. They'd find out eventually though. From the video alone, they would be so disappointed in him—and he wouldn't blame them. He considered being proactive about it and telling them first, so that they'd have his side of the story from the beginning.

Jace spotted a familiar, small silhouette striding near the corner of the greenhouse. He whistled loudly, and Saint crossed the lawn to meet him, holding a phone and a folded piece of paper.

"Let me guess," said Saint. "The real meeting isn't for another two weeks."

Jace tossed him a plastic grocery bag. Saint pulled out the Zero Supremacy hoodie and smiled.

"Are you breaking up with me?" he asked.

Jace stood upright and unfolded his arms. "Why did you do it?"

Saint paused and cocked his head. His smile faded. "Do what?"

Jace pushed him backwards. Saint stumbled, dropping the phone and paper. His glasses nearly fell off. He regained his balance.

Jace stepped forward. "Who made the video?"

Saint looked confused. "What do you mean?"

"The edited one. Of me and my friends at your protest."

"Oh, *that*," Saint swallowed, turning slightly, as if he might sprint away. "I...don't know who made it. Paladin texted it to us a few days ago. We thought it was funny. Are you on our group texts now or something?"

"It's all over the place," said Jace. "Even on the news."

"Wait. They posted it?" The surprise and consternation on Saint's face was genuine, and Jace wished he hadn't pushed him.

"All of this is really messing up my life, Saint. My scholarship. I'm even losing my friends. You guys are liars."

Saint looked Jace in the eye. "I don't lie."

Jace gestured with his phone. "Well, you didn't stop this lie from getting out."

Saint took a few heavy breaths, fixed his glasses, and held out his arms. "What am *I* supposed to do about it?" he said, louder than Jace had ever heard him speak. "I'm not one of the leaders. I don't know half the stuff they do until after."

Saint tucked the hoodie under his arm and put his hands in his pockets. "I joined the Zeroes because it looked like the right thing to do. Maybe it wasn't. I don't know. But I'm trying." He sniffed and cleared his throat.

Unsure of what to say, Jace simply watched.

"When you see your friends being hurt, you want to go defend them, you know?" Saint shrugged. "My friend's dad was beat up by the police when he was my age. Almost killed. He literally wasn't doing anything. They said he looked suspicious and it just kind of escalated. Then they tried to put him in handcuffs, and he freaked out. Couldn't help it. One of the cops wouldn't stop hitting him. You care about justice, right?"

Jace leaned against the brick wall again.

"I know people like you think stories like that are made up," Saint continued. "But this one wasn't. If it was you it happened to, I'd be standing up for you. So what makes you so much better than me? You say you're part of the Bathwater Brigade, so aren't you supposed to listen to other people? Be friends with people different from you? You're supposed to be masters at that sort of thing."

"How do you know all that?"

"Bathwater's website."

Jace cleared his throat. "To be fair, I never finished my training."

Saint turned and faced the fading sunlight. The outside lights were on, ready for their shift at illuminating this corner of campus.

"I don't know if they'll listen to me," Saint said, "but maybe I can talk to them about it. The video."

"I believe you," Jace said with a sigh. "It wasn't your fault."

Saint took his hand from his pocket and picked up his phone and paper.

"What's that?" asked Jace.

Saint unfolded it. "It's just...I don't know." He held it down to his side and shrugged. "I had an idea about the website layout."

"Hm?"

"I think we can simplify the top bar, how it's organized."

Saint reluctantly handed him the paper. The site had been getting cluttered with each new feature they added. He had penciled an idea for a new menu. The handwriting was awful, but Jace could tell Saint had put a lot of thought into it.

Jace pursed his lips and nodded. "This is good."

Saint checked his phone. "Well, the meeting's about to start."

"Should we get it over with?"

They walked toward the entrance together.

"We don't have to go, you know," said Jace, glancing at Saint. "You're not locked in or anything."

"We're going."

"To be honest, I don't think they'll want to see either of us. You're a sworn enemy to the Brigade, and I have a starring role in the video that might blow it all up for them."

Saint nodded. "That's about right."

"Going to put on your hoodie?" Jace asked. They both smiled.

"We should probably stash it in the bushes," Saint said.

"Hey," said Jace. "Sorry I pushed you back there."

Saint nodded again as they approached the doors.

CHAPTER FORTY-TWO

JACE ENTERED FIRST. T.J. was in his usual spot at the front of the room and saw him come in. "Jace! What's up, bud?"

Everyone turned. Jace gave them a nervous wave. Mari hopped up and down, clapping her hands. She flitted toward him, followed by Eli.

Jace sighed. "Hello, everyone. I brought someone."

Saint walked in.

Mari's face fell. She stopped and shot Jace a questioning look. Eli stopped, too, scratching his head. Thankfully, he didn't appear to recognize Saint from the scuffle at Victor Square.

Amber stood from her chair, hands on her hips. "We're not supposed to bring anyone new until the core members have voted."

Nobody moved.

T.J. stared at Saint, and Saint back at him. A curious smile grew under his beard. "Saint. Good to see you."

The air was thick with unanswered questions, but the group followed T.J.'s lead and treated Saint with forced politeness.

"Jace, can I talk to you for a minute?" Mari said. He followed her up the stairs and into the miniature forest. "What are you doing?"

Jace smiled nervously. "I know it's against the rules. But it was the best option."

"Explain."

Mari's glare caught Jace off-guard, and he laughed involuntarily.

"Do you think this is funny?"

"Sorry. That's just..." Jace cleared his throat. "It was either one Zero tonight or forty."

"What! He's a Zero?" Mari put her hands on top of her head. "There is a Zero Supremacist down there right now? At a Bathwater Brigade meeting? In our *headquarters*?"

Jace shrugged.

"Is this the guy you were doing that community service with? You...what? Got to be friends and...I don't understand." After Jace told her the full story, she frowned. "Why didn't you tell me?"

Jace shrugged. "I didn't want to disappoint you. I thought I could take care of it on my own."

"Well, obviously *that* didn't happen. It's like you tossed a live grenade down there."

She turned and put her hands on her head once again. "We're compromised. *Again*. What do we even *do*? Cancel the meeting. Get everything out of the greenhouse. Tonight. That is, if they don't all show up before we have the chance. Then...I don't even know. Spend the next couple of weeks trying to find somewhere else? If there *is* somewhere else."

"I'm not sure you need to do that," Jace said, hands in his pockets. "I doubt he's planning to tell the others."

"Why wouldn't he?"

"Well, at first Saint hated my guts. And yours. But tonight, I got the feeling that he wanted to come...for *him*. You know? To learn. I'm sure he won't admit it. It's just a lot of little things I've seen him say and do recently."

Mari paced, brushing past purple shrubs.

"Wasn't it you that told me that we should try to reason with anyone?" Jace asked. "Even a Zero?"

"Of course. But let's invite him to our secret meeting *after* we get to know his intentions and his character. Not as the first step! I don't think you realize how close we are to having to shut this all down for good." She gestured toward the stairs. "That, tonight...this might be it for us."

271

Jace held a hand to his chin and looked down at her shoes. She wasn't wrong. "Look," he said. "We have a Zero in the basement. We can either kick him out, which might backfire, or we can treat him like you guys treated me on *my* first day here. Give him the benefit of the doubt."

Mari rubbed her face. "I'm not comfortable with that," she said. "But that's probably the only thing that makes sense at this point. I'll go talk with T.J."

Downstairs, T.J. leaned casually against the wall as he talked with Saint. Saint glanced at Jace and raised his eyebrows.

Mari motioned for T.J. They spoke quietly at another end of the room, joined by Amber and Dylan. Jace watched as Amber went through the same emotions that Mari had. Saint remained where T.J. had left him and avoided eye contact with anyone. Jace stood awkwardly next to him, but neither spoke.

They all sat gingerly in their folding chairs like they might buckle. Saint found an empty seat between Amber and Danica. The Brigade members exchanged glances with each other, and Saint stared at the floor ahead of him. Dylan briefly widened his eyes at Jace, who shrugged in return. Danica coughed. It seemed no one knew how to proceed.

Except for T.J.

"All right," he announced in his usual voice. "Let's get started."

Mari exhaled, smiled slightly, and leaned over to Jace. "Good to have you back, even just for today," she whispered. "And even though you brought a time bomb."

Jace was glad to be back, even under these circumstances. It felt like he was home. He had pictured his arrival going much worse—even if Saint hadn't accompanied him. Jace was Trombone Boy, a star of the video that apparently made the Bathwater Brigade look like monsters.

Mari had once told him that the Brigade didn't distance from people because of their past—they were interested in who you are *now*. He had definitely hit a growth spurt in judgment the last few weeks. Not only that—his whole worldview was changing. It wasn't that he believed the opposite of what he thought before. It was more like he had been squinting and bumping into things his whole life, and he had finally been handed a pair of glasses.

"We'd like to welcome my old friend Saint to our meeting today," T.J. said, and smirked. "We might as well say it. He's a current member of Zero Supremacy."

Eli blinked, then turned to Saint. "You're switching sides, then?"

"Sides?" T.J. said, before Saint could speak. "Let's just call this an educational field trip. There are no sides here."

"Maybe he could belong to both," suggested Danica. "Why not? As long as he's not screaming or violent."

Saint raised an eyebrow.

"Is no one worried that he'll bring all his friends here?" Eli asked.

"That's not going to happen," T.J. said. "We've talked. I'll vouch for him. And the core just voted on it, anyway. He'll hang with us tonight."

Mari whispered, "T.J. locked the door, just in case we have more uninvited visitors."

"Wait," said Danica. "Was it *you* that wrote that message on the board?"

Saint smiled sheepishly.

"But..." she began. "You knew about this place for *weeks?*"

T.J. checked his watch. "We need to get started. You remember the rules we talked about, Saint?"

He nodded again.

The topic of the day was the border wall between the United States and Mexico. Dylan and Danica took the front. They were a little wary at first and repeatedly glanced at Saint. It didn't take long, though, before it felt like a normal meeting again.

As usual, both sides brought up excellent points, many of which had never occurred to Jace before. Dylan wanted them to be a welcoming nation, and to him, a giant fence didn't seem to fit.

Mari said that she and her immigrant family were in favor of a wall, which seemed to surprise most everyone there, as long as we had an open and welcoming immigration policy. And Danica illustrated what Jace found to be the most thought-provoking point of the night.

"Let's say you wake up in the middle of the night to screaming," she said, "and outside a guy is chasing Eli around your yard with a knife. What do you do?"

"Why me?" said Eli. Danica gave her classic, shy smile.

"Let Eli in!" said Dylan.

Danica nodded. "You open the door and save Eli. But once he's safely inside, what do you do?"

"Close the door?" said Jace.

Danica pointed to him and grinned. "Yes. Some of the people that are coming here are running from bad people. If it's easy for the bad guys to sneak across and find them, they might not see America as a safe place."

Saint nodded occasionally, and a smile crept to Jace's face more than once that meeting. He'd missed being with his friends, and the surprising excitement of exploring ideas in new ways.

As they were finishing, someone tried to open the door from the outside and then knocked. Jace stood and whipped around, his heart racing. "It's Kendric!" yelled a muffled voice. Dylan let him in.

"Jace thought you were an armed Zero Supremacy gang," Dylan said with a laugh. Saint grinned. Jace eventually joined in the laughter, and Eli patted him on the back.

Kendric remained serious. He marched up to T.J. and discussed something in urgent whispers, gesturing with the binder in his hand.

"I've got to be honest," Jace said to Mari, "I'm surprised you let either of us stay for the meeting."

Mari breathed deeply. "I'm glad you came." Then she raised an eyebrow. "You do things that make me wonder sometimes, but I see something in you that you probably don't see in yourself yet. I think you could help us make a difference at Cale."

Mari noticed that nobody was talking with Saint, so she crouched next to him and started to chat. Mari even laughed occasionally, and Saint smiled and nodded politely.

T.J. walked back to the group wearing Kendric's contagious frown. "May I have the attention of the Brigade? This will be our last meeting for a while."

There were a few gasps.

"How come?" asked Amber.

"Article Twelve," Kendric said.

"What?" Dylan said. "Are you serious?"

"What for?" said Mari as she returned to her seat.

T.J. shook his head. "We'll find out Wednesday. We're supposed to meet them at 2 P.M."

"Meet who?" asked Danica. "What's Article Twelve?"

"We're meeting the administration," said Kendric. "We're basically under investigation."

"For what?" she repeated.

"We don't know. They'll tell us in a few days."

Jace sat still. They all knew the reason, though they were too polite to say it. This was because of him. And technically Eli, though he apparently felt no responsibility for his part in the video.

"We can't meet when we're under investigation?" asked Eli.

Kendric nodded. "Right. Well, the core members still can, but we can't hold these meetings until we're cleared."

Eli looked at Danica and squeezed her hand. "How long will that last?"

Kendric shrugged. "I'm guessing these things take time."

"We're meeting in secret already," said Danica. "Why not just keep meeting? Who would find out?"

"No," said T.J., "that could make things worse. We've got to follow the rules."

Amber tilted her head in Saint's direction. "Should *he* be here for this?"

T.J. looked at Saint. "Not that we don't all have complete trust in you yet, but..."

Saint smiled and stood. "I get it." He cleared his throat. "Thanks for having me, guys." He walked out and quietly shut the door behind him. Amber listened at the door for a moment and then nodded and returned to her seat.

"So," said Dylan, "do you think we should clear everything out of the room? We don't want anything to happen to it."

T.J. shook his head. "I don't want to retreat anymore. Let's not abandon the only home we have." He sat in his chair, looking tired.

"We're coming with you Wednesday," Danica said. Eli squeezed her hand.

"Thanks," Kendric said. "But I think our chances are best if we stick to the core members. We'll let you know how it goes."

T.J. ended the meeting early, saying that he and Kendric had some planning to do.

As they left, Mari paused in the doorway and took in the room. Her eyes met Jace's, and she forced a smile. They climbed the stairs and started toward the dorms through the cool night air. The stars glimmered in the gaps between streetlights.

"Well, this stinks," Jace said.

"For sure."

"Anything I can do?"

"Probably not. I can let you know what happens."

Jace felt a helpless energy. He wanted to do something. Anything. But the university had tied his hands with this scholarship.... He sighed. "Be sure to tell them the video was edited. I'll send you the one that shows the whole story."

"Okay."

"You're mad, aren't you?"

Mari stopped. "No, I'm really not." She smiled, this time genuinely. "Just focused, I guess. Thinking. Sorry."

They resumed at a slightly slower pace.

"So, were you freaking out a few weeks ago as Saint walked down the greenhouse stairs?" she asked.

"Completely."

"Tell me more about that Zero Supremacy meeting you went to."

Her eyes lit up as he dramatized the chase into the parking lot.

"Jace!" she said. "That's like Jason Bourne stuff." She turned thoughtful. "In the last few weeks, you were doing as much for the Bathwater Brigade as anyone."

She looked up at him. Admiration flickered in her eyes and something else Jace was hesitant to name. His heart skipped a beat and he cleared his throat. "Well, turns out Saint is probably not the threat I thought he was."

"He said you're his friend. Is that true?"

Jace blinked, then nodded. "Yeah. I guess you could say that."

She smiled again. "He said you're working on a project together. A website."

"Yup. I'll have to show you when it's further along. So, what do you think of Saint?"

"Just that he seems to be genuine and open-minded."

"He's changed a lot in the past few weeks. A *lot*."

She chuckled. "As people do."

"I'm honestly amazed that we still held the meeting with him there! Did *not* see that coming. And how nobody chewed him out for being a part of the problem. Or tried to show him how Zero Supremacy is stupid. I guess those things would have pushed him away, wouldn't they?"

"Did you expect anything else from a room of Bathwater Dojo black-belts?" Her demeanor turned gloomy again, and they finished their walk in silence.

"This investigation thing is a big deal, isn't it?" said Jace as they stood outside her dorm.

"Yes. This might be it for the Bathwater Brigade. Forty years, and now it's done." She looked away, but not before Jace saw the glassy reflection of her tears.

"I hope not."

She nodded and climbed the steps.

"Hey, Mari?" She turned. "I'm serious. Let me know what I can do." Jace held out his hands. "I'll put myself between the cannons and the Brigade. Just tell me where to stand."

She gave the barest hint of a smile. "Thanks for offering. Really." Head down, she walked inside.

Frustration threatened to bury him and he sank onto the bottom step in sudden exhaustion. There *had* to be something he could do. He wouldn't take this. He wouldn't let them win. He picked up a rock from the edge of the sidewalk and hurled it into the trees. It cracked loudly against a trunk, echoing against the indifferent buildings of Cale University.

Jace just sat there in the dark, breathing, staring out at grass so black he could barely see it. It was as if he were sitting at the edge of a cliff and that the answer was out there in the dark, out of sight and just past his reach. He felt paralyzed. He didn't know for sure what he could do to help, or what was even in his control. But he needed to do *something*.

He pulled the token from his pocket and traced its familiar shape and the rough spot where the dots contained the coded message.

If it is to be, it is up to me.

He had always rolled his eyes when his dad had said it. But maybe it was time to embrace it. He stood up, toes at the edge of the sidewalk. His friends were in trouble and regardless of whatever percentage of the blame was his, he was going to do something.

He was ready to fall.

The next day, Rob came late to rehearsal. He didn't make his usual wise-cracks. He didn't flick Jace's ears with his drumsticks or toss bits of paper into the bell of the tubas. He didn't even drum on the sole of his shoe during the boring stretches.

Jace didn't try to speak to him. Not yet.

As soon as they finished rehearsal, Rob picked up his stuff and left. India followed, turning to give Jace a sympathetic frown and a silent, "Sorry". Jace nodded in return.

As the clack and clatter of instruments being put away mingled with the hum of voices, Jace sat still and watched Dr. Kline. Eventually the room emptied, and the band director retreated to his office.

Jace pulled out his phone and made a call.

"Hi Mari," he said quietly when she answered. "Have a second?"

"Sure."

"Great. Hang on."

Jace stood and strode to Kline's office. The band director sat at his desk, scrolling the mouse wheel at his computer. Jace knocked on the half-open door. "Dr. Kline?" He held his phone to the side of the door frame.

"Yes?" Kline didn't bother to look away from his screen.

"I'm all in with the band, but you can cancel my scholarship."

Kline's head jerked up and Jace heard Mari gasp on the phone. Dr. Kline raised an eyebrow. "Do you have other options?"

"I'll probably get a part-time job to help. Maybe drop a few classes. I don't have it all sorted out yet."

Kline leaned back in his chair and opened his mouth. But Jace spoke first.

"You're looking at a proud member of the Bathwater Brigade."

CHAPTER FORTY-THREE

ON WEDNESDAY NIGHT, Jace, Danica, and Eli met at Primo Campania. The sounds of the busy restaurant filtered into their private room while they waited. Jace straightened in his high-backed wooden chair when a waiter, whose face looked far too old for his blond-tipped surfer haircut, finally came to their table.

"I'm ready," said Eli.

"Don't you think we should wait to order?" said Danica.

Eli looked at his watch. "They're over an hour late. I'm starving."

The Bathwater core had gone to meet with the Cale administration, and were supposed to meet here afterward. Jace didn't love Italian, but Wayne Berry, the owner and also once a Bathwater member, treated them well. He had a room he allowed them to use whenever the restaurant wasn't too busy, pressing a yellow sticky note to the door with the penciled silhouette of a rubber duck.

Eli ordered a calzone. Jace thought of Rob, who viewed eating out as an adventure. His best friend avoided the tourist trap favorites, and took the back roads through the menu, searching for gems that others passed by.

"And you, sir?" the waiter asked him in a far too chipper voice.

"What is the least-ordered thing?" asked Jace.

The waiter leaned over his shoulder and squinted at the menu.

"I'd say the liver and onions. I don't recommend them."

Jace handed the menu back. "I'll take it." Danica recoiled.

The waiter shrugged and noted Jace's order.

Eli smiled at Jace. "He'll come around." Eli knew about Rob and the hoodie. He'd heard both sides and seemed to be firmly planted in the middle, determined to keep both friendships. "Have you guys talked since?"

Jace shook his head.

"They're on their way," said Danica, looking at her phone.

"Did they say how it went?" asked Eli.

"No."

They had hope, though. T.J. and Kendric had been contacting the media about the video, informing them it had been deceptively edited. They'd sent emails with the accurate video in hopes they'd see retractions, posted comments and links in many of the social media posts, and most importantly, denied having anything to do with the banner in the first place.

A few minutes later, the Bathwater Brigade core members entered the room. T.J. nodded to the group, Amber waved as she walked next to Mari, and Dylan and Kendric trailed in.

No one smiled.

They took the empty seats at the long table. Mari's gaze met Jace's. She gave her head a tiny shake. T.J. looked exhausted. He put his massive arms on the table and threaded his fingers through his blond hair.

"So, everything's fixed?" said Eli. "We're good to go?"

T.J. remained in his position for a moment, then slowly turned his head to look at Eli. He smiled tiredly. "Unfortunately, there is more than one meaning of the word 'fixed'."

"What took so long?" said Jace.

"It actually went quick," said Mari. "They just started really, really late."

"I think they did it on purpose," Kendric said. "And they barely looked up from their laptops."

"So, who was there?" asked Danica.

"Us and about five administration officials," said T.J.

"Janet Thompson?" said Jace.

T.J. nodded, and Jace rolled his eyes.

Waiters served food and took orders from the newcomers. No one else spoke until they left.

"Well?" said Eli.

T.J. set a black folder on the table and pulled out a sheet of paper.

"We were right," he said. "We can't have regular club meetings until the investigation is over."

"And only if it goes in our favor," Amber added.

Eli held up his hands and glanced around. "What are they even going to investigate? We haven't been having meetings, and they already made us take down the website."

Kendric answered. "They have access to all the content. I guess there were some complaints."

"No surprise there," said Jace.

"That Zero, Saint," said Danica. "Do you think he's a part of this?"

"I don't think so," said T.J. "We've been talking."

"What did they say against the Brigade, though?" asked Jace. "Even if they still have investigating to do, they had to have some reason to put us under Article Twelve in the first place."

For Jace, it felt good to say "us" again. Mari must have noticed, too. Her concerned expression briefly allowed a smile.

"They mentioned a few things," said Kendric. "They don't like that we leave the full names of people off the meeting minutes."

"That was never in the bylaws," said T.J. "We don't need to."

"It doesn't make sense," said Amber. "We don't even have to post any public minutes at all, much less the entire conversations. That's garbage."

"We used to post the full names," said Dylan. "The Zeroes were harassing Bathwater members, though. We went to just one initial. Who the people are isn't important—it's the discussion."

"Why don't we just stop posting minutes?" asked Eli.

"A lot of people read the discussions we have," said Amber. "They comment and make suggestions, too. It's what is holding the larger Bathwater community together right now."

Danica nodded. "I like reading through them. Fresh perspectives on the world, you know? I hope we don't have to take them down permanently."

Jace pulled up *BathwaterMeetings.com* on his phone. There was a picture of a rubber duck with a speech bubble saying that the site was down per Cale administration until further notice.

"So, did you tell them the *reason* we're not posting full names?" asked Jace.

"We'll have a chance later," said T.J. "There's a hearing Friday where we can make our case."

"In just two days?" asked Jace. "Can we all go to that one?"

T.J. grinned.

"They weren't going to let you," Amber said. "But Kendric read the fine print of Article Twelve, and he found out that we can request that this be a public hearing. So, we did. Now they have to allow anyone that wants to come."

"That's both good news, and bad," said Kendric.

"Right," said Jace. "Zeroes can come too."

Kendric nodded. "I'm glad it's public, though. If they're going to take us down, we want all of Cale to witness it."

"But wait," said Mari sarcastically. "There's more."

T.J. winked at Mari. "We're apparently too exclusive," he said. "They say we don't allow Zero Supremacy members into our group. And we're not posting meeting locations and times."

This brought laughter. "What?" said Eli.

"I know," said Kendric, rolling his eyes.

"Do they know why we had to get away from the Zeroes?" asked Eli. "Plus, Saint's a Zero, and he came."

"Today wasn't the time to bring that stuff up to them," said T.J.

"The good news," said Mari, "is that we think this should be easy to resolve. Especially if we have a public forum to make our case."

"What if the Zeroes come and make a scene?" asked Eli.

"Think about it," Mari said. "That would only help illustrate our points."

Eli nodded. "Oh. Cool."

"So, is that it?" asked Jace. "No mention of the video?"

"Nope," said T.J. "Not directly, anyway. It was funny. They wouldn't bring it up. Just these technicalities."

"Did you get to say anything at all?"

"Well, I said that if we could meet where there was security nearby, then some of these other problems should go away. Then they said that if we can only exist with security officers there, they don't really have the budget for us."

"Nice."

"Yeah," said Amber. "That's like telling a kid that's being bullied that if he can't figure out a way to stop getting bullied, he'll be expelled."

The rest of the food came, and the mood lightened a little.

"So, what's next?" asked Eli.

T.J. finished his bite of spaghetti and sausage. "Spread the word, I guess. Just show up Friday at 4:00 P.M. at room 220 in the Administration Building. When they took our website down, they also took away the ability for us to send out mass emails to our subscribers. But if we search through our personal emails, I think we can reach most of them."

"In other news," Kendric said, "*Texas Late Edition* is doing a story on this. T.J. told them we're not involved with that video, and that it's fake anyway, but they still want to interview one of us."

"Hmm," Mari said. "Are they going to be fair?"

"Well, they're not exactly known for getting it right," T.J. said. "So, two questions. First, should we do the interview?"

"I think we have to," said Amber. "It will just make us look bad if we refuse to talk to the media. Plus, with our side out there, we should get some community support."

Others nodded.

"All right," said T.J. "Now, the hard question. Who should do it?"

Mari had been studying the untouched plate of Chicken Alfredo in front of her. "I'll do it."

"Sounds good to me," said Amber.

"I'll forward you their contact information," said Kendric.

"Actually, why don't I schedule it?" said Dylan. "Since I'm the media outreach guy."

Kendric shrugged and tapped into his phone.

"Want any of us to come with you?" asked Amber.

"I think Jace and I can handle it." Mari gave him a Mona Lisa smile.

Jace nodded and gave everyone a thumbs up, wishing he didn't have a mouth full of food. He sat up a little straighter in his chair.

"Wait." Mari's smile disappeared. "Is that liver?"

CHAPTER FORTY-FOUR

THE NEXT MORNING, Mr. Oatley called Jace and told him they could finish later that day if they wanted to. Jace definitely wanted to.

Jace found Mr. Oatley on a stool in the Maintenance Building. A cane leaned next to the counter. His hat was in one hand, and he rubbed his face with the other. Saint sat on a chair in the corner.

"How was your surgery?" asked Jace.

"Fine, I guess. Each time I move, though, it feels like I'm hugging a rosebush."

"Ouch."

"You sure you're ready to work?" said Saint.

"I don't like grass growing under my feet, son." He took a few tired breaths. "But since I ain't feeling too great, we're going to have a change of plans. An evening with you two has never sounded all that appealing, anyway. Put together, y'all are about as exciting as a mashed potato sandwich." Mr. Oatley gave a chuckle which turned into a cough. His face contorted in pain. "Just do all you can in the Administration Building tonight. Lord willing, y'all might do more good than harm today."

On the walk to the Administration Building, Jace pulled out his phone and started typing a text to Rob.

Ever made a mashed potato sandwich?

He stopped himself before sending it, and put his phone away. They still hadn't spoken, and the longer they waited, the harder it was going to be to make up lost ground. Jace had a suspicion that he was going to have to make the first move. That was fine, but he didn't know where to start. Maybe a mashed potato text *was* the best place.

He sighed. Life was complicated. He glanced at Saint. "So, what did you think of the Bathwater meeting?"

Saint shrugged. "Kind of boring."

"Told you. Thinking of coming to another one? I'm guessing they'll let you."

"I don't know."

"If there *is* another one."

"Paladin is asking all Zeroes to come to your hearing tomorrow," said Saint.

"I figured." Jace sighed. "The website design is looking *really* good, by the way." He grinned. "I would have gotten it to that point myself, though, if I had more time."

Saint smirked. "Sure, you would have."

"Did your friend finish entering the precincts?"

Saint chuckled. "Nah. He's probably the wrong guy for that. Way too slow. Plus, there are about ten times more law enforcement agencies in Texas than we thought."

"Do you think this could get bigger than Texas?"

Saint looked over his shoulder. Then he whispered, "Mr. Oatley will have you hogtied if he hears you say something's bigger than Texas."

Jace laughed.

"But yeah, I've been wondering the same thing." Saint hitched up his tool belt. "Once we test it here, we can see if we want to go nation-wide. I've built the infrastructure so that we can scale it pretty easily."

"Smart. I was thinking we could make a companion mobile app, too. But we should probably finish the website first and see how it does."

"Yeah," Saint said. "You still haven't even gotten your Javascript right on your form validation. Let's look at that Saturday."

"Sounds good."

At times, Jace was tempted to just let them take the project over, since Zero Supremacy had plenty of manpower, and Jace felt like a little brother tag-a-long when it came to the coding of the site. However, he did seem to bring something unique and valuable to the project. Saint noticed it, too, though nothing was ever said. Jace was able to craft the content in a way that kept it from becoming one-sided. He was slow, sometimes spending an hour on a single paragraph, but eventually he hit that perfect tone with his words so that nearly anyone reading the website would feel welcome. They discovered that even the way you mention a statistic could be polarizing and alienate half their visitors. It was like walking a tightrope, and Jace was getting plenty of practice.

Jace imagined the next Stephen Hobbs and tried to reach him, knowing that if the site only focused on the *problems* with law enforcement, it could fuel the distrust and become part of the very problem he was trying to fix. If it turned into a celebration of police and American flags, though, it would never get the attention of half of the group that needed it the most.

Saint pointed things out that Jace missed or that he disagreed with, and they'd hash it out in the computer lab or over text. Saint wouldn't let anything through without his approval, since the Zeroes on the team assumed Saint was writing it all himself. He had Jace revise most of the early pages many times.

Jace smiled. In just a few months, he went from secretly working *against* Zero Supremacy, to secretly working *with* them.

"Oh," Saint said, "one of the Zeroes got talking to his aunt about this, and she's actually really excited about it. You could say she's well-known in the area. If we build it right, she might even help us get the word out."

"Oh, nice. Is her name Janet Thompson?"

"No. It's Deborah Hobbs."

Jace laughed.

Saint didn't.

"Wait. Really? Stephen's mom?"

Saint nodded. "She thinks we're on to something. I gave her access to look at it, and she's been asking a lot of questions."

Jace blinked. "Wow. Does she think something like this could have helped Stephen?"

"I don't know. We haven't brought that up with her."

"Yeah."

When they got to the Administration Building, employees were turning off lights and shutting their doors. Jace and Saint stood in the lobby.

"Well, let's start," Saint said.

Jace cocked his head. "You know, I think I'll start on the third floor. On my own. There's something I want to check out."

Saint shrugged. "All right." He walked to the first door on his left while Jace started up the staircase.

"Oh," Jace called out. "I had an idea for what to call it, and the domain name is actually available. *Civilian Academy*. What do you think? The police have their academy, and now the civilians have theirs."

Saint nodded slowly, then grinned. "I like it."

At the top of the stairs, Jace quietly walked to the waiting room where he'd sat on the day he'd first met Saint and Mr. Oatley. He smiled. It felt bittersweet, like the last day of school.

He sat in a chair and texted Mari.

Guess where I am?

What? Where?

Thirty feet from Janet's office.

He ended that with an emoji of a devilish grin.

She called.

"What are you *doing*?" she asked.

Though nobody was around, Jace ducked and whispered into the phone. "Looks like her office door needs some maintenance. Want me to, uh, watch out for anything?"

"You're really there at her office?"

Jace smiled. "Mr. Oatley said we should work the Administration Building. I thought this was the perfect place to start."

"Jace...skip her office. Please? What do you think you'll find, evidence that will help us? Nothing you do can change her mind. You can only make things worse."

Jace chuckled. "I know. It's just too perfect though." Part of him wanted to pull even a small prank, just to say he did. He could flip all the books in her bookcase backwards, so the spines were facing the wall, or turn her computer monitor upside down, or just leave a simple note, like Saint did on the greenhouse whiteboard.

Mari was right, though. A Bathwater Brigade member pulling a prank on the head administrator just days before she decided whether to shut down the Brigade? He sighed. "I won't go in there. I promise."

"Thanks. I need to go. See you tomorrow."

Jace listened to music as he began working the hinges and hardware of the first office door in the hallway. As he approached Janet's closed door minutes later, he felt the vibrations on the wall as something banged against it. He removed his earbuds. He was surprised to hear muffled voices and the word "bathwater."

Jace crept into the vacant room next door, shut the door most of the way, and put his ear to the wall.

"Is this what you were looking for, then?" a man said. His voice sounded tinny, like he was on a speakerphone.

"I believe it is," said Janet's crisp, no-nonsense voice.

"The Brigade is a hard thing to kill, you know," said the man. "There are really only two ways to do it. Either get them on a technicality, or have the community come at you guys with torches and pitchforks, forcing you to shut them down."

"The furor from the video," said Janet.

"Right."

"So why has it taken this long, then?" This was a new voice, another woman in the room. Her voice was younger and harder than Janet's.

"Look at their history," the man said. "Every time they've broken a rule, the community has rallied around them. And each time the community has been against them, they weren't breaking any rules."

"So, you need both at the same time," said Janet.

There was a momentary silence.

Jace was pretty sure he had heard the man's voice before but couldn't think of who it was. The speakerphone was throwing him off. But he sounded young. And it definitely wasn't Saint.

"Still there?" asked the man.

"I think we've finally done it," said the younger woman.

"By the time next semester starts," said Janet, "the Bathwater Brigade won't even exist."

"They won't see it coming," replied the younger woman. "I think I'll wear black tomorrow. It will be nothing less than a funeral."

"And next week is the burial," said Janet.

"Anything else you need," said the man on the phone, "just text me."

"Thank you," said Janet. "You have been *incredibly* helpful."

"And a true friend to justice," said the other woman.

The man chuckled. "See you guys at the hearing."

An annoying beep signaled the end of the phone call. The sound of chairs rolling across the floor and murmured thank yous and goodbyes had Jace springing into high gear. He dashed into the doorway, crouched next to the bottom hinge, and inserted his ear buds. A young woman left Janet's office and turned right without seeing him. Her hair was short and nearly white. As she turned at the end of the hallway, Jace saw huge glasses.

Paladin, he thought. *Janet Thompson is working directly with Zero Supremacy!*

He turned back to his cloth and can of lubricant. The guy on the phone was probably a Zero, too. If Janet left her office, maybe he could sneak in and look at the recently dialed numbers on her desk phone. Mari would understand.

Jace reached to put the lubricant back into his tool belt and saw blue high-heeled shoes just three feet away.

With a yelp, he fell backward into the room. Janet glared at him. She held a flat, black folder at her side.

He took out his ear buds and nervously chuckled. "Sorry. Scared me."

"What are you doing here?" she demanded. Her words were forceful and hushed though nobody else was around.

"What am I doing here?" he repeated back to her. He stood, pointed at his tool belt, and held his arms out in a shrug. "You're *making* me be here."

"Oh," she said.

"Mr. Oatley said we should come to your building today."

She pursed her lips. "Please work on the other floors. I'm busy up here."

He shrugged again and strolled away. Janet entered her office and locked the door behind her.

Jace found an empty conference room on the second floor and called Mari again. He told her about the phone call, and that a major surprise seemed to be coming at the hearing.

"Do you have any clue on what it is?" Mari asked.

"No. But it might come in a black folder."

She sighed. "I guess we just show up and see."

"All right. You sure I shouldn't wait until Janet leaves? I think I know where Mr. Oatley's keys are."

"No!" she said. "It's not even close to worth it. You'll get caught. You'll get arrested, and it will be all over for the Brigade. I'm going to do everything I can to save this club. But if people are resorting to dishonesty to try to cancel us, then all we can do is stand on our morals and speak. We won't get our hands dirty. It will say more about Cale than us."

"We need you in Congress, Mari."

She laughed. "Thanks for talking to me this time instead of trying to fix things all on your own. See? Don't we make a good team?"

"Yeah," Jace chuckled. "We do. See you tomorrow."

He waited for her to say, "see you then," but she surprised him.

"Hey, Jace. You're a good guy."

He smiled. "Thanks."

When the shift ended, it was well past dark. Jace couldn't find Saint, so he went back to the Maintenance Building alone. There was a note on the door in shaky handwriting. "Leave your stuff inside and lock up. Nice and neat, not all cattywampus. Good job."

Jace wanted to say it was Mr. Oatley that left the note, except for those last two words. He smiled wistfully. He was glad they were finally done, but he wished he had the chance to look Mr. Oatley in the eye and shake his hand.

CHAPTER FORTY-FIVE

FRIDAY DAWNED BRIGHT AND COOL. Though the sun was out, Jace was barely sweating. Fall weather made outdoor existence at Cale almost tolerable. He tried to convince himself it was a sign.

"*Texas Late Edition* decided not to interview Mari, then?" asked Danica as they walked toward the Administration Building for the hearing.

"Yup," said Jace. "Even though our schedule was wide open, Dylan said they couldn't work us in. TV stations, right? You'd think they'd want the interview they asked for."

"So, do you think Cale can really shut us down?" Eli asked.

"Mari doesn't think so," Jace said. "I mean, they can always look in our archives and find something dumb that someone said, but if you look at the spirit of what we do, we have nothing to hide or be ashamed of."

Danica nodded. "We're exactly the kind of club that a university should want."

They turned a corner, and the three-story Administration Building came into view.

"That's a lot of red over there," said Eli.

A group of at least fifty stood outside by the entrance, and most if not all of them Zeroes.

"Is there another entrance?" said Jace.

"Not sure," said Danica. "But I doubt they'll try anything today. Just hurry and walk in."

They quickened their pace and aimed for the largest gap they could see. A lanky girl with the classic red Zero Supremacy T-shirt handed Danica a full-page flier as they walked past.

"Duck!" someone yelled.

Eli quickly crouched and looked up, his hand protectively over his head. Danica had reached the door, but turned back.

An overweight man with a black beard walked toward Jace. Scamp, from the Zero Supremacy meeting. "Hey, man," he said, smiling. "Haven't seen you in a while."

"Oh. Hi." Jace turned his head mostly away to keep them from getting a clear view of his face.

Scamp shook Jace's hand. "You going to join us out here for a bit?"

Jace glanced around. Many of the Zeroes were watching. "Nah, I'm going inside to see what happens. See you around, Scamp." Jace followed after his friends with long strides, trying not to look like he was in a hurry.

Eli raised his eyebrows at Jace once they were inside. "Is he someone you met at that Zero Supremacy meeting?"

Jace nodded. "I don't think they realize that we're the ones in the video. Not yet, anyway. We'd better keep our distance."

"Yeah." Then Eli grinned. "Duck, huh? That's your Zero nickname?"

Jace shrugged.

"It's time to drain the bathwater," Danica read aloud, looking at the flier. "Clever." She scanned the rest of the page, and then dropped it in a trash can as they walked by. "I don't think they understand that being against third-wave feminism does not make you anti-woman."

The venue for the hearing had been changed last-minute to a much larger room. Long tables lined the front. Five chairs were spaced behind them. There were probably a hundred chairs opposite, set into neat rows with an aisle down the center. Two workers were setting up more at the back. About a third of them were already filled. An older man, headphones around his neck and covered in cables, aimed a large video camera to the front.

Jace, Danica, and Eli sat together near the back. "Are the rest of these guys here for us, or the Zeroes?" muttered Eli.

"No idea," said Danica. "I don't recognize any of them."

Jace glanced back at the doorway. "I know a few of them, actually. From calculus. But I don't know whose side they're on." Jace nodded at one classmate in particular, a short kid from Pakistan, and noticed that he had a small rubber duck keychain attached to his backpack.

"Nervous?" asked Eli.

Jace smiled. "A bit."

The noise grew as people, some older but most probably students, streamed in and talked with each other. Wayne from the Italian restaurant came, and it looked like he brought some of his employees with him.

"Jace."

He turned to see India alone in the row behind. "Hi!" he said.

She gave him a kind smile and put her hand on his arm. "Sorry about Rob."

"Thanks. We've known each other for like fifteen years, so it's not the first time one of us has gotten mad. Has he ever told you what happened the day he told Sierra Carver that I had a crush on her?"

She laughed. "No. I'll ask him."

Jace leaned on the back of his chair and sighed. "He has some fair points."

"I've talked to him. And Eli. I know what you did and why."

Jace nodded. "I respect him and his family so much. It hurts that he thinks I don't. Maybe he's right about this and I'm wrong. I'm still trying to work it all out."

India smiled sympathetically. "He'll come around."

Jace nodded.

"Well, I'm here as a cheerleader, but also, after Eli told me about all this going on today, I thought this might help."

She handed Jace an envelope. "She emailed this to the administration and asked me to hand a copy to Jace the Trombonist. You may want to have someone read it out loud today."

Jace opened the envelope, pulled out a signed letter, and read it. His eyes grew wide. "Thank you!" Jace said. He hugged India. "Are you going to hang around?"

"Yeah. I want to see what happens."

"Great. Sit up here with us."

A river of red streamed through the doorway on their right. Zeroes took the entire second and third rows from the front. Paladin sat among them, wearing black. There was no sign of Saint.

"They don't seem that angry today," said Eli.

"They could have something planned for during the meeting," said Jace. "Or they could just be on their best behavior." He noticed Mari step into the room, followed by T.J. and the other core members of the Brigade. They greeted several other students in the audience as they made their way to the front. Still holding India's letter, Jace scooted out of his aisle and joined them.

"Hey, man," T.J. said.

"You ready for this?" Jace asked.

"We just tell it like it is, you know? Nothing more than that. We should sail through."

"Yup. But just in case, I think you need to read this to them." Jace nodded toward the front of the room and handed him the letter.

He turned to see Mari. She looked nervous. He pulled out his wallet and flashed his driver's license at her. "Ma'am? I'm going to have to see all your writing utensils. And you'd better have the receipts."

She grinned. "You know I support law enforcement. But if you're going to be this annoying..."

Jace smiled, pleased that she seemed more relaxed now. "So where do you guys sit?"

"They're having us sit in the audience. I think it's a power play." She leaned closer and lowered her voice. "Keep an eye on Mr. Rodriguez. He's one of the administration. T.J. says he's on our side."

Hands on hips, Jace scanned the room. "So where did all these people come from?"

"Other than the Zeroes?" Mari said. "A lot of them are Bathwater supporters. I'd like to introduce you to some of them after. I don't know about the rest. They could be more supporters, or people upset about the video."

Janet Thompson walked in and sat at the front, putting a binder and a stack of other papers in front of her. She wore a blue dress. *Red would have been too obvious*, Jace thought. She scanned the room.

Four others gradually joined her at the table. A man and a woman sat to her right, and two men at her left. Jace guessed that the one immediately to her left was Mr. Rodriguez, a lean Hispanic man with charcoal slacks, a purple dress shirt, and occasional gray strands bristling among his dark hair. He was the only non-white member of the administration.

"I'm feeling good about this," Jace said. "You?"

She nodded, but slowly. "I've been thinking about that phone call, the one you overheard at Janet's office. We'll find out in a few minutes, I guess. I usually like surprises, Jace, but not today."

"Are you sure?" asked Jace. "T.J. is holding one right now that you might like." Before she could ask any questions, he turned back toward his seat.

"Hey, Duck." Scamp was sitting near the end of the row. "Come here." He looked serious.

Jace hesitated, then walked closer. If he remembered correctly, Saint said Scamp was the one doing the data entry for the Civilian Academy, and Jace was half tempted to ask how that was coming.

"So, you're part of the Bathwater Brigade?"

Jace pursed his lips and nodded. A few Zeroes watched the conversation. "Yeah. Well, I wasn't before, but I am now."

"What were you doing at our meeting?"

Jace sighed. "I just wanted to see what it was like. To see if you guys really believe what you say."

"What. You don't believe us?"

"I do now," Jace said.

The room quieted. One of the five administrators, a bald man in a black suit, stood at the front with a wireless microphone in hand.

"I can tell you more after." Jace walked away, half hoping he'd never see Scamp again. He wouldn't mind getting to know him, but Jace had no idea what would happen once Scamp learned who he really was.

Eli patted Jace on the back as he stepped past. There were about twenty seats left, and people were still trickling in. He watched as T.J.

passed the letter down the row for the core members to read. Mari turned in her chair and scanned the assembly until she found India. She put her hand over her heart and mouthed a sincere, "Thank you."

Janet looked out over the room, her eyes snagging on Jace. He gave her a humorless smile. He knew she had something up her sleeve, but now the Brigade did, too.

The old man pushed a button on the bottom of the microphone. "Students, faculty, and visitors of Cale University. Welcome." He introduced himself as Dr. Kennedy, one fifth of the board that would review the sanctioned status of the Bathwater Brigade. He also introduced the others at the front table. Dr. Van Leeuwen, Mrs. Cannon, Dr. Thompson, and Mr. Rodriguez.

Dr. Kennedy clarified the rules of Article Twelve, and he read the names of the core members of the Brigade, asking each to raise their hand. "Today, we lay out the reasons we believe the Bathwater Brigade is incompatible with our university, and we will allow core members of the club to respond. The decision will be announced here exactly one week from now."

"What if they decide to shut us down?" whispered Eli. "Can we appeal or something?"

"This *is* the appeal," Danica said.

"Can we sue?"

"I don't think so. They have the right to control which clubs they allow on campus."

"Oh," Eli said, frowning. "I hope we win."

CHAPTER FORTY-SIX

JANET PUT on a pair of narrow reading glasses and read a brief history of Cale University. Leading the way in Texas since 1958, the university had championed equality, diversity, and social justice. She then described the video that had been giving the university so much attention—the wrong *kind* of attention—including calls from outraged alumni and citizens. She acknowledged that the video had been edited, and that it wasn't directly linked to the Brigade, but that all of this had caused them to review the standing of the club.

"Let's begin here," she said, briefly glancing at T.J. "According to your own records on February 17th of this year, the Bathwater Brigade urged that women *not* get pay equal to men."

The crowd murmured. Jace sat taller, so he could better see the front row. Mari and Kendric were whispering. Amber shrugged, and T.J. raised his hand half-way.

Janet cleared her throat. "Just two weeks later, on March 2nd, you suggested that every professor should carry a gun."

The murmur grew louder. T.J. stood and spoke loudly, since he had no microphone of his own. "Can we respond to these one at a time?"

"Let's get another mic in here," said Dr. Kennedy. They waited while a thin man with a goatee and a tucked-in T-shirt speed-walked a second mic to the front and handed it to T.J.

"First," began T.J., "let me say that we're an intellectual society that explores ideas. We try to get as many perspectives as we can, and search for intersections and common ground that others ignore. Just because something is said at one of our meetings doesn't mean that the Brigade, or even one of its members, is advocating for it. And sometimes it's just a sarcastic comment, too. Kendric, here, has all the video of our meetings for the past two years. He can instantly look up any clip you have the transcript for, so you can see the proper context for yourself."

Kendric sat with a laptop in front of him, fingers on the keyboard, like a golden retriever waiting for a stick to be thrown.

"That won't be necessary," Janet said, moving on. "I think it's sufficient to say that you don't shut down offensive speech or publish the names of attendees so that we can deal with them."

"You make it sound as if we have white supremacists as members."

"You don't, then?"

T.J. laughed. "Of course not! They hate us. Bringing different people together isn't exactly their thing."

"So, why not list the identities of the students in your meeting minutes?"

"To keep our people from being harassed by my friends in red behind me. But also, our meetings are the first time that many attendees have thought through some of our topics. Sometimes, you need a little room to sort through what you believe. A safe space, if you will. Be a devil's advocate and explore a few sides of the issue. And you might bounce off a dumb comment or two as you think out loud and settle on what your position is. Unless it's truly alarming or offensive, there is a danger of striking too hard and ostracizing someone when they have a thought that you and I might not like."

Yes! thought Jace. *He's going to kill it.*

T.J. continued. "Keep in mind, we're not going for consensus. We invite students of all backgrounds to come. In fact, we might even be your most diverse club on campus."

At this, Janet frowned and narrowed her eyes. She flipped to a bookmarked page in her notebook. "Diverse enough, even, to allow a racist in your midst?"

T.J. cocked his head to the side. "You keep alluding to that. I don't believe we've ever had a racist attending our meetings—"

"April. Of this year."

T.J. paused. Then nodded. "I think I know what you're talking about. You're right, those were racist comments."

Eli and Danica gave each other confused looks, and whispers emerged in the audience.

Janet folded her hands in front of her. "I don't know why you think a member of your group supporting racism isn't directly against Cale's core policies."

T.J. nodded. "This person thought we should all separate and stick to our own race. We were, all of us, confused that such an idea could even be considered." He shook his head. "He wasn't a member, though."

"But it appears you let him stay at the meeting. Why?"

"Did you read all of the notes for that day?"

Janet didn't answer.

"I wish the website was still up so everyone here could read the notes in full context. That was one of our proudest moments."

"Oh?"

Rodriguez shifted in his seat, and Kennedy narrowed his eyes, leaning forward.

"By the end," said T.J., "we'd convinced him that he was wrong. Well, he didn't change *all* his views in one night, but our meeting put him well on his way."

Janet's expression remained unchanged. "Many would say some ideas don't deserve a chance."

"Do you understand what I'm saying?" T.J. said. "We gave *him* a chance—not his ideas. That day the Bathwater Brigade did more than just take a stand against racism. We won a battle against it, in what I think is the best way possible. We defeated the racist but saved the person. We won him over."

"You think a racist can change?"

T.J. blinked. "Well, yes," he said. "Don't you? Have you heard the story behind the song 'Amazing Grace?' It was written by John Newton, a slave trader turned abolitionist. People grow and change their philosophies all the time, even from ideas that are horrible and racist. If the guy who had attended our meeting consistently said racist things, then of course we would have asked him to leave. But we saw that he was changing, and we're also not a group that likes to brand people for ideas they've had in the past."

Jace cheered inside. He saw several heads nodding in front of him. He glanced at Eli, and they grinned at each other.

"Game over," Eli whispered.

T.J. reached for a stack of paper. "If I may, I have letters from Bathwater Brigade alumni. They describe the positive impact it had on their education, and how they've used the skills taught in the club throughout their lives. Could I briefly read two excerpts?"

Janet started talking almost before he had even finished his request. "You may set the letters here on the table." T.J. did.

Mr. Rodriguez glanced at Janet and gestured for the mic. "You said that common ground is ignored by everyone else. Why do you say that?"

"To me, common ground is where two very different people work together on something they already agree on. Like when environmentalists and right-wingers see eye to eye on nuclear energy as a solution. Isn't it great? We *should* all be trying to stand on common ground whenever we see the chance. It should be our favorite hangout."

Rodriguez nodded thoughtfully.

T.J. took in a breath. "But there are people lurking in the shadows, and they chase people off. They make us think common ground doesn't exist—that no matter what you've heard, the other side really isn't interested in working with you. Look here, on the news—someone on the other side is making fun of you. Or they turn it into a no man's land, with razor wire and land mines, making us afraid to approach it."

The room was silent.

"Land mines laid by whom?"

"Politicians." He pointed toward the news camera in the corner. "Media." He nodded toward the table in front of him. "Campus administration. Others. They each have their own reasons—ratings, votes, money. They don't want us talking together."

"Don't want *who* talking together?"

"Rich and poor, Republicans and Democrats, black and white, progressives and conservatives, Christians and atheists. I'm speaking pretty generally here, but haven't you noticed it? They highlight our differences. They try to keep us apart, fighting and hating each other, so they can hold onto the power that rightfully belongs to us, the people."

"Thank you," said Rodriguez, handing the mic back to Janet. He gave T.J. a slight smile, and a tiny nod of encouragement.

"We need to get through this list," Janet said without looking up. "You meet in secret, and this is against the charter."

Jace shook his head. He thought T.J. had just hit on what just might be the bullseye of the problem, and Janet wanted to go chase some technicality instead of discussing it.

T.J. humored her. "It depends how you interpret that part of the charter. And we meet in secret only because we've been forced to. We're simply waiting for you to provide the security we need. We welcome everyone, but certain individuals come to our meetings only to shut them down, and the administration hasn't been holding them accountable."

Many in the audience murmured agreement.

Janet sniffed. "A club that needs constant security is probably not the best fit for Cale."

T.J. reached down and picked up India's letter from his chair. "On that topic...could I share a brief message, written by one of Cale's most generous donors specifically for today?"

Jace and India exchanged glances. India's eyes were wide and hopeful.

"We don't have the time," said Janet, smiling insincerely. "Let's move on, please."

"Just this one," said T.J. "I insist." The audience shifted and whispered. Dr. Kennedy placed his hand on Janet's wrist. She glanced at the others, who nodded at her. She tried to keep her game face while she motioned for T.J. to go ahead, but her scowl showed through.

"Thank you," he said, unfolding the paper. He cleared his throat and read the letter aloud.

To Cale Administration,

As a proud graduate of this institution, I have always admired its commitment to the freedom of expression and diversity of thought. This is no small reason why I have cheerfully donated twenty-three million dollars over the past thirty years.

I have recently learned of the Bathwater Brigade and have personally interviewed some of its members. Though I don't agree with all of them on all topics, they have impressed me with their knowledge and skill. They can navigate the varied perspectives on topics that even seasoned adults find difficult and emotionally triggering. I trust that encouraging your students to learn and practice how to handle the views they'll find in the real world is your highest priority.

I will gladly pay for any security required to get these meetings back in the open where they belong. I will even offer to attend them when I get the chance, and I will report any concerning or dangerous ideas that I feel the Brigade hasn't properly handled.

Sincerely, Florence Hughes.

There were more murmurs from the audience. Eli hugged India. Jace gave them a thumbs up.

Janet was unimpressed. "I don't believe that your bylaws allow for non-students to attend your meetings."

"No," said T.J. "But I'm sure that can be arranged. At the very least, temporarily." He turned, and the core members nodded emphatically. "In fact, I'd like to invite the five of you to come to some of our meetings."

"No," Janet said.

T.J. cocked his head. "I think you'd have a different view of us if you came."

"We will *not* be attending," she said. Her voice intensified, and she placed both palms on the desk.

"But why?" T.J. took a small step forward. "You'll see that our only agenda is to share ideas—"

Janet jumped from her chair. "Some ideas get people killed!" Her shout echoed through the stunned room as she stood there, bracing her hands on the table, breathing heavily. She and T.J. stared at each other.

"The suppression of ideas can get people killed, too," T.J. calmly responded.

After a long silence, Dr. Rodriguez gingerly lifted the mic. "I have one question. Here we are discussing whether your club is a good fit for Cale. Have you considered doing this off-campus? You might have a bigger audience."

"I hope there is a club like ours off campus," said T.J. "But we would choose to stay at Cale a hundred times over. We feel that intellectual diversity has been a hallmark of higher education in the Western world. We feel that our club embodies this value."

Many in the audience nodded as T.J. continued. "The responsibility begins at the top. We believe that Cale's students, faculty, and administration should firmly support the Bathwater Brigade, which is simply a group of its students who dare to think in new ways and peacefully challenge each other. The university would do well to follow the historic tradition of shielding her bold thinkers from attacks by the outside." He looked at Janet. "Today, it seems, the situation is reversed."

"Thank you," said Rodriguez.

"Wow," whispered Eli. "Glad T.J. is on our side."

Someone near the news camera began clapping, followed by others. Many in the room joined the applause. Janet surveyed the room, expressionless. T.J. sat back down. The clapping stopped, and chatter took its place.

"I can't imagine them canceling us after that," said Danica. "Is it over?"

Jace shrugged.

"I just hope they all have an equal vote," said Danica. "Dr. Thompson still looks like she hates our guts. She's all over the place. It's like she's grasping at all these ridiculous reasons to shut us down because she won't tell us the real one."

The loud tapping of a hand on a microphone caught their attention. "Excuse me," said Dr. Kennedy. The room quieted once more. "We need to wrap up."

Janet raised a finger. "One last item," she calmly said and lifted a simple black folder. Jace sat forward as his pulse quickened.

"Cale University student organizations have charters that contain carefully-drawn boundaries around their influence. With a few exceptions, our clubs should refrain from affecting the community, elections, things like that. Are you aware of this?"

"Yes. That's right," T.J. said. "Our efforts fit well within those boundaries, as you call them."

"I'm confused, then, by this flier of yours." She pulled a sheet of paper out of the folder.

"The Pro Voter one?" whispered Danica. "This will be easy to explain. She must not have read all of it." Eli nodded. Jace sat forward with his hands at his mouth.

Janet asked the other four administrators to pull out their copy.

"Dr. Kennedy, would you read the title?" She seemed to relish the moment.

Kennedy looked down through his glasses and read, "Cops Aren't Racist".

"Thank you. Dr. Kennedy, you have read through this flier. Could you summarize the content for us?"

He put the flier by his side and addressed the crowd. "It has various statements about race, black history, and police shooting statistics. Very poor quality, if you ask me."

Jace and Eli looked at each other.

"Oh my gosh," said India, hand covering her mouth. "I think that was the one Rob had."

T.J. raised his hand. Janet only glanced at him with a smirk.

"Can you tell me where these fliers were found?" she asked Dr. Kennedy.

"At the New Brig Second District Court."

"And *when?*"

"During the trial of Gina Lambson."

The audience buzzed.

"Why do they think it was a Bathwater flier?" whispered Eli. "We changed it."

Janet addressed T.J. "For a club that is restricted to on-campus influence, is it normal behavior for you to launch campaigns to directly affect public opinion at trials of national interest?"

T.J. stood. "Dr. Thompson, I honestly don't know what flier you're talking about. Can I please see it?"

Kennedy gave him his copy.

T.J. held it up. "It's sort of like one that we handed out a while ago, with some of the same things on it. But this didn't come from the Bathwater Brigade."

"Oh?" said Janet. She held up her copy and tapped the corner. T.J. inspected it once more. He shook his head and ran his fingers through his hair.

Eli closed his eyes. "The rubber duck. The logo thing in the corner. I think we forgot to take it off." Jace rubbed his face.

"This isn't ours," said T.J. "We can't help it if someone takes our flier and changes it for their own purposes. Besides, none of us were even there."

"Really..." Janet said with a smile. She held up a full-page color photo. "Recognize anyone here?"

TJ stepped closer and examined the photo. His shoulders slumped imperceptibly, and Jace's stomach dropped. Janet must have had a photo from the courthouse, and her triumphant smile could only mean one thing: He and Eli were in it. Horrified, Jace's mind raced. He technically wasn't a Brigade member at the time, but Janet wouldn't let that matter.

Janet leaned forward. "Mr. Campfield, after the fascinating lecture on ethics you just delivered, one would think you would agree with the virtue of taking responsibility for your actions."

T.J. held a hand up in frustration. "I'm telling the truth. Our flier had a different theme. And it stayed on campus."

"You seem to have an excuse for everything," she said. "Aside from your society's dwindling integrity, this goes back to the point that the Bathwater Brigade seems to be much more trouble to the university—and our reputation—than it's worth."

T.J. shifted but didn't reply. He looked...smaller than before.

She sat back with a satisfied smile. "If you'd like to provide proof of the claims you've made today, you are free to drop it by our offices.

During the next week, we will deliberate and make our decision on the continued existence of the Bathwater Brigade at Cale University."

T.J. stood before her, head raised, shoulders back.

But Janet wasn't finished. Her lips curled with contempt. "And, the suspension of its president."

"What?" Jace jumped to his feet. So did Mari and Kendric. Loud groans of protest sprang from the crowd. Mr. Rodriguez watched the core Brigade members in the front row, concerned and sympathetic. T.J. shook his head and smiled in disbelief.

Janet raised an eyebrow at T.J. "As you say, responsibility begins at the top."

She turned off the mic, gathered her things, and led her colleagues out of the room.

The meeting was over.

CHAPTER FORTY-SEVEN

THAT NIGHT, the door to Primo Campania's back room had a sticky note with the sketched rubber duck wearing a party hat. Wayne had said he wanted to give them a break from bad news. Two servers brought complimentary appetizers of Wayne's famous Bruschetta and mini meatballs with toothpicks. A silent basketball game played on the large screen at the back.

Jace sat next to Mari. They'd had a long talk after the hearing—particularly about Rob's flier. Jace showed her the text he had sent to Rob, instructing him not to use the Bathwater one. Still, Jace defended his friend. Rob wouldn't have used it when he'd been told not to. There must have been some other explanation.

With the threat of suspension hanging over him, T.J. was a somber celebrity. Everyone offered their support and condolences, though he shrugged them off.

"Doesn't feel like time to celebrate," said Jace.

"We held our ground," Mari said with a weak smile. "I think that's something to celebrate."

"So, T.J.," Eli said, "when they accused us of not allowing certain people to come to our meetings, why didn't you tell them about Saint?"

"It wouldn't have changed Janet's mind. Besides, it's not my news to share. If I had, he'd have been in literal danger from some of the Zeroes. And he would have felt pressured to choose between us and them." T.J. stroked his beard. "I don't know if he's far enough on our side that he would choose us. Plus, I'm perfectly fine if he never officially joins. I'm just glad he's thinking. And listening."

"Someone should send a thank you note to India and Mrs. Hughes," Danica said.

"The great thing about it," said Dylan, "is that when the Zeroes meet strong security at a few public meetings, they'll learn their lesson and stop coming. It will be nice to be back to normal and have everybody come to the meetings again."

Amber cleared her throat. "I like how you're planning our next meetings, but I don't think we'll get that far."

Dylan put an arm around her. "Hey. We gave them like ten pages of stuff this afternoon. We went through all their concerns. I really think they'll change their mind."

Danica said, "So, T.J., did they tell you what suspension means, exactly? Just pause your classes for a semester?"

"Some of those classes are only held once a year," said Amber. "And of course, he wouldn't be allowed to be in the Brigade." She looked up from the untouched food in front of her and watched T.J. balance a spoon on his finger. "They gave us one more option Wednesday," she said. T.J. gave her a stern look.

"What's that?" asked Danica.

"If we all quit right now—you know, pretend the Bathwater Brigade never happened—then they won't suspend T.J."

"So, it's a gamble," said Jace. "If we're toast anyway, then quitting now will help T.J. A lot."

Some of them shifted uncomfortably. T.J. set the spoon down, sat up straight, and folded his arms. "Nope," he said. "Not an option."

"But," said Amber, "this is a big setback for your career. You've worked so hard. You already have a firm ready to hire you."

"I really don't want to quit," said Eli, "but maybe we should take the offer."

Jace glanced at Mari. She stared at the floor. He nudged her arm. She only shook her head.

T.J. looked up. "Like I said, the Bathwater Brigade won't die on my watch. Even if I have to wait a bit to finish school."

"You know it's a bigger deal than that," said Amber.

"Look at Jace," said T.J., nodding toward him. "He gave up a scholarship to be here."

Amber smiled at Jace and then turned back to T.J. "That *was* a big sacrifice. But it's not the same."

"I don't know what the right answer is," said Kendric. "But let me remind you that we make these decisions by core vote. You don't call the shots yourself, man."

"No." T.J. set his jaw and locked his icy gaze onto Kendric.

"Do we have to decide now?" asked Danica. The tension drained from the room, and T.J. clapped Kendric on the back. They agreed to resume that discussion later.

"Speaking of community support..." said Eli, reaching for his backpack. Danica grinned as Eli pulled ten rubber ducks of various sizes and shades of yellow from his pack.

"There was a box of these on a dumpster in the back of the Administration Building," he said. "I saw some on the ground when we were walking out."

Kendric smiled. "Maybe Janet bought some ducks just to throw away. Like voodoo dolls."

Eli tossed a folded piece of paper at him. "There were some of these, too. This was taped to the big duck."

Kendric unfolded the paper and read aloud.

To the Cale University administration. My son joined the Bathwater Brigade six years ago when he was a student there. I don't know what infractions may have caused them to come under your investigation, but I can't begin to tell you the valuable lessons that he has learned by his membership.

Kendric looked up and smiled.

"Taped to the duck?" laughed Dylan. "Did they try to throw it through the window?"

"The alumni social media pages are encouraging everyone to

support us," Mari said. "They probably organized an effort to mail ducks to the administration. It's just that they didn't know the administration has already made up its mind."

"Wait a minute," said Eli. "I've been seeing rubber duck keychains attached to backpacks. Do you think those are students showing support for us?"

T.J. turned up a side of his mouth. "Pretty sure."

"Well, *this* is interesting," said Kendric. He nodded at the TV.

The basketball game had ended, and the *Texas Late Edition* logo was now in the corner of the screen. They instantly recognized the infamous video of the banner, the confetti, and the trombone slide.

"Turn it up!" said T.J.

By the time Eli dashed to the television and found the volume, Paladin was on screen, sitting in some large office or library. The host introduced her as the leader of a local group working for social justice and equality. He never mentioned Zero Supremacy by name.

"Ugh," said Amber. "She's on TV all the time. 'A young person fighting for important causes.' They make it seem like everyone her age thinks like her."

"She even gave a TED Talk once," added Mari. "Some of it was pretty good." They turned their focus back to the television.

"Are they racist?" the host asked Paladin.

"I don't want to put that awful label on anyone," she replied. "But the evidence is out there."

Eli, who had just taken a drink, choked and groped for a napkin, nearly spewing water onto the table.

"Wow," said Danica.

Paladin continued. "They don't want to acknowledge America's racist history."

"Even in their meeting archives," the host narrated, "we found racist comments. We won't repeat them here."

"Let me guess," said Kendric dryly. "They found the transcript where we convinced that guy not to be a racist anymore. That was the *one* time. And if they'd just read it in context, they'd see that it was a win for our club."

313

"How did they get access to the archives?" whispered Danica. "They took the website down."

"Should a club like the Bathwater Brigade exist on a modern campus?" the host asked Paladin.

She replied, "There are some wonderful people there. I know some of them. But that kind of thinking doesn't belong in a modern university."

"How about you show footage from Zero Supremacy riots?" Eli shot back. "Those guys are from the Dark Ages."

Stunned, Jace turned to Mari. She looked utterly defeated.

Janet Thompson was interviewed in the shade, strands of her blond hair flowing in a light breeze. Jace didn't remember much of her interview, except that she assured the host that her university was forward-thinking and on the cutting edge of justice and equality.

The moment the segment was over, Eli turned it off. Silence hung in the air.

"They did the segment anyway," Kendric finally said. "I can't believe it."

Dylan shrugged. "I don't know what to tell you."

"They left us out on purpose," said Jace. "We couldn't even defend ourselves. And how do they twist everything like that?"

"They're masters at their craft." Amber shrugged. "They can take a set of facts and tell any story they want. And they don't even have to lie."

Mari laid her head on her folded arms, her shoulders shaking. Amber knelt beside her and rubbed circles on her back.

Wayne walked through the doors and clapped his hands together. "Well? How is everyone?" He took in the room. "Oh. Not so good?" He pulled up a chair to the table and sat down. Kendric told him about the news story.

"Well," Kendric finished, "it's clear how Janet Thompson will vote."

Wayne chuckled and shook his head. "Janet Thompson," he repeated.

"What's her problem with us?" asked Eli.

Another somber pause hovered over them.

"I'm sorry, guys," said Jace. His voice cracked. "About the video. The flier. Everything."

"Hey, man. You're good," said Kendric. "It's not just about you. This has been brewing since before you started here."

Something clicked together in Jace's brain. He frowned. "When did it start, exactly?"

Amber sighed. "The Zeroes really kicked it up a notch in the middle of spring semester, I'd say."

"Even if it all crashes down," Kendric said, "it will be nice to finally get it over with, you know? Then we can start building something again instead of running."

"Build what?" Amber asked. "Where?"

Kendric shrugged. "I don't know."

"February," Jace said, looking at his phone.

They turned to him. "What?"

"That's when Janet started working at Cale." He looked up at them. "Interesting timing, isn't it?"

Dylan chuckled. He was leaning his head on the high wooden back of his chair, with his arms folded. "So, you think Janet Thompson gets hired on, and gets right to work on using her influence to crush the Brigade? Surely she has better things to do."

Jace shrugged. "I don't know. A lot of our problems lead to her, though. And she seems almost giddy that our fate is in her hands right now."

T.J. stared at the napkin ring he was playing with. "Why do we need to wait around for *them* to make all the decisions?"

"What?" said Dylan.

"How about we take control and up the ante? Get a different kind of press."

"No idea what you mean," Dylan replied.

"I could quit."

"Offer to step down as president?" said Kendric. "Not sure that would change anything."

"No." T.J. leaned forward. "Step down as a student."

Heads jerked.

"Leave the university completely?" said Amber.

T.J. calmly nodded. He set the napkin on the table and folded his arms.

Amber put her head in her hands. "T.J. We might be talking *years* of setback. Tens of thousands of dollars. I don't think you can just walk into another college and continue where you left off." His expression remained. "What's dad going to say?" No reply. "T.J.!"

He slowly leaned forward and addressed the rest of the group. "Tonight, I'll announce that if Cale decides it can't handle a few students having a quiet discussion about important things, then I'm not interested in staying here."

Jace exhaled loudly.

"Wow," said Kendric. "That would take this to another level. If you're serious about this, I'll help you spread the word."

T.J. nodded. "We'll *show* them we're serious. We're not just some club. If all colleges had a Bathwater Brigade, don't you think we'd see a better world out there right now?"

Heads nodded, including Mari's, her eyes still red from crying.

Amber put her hand on her forehead. "But quitting! Your degree!"

T.J. sighed. "Think it's going too far? Any of you core members going to try to vote me down on this?" No one responded. "Good. It doesn't matter, anyway. This isn't a Bathwater decision. It's a personal one. Believe me—it's personal."

"I can help," said Wayne. "You do that, and I give you free Bruschetta for life."

T.J. grinned. "If I had known that, I would have dropped out of college years ago."

For the first time that hour, they laughed.

CHAPTER FORTY-EIGHT

THE NEXT DAY, Jace leaned against his car in his dorm parking lot, freshly showered and wearing sunglasses. He smiled as he put his phone back into his pocket. Mr. Oatley had called. After a meandering conversation which included complaints about Jace's speed and quality of work, Mr. Oatley said he needed some extra help with sprinklers in the spring, if Jace was interested and could keep the cattywampus to a minimum. It just so happened that Jace was looking for a job.

Mari approached from the side, carrying a small yellow hiking pack. "Funny thing," she said. "Apparently the administration office is sneaking letters into students' backpacks now."

Jace shrugged. "Saving on postage, probably."

She held a folded piece of ruled notebook paper and read aloud.

From Cale Administration, to Mariana Munoz.

Since we hope to stomp out your little Brigade soon, we feel that now is the time to give your friend, Jace, the final dojo lesson. Please do this on Saturday. Meet him in the parking lot of his dorm at 3 P.M.

Yours always, Janet Thompson.

She eyed Jace. "It's interesting that you and Janet have the same handwriting."

"Pretty sure she's been trying to copy mine ever since she saw the signature on my university application. It's pretty impressive."

Jace relished Mari's laugh, his chief goal for the afternoon. She'd worn a worried frown for most of the last twenty-four hours, and his heart ached for her.

They drove to the trailhead and began walking.

"You saw the group chat, right?" said Mari. "T.J. got invited to be on the Hans Hansen show."

"Yeah. A national show! How'd we luck out with that? T.J.'s going to do it, right?"

"Yes. Even though Hans Hansen is a conservative show."

"What's wrong with that?"

"Nothing really. We'd just rather have interviews on a few different platforms, so it doesn't seem like the Bathwater Brigade is one-sided or political. We're hoping the other side will see his interview and want to talk with him, too."

The leaves crunched under their feet as Jace told Mari details of the Civilian Academy website he and Saint had been working on, his voice brimming with excitement. He handed his phone to her, and she gushed over the quality of the work and the importance of the message. "This is what we need right now, Jace!"

She handed him back his phone. "You're getting really good at Bathwater principles. Your work with Saint, the website, all of that." Then she laughed. "And did you ever think you could have a conversation about feminism with a feminist? You're pretty amazing, you know that?"

Jace sighed. "It's true."

She hit his arm. "What happened to 'No Egos'?"

"We're not in a Bathwater meeting, are we?"

Mari pulled a piece of fabric from her pack and tied it around her head. "Now we are."

Jace grinned. "Sensei Mari. Let's do this."

They reached the top of the trail and sat on two large rocks.

"Young apprentice," Mari said, "tell me what you have learned. First lesson, how to surprise your opponent. Go."

Jace thought of his silly sword fight with Dylan all those weeks ago. "Discard your weapons. Also, admit it if you don't know something. It stuns your opponent, and they often follow suit."

She nodded. "This prepares both of you to battle against ideas, not people. Shock them into thinking in a different way."

"Second lesson," she continued, "you learned how to know yourself and your opponent."

"Yes," he said, trying to remember. "The puzzle box thing. Worldview, right?" When she nodded, he said, "I need to carefully consider new information before just throwing it away, even if it doesn't make much sense to me at first."

"Yes. And..." She reached in her pack and held out a metal figure of a man.

"Oh, right," he said. "The steel man. The more I can understand their argument—what they're really thinking and feeling—the more effective our combat will be."

"Yes," she said. "We call it engagement though. Not combat."

He gave her a thumbs up.

"Speaking of engagement, now to lesson three."

He remembered the bridge they had tried to build. "When we ignore the traditional boundaries and work together, you can actually get something done. And it's easier than you think."

"And do you remember a certain Founding Father?" she asked.

"Benjamin Franklin!" he said with a laugh. "The language of persuasion. At the present time, it seems to me that we're ready for the final lesson. If I'm not mistaken."

She chuckled. "Keep working on that until it feels natural." She composed herself, and dramatically said, "Today, you learn to *win*."

This was over-the-top cheesy, but Jace was genuinely excited to see what was next.

Mari pulled eight drinking straws from her pack, handed four to Jace, and invited him to crouch next to her. She asked him some easy math questions and asked him to set a straw in the dirt with each answer. Jace didn't know why they kept doing math questions in the dojo, but at least it wasn't college-level equations.

By the end, he had placed four straws neatly in a row. She did the same, except that one of hers was tilted. Jace absent-mindedly reached over to straighten it.

"Stop!" she said. They both stood. "Why did you touch one of mine?"

"I don't know. I was just fixing it."

"That is not for you to do," she said. "You must learn to allow people to be different. Resist the urge to make people be what you think they should be."

"But...why would I be talking about all these ideas with them if I'm not trying to get them to change?"

"Ah," she said. "Is that what winning is to you? To get the other person to change?"

"Maybe?"

"After a thoughtful discussion, what if it is *you* who changed? Is that a loss?"

"No." Jace thought again. "If I come out of it with some changed ideas of my own, I guess that's a win, too. Maybe a bigger one, actually. I would have worked on my worldview." He looked back at the straws, and grinned as he fought the urge to straighten the one that was out of place.

"Don't do it," Mari teased. "As part of your training, we're going to leave them as they are until we hike back down."

They sat on the rocks again, the tilted straw apparently being the point of the exercise.

Mari smiled. "So, what *is* a win?"

"Probably when we're able to have an honest conversation. No matter the results."

"Yes, apprentice." She gestured toward the straws on the ground. "Persuade and discuss. Even argue. But let your opponent control their own straws and move at their own pace, or no pace at all. Let them be inconsistent, or even flat-out wrong. If you're for intellectual diversity, you shouldn't demand that they think the same as you."

Jace nodded, eyebrows raised. "Great point."

"The second component of winning is to end each engagement better friends than when you started."

"Sounds nice. But what if you're not friends to begin with?"

"Then you want a friendship to start."

"What if the person is just a colossal jerk? Yelling at you and even making up lies. Not listening to a thing you say. Are we supposed to build a friendship there?"

"If you can."

"How is that supposed to happen?"

Mari tossed a pebble at him, on the edge of laughter. "Jace. Think! What about Saint? You had quite a rocky start and it wasn't perfect. But I think you already know how to turn enemies into friends."

Jace cocked his head. "Yeah. I'd say it was him just as much as me, though."

"I know."

Jace smiled thoughtfully, a gentle swell of personal pride warming his chest.

"So, here's what I do." Mari shifted. "If the other person isn't listening to me, and things are going nowhere, I usually just thank them for their time and for giving me some points to think about."

Jace put his hand to his chin. "Dr. Adelson comes to mind."

"Now that you say it, yes," she laughed. "And remember the first dojo lesson where we learned that we don't always have to fight them? Ending the conversation this way is another surprise to them. It's kind of fun, actually. Puts you both in the perfect position for the next time you talk."

"What if there won't *be* a next time? Do I still try to make friends?"

"Yup."

"Even if they don't see it my way at all?"

"I like to keep friends who think differently than me," she said.

"What if *they* don't want to part as friends?"

She grinned. "Do it anyway!"

"You make it sound so easy."

"You plant a seed in them, even if they were a jerk to you. Eventually they could open up. Maybe with someone else later on."

Jace nodded. "I've got to be honest—I feel like I need to have the last word a lot. I want to keep hammering until they admit how stupid they're being."

She laughed. "I know what you mean. But think of when your parents are in a bad mood and criticize everything you do. After a while, you're not that interested in their advice anymore, are you?"

"You're right. So, knowing when to back off the argument for a while and continue later is super important to keep friends." He studied her face. "I'll need a lot of practice to reach Mari Level on this."

"I struggle with this one sometimes," she said, her cheeks coloring. She pulled her feet close and wrapped her arms around her knees. "Remember when you quit the Brigade? I mean, it was understandable with your scholarship and everything. But it was still hard to strike the balance. I was disappointed in the situation, but I wanted to keep your friendship, too. I tried to still be there for you and give you space. I'm not sure I did it right."

They looked at each other. "I think you did."

Jace's phone buzzed, killing the moment. "Oh my gosh, these guys are idiots. Perfect timing."

"Who are they?"

"Some of the people trying to get all our members kicked out of Cale. One is a professor here. Callahan. Such a moron. He keeps talking about the protest video."

"You're arguing with them online?"

"Let's say I'm just offering some points of clarification."

"Don't forget the dojo lesson. Use what you've learned."

He looked at her. "On Twitter?"

"I don't know about you, but when I argue online, it's sort of like fast food. Feels good at the moment, but you usually regret it later."

"They don't even *care* what the truth is. Callahan is all over the place. Every time I give him a valid point, he switches to another topic."

"Still. See if you can practice what you've learned." She sat up and shook a finger at him while she tried not to smile. "Do I need to follow you around with my dojo headband?"

He sighed. "No. But I sort of like how you look in it."

Mari grinned. She stood from her rock and pulled a stick of licorice from her pack. "No phones allowed in the dojo. Here. Stand for the final lesson."

Jace obeyed.

"You're trying to bring me to your side, right? Get me to see things your way?" She handed him an end of the licorice. "Here. Pull me to your side."

He pulled. The licorice broke. "Oops."

"This," she said, holding up her piece of the broken licorice, "was our friendship."

"Crap."

She got another piece. "Try again."

This time he was careful to judge the tension. She let him pull her until she had to take a step to keep from falling forward.

"Well done, apprentice. You made progress, but you knew when to hold back. See? With our friendship still intact, you have the chance to engage with me again."

He tried once more and she came another step, licorice unbroken.

"I get it," he said. "Cool."

Jace cautiously pulled again. She stepped closer, only inches away.

He cleared his throat. "So, an important part of winning is remaining friends?"

She nodded, her face tilted up to him. Something vulnerable fluttered through her eyes. Jace's heart tripped, then resumed at a faster pace. Her eyes drifted closed. He dipped his head and gently kissed her.

Jace raised his head and his fingers slid from her arm to her hand. "I think this is my favorite dojo lesson."

Mari smiled wide.

CHAPTER FORTY-NINE

JACE PULLED his hood up over his head. It was noticeably darker and cooler than it had been at this time of day, even a week ago. He squinted into the face of the north wind and hurried toward the greenhouse.

Possibly for the last time.

It was Wednesday, just two days ahead of the announcement of the decision that Cale administration had probably made weeks ago.

In the basement, the chairs made a full circle. T.J. was there with a few others. They were congratulating him on an impressive haircut and on a flawless interview the night before.

It had been via satellite. T.J. had driven to a TV station in Houston. They set him in front of a backdrop of fake bookshelves facing a screen and a camera. Hans Hansen had clearly been sympathetic to the Brigade, and with each new detail he learned of the club's goals and rules, he seemed to like it more. Hans had described the Bathwater Brigade as a Cale University tradition that spanned generations and was now under attack. He had introduced T.J. as the senior college student willing to drop out of school to help save it.

Jace slapped a firm hand on T.J.'s shoulder. "That was awesome! You nailed it, man."

"Is it true that Hans wants to talk about organizing the Bathwater Brigade nationwide?" asked Kendric. T.J. nodded.

Eli held the door for Danica as they entered the basement. Mari arrived just before 7:00 P.M. She stood near the doorway for a while and took in the room. When her gaze met Jace's, she gave him a sad, fleeting smile and sat in the chair next to him.

"I'm hungry," Jace said. "Can you just give me more licorice, or do I have to practice dojo lessons for that?"

She nudged him and grinned. "I'm good either way."

T.J. looked around the room. "Okay, we're all here. Now to be clear, in case Janet Thompson has bugged the room, this isn't a *regular* Bathwater meeting. Only the core members were officially invited. Anyone else that's here found out and came anyway."

They nodded and chuckled.

"Have you heard from Rodriguez?" asked Kendric.

"Yeah," said T.J. "Just a little while ago."

"And?"

"Status quo. They saw the Hans Hansen clips. Didn't change anything. He says he'd be shocked if they didn't vote against us."

Kendric's face fell, and a few others groaned.

"You look happier than I would expect," Mari said to T.J.

He smiled. "I got an interesting email a few minutes ago."

"Was it from God?" Amber said. "I think that's the only thing that will help at this point."

"Nope." He winked at her. "Close, though. It was Rich Weaver."

"The senator?"

He nodded.

"He's great," said Amber.

"Rich contacted us, said he might be able to help. Said I could call him." T.J. leaned back in his chair. "What do you guys think?"

Jace looked at Mari and shrugged. Amber glanced around. "Well...yeah! Let's call him. It can't hurt, right?"

"Would that mean we're getting into politics?" asked Eli.

"Not necessarily," said T.J. "We can talk to anyone we like. We just can't encourage anyone to vote for him."

Dylan gave a thumbs up. "Well, go on. Give him a call!"

T.J. nodded. "I'll go up where there's cell reception." He left the room. They heard him go halfway up the stairs and then return. He poked his head back through the door. "What. Nobody's coming with me?"

They laughed and raced for the door.

T.J. found an open spot between a long table covered with flowers and a row of potted ferns on the ground. They formed a circle around him. He glanced at everyone as he pulled up the email on his phone. He found the phone number and put it on speaker. He breathed deep and flicked his eyebrows at Mari. "Here we go."

Two rings later, a man answered. "Weaver here."

Mari, who was holding onto Jace's arm, squeezed harder.

"Hi, Senator. This is T.J. Campfield. From the Bathwater Brigade. I'm here with a few friends."

"Oh, great! Thanks for getting back with me, T.J. You've been getting quite a bit of attention lately. Stirring things up in the right ways. I like it."

"Thanks."

"Are you going on any more TV shows?"

"Two more reached out. But they won't air until after the final hearing."

"All right. So, how's it looking for you, there? Think the school will back off?"

T.J. sighed. "Doesn't look like it, unfortunately."

"That's too bad. Well, look. Let me get right to it. I'm friends with the president of the university. Camden and I golf at least once a month. He owes me a favor."

"Really?"

"One hundred percent. I'm confident I can work something out with him. I hear that some of the other administrators aren't too keen on you guys, but no administrator will go against a directive from their president."

Eyes grew wide in the group. Amber silently clapped. Dylan put his fist in the air.

"That would be amazing." T.J. gave a short laugh.

"When is the big day for you all?" the senator asked.

"They announce their decision in two days."

"Okay. I can call him tonight."

"Thank you so much," said T.J.

"Always happy to help. You're doing important things, you know that?" Before T.J. could answer, Weaver said, "One last thing."

"Yeah?"

"I'd sure like your support this election."

The greenhouse went silent.

"Hello?"

T.J. cleared his throat. "To be clear," he said, running his fingers through his hair, "you'll need our campaign support for you to help us out?"

"I'm afraid so, guys. I only have so many favors I can call in. I wish the world didn't work this way, but it does. It's neck and neck this election, and if I had you sharing your endorsement on a few of these interviews you're giving...well, it just might make the difference I need."

"Give us just a minute." T.J. put the call on mute. He pinched the bridge of his nose with his free hand and then looked at the core members. "Well?"

"Is there even a question?" said Dylan. "It's either this, or the Brigade is done."

Amber stared at the ground, a hand to her chin.

"We can't," said Mari with a sad shake of her head.

"But if it saves the Brigade..." said Eli, to no one in particular.

Kendric frowned.

Dylan's breathing quickened. "You guys are idiots. We're drowning here, and we just got thrown a life preserver. People will understand. Who cares if we do it this once if it means that we get to keep meeting? Just...let's get through this election and then reevaluate things."

"There's a Bathwater saying," said Kendric after a pause. "A win where we have to abandon our principles isn't a win."

T.J. locked eyes with the core members, one by one. He skipped Dylan. Some hesitated, but in the end, they each shook their head.

T.J. took the call off mute.

"Senator?"

"Yes."

"We're sorry, but we can't support you or anyone else in the election."

There was a pause. "That's unfortunate, but I understand. Well, I wish you all good luck."

T.J. clenched his jaw. "Thanks."

Weaver hung up.

T.J. put his phone in his pocket and looked around.

"Um, what just happened?" asked Danica. "It sounded like he just shut down a business deal."

"To him," said Kendric, "I guess it was."

"I think I'd like to sit down," said T.J.

They trudged down the stairs.

CHAPTER FIFTY

"I GUESS we're in the same situation we were in twenty minutes ago," Eli said. "But it feels much worse."

"Well," said Jace. "What now?"

No one answered.

Dylan stared at the floor. "You're all morons."

"Wow," said Amber. "Thanks, Dylan. What did you expect us to do?"

Mari shook her head. "Even if Janet is fine with us campaigning, it goes against what we are. We'd lose our essence. You know that."

Dylan laughed. "Essence." He stood and paced the room, holding the sides of his head. "I don't believe you just did that."

"Why do you want to support him so badly?" Danica asked.

He stopped pacing. "I watch election after election. Each time I think Washington D.C. can't get any worse. But it does."

"We know," said Kendric. "That's why we're here."

"But what are we *changing*?" Dylan clenched his fists. "All we do is talk, talk, talk. Where is the action? The party with the most seats in Washington makes the rules. That's how the game is played. And it doesn't even matter who the politician is or what their principles are. Don't you get it? Weaver could have turned things around. And he's even a decent guy, I made sure of that. Someone I thought you'd really get behind, you know?" He shook his head. "You talk about policies. This was your chance to influence them."

"We're in the same fight, Dylan," said Mari. "You're talking downstream, at the voting booth. The Bathwater Brigade is upstream, where philosophies are formed. We need both."

Jace said, "You can still support candidates on your own, you know? I mean, I'm going to vote for Weaver. At least, I *was* going to..."

"Maybe Bathwater isn't a good fit for you," Danica said earnestly.

Dylan laughed again. "Do you know how much good we could have done, right here? Weaver is *barely* behind in the polls. Have you looked at who he's running against? Harper? His party is guaranteed to run this country into the ground. With all the media attention we've been getting, we could have made the difference."

"For being part of the reason we're in this position," said Eli, "you're getting pretty upset with us."

"What do you mean?" asked T.J.

"He's the one that made the flier," Eli said.

"The cops one?" said Mari. "From the trial? We thought it was your friend Rob that made it."

Eli nodded. "Rob got talking to him, and Dylan said he could help him out. I thought you guys knew."

Mari stood and stared Dylan down. "*You* made that awful flier? With our logo still on it?"

"So I'm not a graphic designer," Dylan said with a shrug.

"You are a core member of the Bathwater Brigade," said Mari. "You know better."

Kendric stood. "This isn't making sense, man."

T.J. narrowed his eyes. "Dylan. Did *Texas Late Edition* really cancel our interview?"

Jace grabbed Mari's arm, eyes wide. He slowly stood. "Wait. Were you on a conference call with Janet Thompson last week? Just before the first hearing?"

"No," Dylan said with a look of disgust.

"It *was* you. I was there."

"In Janet's office?"

"Who said it was in her office?" asked Mari.

"Show us your call history," said Jace.

T.J. stood, arms folded. "Just tell us what's going on."

Amber looked like she was about to cry.

"You were supposed to accept his help!" Dylan yelled. He shoved the folding chair in front of him. It collapsed with a metallic crash that echoed off the concrete walls. The rest of the Brigade rose to their feet.

"You played us," said Kendric.

Dylan whipped around and pointed at him. "No. I played Zero Supremacy. And Janet Thompson. Once Weaver got involved, they would have *had* to back down. We could have defeated them for good! We could have gotten out of this crappy basement and everything would have been normal again."

"With the bonus of forcing us to betray our principles to get your favorite candidate elected," said Mari.

Dylan held up his hands. His face changed from angry to pleading. "I did it for you. For all of us. He was our only shot. And I knew you guys wouldn't go for it unless things got really bad for us."

"So you made things really bad for us," said Jace. "Nice."

"All I did was speed up the inevitable. Janet was going to find some reason to shut you down anyway." Dylan shoved his way through the circle of chairs again and got in T.J.'s face. "Are you telling me you'd rather throw away your education than bend the rules of a stupid campus club?" Dylan waited, breathing hard. The pause was so long, Jace wasn't sure whether T.J. would respond at all.

"I don't care about the sculpture club," said T.J. "Or Cale's school spirit club. Or any of the rest. But when it comes to this one, yeah, it's worth something, Dylan. Principles are worth something. I thought you got that."

Eli put his arm around Danica. Mari and Kendric closed ranks around T.J.

T.J. took a step forward, crowding Dylan back. "I'm playing the long game, Dylan. And maybe it's selfish, but in sixty years, I'll have a lot of time to think. We don't get many chances to make an impact like this in the world. If I let the Brigade fizzle out, or fundamentally change what it is, then I'll regret this moment for the rest of my life."

T.J. lowered his head and his eyes bored into Dylan. "I guess we're both being selfish right now. But only one of us has to leave through that door."

Dylan turned an ugly red, and his hands balled into fists at his side.

"Don't do it, man," Kendric murmured. "T.J. will take you apart."

Dylan trembled on the brink for what felt like an eternity. His breath came in ragged gasps.

T.J. spoke again, his voice hard but calm. "Leave. Right. Now."

With a sneer, Dylan spun away and stormed toward the door. He grabbed the back of another folding chair and launched it, spinning like a discus to the back of the room. A leg of the chair punched through the canvas painting of the football player before it clattered to the floor.

Jace moved to stop him, but Mari held his arm.

Dylan stalked out of the room, slamming the heavy door behind him. Dust floated from the ceiling as the booming echo faded.

"Woah," whispered Eli. "That was intense. I thought that only happened in movies."

Amber held her hand to her mouth. Choking back tears, she rushed toward the door and then stopped. She came back and collapsed into her chair. Mari sat next to Amber and gently hugged her.

Jace picked up the chairs while Danica inspected the painting. "We can fix it from behind, I think."

Once more, they slowly took their seats. T.J. breathed in and then out through pursed lips. He rubbed his face. "What a week."

"Well?" said Jace. "What now? How can we make this even worse?"

T.J. smiled and reached for his bag. "I thought we might find ourselves here." He pulled a piece of paper from a blue folder.

"What's that?" asked Kendric.

"My resignation."

Mari gasped. "Oh no," said Amber.

"Quitting college, then?" said Eli. "You're really going for it?"

T.J. nodded.

"What does it say?" asked Kendric.

"Just some more of what we talked about in the hearing. What a university should be. And that if Cale can't handle a couple of students talking about tough subjects, then it's not where I want to wear the cap and gown."

Amber said, "I know what you mean about regrets, but you quitting isn't going to change Janet's mind. Either way, you know we're not going to win. Right?"

T.J. set the paper down and raised an eyebrow. "On what timeline?"

"What do you mean?"

"Remember when we went to England that one summer with Mom and Dad, and they dragged us to every church in the U.K.? And how, even after seeing all those other churches, York Minster Cathedral still took our breath away?" Amber nodded. "How many years did that take them to build?"

Amber shrugged. "A few hundred, I think."

"Workers showed up each day, knowing they'd never see it completed. Same with the architect. Every single person at the ground-breaking ceremony was in the cemetery by the time of grand opening." He reached over and squeezed her hand. "Some things are worth working on and sacrificing for, even if it doesn't help me personally in college. Or ever."

Kendric sighed. "As they say, Moses never got to see the promised land."

Jace tilted his head and narrowed his eyes at T.J. "I was about to say you're no Moses. But if you grow that beard just a little longer..."

"You're saying this is bigger than us?" asked Eli.

T.J. sat forward. "I'm getting emails from all over the country. We're not the only ones, guys. I mean, we're the only Bathwater Brigade, but there are other university clubs like it that are struggling to survive. In Maryland, Oregon...They're getting shut down, too. We're in the spotlight right now. Our story is still growing. And our support. Even after it's all over for us, our story will be there." T.J. held up his paper. "This probably doesn't help *us*. But maybe it can help *them*."

"By becoming a martyr?" asked Jace.

"Yes." Then he added, "I'm only following through on what I said I would do. It's working. Me dropping out of Cale is getting attention. This movement, this idea of diversity of thought, it's bigger than Bathwater. It's bigger than Cale."

"He's right," said Kendric. "If you read history, the universities are where the destinies of nations are born." He looked at T.J. and sighed. "I don't think you're overselling this, man."

"But your degree!" said Amber.

He shrugged. "I figure it will set me back at least a year. Look, it's not like I'm laying down my life here. Do you know how many guys my age actually died to make sure America is free and under the banner of good principles? Ten years from now, I'll be an architect either way. Yeah, it's a hassle, but lots of students take a few extra years to get their degree."

"So, what will you do?" asked Eli.

"Not sure yet. But I guarantee I'll be going somewhere that will tolerate a new chapter of the Bathwater Brigade."

"But we won't have you with us," said Mari.

T.J. solemnly nodded. "That was the hardest part."

"Can I read it?" asked Kendric. T.J. handed him the paper, and Kendric pulled a pen from his backpack.

"What are you doing?" asked T.J.

"Word hog. You didn't leave much room for anyone else to sign," Kendric said. He put his signature next to T.J.'s.

T.J. stood. "Oh, no you don't. This is *my* thing."

Kendric stood, handed it back to him, and somberly shook his hand. "Don't worry, I've thought it through. I'm with you, brother. You can't live it up with a new Brigade somewhere else and leave us with Janet Thompson. And why is it a good idea for you to resign, but not for me? Won't we get more publicity by having two of us dropping out together?" Then he smiled. "Or do you just want the whole spotlight for yourself? You really *are* being selfish!"

T.J. looked defeated. Or maybe relieved. "Thanks, man."

Silence fell on the room again, but it was the quiet of coming goodbyes and new, hopeful beginnings rather than the depressing silence of defeat.

Amber held out an impatient hand and T.J. reluctantly gave her the paper. "I was going to sign anyway if my idiot brother decided to go through with his ridiculous plan."

Eli signed next, then Danica. She handed the paper to Mari.

Jace nudged her with his elbow. "Hey, maybe you, me, and some others could go to Lone Star College or something. Start our own Bathwater club." Then he smirked. "Plus, this way we can get out of next week's botany final."

She didn't laugh. She just stared at the paper, her hand trembling a little.

Jace's stomach pitched uneasily. "Mari?"

She clutched the pen. "I'm not going to sign."

Jace blinked. "You're not?"

"No. It's a big deal, Jace. Our college degrees are a big freaking deal."

"But...I thought you would be the first one. What about your aunt Yanni? And helping America remember who she is and all that? The washed-up hero. I mean, you're the one that got me where I am, here."

She blinked back tears. "Jace, we can talk about it another time." She exchanged glances with T.J. "And promise me you won't sign this just yet."

"Wait!" said Danica. She held up a hand.

"What?" said Eli.

"Shhh..."

They heard footsteps on the stairs.

Lots of them.

T.J. quietly dashed to the door and locked it.

The Brigade members glanced around nervously. Eli stepped in front of Danica. Amber picked up a folded metal chair. "Zeroes!" she whispered.

"I thought it might end this way," Jace muttered. His breathing quickened. He and Mari looked at each other.

The footsteps stopped at the landing on the other side of the door. A loud knock echoed through the room. T.J. listened. They heard voices. And the clink of keys. Jace tensed.

"T.J.," Kendric whispered. "Turn off the lights."

He didn't. Instead, he held up a finger.

"T.J.!" Amber hissed.

Then he unlocked and threw open the door.

CHAPTER FIFTY-ONE

IN WALKED Wayne Berry from the restaurant.

With a big smile, he raised his arms wide as if inviting an enormous group hug. "Hello! We thought nobody would be here."

Jace slumped and exhaled.

Kendric still stood in a defensive position, holding one of the foam swords from the first dojo lesson. "Kendric!" whispered Mari. He snapped out of it, and with a sheepish smile, cast the toy to the side and cleared his throat.

More people followed Wayne into the room. A portly woman with medium-length brown hair and a kind face. A tall, thin man with neatly trimmed gray hair and beard. A woman who looked Japanese. Twelve of them in all, between the ages of forty and sixty. They smiled at the gaping students.

"We didn't mean to interrupt," said the first woman. "It appears we may have frightened you." A few of them chuckled.

"T.J., everyone," said Wayne, "please let me introduce you to a few of the Bathwater alumni."

Mari gasped. Kendric smiled. The students walked over and shook hands with each of the guests.

"We're *so* glad you came by tonight," said Mari. "What brings you here?"

"We heard something big was happening in a day or two," said the tall man with the gray beard. "Thought you could use some moral support. More are flying in tomorrow."

Mari smiled bigger and blinked back tears.

"I'm Ilene Corey," said the woman standing next to him. "And this is my husband, Norwood. We were in the Bathwater Brigade in the late seventies."

The buzz of conversation filled the room as the two groups mingled.

"Hold on!" said Wayne. They quieted. "We need to organize this. Everyone introduce themselves one at a time, and then we can be done with it. I'm Wayne Berry. I joined the Bathwater Brigade in 1977. I live here in New Brig."

He nodded to the girl on his left.

"Amber Campfield."

"T.J. Campfield."

"You two married?" asked someone.

"Nope!" said T.J. immediately, apparently knowing that question was coming. "Siblings."

"Jean Pendrod. 1985."

"Miyashiro Ayumi. 1991."

"Warren Hollis. 1984."

"Clarissa Glenn. 1976. But I was Clarissa Donnelson back then."

Kendric stepped forward. "You..." he began. He pointed at her. "You started the Bathwater Brigade."

Clarissa smiled brightly and nodded.

The students shifted quietly, looks of stunned excitement on their faces. Mari took a few steps forward, then nearly lunged at her with an embrace.

Clarissa recovered and patted Mari on the back, smiling at her alumni friends. "It was only me and a few friends at first. I never dreamed it would grow into this."

"You created something the world desperately needed," said Norwood.

"Stumbled onto it, rather," replied Clarissa humbly.

The seasoned guests strolled around the edge of the room, talking excitedly with the students and each other as they admired the artwork and examined the photos of past Brigades. Occasionally, they would snap a picture of one of them standing next to a photograph and pointing.

T.J. and Clarissa put an arm around each other for a photo.

"Awesome," said Eli. "The first and last Brigade presidents." Danica shot him a glare. "I mean, the first and *current* Brigade presidents."

"What is it, Norwood?" asked Ilene. Her husband crouched in the corner, with a wistful smile and hand to his beard.

Norwood lifted the Worldview box. He opened it and nodded.

"Your box!" Ilene said.

"You're the one that carved it?" said Kendric.

"Yep." He turned and examined it with a look of satisfaction. "You guys kept it pretty nice!"

"It has helped hundreds of students like me learn a valuable lesson," Kendric said. "And that's only the actual members! Then those members teach and influence others in their classes, jobs, families..." He shook his head. "You have helped thousands see and understand each other better. Thank you."

"Do you all have plans right now?" asked T.J. "Because we would absolutely love for you to stay for a while."

Ilene smiled. "We were hoping you'd say that."

They added more chairs to the circle. Amber pulled some of the old archives from the filing cabinet and sat with a few of the visitors, parsing through photographs, newspaper clippings, and old meeting notes.

They laughed as they exchanged stories and nodded as they told of their struggles. A few of the alumni could still recite the dojo lessons in order, and they told how it had helped them throughout their lives. Two of them were company presidents, one a renowned author, and a handful of them ran successful charity or nonprofit organizations.

"It's so peculiar," Mari whispered to Jace. "I feel more connection to these strangers than most of my classmates." He wanted to squeeze her hand, but it still felt like she had let him down, and he hadn't had time to process those feelings yet.

"So," said Norwood. "How's it looking? You know, for tomorrow."

T.J. put his hands on his knees and took a deep breath. "Well, it's been a roller coaster. But it's likely that you're sitting at the last meeting of the Bathwater Brigade."

"*More* than likely," said Kendric.

This was met with groans from the alumni.

Amber said, "But we are so glad you're here with us for it. A poetic ending."

The students told the entire story. The Zeroes, the reason for meeting in the basement, the video, the flier. They showed them Florence Hughes' letter and told about the call with Senator Weaver.

"I feel bad for Cale University," Wayne mourned. "It will never know the gem it has lost."

"The *world* has lost," corrected Ilene.

They all nodded.

"Oh no." Amber's whisper cut through the moment's silence.

"What's up, Amber?" said T.J.

Her eyes were wide as she stared at a strip of newspaper. "Apparently you guys had a display on campus. 1979. It was about gun control."

"I remember that," Clarissa said. "There was a big clamor for gun laws at that time. Ilene, do you remember?"

Ilene looked up at the ceiling tiles for a moment. "Yes. We were out there with some statistics and other considerations for why those particular laws just might make us less safe instead of *more* safe. Funny how upset some people were with us."

"Sounds like something we would do," said T.J.

Amber nodded. "Yeah, but look who stopped by." She showed T.J. "Read the caption."

He raised an eyebrow, then leaned forward with a hand over his mouth. "Janet Thompson."

Danica turned. "What?"

T.J. put the clipping into Ilene's outstretched hand.

"Is she the one..." began Norwood. Ilene glanced at him and nodded.

"Does one of you know her?" asked Clarissa.

Jace chuckled. "Oh yeah. She's the administrator trying to shut this down."

Clarissa frowned. "She's in Cale University's administration now? Really..."

They passed the clipping around the room. A young, angry woman was yelling at three students standing behind a table.

"Same hairstyle," remarked Eli. "Was she a Bathwater member once or something?"

"No," smiled Norwood. "But the gun control issue really got her attention. She was pushing for that legislation. It was going to restrict the types of firearms you could buy or something like that. As you can see in that photo, she didn't like what we were doing."

Ilene groaned. "She got a big group together. They followed us around, demanding we stop talking about it. She made threats and said horrible things. She eventually got suspended." Amber, Mari, and Jace glanced at T.J. "We never saw her again."

"The weird thing about it all," said Clarissa, "is that some of us actually agreed with her about the legislation. But we all felt that one side of the argument wasn't being represented. We wanted to make sure we had our eyes open wide, and that we weren't going to accidentally throw out the baby with the bathwater."

Jace nodded. "So, why was she so angry?"

"No idea," said Ilene.

"Don't you remember?" said Clarissa. "It was because of her uncle."

"Oh, that's right. It was personal. She had an uncle that got into an argument one night. The person he fought with shot and killed him."

T.J. grimaced. "That's rough."

Wayne sighed. "This is all making a little more sense. Remember when she said that some ideas get people killed?"

T.J. nodded.

"I feel so bad for her family," said Danica, sitting on her hands, her short legs barely touching the floor. She looked up. "Did she really come to work at Cale just to get at the Bathwater Brigade?"

Mari shrugged. "I don't know what to think anymore. But she's here now, and it looks like she's calling the shots."

Norwood leaned forward. "So, I hear you're quitting school," he said to T.J. "Saw you on Hans Hansen. That's quite a thing."

340

T.J. nodded.

"Really going to do it?"

"Yeah. After they announce the decision. A few others here think they're going to quit, too." He glanced at Kendric and rolled his eyes.

"You really think it's not going to go your way."

The students nodded.

Ilene nudged Norwood. They glanced at each other. She reached into her bag and handed him a thin binder. He pulled out two pieces of paper. Leaning forward in his chair, he looked at them for a moment. Then he handed them to T.J.

"Here. We'll add these to the mix."

T.J.'s mouth fell open. "Your diplomas!"

"It's not like it changes our life," said Ilene. "It's not a sacrifice compared to what you're doing. But we wanted to do something."

Norwood took the diplomas back and glanced around the circle. "A bunch of us brought them here. We'll hand them in at the administration office right after the trial and make a short statement. That is, if it all goes south like you're thinking. We already notified the local news. They'll be there." There were solemn nods from the alumni.

"This is...amazing," said Amber.

"We want to make sure people know what happened here."

Eli nodded. "Playing the long game."

Norwood winked at him.

Eli reached back and grabbed T.J.'s letter. "This is our resignation."

Jace casually stood. "Here. I'll hand it to them."

Before Mari could react, he snatched a pen from Kendric's open backpack, set the letter on his empty chair, and signed.

CHAPTER FIFTY-TWO

THE NEXT MORNING, the weather was calm and pleasant. So were Jace's nerves as he strolled through campus carrying his backpack and trombone case.

Everything looked different, now that his time at Cale was short. He was mentally detaching himself from what was here. He knew what would happen at the hearing tomorrow, and he was beginning to accept what just days ago was unthinkable.

Long after the alumni had left the night before, Amber had posted a picture of the final paragraphs of the Janet Thompson newspaper clipping in the group chat. "We should have read to the end." Janet was quoted in the article as saying some very nasty, and even racist things about them. Eli was elated. "People get fired for this. It was under our nose the whole time!" he'd responded to the group. "All we have to do is bring this to the media, and she'll have to resign for sure. Maybe T.J. can go on Hans Hansen again."

But Jace knew it would go against the Bathwater Brigade's standards to dig up statements made in the distant past that the person might not believe now, and may not have even believed back then. They wouldn't take that road. Even when it could have saved them.

Jace had smiled sadly and wondered who would be the first to type it.

It was Danica.

A win where we have to abandon our principles isn't a win.

They were out of options now. The Bathwater Brigade was done, and partly because of Jace. But the Texas sun would rise again. They'd each find new ways to challenge conventional thought. Jace wondered whether he would be the only Bathwater member wherever he ended up, and whether he had the personality to start a similar club himself. It would never be the same without T.J., though. Or Eli, or Kendric.

Or Mari.

They hadn't spoken since she told him she was choosing a Cale diploma over the Brigade. Her decision was a completely rational one, and it surprised him that he felt a little hurt by it. He decided he'd let her make the first move and come to him with an explanation, when she was ready. Hopefully, it would happen during his now very limited time at Cale. For now, though, he tried to put her out of his mind.

A chubby kid with shorts, a white T-shirt, and high socks sat alone on a bench while others walked past. He leaned forward with an elbow on his knee and his fist under his chin. With the other hand, he held a long wooden stick which he had attached to a homemade sign. "I think, therefore I am...unwelcome at Cale." A yellow rubber duck was drawn in the bottom corner.

Jace smiled and stopped to talk with him. He was a local high school student. His older brothers and sisters had all been members of the Bathwater Brigade, and he'd hoped to join next year. His entire family planned to attend the hearing the next day. Jace gave him an encouraging pat on the shoulder and resumed his walk.

He went into rehearsal. Rob was on a chair, leaning back against the wall in precisely the way Dr. Kline had instructed him not to. Their eyes met. Rob nodded at Jace before returning his focus on the drumstick that he was flipping in the air. It wasn't much, but it was something. Jace wondered when he should tell Rob that he was leaving, and whether he would even care.

. . .

The lists of police training and policies were looking great on the *Civilian Academy* website, but one of the Zeroes had complained that some of the descriptions were technical and boring. Jace had the idea to make it so the viewer could switch between *Technical Mode* and *Regular People Mode*, with a summary in everyday language, and he and Saint worked on it in the computer lab later that afternoon.

Jace clicked the save button after copying the last of New Brig Police Department's Use of Force policies into *Civilian Academy*. He glanced over at Saint who was frowning at his monitor. "We need one more addition." He leaned one arm over the back of the office chair.

"What *now*?"

"A section to explain the reason for each policy," Jace said. "You always see people criticize the police for doing this or that, but you hardly ever hear whether they were following their training. And if so, what the training is even for. We could even have bodycam and dashcam videos right on the page that illustrates what could happen if they didn't have that policy."

"Hmm. An example?"

"Like when the police shoot more than once. Everyone says they shouldn't keep shooting. But I've seen videos where the suspect still goes after them even after a couple of shots. I don't know, it would just be nice to see their side of it before we get too upset at them."

Saint's eyes hadn't left his screen. "Maybe," he muttered. "But if so, we'd better add one more section: the criticism of the policy. Show the other side, right, Bathwater Boy?"

"That's fair." Jace swung his chair around in a full circle, his legs crossed. "Maybe anyone could comment on it. This could be the community's main platform to push for change."

Saint raised an eyebrow. "Don't feature creep on me. Community interaction is phase two, remember? At first it will only be informational."

Jace nodded. "True. And for the extra info about the policies, we'd probably need to get cooperation from the police. Like that's going to happen."

"Deborah's way ahead of you."

Jace grabbed the edge of the desk to stop the swing of his chair. "She reached out to a police department?"

"Yup. She knew that to get the website how we want it, we'd have to work with them eventually. Last week she asked if I'd be okay with her reaching out to a few departments to get a relationship going. I knew you'd be fine with that." Saint finally looked away from the monitor and rubbed his eyes. "She keeps talking about having a diverse coalition. You know, getting lots of different groups behind this. She thinks we'll get more attention that way."

"Like an alloy."

"You mean *ally*."

Jace chuckled. "No. When you want to make metal stronger, like for a bike frame, then you mix it with different kinds of metal."

"Are you sure that's how it works?" Saint asked.

"My dad's a machinist."

"Oh, right."

Jace grinned. "We should get the Bathwater Brigade officially on board. Bringing different perspectives together is our main thing, you know. Just think...the ultimate diverse coalition! The Hobbs family, the police, Zero Supremacy, and the Bathwater Brigade."

Saint laughed. "You know, she might actually go for that."

"Too bad we'll be disbanded before we get that shot." Jace sighed and picked up a stray rubber band someone had left on the desk. "Well, it's great she's good with at least involving law enforcement on this. I mean, we talked about doing it eventually, but I didn't think Zero Supremacy would actually put up with that."

"Some of them won't." Saint turned his chair and leaned back with his hands folded behind his head and sighed. "Something's happening with Zero Supremacy, Jace. It feels like things are shifting. Lines are being drawn, you know?"

"Oh. Because of the Civilian Academy?"

Saint grimaced. "I think it began before that, but this seems to be speeding it up. It's not like all of Zero Supremacy is working on the website, but they all feel like their name is on it. And some of them are really uncomfortable saying anything about the police that's not..." He trailed off.

"Calling them Nazi pigs?"

Saint smiled and looked up at the ceiling.

Jace lightly punched him on the arm. "If you're looking for a new club to join, I'm pretty sure the Bathwater Brigade would be glad to have you."

Saint laughed. "You're asking me to jump ship onto the Titanic, literally as it's sinking."

"Fair point." Jace watched the tiny blinking lights down the row of computers, the monitors all in sleep mode. "Deborah's still going strong, then?" Jace said.

Saint raised his eyebrows, looked at Jace, and nodded. "She's on fire. Like, spending as much time with it as you and I are. I think this is her way of coping with the death of Stephen. We're having all the meetings at her house, now. She's a natural leader."

"We're lucky to have her on the project, that's for sure."

"She wants news stations to mention *CivilianAcademy.com* when they report on police shootings—especially ones that could have been avoided. The same way they give out the number for the suicide or domestic abuse help lines at the end of some news stories."

"Awesome," said Jace. "With her behind it, the news stations might actually do it."

Jace accidentally flipped the rubber band he was playing with, and it flew to the other side of the room.

"So, does it still look like the Bathwater Brigade is over?" Saint asked.

"Yeah, we're toast."

A month ago, this news would have had Saint jumping for joy, but now he only asked, "Even with that rich lady offering to pay for security and all that?"

"I think they're mainly just worried about the school image. They *really* didn't like that viral video. They think it makes the whole school look racist." He smirked. "You're in it, too, right? In the background somewhere? That's got to be cool for you, being in the video that took down the Brigade."

Saint smiled a little, nudging his shoe against the edge of the desk to give his chair a bounce.

Jace chuckled. "I think the only person on this planet right now that Janet would listen to is Deborah Hobbs. But I doubt that anything

Deborah would say right now about the Bathwater Brigade would be positive. She must hate us."

"I don't know about that," said Saint, examining his shoelace. "She'd probably surprise you."

They were silent, the subtle whir of computer fans the only noise in the room.

Jace and Saint looked at each other. Jace's smile faded. Saint tilted his head and narrowed his eyes.

"Do you think..." began Jace.

"Couldn't hurt to try."

Jace sat straight up and planted his feet on the floor. His eyes were big. "When do you meet next?"

"Tonight."

Jace tunneled his fingers through his hair, then he laughed. "Hi. I'm the guy that apparently made fun of your late son at his memorial. How about you do me a huge favor?"

Saint's smile widened. "You could probably word it differently."

"But if I show up at your meeting, then everyone would know you've been working with me," Jace said. "That wouldn't be good for you. Maybe I could write a letter, and you can say you found it on her porch."

"I can give her a letter," Saint said.

Jace stared at his monitor, frozen.

Saint checked his watch. "Might want to get started."

Jace nodded, clicked the mouse a few times, and began to type.

CHAPTER FIFTY-THREE

JACE AND ELI enjoyed a game of pool on what was probably their last night as Brigade members. Two paper plates with half-eaten sweet rolls were on the wide windowsill.

"So, what do you think?" Eli said.

Jace strolled around the table, looking for his best shot. He had only been half listening. "You're going to buy one hundred bars of soap. For *what* again?"

"No, *we're* going to buy the soap. Bars of Petals of the Maldives are on a massive sale right now at the main store. We'll pass a box to all the Bathwater fans with this paper."

Jace glanced at Eli's handwritten note.

Do not open until you hear a loud sneeze at the back of the room.

Eli grinned. "Then the whole place will smell like bath soap!"

Jace smiled a little. "What's the name of *this* operation?"

"Operation? Nah, this one's just a prank."

Jace's smile faded. He didn't know what would happen after the meeting, after they submitted their resignation. It was quite possible he'd never set foot in band again. He wouldn't miss band much, but he didn't know if he'd ever get a chance to break the awkward stalemate with Rob. The longer they went without speaking, the more distant they felt.

Jace missed the pocket that he thought would be an easy shot and straightened. "I don't know, Eli. It would be fun, and it's *definitely* going to annoy Janet, but it won't help the Brigade."

Eli sighed and put the note back in his pocket. "So Mari's staying at Cale, huh? Danica and I were a little surprised."

"It was a surprise to me, too." Jace sat on the edge of the table. "Maybe dropping out is stupid. But I know I'd regret it if I didn't sign. I'm kind of mad at her, but I shouldn't be. She's not doing anything wrong. I just hoped that we'd have longer to see where things went with us, you know?"

Eli gave him a pat on the back and then lined up his shot. "I've been there. Lots of times."

"I thought we'd go down in a blaze of glory together and start fresh somewhere else."

"You just need a few days," said Eli as he hit a striped ball into a side pocket.

"Right," said Jace. He stood, grasped his cue stick, and walked to the other side of the table. He stared at the balls for a minute before he smiled. "Thanks for bringing up Mari. You're trying to mess with my head, aren't you?"

"Whatever it takes to win." Eli grinned. "You make it so easy."

Jace checked his phone. 10:05 P.M. That Civilian Academy meeting had to be over by now, and he hadn't heard anything from Saint.

"Arguing with Professor Callahan again on Twitter?" asked Eli.

"No." Jace sized him up. "You'd call me crazy if I told you."

Eli set his cue down. "Let's hear it."

"You sure? This will take a few minutes to explain, and you'll lose your momentum on your winning streak."

"Let's get out of here."

They cleaned up the game, left the Student Union Building, and strolled around the outside of the football stadium. In the dark, Jace explained about Deborah, the Civilian Academy, Saint, and the letter.

"Woah. Can I read it?"

"Sure." Jace pulled it up on his phone. When he'd written it, he'd felt like he should begin the letter with an apology about Stephen's memorial. If she responded to the letter, then she'd find out eventually that it was him on the roof with the banner, and Jace thought that information was better coming from him sooner rather from someone else later. But he had stared at the keyboard for twenty minutes without finding the right words. In the end, he'd just left it out.

Eli read aloud.

Dear Mrs. Hobbs,

I've heard about the website you're building, CivilianAcademy.com. It's an amazing idea and I think it will do a lot of good in the world.

Eli glanced at Jace. "Complimenting yourself, here?"
Jace grinned and shrugged.
Eli continued reading.

Let me introduce myself. I'm a member of the Bathwater Brigade here at Cale University. You may know about us already. First, let me say that if you've heard anything bad about the Brigade, there is probably more to the story.

Eli smiled. "True." He continued.

Most people seem to be annoyed at differing opinions, but our club seeks them out. We see them as opportunities, and we practice how to have respectful and productive conversations with people very different than us. Some of the best friendships and world solutions can be found when opposites come together. Except when they do, they discover they're not really opposites at all. We are so much more alike than most of us realize.
I understand that to achieve your goals on the Civilian Academy, you'll need to get people to work together who normally wouldn't

see eye-to-eye. The Bathwater Brigade would be happy to discuss joining with you on this great project.
However, we will not be able to join you if we are shut down tomorrow morning. If you would like our help, put in a good word for us with Janet Thompson by calling the number below before 9:30 A.M. Please consider it.

Sincerely, Jace Kartchner

Jace watched Eli, gauging his reaction. Only his silhouette was lit by the bright lights of the Maintenance Building behind him.

Eli put a large hand on Jace's back, let out a deep breath, and gave a raspy chuckle. "Man. I bet you never thought you'd be writing a letter like that. Bold move. What are the chances she'll call?"

"I don't know. Twenty percent? Maybe fifteen."

"Maybe Saint knows. If he gave the letter to her."

Jace nodded. "I'll text him."

How did it go?

While they waited for a response, Jace and Eli completed the walk around the stadium, discussing predictions about what would happen at the hearing the next morning. Five minutes later, Saint texted back.

Where are you?

Just finished playing pool. The doors here swing remarkably quiet, by the way.

Can you come to 252 Poplar Ave?

Jace frowned and glanced at Eli, who was looking over Jace's shoulder.

Why?

Deborah wants to talk to you. Now.

Jace's stomach sank to the toes of his shoes.

Serious? It's 10:30 P.M.

We'll be waiting.

"Oh, crap," said Eli. "You really going?"

"I don't know," said Jace, his breath coming fast and shallow.

Eli folded his arms. "You got invited to go visit some Zeroes. At the home of the guy that was killed, whose vigil we allegedly crashed."

Jace nodded, wide-eyed.

Eli raised an eyebrow. "To someone not familiar with the situation, they might predict that you die. Literally. Tonight. Doesn't this sound like a classic setup?"

"You're not following the *no negativity* Bathwater rule," Jace said. He meant it as a joke, but neither of them smiled.

"If Rob was here, he'd spontaneously combust."

Jace pursed his lips and looked at the asphalt. "I have to go there."

Eli nodded somberly. "I know."

Jace began to walk away. "I'm sure nothing horrible will happen. But I'll text you the address, just in case you don't see me tomorrow."

"Want me to tell T.J.?"

"Nah," Jace said. "There's only a slim chance anything good will come out of this. No reason to get hopes up. I just have to try."

"How about Mari?" Eli called out. "Want to check with her before you do something dangerous like this?"

"That's the perfect reason *not* to tell her."

It was almost 11:00 P.M. by the time he pulled up to the house. There were three cars in the single-lane driveway and two parked on the curb. One of them was Saint's Jeep.

Jace purposely left his jacket in the car, so they wouldn't wonder whether he came armed.

He walked up the cement steps to a covered porch. He opened the screen door, hesitated, and then lightly knocked on the wooden one. Footsteps. A figure in the murky glass at the top of the door swayed and grew larger. The door opened partway.

A deep voice said, "Jace Kartchner?"

Jace cleared his throat. "Yes."

The door opened fully. A tall man, about a generation older than Jace, motioned him in.

Jace stepped inside.

A brick fireplace to his right caught his attention. There was a horizontal rectangle where the brick was slightly lighter, evidently where a television had hung for years. Now, an impressive portrait of Stephen Hobbs took its place. Noble. And hopeful.

Saint—the only other white person in the room—sat on a leather love seat with hands in his pockets. Two boys about Jace's age sat on a couch. Between them was a woman.

Her.

Jace hadn't seen pictures of her from before. And he wondered how much of the care and worry and exhaustion on her face had appeared the night her son died.

They looked at him. Nobody spoke.

Jace swallowed and met Deborah's eyes, deep brown and weary with sorrow. "I'm sorry," he said. And then something else stirred in his depths. Between one breath and the next, emotion and tears spilled from him. The man guided him toward a chair. Jace collapsed in it and quietly sobbed. "I'm sorry," he said again.

He wasn't even sure what he was sorry for. Partly for crying. Partly for the operation with Rob and Eli. But mostly because, no matter who was at fault, or what could have been done differently, a family was made to bear this tragedy.

Deborah quietly knelt beside the chair. She sighed, put her arm around him, and squeezed.

"It's okay," she whispered. "It's okay now."

CHAPTER FIFTY-FOUR

EARLY THE NEXT MORNING, the chubby kid was there again on his bench, thinking and holding his sign. Jace joined the people streaming past, all moving the same direction.

Around the corner and up the path, a large group milled around the entrance—mostly students. Some carried homemade signs, though about twenty of them were identical and professionally printed with *Drain the Bathwater!* in large text along with a cartoon rubber duck lying on its side with X's for the eyes.

All this support for the Bathwater Brigade was heartening. Jace's smile slipped into a yawn. He'd been at Deborah's house for a long time last night and was feeling it this morning. But it was a good tired. Like he had been up all night cramming for a final for his most difficult class, knowing he'd probably fail, but he did his best and at least it would be over soon.

As he made his way through the crowd, he saw a table with rubber ducks of various sizes. A sign taped to the table read *Small ducks $2. Large ducks and key chains $3*. Eli sat behind it. Three Zeroes in red shirts stood in front, arguing with him. Jace waited until they left.

"If you believe that, you're a moron," Eli called after them.

Jace walked behind Eli, put hands on his shoulders, and said low in his ear, "Trying to win? Or win them over?" He patted him on the back and resumed walking.

"Wait!" said Eli. "Come here for a minute."

The Zeroes left. Jace returned and crouched next to Eli.

Eli lowered his voice. "Did you hear anything new this morning?"

"No."

"Do you think she called Janet, then?"

Jace shrugged. "She said she'd think about it."

"Danica's upset about everything," Eli said. "Freaking out."

"She can still take her name off the resignation letter. She knows that, right?"

"That's not what she's worried about. You remember that Bathwater is the whole reason she even came to Cale, right? She says the Brigade is the best thing in her life right now."

Jace smiled. "Then you'd better up your game, Eli." He looked over at the double doors leading to the hearing that would change his life for the next four years, maybe even forever. How could you predict the way the current of time and circumstance might affect you? "It's sad, thinking it will all end. But we tried our best." Jace saw more Zeroes coming over to Eli's table. He patted Eli's shoulder again and walked away.

"Jace. I need to tell you something," Eli called after him.

Still walking, Jace gave him a thumbs up. "In a few minutes. I'll save you a place inside."

Closer to the entrance, he passed near a news reporter on camera. He heard the word 'Bathwatergate' and rolled his eyes.

Eight boys stood near the doors, bare-chested, with towels around their waists. Each had a large, blue letter painted on their chests. They stood roughly in a line, spelling BATWATER. Letter H spoke to a security guard at the door, trying to get in dressed as they were. Letter R dropped his towel briefly, thankfully revealing basketball shorts. His scream and the speed at which he retrieved his towel made the others laugh.

Jace paused at the door and looked to his right. A cement panel among the brick displayed the name Louis Melick, and the year 1991. And below that was a very slight, almost imperceptible imprint of a rubber duck. Here. On the Administration Building. Jace ran his fingers along the cornerstone and smiled, wondering if Janet knew.

Room 232 was packed with as many chairs as it would hold. About seventy-five people were there so far. Among them were the Bathwater Brigade core members. They stood talking near the front.

Mari saw Jace and approached him cautiously. "You look tired," she said.

Jace rubbed his face. "I was campaigning for Rich Weaver all night. Putting his fliers on doorsteps—at least until my flashlight ran out of battery."

"No, you weren't!" She pushed his shoulder.

Their smiles evaporated as Jace took in the room. "Well, this is it." He saw Wayne and the rest of the alumni sitting together near the back. He waved. They smiled and waved back. A few held up pieces of paper.

Mari sighed. "I'd like to be there when they turn in their diplomas."

"You never know," said Jace.

"You mean the decision? Yeah, we do, unfortunately. We had thought at least Kennedy might swing to our side, but the vote was four to one."

Jace's stomach sank. "They already voted?"

"Yes. Today, our only job is to stand here and make sure Texas knows what happened."

"So, this is the Bathwater Alamo."

"I like that." She leaned on the chair in front of her. "Jace, can we talk this weekend?"

"Might have to be over the phone. I have a feeling Janet might personally escort the rest of us off campus property later today. Looks like I'll be starting my Thanksgiving break early."

"I don't think it's going to happen like that, exactly. But how about this afternoon, then?"

He shrugged. "Okay."

She smiled again and he followed her up to the front to greet the others. We wished them good luck, then he made his way over to the far side of the room. He crossed his ankle over his knee and watched the entrance.

Eli and Danica walked in. They talked with Amber, Mari, and T.J.

at the front before making their way to Jace. Eli set his box of ducks by his feet.

"How many did you sell?" Jace asked.

"I made about thirty bucks," Eli said with a satisfied smile. "I'll try to sell more after."

"Clearance sale?"

Zeroes streamed in—more than last week. They took a few rows in the middle. Jace spotted Saint among them, and pulled out his phone and texted him.

Did she make the call?

Saint turned to look behind him and found Jace. Then he turned back around and replied.

No idea.

India came next. Danica waved her over.

One by one, Cale administration occupied the five seats at the front behind the long tables. Jace watched Mr. Rodriguez closely. He exchanged sober glances with T.J.

She didn't call. Jace realized how high his hopes had been.

Seats filled, and the chatter volume grew.

Then Jace sat up straight. Rob stood in the entrance, his long hair pulled back, sunglasses on his head. He looked out over the crowd. Eli stood and waved.

"Eli?" said Jace. "What's going on?"

"Oh. I made Rob promise to come."

"Why?"

"I thought if he could see what Bathwater really is and what we're fighting for, that might help you two be okay again. Today looks like our last chance."

Jace smiled. "This will probably get awkward. But thanks, Eli. Really."

Rob studied the room again, then flashed his friends a devious grin. He leaned over and spoke to the Zero on the end of one of the rows. One by one they stood or turned their legs to the side as Rob brushed by. There were no empty seats in the row.

Jace and Eli laughed.

Rob did this all the way into the center aisle and continued to inconvenience the Zeroes on the other side. He nearly tripped a few times, apologizing as he went.

"Good Lord," said India.

A full minute later, Rob completed the trek to his friends. Danica moved so that Rob could sit between India and Jace. Rob paused when he saw where the empty seat was, but he sat down anyway.

"Just don't go out the way you came," said Eli. "You'll get beat up."

"Maybe not," said Rob. "They're so well-behaved today. It's like the beekeeper is blowing smoke on them."

Jace smiled to himself. Eli was right. No matter what happened at this hearing, this could be his best—and last—chance to show Rob the true heart of the Bathwater Brigade. And that Jace *did* back Rob, his family, and good police everywhere.

Janet had taken her place at the front, wearing a Zero shade of red. She leaned back in her chair, a pleased smile on her lips.

Rob leaned over to Jace. "How good are you at forgery?"

"What?"

"If we hurry, I can slip them a note from the president of Cale, telling them they have to keep your club around, and to use this meeting to announce their resignations instead."

Jace grinned. "We're so desperate, it's almost worth a shot."

Rob was quiet for a minute, then sighed. "Our last conversation left things hanging. We should talk."

Jace nodded. "I agree."

"I mean, I know we had a disagreement. But you didn't have to drop out of college. You need a thicker skin, man."

Jace smiled. "Eli told you about that?"

"Rehearsals without you to torment? I won't be able to stay awake." Rob turned to look at him. "Hey. But if your Bathwater club is over, what do you think? Are you back on for a few more Zero operations before the semester's out?"

Jace leaned forward and rubbed his eyes. He thought of those movies where a man's life is destroyed, his family is taken from him, and he has nothing left to lose, so he goes renegade against the bad guys. Lashing back against Paladin and Janet and those who had smashed the Brigade out of existence? That would feel so good.

Then he pictured the greenhouse basement. The friends he had made, and the lessons that once were so foreign to him, but now seemed second-nature. Self-evident. They had begun to be a part of him. No, he knew too much. He would gladly engage with Zeroes, but the operations would be of a different kind.

Jace thumped Rob on the back. "We'll talk after."

Janet stood. "Ladies and gentlemen, if we can begin?" She waited for the chatter to fall silent. "Thank you. We'll keep this brief. As you know, we are here to deliver our verdict on whether the Bathwater Brigade will remain a club of Cale University."

Noise from the crowd grew again, but this time in spreading murmurs and whispers, and people shifting in their seats to view the doorway.

"We have carefully considered all the facts..." Janet trailed off. Nobody was listening to her.

A black woman stood, looking out over the room. Jace stiffened, mouth open. Whether or not Deborah Hobbs had called ahead of the meeting, he might never know.

But she had come to watch.

CHAPTER FIFTY-FIVE

SOME OF THE Zeroes smiled and waved to Mrs. Hobbs, and she waved back.

"Wait," said Rob. "Is that..."

"What's happening?" said Danica.

Two tall men flanked Deborah. Together, they started toward the back of the room. Five more followed. All eight were black, of various ages. Jace recognized some as members of her family. Maybe they all were. Janet Thompson beamed.

Mari turned to find Jace. Their eyes met. She looked worried, her brow furrowed. Jace could think of two very different possibilities for why the Hobbs family had come. He gave her a wide-eyed shrug.

Mrs. Hobbs found some empty seats next to each other, near where the Bathwater alumni were sitting. Norwood and a few others smiled graciously and shifted seats to make more room.

"They came to see you fry," Rob said. "Gina slipped away, and now they're here for you."

The rustling at the back quieted, and Mrs. Hobbs gave an apologetic wave.

"Thank you," Janet said, smiling at Mrs. Hobbs. "Welcome.

Normally this would only last a few minutes. Due to the level of interest, we have prepared a statement which I will read. Afterward, we will allow the Bathwater Brigade an opportunity to make a brief statement to comment on the decision.

"We understand that there are others among you who would like to comment or ask questions of us." She looked around the room. "There will be no opportunity for that in this meeting. However, anyone is welcome to submit feedback on our website." She read a long web address, including the three w's at the beginning.

Jace glanced around. Danica was squeezing Eli's hand.

"Drumroll please," whispered Rob.

Janet Thompson adjusted her glasses and held up a clipboard.

"Excuse me," said a voice from the back. There was a rumble in the room as everyone turned to see who the speaker was. Mrs. Hobbs raised her hand. "Could I ask a favor? I'd like to make one brief comment."

Janet glanced at her colleagues behind, and then smirked as she nodded.

"Oh, crap," whispered Eli.

Kennedy started towards her with microphone in hand. She met him near the front. He stood to the side, hands folded in front of him. Her family followed and stood behind her. A man with a badge around his neck and a large, expensive-looking camera moved back and forth near the front of the room clicking photos. The video cameraman folded his equipment and kept his eye on the Hobbs family as he searched for a new position.

"Thank you," Mrs. Hobbs said. "Members of the administration, some of you know me and are aware of the tragic events that took the life of my Stephen on the twenty-first of August last year. I'm Deborah Hobbs, his mother.

"No mother wants to bury her son. But I know from experience that when it does happen, a force awakens inside of her, and she will do whatever is in her power to prevent it from happening to others."

She spoke deliberately and a little slowly, just as she had at Victor Square.

"You may have seen news reports that my son was holding a cell phone when they shot him. The police claimed they had mistaken it for a gun." Rob clenched his jaw.

"Do you know what he was doing with it? He called *me*." She held up her phone, and her voice choked with emotion. "I didn't answer. I was in the shower after getting home from work. He left a voicemail. He was panicked and could hardly speak. He said he was being chased by cops. He said he was sorry. Even though I wasn't on the phone with him, he kept asking, 'Mom, what do I do? What do I do?'"

Many in the audience were visibly affected. A woman in front of Jace put a hand to her face, and the man sitting next to her frowned and shook his head. Rob seemed to soften a little. The room was silent.

She gestured to her side, where the Zeroes were sitting. "I have been working with many of these people." Some of the Zeroes politely smiled and nodded. "We are creating an organization that will save lives. We're calling it the Civilian Academy. It educates the community on current police procedures, especially when making arrests. The more we all understand what the police are supposed to do and why, the more likely it is that we can think clearly and calmly. We can save the argument for our court system instead of on the street where tensions are high and weapons are drawn. We will soon reach out for partnerships with the media, schools, and even police departments."

The administration nodded, and murmurs of assent briefly circled the room. Rob sat back in his chair, arms folded. He turned to Jace. "Did she just say that Zero Supremacy is going to partner with the police?"

Jace nodded and smiled. "I'll tell you more later."

"Woah," said Rob. He looked forward, thoughtful.

Jace couldn't believe she was doing this. Besides the Hobbs family, only he, Saint, and Eli knew what was coming next. He watched intently. He didn't smile. But anyone could have seen the optimism in his face.

Deborah said, "But I did not come here today in order to step in front of a news camera and plug my new website." Kennedy smiled and briefly bowed his head. "In order to get something done, you need to get others behind you. If you want to be noticed, you need to get not just individuals, but groups and organizations on board. And if you want to make *waves*, you need a *diverse* coalition. Zero Supremacy partnering with the police is a good start, but there's another group that deserves a seat at the table. Perhaps even the seat at the *head* of the table."

Janet sat back in her chair with one arm across her stomach and the fingers of her other hand resting against her lips. Her eyes never left Deborah.

Mrs. Hobbs continued. "I have learned that the Bathwater Brigade has also been involved in the Civilian Academy. More than involved. In fact, it was their idea. They have also been the main force behind the unbiased content of the site." There were a few gasps from the audience. Heads perked up, especially among the Zeroes.

"Saint told her," Jace murmured incredulously.

"I can think of no coalition that is more diverse, and thus as strong, as Zero Supremacy joining with the Bathwater Brigade," Deborah said. Heads nodded in agreement, even among the Zeroes. But several others shook their heads.

"Members of the Cale University administration, you are ultimately in charge of determining what is best for this school," Deborah said. "But I want you to know that I have reviewed your issues with the Bathwater Brigade, and I have personally met with one of their representatives. I have studied the content they have written for the Civilian Academy, and I am impressed with their fair treatment of such a complex matter. Any group that encourages the careful study of all sides of an issue, and produces students that build bridges and solve problems, is a group that any university should be begging to stay. If it were up to me, I would keep them around. In fact, I ask you to. Thank you for your time."

Janet stood so quickly that her chair tipped back, nearly falling over. The other administrators looked stunned. Commotion broke out in the audience, especially in the ranks of the Zeroes.

T.J. whispered to Kendric, and Kendric shrugged. Mari got their attention, and they both leaned toward her while she told them something. Jace just smiled to himself.

Janet recovered and called Kennedy over. They spoke for a minute, and he nodded. "Mrs. Hobbs," he said into the microphone, halting her return to her seat, "we have a few questions for you, if that's all right."

She turned back and Kennedy handed her the mic. He activated another one and gave it to Mr. Rodriguez. The room hushed.

"Your new organization is intriguing," said Mr. Rodriguez. "Civilian Academy, was it?"

"Yes."

Rodriguez looked at the rows of Zeroes. "Do you trust the justice system, then?"

"Myself? Not entirely."

He closed his mouth and nodded. "Thank you."

Kennedy took the mic back. "I believe you said that Zero Supremacy would like to work with police departments," he said. "Did I hear you correctly?"

Deborah smiled. "Indirectly through the Civilian Academy, yes. I've been hearing surprised reactions from both sides. The Academy isn't pro-police, though. Believe me, I have some problems with how the police acted with my son. Major problems. Those are still being worked out.

"But it's also not pro-criminal. Some have said that they're afraid this will help law-breakers escape justice, which simply isn't true. The Civilian Academy does not assume guilt or innocence. That's the job of the judicial system, and we simply want to get everyone safely to a courtroom."

Kennedy nodded politely. Rob's brow was furrowed, and he absent-mindedly tapped a quiet rhythm on his leg.

Janet Thompson reached for the mic. "We have become aware of an event to honor your son a few months ago. You may not have heard, but this was mocked and disrupted by members of the Bathwater Brigade."

Jace felt his face grow hot. He clenched his jaw. *She knows that's technically not true*, he thought.

Deborah surprised Jace by turning and looking at him. She smiled. "What happened that day has been taken care of."

Jace swallowed and nodded.

Janet glared at Jace, and then turned back to Deborah. She pulled out her binder and flipped through the pages. "You may not be aware of some concerning statements that have been made in Bathwater meetings," she said. "Some of them would surely dismay a person of color like yourself."

Deborah held up her hand. "The racist? Oh, I've heard all about it. I understand those comments were made in ignorance and that the Brigade helped that person see clearer. I may still find plenty of statements I disagree with, but here is what we want everyone to know. We are all very different—the police department, Zero Supremacy, the Bathwater Brigade, and the Hobbs family. None of these groups agrees completely with any of the others. If you draw our circles in a Venn diagram, some circles barely touch at all. But we have discovered a thread that connects all of us.

"We're not asking anyone to change what they believe or what they stand for. But when an arrest is imminent, each of these diverse groups just wants everyone to be safe, and to sort it all out on another day and place." She paused, and when she spoke again, unshed tears were in her voice. "My son didn't know what to do when the police were chasing him. Or at least, he had forgotten. The work that Zero Supremacy and the Bathwater Brigade have done on the Civilian Academy could have saved his life."

Janet looked like she had more questions, but Kennedy quietly reached for her mic, which she reluctantly gave up. The rest of the administration had been busy on their phones, looking from their screens to one another, apparently texting each other.

"Please give us one moment, thank you," said Kennedy. He turned off the mic and spoke with his colleagues. Janet's movements were sharp and negative, but the others seemed to be speaking over her. Whispers in the audience grew into a low murmur.

"Oh my gosh," said Danica. "Are they rethinking the decision?"

Jace shrugged.

"Was she looking at *you*, Jace?" asked Rob. "Have you talked with her before?"

Jace nodded. "Yeah."

Rob raised his eyebrows and Danica said, "Okay, we *definitely* have to talk after."

Kennedy turned on the mic. The room grew silent again. Jace's heart pounded.

"This will conclude our meeting," said Dr. Kennedy.

Groans arose from the audience. Someone shouted, "What's the decision?"

"We have decided to table this indefinitely."

Eli turned to Jace. "What does that mean?"

Danica clutched Eli's hand. "It means you won."

There was a "woo!" from the audience. Someone started clapping, followed by others. T.J.'s celebratory fist shot into the air at the front. Mari jumped up and hugged Amber. Kendric grinned as he held up their resignation letter and crumpled it in his hands.

Jace pulled in a slow, shaky breath. Suddenly exhausted, he leaned forward and ran his fingers through his hair. Head down, he closed his eyes tightly and wiped them with his shirt.

Eli and Danica excitedly patted him on the back. "We did it!" Danica said.

Jace waited for his emotions to pass before he stood and looked around the room.

Some of the Zeroes were visibly upset. Others looked either indifferent or confused. Paladin looked furious. She began pushing and pulling on them to leave the room. Probably so their anger wasn't caught by the news cameras.

Saint stood apart from the other Zeroes, a frown creasing his forehead, but when he saw Jace, he smiled and nodded. Jace mouthed, "Thanks."

Mr. Rodriguez shook T.J.'s hand and laughed.

Seeing his friends happy, Jace's spirits were so light he felt he could jump to the top of the building. "There's the smile," India said, punching him lightly on the arm. "I was beginning to think you were disappointed."

Rob put a hand on Jace's shoulder. "Not bad." Jace's grin widened.

"Jace! Danica! Eli!" Mari called over the noise and motioned for them to come to the front. As they made their way around the edge of the room, Jace nearly bumped into a woman wearing red. Janet Thompson stopped and glared at him, her mouth small and tight. "Congratulations. You've just reopened the Pandora's Box."

Jace stood, relaxed and calm. "Have some faith in your students.

And watch what we build together." She stared at him, and then stormed off. "You're welcome to join us any time," he called after her.

T.J. walked up to Jace and slapped his back before pulling him into a quick hug. "So, you're calling the shots now?" he grinned. "Setting up alliances and big sophisticated projects?"

"I figured you guys would think it was all right if we work on the Civilian Academy with them. I can just do it myself, if you want."

"No way," said T.J. "It sounds awesome. I'm in."

"This was all *you?*" Amber said, nodding toward the Hobbs family.

"Yeah," said Jace. "And that guy over there." He motioned toward Saint, a few rows behind them.

Amber looked at him with an expression he'd never seen on her face before: admiration. "Nice job."

Jace picked up T.J.'s crumpled letter and smoothed it out. "Hey guys. We'd better keep this on us. If Janet gets ahold of it, she'll still honor it."

Eli laughed. Jace looked at the list of signatures. Seven in total. His smile faded. At the bottom was a neat, flowing signature with familiar handwriting.

Mariana Munoz.

Jace looked up. Mari was watching him. He held up the paper, and she smiled. "Changed your mind?" he asked as she made her way over to him.

"No." She bit her lip. "But I lied a little."

"I don't get it."

She stepped closer.

"I was always going to sign."

He slowly grinned.

"But dropping out of college is a big deal. Not just for you, but for your family. I might have overstepped my bounds a little, but I felt sort of responsible for bringing you into the Brigade, and I had to take myself completely out of the picture for a minute."

"To make sure I was doing it for the right reasons..."

She nodded sympathetically. "Do you understand?"

He grabbed her in a bear hug and lifted her off the ground. "My worldview box makes sense again."

She laughed and kissed him.

"It's not all good news, guys," said Kendric.

Jace set Mari down. "Why not?"

"I already turned in my notice to the landlord."

They all laughed.

Jace said, "I know of a dorm with plenty of room."

CHAPTER FIFTY-SIX

THAT EVENING, the alumni insisted on taking the students to dinner —of course, at Primo Campania. They hailed Jace as the hero. T.J. hinted at the recent vacancy in their core leadership, and Kendric even vowed to attend Jace's upcoming band concert.

Their spirits were high as they talked over each other, making plans for the next phase of the Bathwater Brigade. Eli spent most of his time on his phone seeing what it would take to set up an online store for rubber duck keychains. T.J. stepped out to take a call from a college in Maryland who wanted to fly him out to speak on a panel about intellectual diversity. Kendric talked with Norwood at length about his plans for the Unity Department, that event he wanted to set up on racial and cultural diversity.

There was an element they didn't want to lose, brought by this new connection between past and present. They all agreed that they should have a Bathwater reunion every other year and joked that they should hold it in the Administration Building. Clarissa and Kendric volunteered to gather contact information of as many alumni as they could.

It was dark by the time they reluctantly parted, and Jace walked Mari to her dorm.

"You never told me what happened with Rob," Mari said. "I saw him there today. Things back to normal with you two, I hope?"

"I think he has to process, you know? But before he left, he said that I just might be the biggest Zero Supremacy buster he's ever seen."

Mari grinned. "In a way, I guess you are."

"This might be crazy, but I want him to join us. On the Civilian Academy."

She gasped. "You think he'd work with Zeroes?"

"He might. We'll need someone to make sure the police are represented fairly." Jace shrugged. "I'll see how things go with him."

She smiled up at him, admiration shining in her eyes. They arrived at her dorm. She hugged him tight.

"Oh, almost forgot this," Jace said as he handed her an envelope. "I don't know why they keep delivering your letters to me."

She accepted the letter. "Looks official." Her curious but skeptical gaze remained on him as she opened it. She read aloud, breaking into laughter occasionally.

OFFICIAL CALE ADMINISTRATION

Mari Munoz,

Since it seems your Bathtub Brigand—or whatever it's called—is here to stay, we turn our focus back to bigger matters.

You are no doubt aware that Jace Kartchner has paid his debt to society and to this grand institution for his disastrous bowling score. However, we are determined to never allow such a terrible score to happen again.

We have randomly selected you as his parole officer. During the upcoming Thanksgiving break, you are to check in with him at least once a day. Texting will do, but video chat is preferred. If it appears that he is in a bowling alley, contact us immediately.

Thank you for helping us preserve the integrity of the sport, the university, and the office of the administration.

Janet Thompson's supposed signature was large, and about seventy other small squiggles covered the bottom half of the paper.

"More people signed this than the Declaration of Independence, huh?"

Jace shrugged. "Looks like they take this seriously. I'd do as you're told."

After Mari had gone inside, he took the long way home, strolling around the edge of campus. It had been an exhausting day, but he wanted some time to think in the dark autumn air and relive the morning's victorious moments. The skin on his arms was cool. He should have worn long sleeves.

He pulled up Twitter. Professor Callahan had tagged him on five posts since he looked last, picking fights on the death penalty, religion, and spending on education—none of which he could have known Jace's opinion on. Someone Jace didn't recognize called him out as well.

Admitting defeat, bath boy? Haven't heard from you in a while. Why did you stop?

Jace weighed his phone in his hand and looked at the stars. Then he smiled.

Because I wasn't talking to the professor.

Red and blue lights flashed ahead. Curious, he walked toward them. When he realized where they were coming from, he started running.

Three police cars, a fire truck, and an ambulance filled the otherwise empty greenhouse parking lot. Officers and other first responders walked between their vehicles and the building.

"What happened?" Jace called out to no one in particular. "What's going on?" No one answered. As he rushed toward the greenhouse,

EMTs pushed an ambulance cot out through the entrance. The glass doors had been shattered, and someone had swept a path through the tiny shards.

Jace's heart raced. The only people he'd ever seen in the greenhouse at night were his friends.

One of the EMTs held out her hand. "Sir, please step back."

"Jace?" The whisper had come from the gurney.

Jace looked closer at the badly bruised face, the swollen eye, and the bandages. "Saint?" His hands eventually rested on top of his own head. "What...*happened*?" Jace walked beside the cot as the EMTs pushed it toward the waiting ambulance.

"Zeroes," Saint said. "After the hearing, some of them couldn't handle it. Paladin had found out about the greenhouse, and a bunch of them came and broke in. Busted everything up. I think Paladin's done with Zero Supremacy. And a bunch of others. That's probably for the best."

"What were you doing here?" Jace asked.

"I tried to get them to stop. I think I lost my phone down there."

"Oh, Saint." Jace looked away and choked back tears. "What did you do, then?"

The EMTs had reached the ambulance. "We've got to go," they said to Jace.

"Wait," Saint said. "Give us a minute." The EMTs reluctantly stepped back. "I pulled the fire alarm."

Jace let out a quick laugh. "I always figured you would be the one to pull the fire alarm at Bathwater headquarters."

"Then I bravely ran upstairs to get away. I..." Saint pulled in a labored breath and grimaced. "I didn't make it."

Jace's chest squeezed tight as he looked at what the Zeroes had done to Saint. "What were you thinking? This wasn't your fight. You should have hidden in the bushes and called the cops."

"Maybe. But I told you a long time ago. I fight for the truth...as I see it." He took a few more shallow breaths. "And I stand up for my friends."

Jace cleared his throat, wiped his eyes, and smiled.

"All right," the EMT said, moving forward. "We need to get him to the hospital." On the count of three, she and her partner loaded Saint into the ambulance. Her partner jumped in and she slammed the red doors. "We're taking him to Brooks Regional."

"Will he be all right?"

"Probably nothing life threatening. It's a good thing he pulled the alarm."

Jace remembered Saint's cell phone. "Hang on." He ran to the greenhouse. Inside, an officer told him he'd better leave.

"My friend got beat up down there," Jace said, out of breath. "They're taking him to the hospital, and he needs his cell phone."

The officer eyed him for a moment and then agreed to accompany him downstairs.

Jace stopped at the entrance at the bottom of the stairway, next to the dented door with a mangled handle. For a moment, his mind refused to comprehend what he was seeing, and he took a small, involuntary step backward. It was worse than he had expected. They had broken most of the artwork and thrown it into a pile in the middle of the room. Dents and holes in the sheetrock surrounded the fragments that remained hanging.

They had dumped out the contents of the filing cabinet, also heavily dented, and the door of the soda fridge was broken off. Papers, photos, and bits of glass littered the pile and the surrounding area, and the floor had sticky streaks of soda crisscrossing the bare cement. Jace picked up a dark, splintered panel of wood and turned it over. Sorrow rolled through him. It was a side of the Worldview Box.

"It looks like they tried to light it all on fire," the officer said, shaking his head. "Morons."

"Did they get away?"

"We caught a few. They're on the way to the station right now." He helped Jace look for the phone. "Why don't you call it?"

"No reception down here. Trust me." They searched for about five minutes but never found it. Jace gave him his contact information in case it turned up later.

Jace hurried upstairs, but the ambulance had left.

He sat on the curb, pulled up the Bathwater group chat, and debated what to say. He was never good with serious situations. He typed out, *We wanted a fresh start, and we definitely have one.* Then he erased it.

Come to the greenhouse ASAP. He erased that, too.

Jace leaned forward, rubbed his eyes, and sighed. He was utterly exhausted. Not even one semester done, he felt as if he'd earned two college degrees.

He rested his arms on his knees and stared out at the darkness, replaying what Saint had said.

Fight for the truth as you see it. Be humble enough to *change* how you see it. And stand up for your friends.

What was there to aspire to higher than that? He shook his head and smiled. This was the most powerful dojo lesson yet. Taught by Saint. The Zero.

Jace finally settled on a message and sent it.

A friend needs our support. Meet me at Brooks Regional.

He nodded to himself, exhaled, and jogged toward his parking spot through the cool Texas night.

EXPERIENCE MORE...

bathwatermeetings.com

Made in the USA
Las Vegas, NV
17 December 2020

13836633R10212